THE 530-YEAR HAVERIĆ BEY'S FAMILY

GENEALOGY AND HISTORIOGRAPHY

Dr Dzavid Haveric

Lulu

ISBN 978-0-9580103-7-5

USA

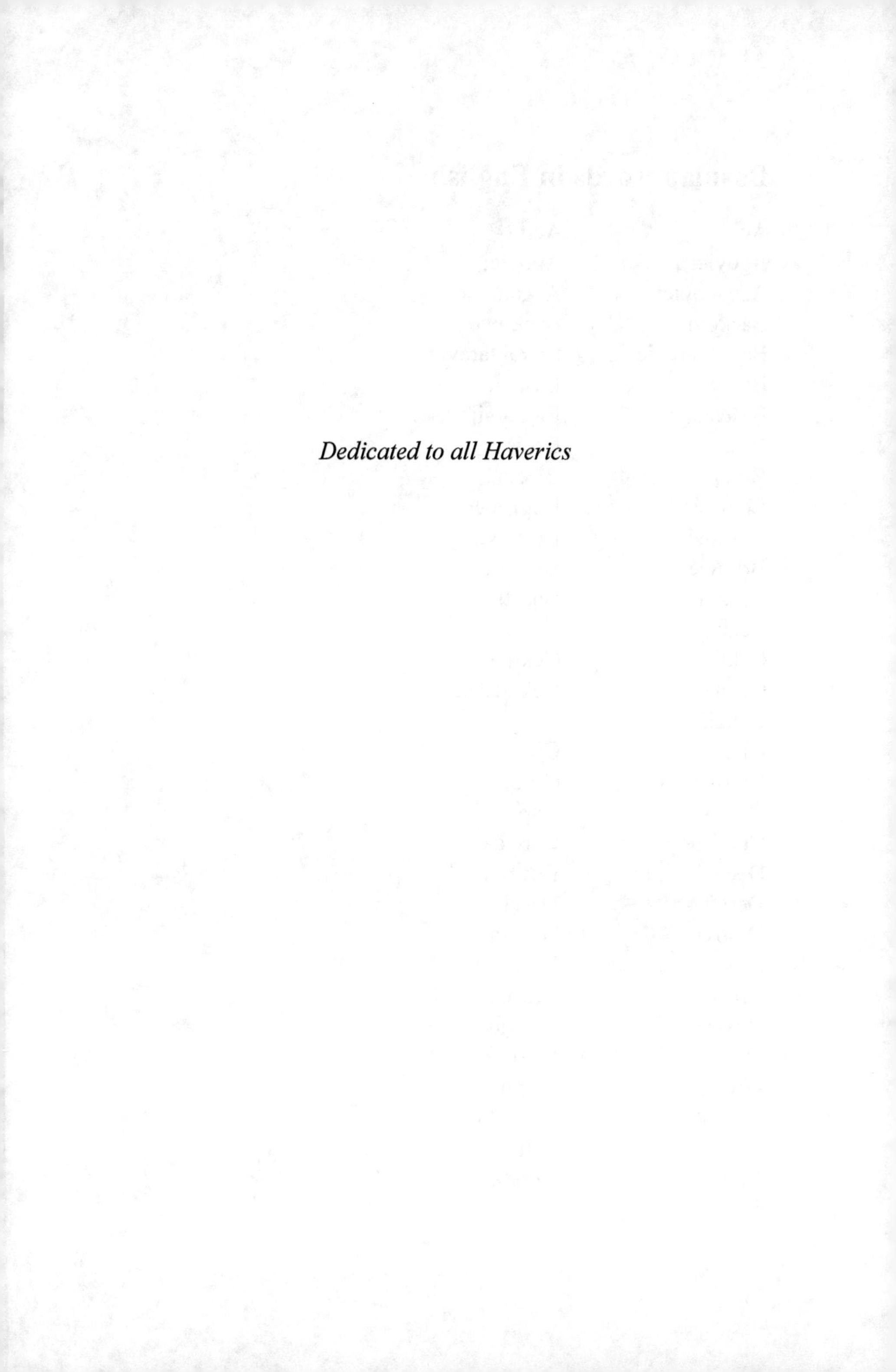

Dedicated to all Haverics

Bosnian words in English:

Aćif	Acif
Agovići	Agovici
Azganovići	Azganovici
Backović	Backovic
Bajraktarević	Bajraktarevic
Bašagić	Basagic
Baščaršija	Bascarsija
Bećir	Becir
Bibezić	Bibezic
Bogišićev	Bogisicev
Bošković	Boskovic
Brković	Brkovic
Bušatli	Bušatli
Ćazim	Cazim
Ćeklići	Ceklići
Čekmedža	Cekmedza
Čengić	Cengic
Čirgić	Cirgic
Crnojevića	Crnojevic
Ćuprija	Cuprija
Ćurčića	Curcica
Đečević	Decevic
Derviš	Dervis
Dinoša	Dinosa
Drač	Drac
Drače	Drace
Džavid	Dzavid
Džefa	Dzefa
Džemal	Dzemal
Dževahira	Dzevahira
Folić	Folic
Gondža	Gondza

Goričani	Goričani
Gradaščević	Gradascevic
Gruž	Gruz
Hadrović	Hadrovic
Hadžiabdić	Hadziabdic
Haverić	Haveric
Havuša	Havusa
Ibrahimagić	Ibrahimagic
Jovičević	Jovicevic
Kalezići	Kalezici
Kalići	Kalici
Kaluđer	Kaluder
Karađordević	Karadordevic
Karađuzović	Karaduzovic
Kolašin	Kolasin
Krleža	Krleza
Krnić	Krnic
Krojacka	Krojacka
Kruševac	Krusevac
Kruška	Kruska
Kučuk	Kucuk
Kuče	Kuce
Kulišić	Kulisic
Lačević	Lacevic
Lisičić	Lisicic
Lješkopolje	Ljeskopolje
Ljumanović	Ljumanovic
Memić	Memic
Memović	Memovic
Mikulić	Mikulic
Morača	Moraca
Muhić	Muhic
Nešo	Neso
Nikšić	Niksic

Njegoš	Njegos
Omerbasić	Omerbasic
Omerčahić	Omercahic
Oslobođenje	Oslobodenje
Papović	Popovic
Pavičević	Pavicevic
Petrović	Petrovic
Radusinović	Radusinovic
Ramadanović	Ramadanovic
Redžep (Redžo)	Redzep (Redzo)
Roganović	Roganovic
Ruždija	Ruzdija
Šaćir	Sacir
Šećer	Secer
Šeko	Seko
Šemsudin	Semsudin
Seoča	Seoca
Sijerčić	Sijercic
Šipad	Sipad
Špiro	Spiro
Spuž	Spuz
Stanić	Stanic
Stara Varoš	Stara Varos
Stećci	Stecci
Tabački	Tabacki
Talirević	Talirevic
Večernji	Vecernji
Vranić	Vranic
Žabljak	Zabljak
Ždrebanika	Zdrebanika
Želimir	Zelimir
Zlatičanin	Zlaticanin
Zotović	Zotovic

CONTENTS

Acknowledgements

I am thankful to *all* Haverics, Haveris, Haverikus and Tanbays who provided valuable information, documents, photos and stories for the book. For similar support, I thank to Dr Enver Backovic and Ramadan Zaganjor, the cousins from their mothers' sides, Haveric. For archival data written in different languages, I thank: for data in Albanian, Agim Haveri and Dr Nathalie Clayer; data in Arabic, Dr Ismail Albayrak and Dr Ismet Busatlic; and data in Osmanli/Turkish, academic Dr Serbo Rastoder. For their support I thank to Sead Mandic, Vahid Goga, Ali Ymer, Atvija Kerovic and Dzemo Redzematovic. My thanks also go to the staff of the State Archives of Montenegro, Cetinje and the National Library of Montenegro, Podgorica. Special thanks go to Vicki Snowdon for editing and Barbara Peak for pre-editing the manuscript. For book reviews/endorsements, I cordially extend my thanks to a distinguished academic Dr Ferid Muhic, my colleagues Prof. Salih Yucel and Prof. Ismail Albayrak, and my cousin Dr Enver Backovic. Last but not least, my loving thanks go to my family.

Exploring family genealogy and histography becomes a captivating voyage through times, counties and identities. In the present time, research and writing about family historiographies and genealogies has received great interest with a move to their revelations. This work on the Muslim bey family's tree is (among) the first in the Balkans written in English and the first in Australia, especially dealing with its multiple branches. Over several years, I have worked and dedicated my spare time to this research and book about the Haveric family with an intention to bring to light its ancestry and historiography. It deals with interconnected familial ties that transcend borders, revealing expansive networks and an old noble heritage.

With the legacy of the Haveric bey family preserved in a book, I also hope to share this among the many other families who have had similar experiences or their friends and all decent readers interested in a related field. For passionate readers, it is clear this type of book includes many ancestorial names, which is obviously the nature of any complex genealogical work. However, beneath the story is shared messages of humanity, which are peace, social virtues and survival acknowledging that people belong to the same species, share common experiences and have inherent dignity.

Foreword

THE GARDEN OF OLIVES

Dr Dzavid Haveric, The 530-Year Haverić Bey's Family: Geneaology and Historiography

In terms of its subject matter, the latest work by academic Dzavid Haveric falls into the genre of family chronicles, while in terms of its methodology it is conceived as a scientific *case study* of the Haveric family. The book represents an extremely valuable contribution to the sociology, culturology and historiography of southwestern Europe, specifically, the central region of the Balkan peninsula over a period of more than five centuries.

The basic meaning defines this genre as a chronicle of the lifestyle, social status and tradition of a family with its genealogical ramifications, as well as the mutual relationships among several families. The main approach to the presentation is a dominantly chronological sequence of formation, development and changes in the life of a family, over a certain period, usually more than a century. This analytical, sociological, cultural and historiographic approach allows for precise insight into the everyday life of the family that is the subject of scientific research and offers a deeper understanding of the ways in which external factors influence the mutual relations of family members. In this way, consistently realised family chronicles go beyond the framework of descriptive sociology based on the research of anonymous social categories, because they revive the dilemmas, reflections, aspirations and challenges of members of a specific family. At the same time, it contextualises these aspects within the precise framework of temporarily and regionally defined social conditions.

This research is dedicated to the changes that the Haveric family went through, in a span of more than 500 years – from the 1480s to the end of the 20th century, exposed through a systematic analysis of the cultural-religious, social and historical circumstances throughout this entire period. The author, academic Dzavid Haveric, follows the chronicle of the Haveric bey's family based on a wealth of first-hand information, through interviews with members of the Haveric family, but also on archival data and family documents, as well as the memories of members from the Haveric family scattered over a wide area of Montenegro, Albania, Bosnia and Turkey. The systematisation and thoroughness of this research dedicated to the genealogy and historiography of the Haveric family can best be seen from the analysis of the etymological root of the family name Haveric.

In search of an answer to this question, the author consulted all available sources and followed all traces in the languages in which the word Haver appears. He concluded that the word 'Haver' in Persian means 'friend', while in Arabic it is known as 'Habr' and has a double meaning: 'educated man' or 'news', and in the same meaning it is also present in the Bosnian language as 'haber'. In Kurdish, the word 'Haver' is 'dawn', or 'morning', while some associate it with the concept of 'honourable man'. In Hebrew, 'Haver' means 'friend'. The word 'Haver' is present in Hungarian and also means 'friend', or 'my friend'. Academic, Dzavid Haveric, also found that 'Haveri' is the name of a district in India as well as that 'Havernek' is the name of a legendary castle on the Euphrates River. In the form 'Havarin', i.e. 'Ḥawariyyun', in the Arabic language means 'helper', 'follower', 'apostle', while in the Turkish language 'Haber' means 'news', 'news'. Considering the way in which academician Dzavid Haveric approached this work and the knowledge he gained from it, there is every chance that the etymological source of the family name Haveric is derived precisely from the meaning of 'friend', 'noble man who helps others'. An historical parallel can be both an inspiration and an illustration for the following conclusion.

Namely, it is known that Rabindranath Thakur (anglicised variation is aRabindranath Tagore), author of the poetry collection *Gitanjali: Song Offerings* (in Bengali: গীতাঞ্জলি), won the Nobel Prize for Literature in 1913 for this work, as the first winner from Asia. At the same time, it was the first Nobel Prize awarded for lyric poetry. Outside the English-speaking world, this book is often translated as *The Gardener*, because Tagore conceived his book as a garden, a garden, from which he offered his poems as a gift, like flowers from that garden. However, it is less known that the great poet was a 'peripatetic poet' – a travelling poet. On one of his travels, in the desert of Iraq, in 1932, Tagore visited a Bedouin camp. When Tagore asked the tribal chief in conversation: 'Who is a true Muslim'?, the chief replied: 'Our Prophet (peace be upon him) said that a true Muslim is one who neither by his words nor by his deeds does the slightest harm to his fellow man…' Impressed, Tagore wrote in his diary: 'I was left breathless because I recognised in his words the voice of essential humanism'.

Following a pathway of one of the family ancestors, who was an olive grower with an estate of a thousand olive trees near the city of Bar in Montenegro, academic Dzavid Haveric, through this family genealogy and historiography, clearly inherited the same noble affinity and gift of his ancestor, the olive grower. The Haverics, gathered in this monograph, all of them and each one individually, were for Dzavid Haveric gold that, from one and the same ancient olive tree, dripped into the corners of his heart and sprouted in his mind. After many years of patient work, with much love and care, academic Dzavid Haveric has cultivated this GARDEN OF OLIVES of his own! Although explicitly dedicated to all Haverics (*Dedicated to all Haverics*), this book is now a wonderful garden, widely open to all people, regardless of their family genealogy, and from its fruits every person may benefit and no one will suffer any harm.

Dr Ferid Muhic
President of the Bosniak Academy of Sciences and Arts
Formerly a professor of Philosophy at the Saints Cyril and Methodius University, Skopje, North Macedonia; also Visiting Professor at Sorbonne, New York's Syracuse University, Florida State University, International Institute of Islamic Thought and Civilisation, International Islamic University Malaysia (IIUM), and several universities in Southern-East Europe.

Introduction

And if all the trees in the earth were pens,
and the sea, with seven more seas to help it,
(were ink), the words of Allah could not be exhausted...
(Qur'an 31:27)

The ancestry tree of the Haveric family derives from common genealogical roots in Montenegro. Its branches were developed in Albania, Bosnia and Herzegovina, and Turkiye, where their descendants have lived for several generations. Their more than 500-year bey tradition is evident in their high posts during the Ottoman Empire, high posts in the time of Montenegrin and Albanian kings, the regions of ruling (*beylik*) the wealth of landownership (*begovat*), successful trading businesses and a beneficiary (*waqf*). It is also linked with their familiar respect by all people regardless of religions and ethnic belonging due to their promotion of tolerance, education, loyalty and defending the counties where they lived. Thus, this work honours their noble heritage during the Ottoman Empire and kingdoms in Montenegro and Albania, reflected in their largely forgotten ancestral legacy.

Like other Muslim families, the Haveric family is connected through blood ties, linked to their surname, the Islamic heritage, a source of ethnic origin before taking other nationalities in receiving countries and certain interests for the ancestry by the generations of descendants. In the Balkan regions, genealogical family trees as, an unwritten rule, are drawn down the male names as a continuation of new branches based on their family surname. In this context, the Haveric family is no exception. However, the Haveric females of those born as Haverics or married a Haveric are respectfully mentioned.

Montenegro, Albania, Bosnia and Herzegovina are part of the Balkans. Some scholars interpret that the Turkish word *Balkan* signifies a 'chain of wooded mountains' composed of two parts: *bal* means 'honey' and *kan* means 'blood'. In times of peace, the beauty of this part of Europe was 'sweet' but came at a 'bloody' price in war because of internal ethnic turmoil, but also nothing less of external imperial impacts. This metaphorical expression illustrates that the Haveric family, like other Balkan families, communities and ethnic groups experienced successes and appreciation, but also struggle and exodus, such as during the turbulent first decades of the 20th century. Despite various historical circumstances, they lived and shared in their multicultural milieu many common values with Muslims, Christians and Jews.

The book timeframe focuses mainly on the Haveric family from its beginning in the 1480s to the end of the 20th century, spanning over 500 years. It shows the family evolution through cultural-religious and socio-historical contexts. This historical narrative is a non-ideological approach, offering a wealth of first-hand information, traces of ancestry, historical facts and many stories from Montenegro, Albania, Bosnia and Turkiye. It also includes old documents and photos along with some literature and old articles mainly deriving from the archival data from Tirana, Shkoder and Podgorica, Bar and Cetinje, as well as data from various heritage sites, thematically assembled in chronological order. The whole work is built mainly on fragmented data, treasured by the family, which I obtained during my visits or contacts in Bosnia and Herzegovina, Montenegro, Albania, Turkiye and the US.

In this work, I do not impose my opinion on the origin of the family, but reveal a contemporary view free from mythologies that were characterised on these themes in many areas of the Balkans. It is in accord with recent works on the arrival of Islam in the Balkans and its impact on the local ethnicities. Many Muslim families in the region did not pay much attention to documenting their ancestry. Their genealogy and historiography were written by non-Muslims, whose sources were often ambiguously 'accepted' by Muslim families, like in the case of the Haverics. Thus, as a Haveric and an historian, I dedicate my humble contribution to writing as far as possible, because this remarkable topic of the 500-year beys' historiography and genealogy deserved for a long time to be revealed. For these who have different views on the family origin, it certainly allows them to retain their opinions. The work may attract not only the Haveric family members and all readers and researchers interested in related fields.

The history of genealogy matters because it helps individuals and families to understand how their family trees were developed, the way they were engaged and what they valued. Writing about the past means 'refreshing the ages', harmonising chronological events and happenings and learning something new. For the future, what we owe our family history is to continue writing it, which may be a task for the young generation of Haverics. It is because there is scarce data, especially where the connection with the genealogical tree has not yet been found, such as through the Ottoman archives. Indeed, some evidence of ancestry remains unsolved. Those Haverics who would like to add more information about their family brunches are welcome to do it in the last section of the book titled 'an addition to my family branch' to keep the information in it that they would like to share.

Today, the descendants of the Haveric family are scattered all over the world, not only in Bosnia, Montenegro, Albania and Turkiye, but Western Europe, the USA and Australia. Circumstances are changes and they no longer bear the title of beys, but are regarded as a distinguished family by many families and friends. However, many Haveric family members still proudly cherish their noble ancestry. New generations of the Haverics are mostly well-educated, contributing to many different fields, such as medicine, science, humanities, arts and business, just to mention a few. This is evident in the many different records where they live locally and internationally. Parents tell stories about the Haveric family and they appreciate this long-lasting tradition. New generations are also curious to know more about other family members and this is what the book also offers.

Dzavid Haveric

Etymology of the Word 'Haver'

Throughout history, Muslim family surnames from the Balkans were exposed to changes due to cultural-religious influences and different states' regulations. In the past, due to emigration, original surnames became 'immigrant' surnames in these new environments. According to the rule of the receiving countries, their surnames were either 'adjusted' (such as in Albania), or 'changed' (such as in Turkiye). In recent times, many Muslim families, however, have preserved their surnames, regardless of their migration from one place to another, one country to another or from one continent to another.

The etymology of the surname testifies to the human's call for ones' primordial roots, the search for the source and place of origin of ones' ancestors. Muslim surnames usually originate from Islamic linguistics – Turkish, Arabic and Persian. Such influences were recorded when the Ottoman State (*Devlet-i Ali Osmaniyye*) arrived in the Balkans. The new government brought a new religion and cultural and linguistic impacts, and a new world view.[1]

The word *Haver* was created by a Persian or Arabic linguistic influence. It was during the time of the Ottomans, who, as cultural carriers, first accepted the word from the East then transferred it when they arrived in the Balkans. The preservation and cultivation of the sound 'h' is one of the most significant and recognisable attributes 'in the phonetics of Muslim family names', such as Haveric.[2] This influence of Oriental languages became a traditional feature for new generations in many different countries. In some historical sources, the word ‘Aver’ also appeared, as a result of the cultural, religious and linguistic groups of the authors, mostly non-Muslim. Aver is not a Muslim term nor an original name for a Muslim family in the Balkans.

Rich etymological sources mention the word ‘Haver’ in many variants and multiple meanings. For instance: In Persian ‘Haver’ means ‘friend’, ‘east’ and ‘sunrise’; ‘Hvr’ pronounced Hivar for a dialogue is also a Persian word; ‘Haver’ – Habr in Arabic means capable, a learned man, a synonym for ‘an educated man and a scholar’ or simply ‘news’; ‘Haver’ is sabah or dawn in Kurdish, while others translate it from the Kurdish ‘honourable’; and ‘Haver’ is also a friend in Hebrew. According to the Hungarian dictionary, the word ‘Haver’ means a friend or ‘my friend’,’ and it means courage, exhilaration and friendship like the frequent exclamation, ‘Haver!’ The Indian word ‘Haveri’ is the name of a district in central Karnataka, India. Havernek is a legendary castle on the Euphrates, an area that is still ancient and was a part of the Persian Empire; ‘Havarin’ is an Arabic word; and Ḥawariyyun, means a ‘helper, follower, apostle’. ‘Haber’ is a Turkish word that means a news or notice. Therefore, the origin of the word in most cases refers to Eastern provenance.[3]

Montenegro, Albania, Turkiye and Bosnia

With the raising of the Ottoman Empire, its imperial domain expanded in many different parts of the world, including the Balkans. The Sultan's titles and Ottoman territories comprised a long list: His Imperial Majesty, Head of the Dynasty, Sovereign of the Osman Family, Sultan es Selatin (Sultan of Sultans), Khakhan (Khan of the Khans), Caliph of the Faithful, Servant of the Cities of Mecca, Medina and Kouds (Jerusalem), Padishas of the Three Cities of Istanbul (Constantinople), Edirne (Andrinople) and Bursa (Brousse), and of the Cities of Cham (Damascus) and Misr (Egypt), of all Azerbaijan, of Maegris (in Ethiopia), of Barkah, of Kairouan, of Alep, of Iraq, of Arabia and of Ajim, of Basra, of El Hasa, of Dilen, of Raka, of Mosul, of Parthia, of Diyarbakir, of Cilicia, of the Vilayets of Erzurum, of Sivas, of Adana, of Karaman, of Van, of Barbaria, of Habech (Abyssinia), of Tunisia, of Tyrabolos (Tripoli), of Cham (Damascus), of Kybris (Cyprus), of Rhodes, of Candia, of the Vilayet of Morea (Peloponnese), of Ak Deniz (Marmara Sea), of Kara Deniz (Black Sea), of Anatolia, of Rumelia (the European part of the Empire), of Bagdad, of Kurdistan, of Greece, of Turkestan, of Tartary, of Circassia, of the two regions of Kabarda, of Gorjestan, of the plain of Kypshak, of the whole country of the Tartars, of Kefa and of all the neighbouring countries, of Bosnia and dependencies [including Karadag, i.e. Montenegro], of the City of Belgrade, of the Vilayet of Serf (Serbia), with all the castles and cities, of all the Arnaut Vilayet (Albania) [then included Karadag, i.e. Montenegro], of all Iflak and Bogdania, as well as all the dependencies and borders, and many other countries and cities.[4]

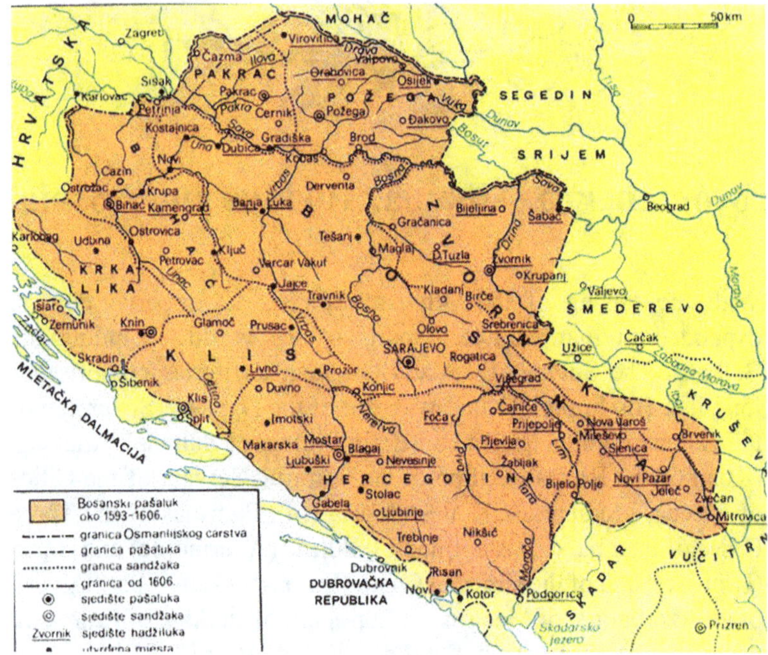

Bosnian Eyalet (Pashadom)

The Bosnian pasha held, under his authority, an area larger than any Bosnian king. In the south, the Bosnian *Pashalik* ('Pashadom') stretched from Dubrovnik to Ulcinj and Bar in Montenegro. The small town of Spuz is near the Zeta River, under the hill that dominates a large part of the Bjelopavlic plain, where, according to some scholars, the Haveric family originated. Even earlier, the first historical mention of the stay of King Tvrtko in Zeta was in 'Spuz in 1379'.[5] Over time, the Ottoman Empire included in its realm most of the Balkan countries, including all of Bosnia, Serbia, Montenegro and Albania.

Under the Ottoman Empire, the places of residence for the Haverics appeared in the three Balkan areas. Those places were in the largest territory of the Bosnian *Eyalet* (Pashalik); the Montenegrin Sandjak (*Karadag*) reorganised them as a separate vilayet of Montenegro, 'Vilayet of the Black Mountain' as well as the Albanian Sandjak. Many other Bosnian Muslim (Bosniak) families in Bosnia, Albania and Turkiye derived their genealogies from Montenegro, including the Haveric family. While some continued to live in those realms, others emigrated to other states.

Montenegrin immigrants from Podgorica, including Haverics, emigrated to Albania, Bosnia and Turkiye (i.e. The 'Turkish part' of the Ottoman Empire which refers to the area within the modern borders of Turkey) in four main periods: 1) During the rule of the *Bushatlins* (the Bushati, a prominent Ottoman-Albanian family that ruled the Pashalik of Scutari from 1757 to 1831); 2) after the Berlin Congress in 1878 and after the Russo-Turkish war between 1877 and 1878; 3) on the eve and during the First World War from 1914 to 1918; and 4) during the Second World War between 1941 and 1945 and afterwards.[6]

In Montenegro, during the Ottoman rule, if not earlier, the majority of Haverics lived or were present in Podgorica, Goricani, Golubovci, Tuzi, Bar, Spuz, Zabljak, Bjelopavlici, Cetinje, Danilovgrad and Niksic. Some Haverics in Montenegro were and are called 'Averic', missing the writing of and voicing sound 'h'. Their genealogical part in the family tree is the longest in history because most Haverics inhabited Montenegro before many of them left to other states. Up to today, there are at least 16 generations of Haverics. Under the Kingdom of Montenegro, ruled by the King Nikola, they also lived mostly in Podgorica. The surname 'Haverić' was created in the time of the former Kingdom of Yugoslavia when most surnames received the Slavic suffix 'ić'. From that time, many Haverics took refuge in other Balkan states.[7]

In Albania, at least 5 or 6 generations settled mainly in Shkoder, Tirana, Durres and Kavaja. They adopted an Albanianised version of the Haveric surname by removing the Slavic suffix 'ic', including Haveri, Haveriku, Haveriqi and Haveraj. The Haveric families from Montenegro consider themselves Albanian but maintain that their common family origin is from Podgorica. In Albania, they lived and worked in the service of the Ottoman Empire and King Zoglu. They also lived under the dictatorship of the President of Albania, Enver Hoxha.

In Turkiye, a branch of the Haveric family came to Istanbul, Ankara and Izmir. Haverics have been present in Turkiye for at least 4 generations. There the family changed its surname to Tanbay ('Tan' means sunrise or 'East' in Farsi, 'bey' in Turkish means a 'man') and Adenis (in Turkish means 'beyond the sea'). Their awareness of belonging to the Haveric genealogy prevails. They lived and worked in government services during the Ottoman Sultans and the Republic of Turkiye under statesman Kemal Pasha Ataturk.

In Bosnia and Herzegovina, many Haverics lived for at least 3 or 4 generations in the city of Sarajevo. Haverics emigrated to Bosnia between the world wars or during or after the Second World War.[8] They lived and worked during the Yugoslav Kingdom, the Socialistic Republic of Yugoslavia ruled by the President Josip Broz Tito, and the state of Bosnia and Herzegovina.

Junus, a Progenitor of the Haveric Family

Most questions related to genealogy start from a logical question: Where are the beginnings of family? This matches the proverb: 'We need to find the source to understand the river'. The complexity of it includes many explanations and stories. Some also denied the family's authentic ethnic and religious identity. Respecting diversity means accepting there are differences among people, including those related to their origin. Here it is important to stress that this contemporary work respects other ethnic groups, such as Serbian, Croatian, Montenegrin and others, and their religious beliefs, but at the same time explores the ethno-religious origin of the Haveric family, from a Bosniak Muslim point of view.

In the Montenegrin history, it was said the Haverics ('Aferics') were a respectable Muslim brotherhood, which had its officers and *kadis* (judges) – 'they originated from a mixture of Slavic and pre-Slavic people' (i.e. Bogomils).[9] The Haveric family tree started with its progenitor embracing the Islamic faith at the end of the 15th century, if not earlier. Unfortunately, the arrival of Islam in the Balkans is often misunderstood and ethnic identities misinterpreted, including those Bosniak Muslims in Montenegro. Islam in medieval times sometimes reached regions of the Balkans, including Bosnia and Montenegro, and its inhabitants, the Bogomils, even before Christianity.[10] Islam would influence the formation of the religious Islamic identity and the ethnic Bosniak identity.[11] Indeed, Muslim religious identity was created at a similar time when other religious identities were formed.[12]

The presence of Islam along the Adriatic coast and its small islands and in the Neretva Valley is recorded as early as the 8th century. Some Muslim migratory waves from the east also were part of the arrival of the Muslim ethnic groups. The arrival of Sufis, traders and explorers contributed to the spread of Islam in the Balkans.[13] For instance, a Turkish historian, Halil Inalcik, said that after much hardship, forty dervish Turkish families migrated to the Balkan Peninsula in 1261. The medieval reminiscence of the Bosnian Kingdom were Bogomils and their beliefs and of tombstones appearing as far as Montenegro. The Bogomils chose to embrace one of the Abrahamic faiths, such as Islam whose main transmitters of the faith were the Turks.

In Montenegro, 107 localities with 3,049 Bogomil tombstones (*stecci*) were recorded. From thin stone slabs to monumental stone blocks many of them bear carved Islamic symbols such as in the village of Vuksanlekaj, near Tuzi, in the region of Malesia located around 14 km from Podgorica. In the middle of the cemetery, an unusual group of old graves indicate the syncretism of the *Bogomilism* (an ancient belief originating from Persia, dualistic Bosnian Church) and Islam. There are around 30 carved tombstones, between 100 and 150 cm high. Carving was on the front and back of the headstones, and on the plate cover. The carved symbols include crescent moons, stars, the sun, human bodies, heads, flowers, rifles and swords, shepherd sticks, snakes and other motifs.[14]

These gravestones in the lower Zeta have many stylistic similarities with tombstones in Bosnia that belong to the second half of the 15th and 16th centuries. Some of them have even more decorative Islamic motifs.[15] The connection with the Bosnian Muslim gravestones (*nishans*) and Tuzi gravestones in the old cemetery and the cemetery next to the Nizam Mosque is also very close.

The region of the lower Zeta is important for the Haveric family because its family members usually lived, traded and ruled for centuries between Podgorica towards the border of the Shkoder Lake, which was also from the direction of the Ottomans' arrival. It has been geographically, administratively and historically recognisable since the Middle Ages, and today its largest part is the territory of the Municipality of Golubovci, which is within the capital city, with Golubovci as its administrative seat.[16] In this region, Haveric ancestors were exposed to early interactions with the Ottomans and subsequently with Islam. Many Bogomils embraced Islam peacefully and spontaneously, 'without coercion by the Ottomans'. Individuals from influential families, including the Haveric family, were 'the first to accept Islam in Montenegro'.[17] As they have authentic ethnic Bosniak identity, their Islamisation is *not* Turkification ('turned' into becoming Turk). Thus, a distinction should be made between the Bosniak Muslim identity and Turkish Muslim identity.[18]

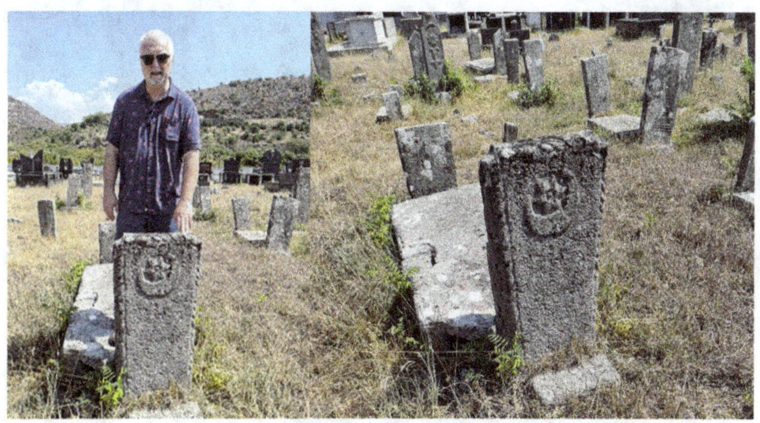

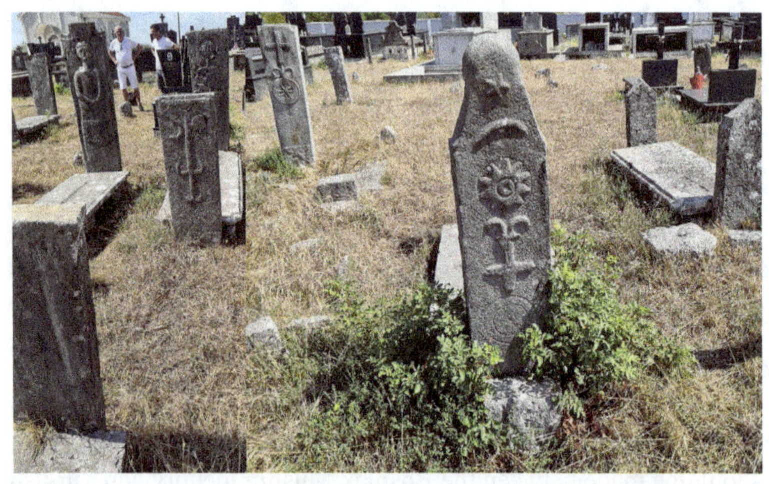

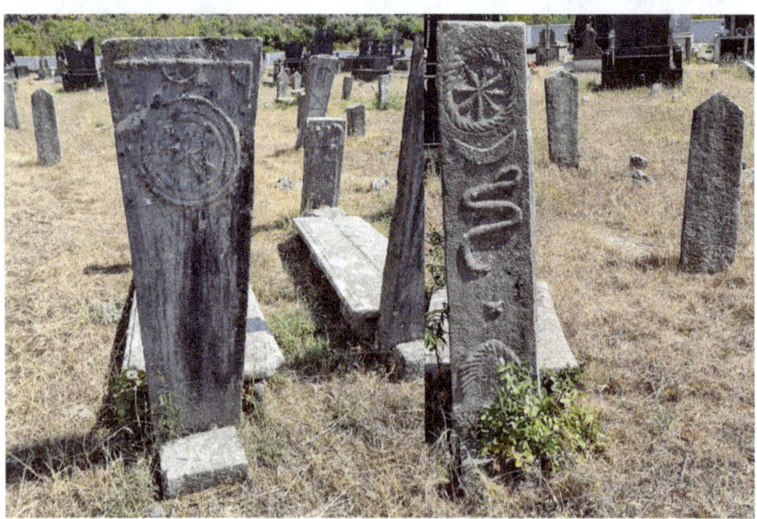

Bogomils' tombstones in the Vuksanlekici Cemetery (municipality of Tuzi)

The appearance of the Haveric family progenitor, named **Junuz**, represents a starting point in the family Islamic history and genealogy, which goes back to the arrival of the Ottomans and their encounters with the Bogomils, if not earlier. As a result of the spread of Islam among the Montenegrin inhabitants, the Bogomils, this process created a unique Muslim identity. Subsequently, medieval Montenegrin family names were translated into Turkish, Arabic or Persian, such as in the case of Haverics. The name **Junuz** does not have a non-Muslim father's name, which is common in Islamised families. This suggests the family is even older than the period of the arrival of Turks or came from Sufi circles.

Among some family members, as well as seen in the works of some authors, it was said that the Haverics wrote chronicles 'from the beginning of their conversion to Islam'. For instance, a historian, Andrija Jovicevic, said that many Haverics were literate and 'everything that was written during the time of the Turks in Zeta was kept until 1918'. Since then, the Haveric family lost a lot of its genealogical and historiographical information, including their accounts about the Turkish rule in Zeta, which were destroyed by the end of the First World War. Despite everything, some authentic fragments of the past and stories about family branches in Bosnia, Montenegro, Albania and Turkiye have been preserved to this day.

A few stories about the acceptance of Islam by the progenitor Junus, which were not shaped by the Haverics have different interpretations, 'coloured' with mythical views and ideologies. Thus, this aspect deserves attention due to it being misleading. For instance, a popular story on behalf of the Haverics is that, in the 15th century, the first ancestor of the Haverics was a monk (*kaluder*) in the Zdrebanik monastery Ilija from Slatina. He became 'Turkish', chose the name Junus and had a son, Aver – the Averici were named after him.[19] According to some Christian Orthodox canons, a monk (*kaluder*) did not have a right to marry. Even after his period of priesthood life, if he was married and had a son, the name Aver is not Muslim. The word, 'Aver', which may be a Christian name, is misleading as a basis for the surname of the Muslim Haveric family. It has nothing to do with the Muslim word 'Haver', which had multiple meanings in Islamic terminologies. In fact, **Junuz** is a Muslim name, which even appears as the name of one of chapters in the Qur'an. The term 'Junuz' may refer to Surah *Yunus* (Chapter 10) in the Qur'an. The progenitor **Junuz** also was not 'Turkified', but Islamised.

'Religious exclusion against Muslims was an ideologically motivated and politically organised process', stated Muhic. 20 The narration that the Haverics' progenitor came from the 'ethnicity or nationality of Serbs or their priest' is most likely ideologically inspired and instructed by *Danilov's Code* from 1855, which recognised a Muslim group in Montenegro, but states, 'There is no nationality in this country except Serbian ... Although there is no nationality in this country except Serbian and no other religion except Eastern Orthodox, every foreigner can live freely and enjoy this freedom and our domestic rights as every Montenegrin and Mountaineer enjoys it'.[21] Although in Montenegro the freedom to practise Islam was recognised even before the Berlin Congress, Montenegrin Muslims were still falsely considered as Serbs or of Serbian Orthodox origin which was nothing else than 'hairdressing history'.[22]

Since then, others have continued writing similar stories about various Muslim families, including the genealogy of the Haverics, linking it to Bjelopavlici and the wider region of Zeta to Spuz.[23] For them, Bjelopavlici could be the place of origin for the Haverics before they moved to Podgorica but they denied their authentic Bosniak origin. The reason for the story could be 'masking' the event of the 15th century when Kaleta Kalezic lost a battle in Bjelopavlici from a certain kadi.[24] The Serbian story was told to create their 'victory' over the Ottomans, despite the fact the Haverics are not Turks, but authentic European Muslims. Those who 'invented' that story believed it was the 'only correct one'; for them, it 'must be right'. For instance, the claim that the Turks did not build a fortification, 'Depedogen', around Podgorica in the 15th century but earlier by Stefan Nemanjic, the Grand Prince of Serbia, is equally false.

In particular, Neso K. Stanic, in 1910, wrote a similar, but the longest story in the *Monument to the Shadows of Podgorica Serbs* considered every ethnic identity is of Serbian and/or Orthodox origin.[25] In his writing, he put the following lines in the mouth of Hamza Salih bey:

> The Haverics are from Bjelopavlici, the village of Slatina; after the Turks conquered Podgorica in 1443, Sultan Mehmed himself came and brought his first headman with him. His name was Emir and Haji Sultan, which means the 'elder of all Turkish hadjis'. Upon his departure, the sultan left Emir behind to spread Muhammad's faith [Islam]. Of the first Turks, only four remained there: Memo from whom the Memovics were descended, Azgan from whom the Azganovics were descended, Ago from whom the Agovics were descended, and Ahmet from whom the Ahmetovics were descended.
>
> I think ours was the name of monk (pope) Ilija Kaluder from the Zdrebanik Monastery – he had two more brothers: Bosko, from whom the Boskovici came and Kalez, from whom the Kalezics in Bjelopavlici and the Kalics Turkic people in Kolasin and we are related to all of them. Monk (pope) Ilija brought with him some Christian books that were placed with the *fermans*

> (decree issued by sultan). Then, our ancestors received these *fermans* from the first Sultans because we were faithful to the Turkish religion, but today we don't have any of those Christian books or *fermans.* Monk Ilija was personally turned to the Turks by the Emir and Hadji Sultan, who gave him name **Junus.** Afterwards **Junus** got married and his wife became pregnant. One morning, a messenger runs to the Emir, as soon as the latter saw him walking cheerfully, he was asked by *hayirli havaz* ('happy voice'), and when he told him that **Junus** had a male child, he blessesed the messenger and orders that the newborn be named Haver, from which we Haverics, for whom he also built a house, he placed a saber in the foundation of the same house, but it is not written in which place in the *tevarih* (chronicle). After establishing 'Muhammad's faith' [Islam] here in Podgorica, the emir went to Donja Zeta to preach there as well; he settled in the town of Zabljak (conquered by the Turks in 1482), and pushed many people there, and gave them large estates and power over heaven, and made a *turbe* (monument) in Zabljak, where he and his family were later buried.

In contrast to Nesic's uncertain writing, not all residents were Eastern Orthodox Christians, which the existence of the Bogomil tombstones clearly confirms. For him, no single Muslim family derived its roots from the inhabitants, who were the Bogomils and embraced Islam. In his mistaken view, they could only have been descendants from the Christian Orthodox Serbs unless they were Muslims from a Turkish background like the four families mentioned in the story.

Despite the mentioned details of 'Nesic's Hamza story', it is more than mere fabrication, although some Haveric family members still believe it as the truth. As for the fabricated story of Hamza Salih bey, in 1910, he could not have known all those details from the past (1480s) because 'he had no saved written traces at that time'.[26] The story is constructed for ideological purposes by a passionate ideologist. **Dr Ismail Haveric** stated, 'Hamza Salih bey certainly couldn't remember 1910 more than my grandfather, **Hadji Hafiz Miftar bey** (1870-1940) and great-grandfather **Jusuf bey**, who had knowledge of the origin of the Haveric family from his father, **Hadji Husein bey**'. He added that 'the ideologists wrote what they wanted for Muslim genealogies as Muslims, including the Haverics, due to their struggles in turbulent times, didn't have the chance to write their genealogy story down. They were robbed, their houses were demolished or burned down, their business premises were destroyed, many were expelled and some killed. With this their written family history 'went to dust'.

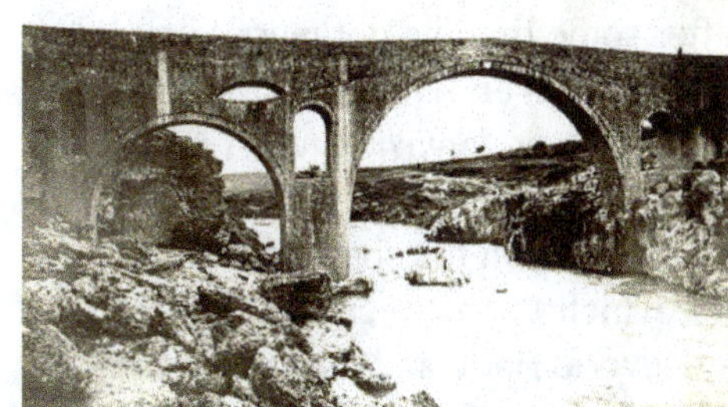

The Vizier Bridge

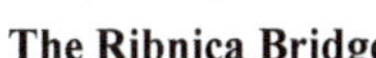

The Ribnica Bridge

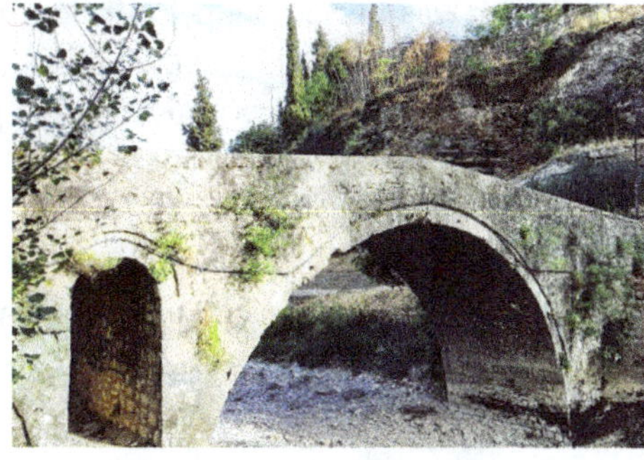

Most importantly, there is a non-ideological story about the conversion to Islam of the Haveric progenitor, re-told by some Haverics, whose interpretation has been summarised:

> … When the Turks reached the shore of the Ribnica River in Podgorica, they camped with their army at the mouth of the Ribnica River in Moraca River. The Ottoman invaders came to Podgorica led by Sultan Medmed II El Fatih, who was accompanied by a certain Arab, Hadji Emir. He met an inhabitant later named **Junus**, in a place where later some members of the Haveric family lived (next to Slatina). In the meeting with Hadji Emir, he expressed his desire to convert to Islam. Haji Emir showed him how to perform ablution and confess *shahada.* He followed it and voluntarily agreed to be a follower of Islam (*Mu'min*). Hadji Emir gave him the name **Junus** and he became a new Muslim (*Muslim-i nev*), and after some time he got married and had a son, whom he named **Haver**. The birth of **Haver** was a *khaber* (*haber*, news), a *hayirli havaz* (happy voice). This is how the name of the family Haveric's brotherhood 'came into being'. On the coast of Moraca, there is still a stone on which this conversion to Islam took place; called the 'Haveric Bath' and then the house of Haveric was built, in whose foundation a golden saber was buried. Haji Emir continued to spread Islam by going to Donja Zeta, Zabljak, where he would die, and there a *turbe* was raised in his place…

A short version of this the most relevant genealogy story narrates:

> The conversion took place in Podgorica when **Junuz**, Haver's father, later a progenitor of the Haveric family,

> got married and got a son named H a v e r (Arabic: 'dawn', *sabah,* also an 'educated man'). It was given by a certain Haji-Sultan, because 'the child was born at dawn'. The Haveric brotherhood (family) was named after **Haver**.[27]

Whether that Arab, Haji Emir, belonged to the Sayid family, who often spread Islam in different parts of the world, is hard to claim nor does this work want to speculate about it.

Fragmented Statistics, 1894

At the beginning of the 18th century, 119 Muslim brotherhoods (families) in Podgorica were recorded, including the brotherhood of Haveric.[28] The later statistic of Bogisicev archive Cavtat, XVI, 4. from 1894 shows that 7 Haveric families lived in Podgorica and 3 Haveric families were in Bjelopavlici.[29]

Genealogy of the 'Mohammedans' of Podgorica 'Rodoslovlje muhamedanaca Podgorickih'

(Bogišićev arhiv Cavtat, XVI, 4. – 1894.god)

	Prezimena		Lokacije	Prezimena		
55.	Brunčevići	-	Nikšića	Brunčevići	1	1
56.	Taljanovići	-	Zete	Taljanovići	1	1
57.	Salahagići	-	Azije	Salahagići	1	1
58.	**Averići**	**-**	**Bjelopavlića**	**Averići**	**7**	**7**
59.	Kerovići	-	-	Kerovići	2	2
60.	Abdići	-	Gruda	Abdići	2	2
61.	Rakići	-	Brskuta	Rakići Šabanovići	2 1	3
62.	Pokrklići	-	Velestova	Pokrklići	3	3
63.	Tuzovići	-	Tuza	Tuzovići	2	2
64.	Adži Ametovići	-	Gradca	Adži Ametovići	2	2
65.	Pirovići	-	-	Pirovići	1	1
66.	Perkočevići	-	-	-	1	1
67.	Bibezići	-	Tuđemila	Bibezići	1	1
68.	Redžići	-	Gruda	Redžići	3	3
69.	Smakovići	-	Gruda	Smakovići	1	1

70.	Cucovići	-	Cuca	Cucovići	3	3
71.	Kapići	-	Pipera	Kapići	3	3
72.	Dedovići	-	Gradca	Dedovići	1	1
73.	Krkanovići	-	Gruda	Krkanovići	1	1
74.	Adži Alovići	-	Lopara	Adži Alovići	2	2

Muslims in Zeta ('Muhamedanci u Zeti')

(Bogišićev arhiv Cavtat, XVI, 3. – 1894.god)

Br.	Bratstva	Bratstva se dijele na manja bratstva	Kuća u bratstvu	Odakle se bratstvo doselilo
1.	Ajdar Kučevići	Begovići; Alunovići Kubasičići	8	Kuča
2.	Redžovići	Redžovići	1	Bjelopavlića
3.	Rkočevići	Rkočevići	1	Kuča
4.	Dibranin	Dibranin	1	Dibre
5.	**Averići**	**Averići**	**3**	**Bjelopavlića**
6.	Usenagići	Usenagići	5	Iz Bajica u Podgoricu, pa u Zetu
7.	Adžagići	Adžagići	7	Iz Bajica u Podgoricu, pa u Zetu
8.	Smajovići	Smajovići	2	Ne zna se odakle su
9.	Omurovići	Omurovići	4	Kuča
10.	Adži Omerovići	Adži Omerovići	2	Budve
11.	Lampirovići	Lampirovići	3	Dobrskog Sela
12.	Mustagrudići	Mustagrudići	6	Gruda
13.	Piranići	Piranići; Elezovići	5	Bajica
14.	Adži Jusufovići	Adži Jusufovići; Mujoadžići	8	Gruda
15.	Ablahovići	Ablahovići	1	Lješanske nahije (Oraha)
16.	Babaasanovići	Babaasanovići	1	Azije
17.	Strinići	Strinići	4	Spuža

Muslims in Zeta in 1894
(Muslimani u Zeti u 1894)
Rodoslovlje podgoričkih muslimana, 1894

Schematic Presentations of the Family Tree

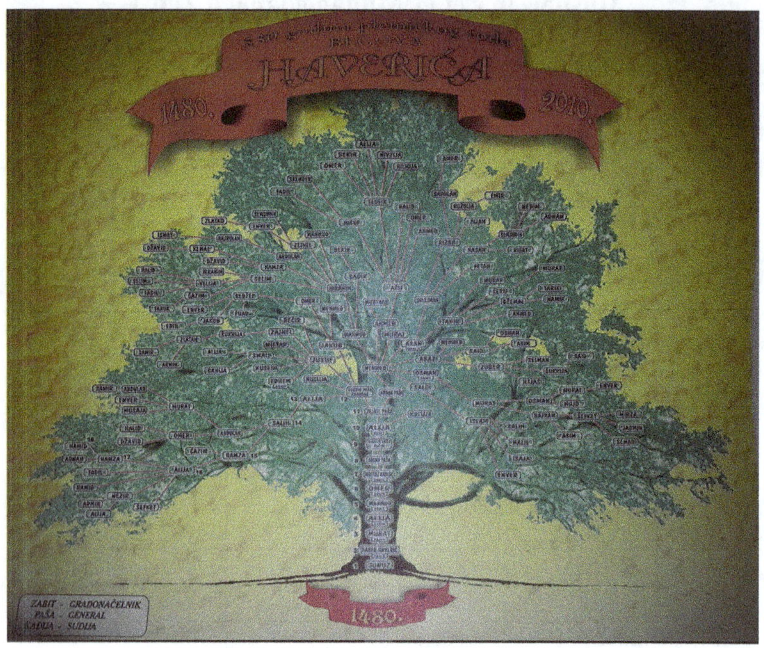

Family tree of the Haveric found in Montenegro

The schematic representation of the Haveric family tree began with the progenitor **Junus** and his son **Haver**. After the first Haver in genealogy there were three more names of Haver in Montenegro, Albania and Turkiye, which also testified to the Haverics' long tradition associated with name **Haver**. After the family archive was destroyed in 1918, the oldest surviving members of the family tried to reconstruct the family tree using their memories and schematic representations.

The schematic representations, oral and written traditions confirm an interest in cherishing the family genealogy. For instance, at the end of the 19th century or beginning of the 20th century, **Sulejman bey** and **Jusuf bey Haveric** made the first reconstructed schematic representation of the Haveric genealogy based on its male linkages. Sulejman bey was an imam and one of the oldest in the Haveric family, who carefully kept memories of the ancestors during his life in Podgorica, then as a *muhajir* (refugee) in Shkodra, as recorded in the family tree. One written source about him said:

> **Sulejman bey** took 'paper and *lapis* (pencil)' and drew a tree and branches. He placed circles on the branches, and wrote the names of Haveric in them. He spoke about the common roots of this large family, and about his work based on the Turkish *tarih* (chronicle) of Haveric. He said that other family branches of Haveric were also developed from that big tree…

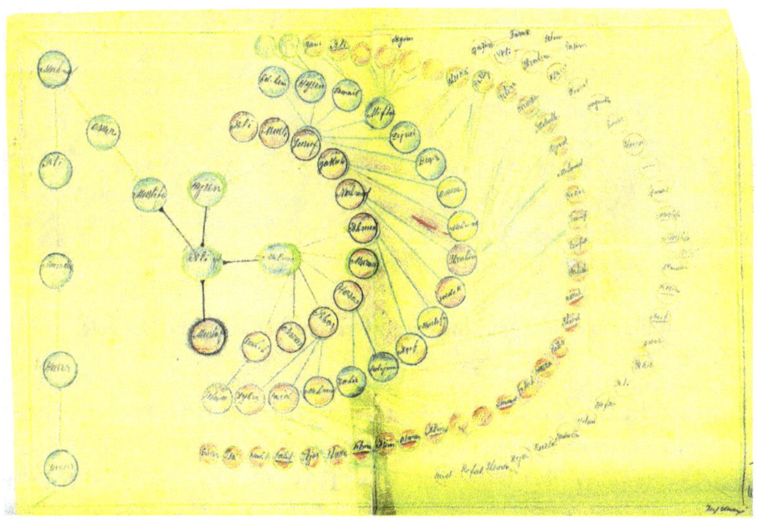

Family tree made in Shkoder

On this account of the Haveric genealogy, which was written in Albania, the Haveric names are written in the Albanian alphabet and **Dr Yumer (Omer) Haveri** wrote about this preserved family tree and the desire to unify the family branches in the entire Haveric family tree:

> It has been a long time since I have written down the roots (family tree, genealogy) of our Haveric family (genealogy), which have been preserved and recorded well by Rizah's father **Sulejman bey** and **Jusuf**, my uncle. I think that your branch of the family tree (part of the family genealogy) is also large and widespread in Albania, Yugoslavia and Turkiye, and I would like, if possible, for you to write down your branch of our family if you know more about it…

Ima mnogo vremena te na moje ruke, imam upisano korin naše familje "Haverića" (genealogia) koja se oderžala dobro od oca Riza Sylejman Bega, i Jusufa, moj stric. Mislim e naša svojta je velika i raširena u Albaniu, Jugoslaviju i Tursku, i volim ako je moguće da ovu granu korina naše svojte pišemo još od vas koji može da zna više (takođe su mi rekli)

A manuscript about the preserved family tree of the Haverics

Oral traditions about the genealogy of Haveric have also been preserved from generation to generation. One of the oldest stories was told by **Selim bey Haveric** to his son **Cazim**

bey, one of the longest-lived members of the Haveric family. **Bahrija Haveric**, who also lived for over 100 years, gave her story:

> I have a load of pictures, but our cousin took them and now he doesn't bring them back to me for four months. I hope he will bring them, as he is still writing. He borrowed the father's data which he recorded about the family tree... The cousin is going to make a book about Haverics...

Hazera, Bahrija's daughter, said a long time ago someone from the family in Albania tried enthusiastically to write a book on the Haveric family. Probably, it was **Agim Haveri** in Tirana who from 1968 started to collect and record individual names and photos of Haverics as well as some short biographies. **Nazira Haveric** was also instrumental in collecting data about the Haverics like **Dr Hilmi Haveric**, both in Albania. Nevertheless, Agim wrote a long list of Haverics scattered across the Balkan areas. He became one of the main archivists for the collection of historical material for the Haveric genealogy and wrote the following lines:

Squeezing the memories

Collecting the remaining memory,
like pieces of hidden pearls,
like multi-coloured but pale petals,
we will try to list them in order
and put those stories on paper,
to perpetuate and inherit,
as a reflection and example between generations[30]

Similar examples in recording genealogy of the Haveric family are evident in Shkoder, Durres and Kavaja by **Fadil Tasim Haveriku**, who collected data from his aunt **Naxija Xeka Haveriku** around 1954. A related effort was made by other Haveriku families in Kavaje and Durres. In Sarajevo, the architect **Semsudin (Dino)** made a schematic representation of the tree in large paper format. **Kemal Hamza bey**, **Fadil Alija bey** and **Dr Ismail Halil bey Haveric** wrote their accounts on the family genealogy. The Haveric families in Podgorica and Bar also cherish their written tradition, especially by **Dr Ismail Haveric**. Family branches in Bosnia, Montenegro, Albania and Turkiye preserved data about the family genealogy, with some rare connections with the genealogical branches, such as the **Tanbay** (Haveric) family.

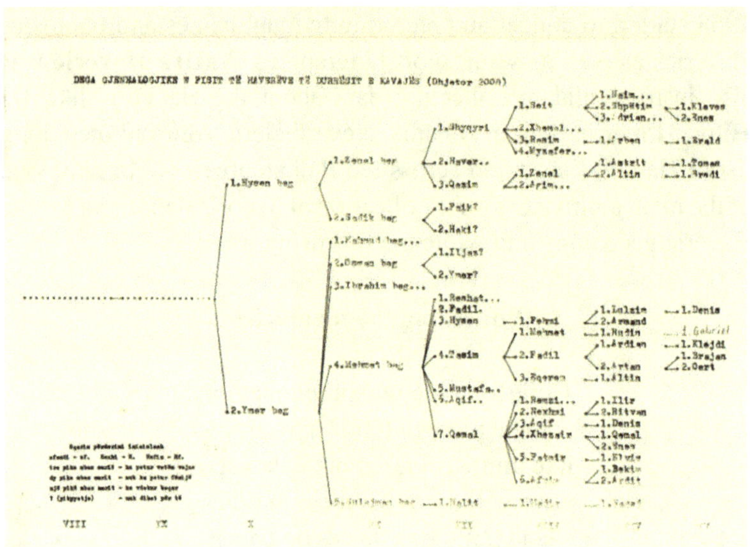

Family tree made in Durres and Kavaja

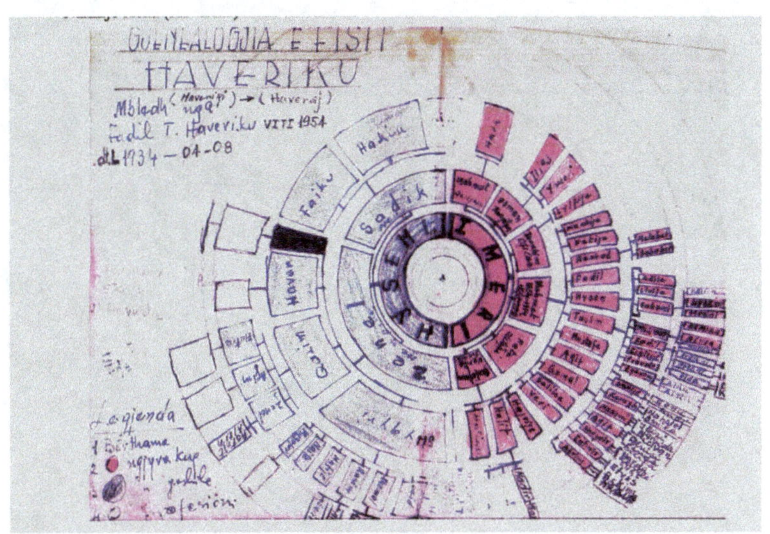

Family tree made in Durres

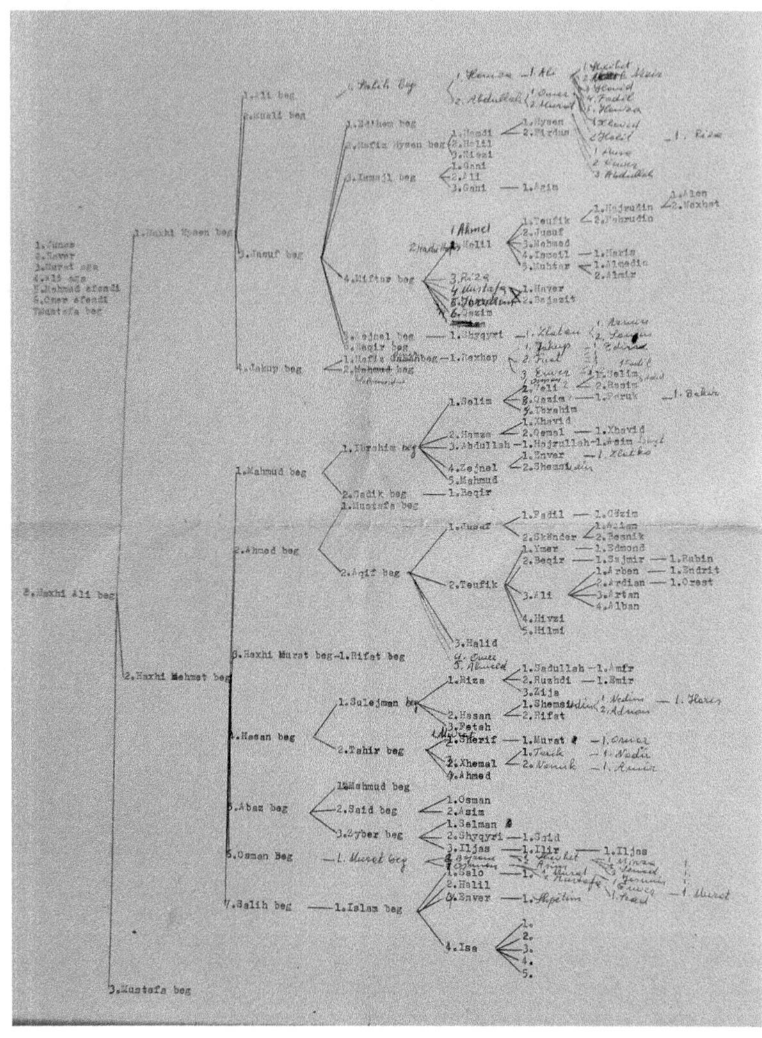
1.Ali beg
1.Haxhi Hysen beg
1.Edhem beg
2.Hafiz Hysen beg
3.Ismail beg
3.Jusuf beg
4.Miftar beg
5.Zejnel beg
6.Beqir beg
4.Jakup beg
1.Hamdi
2.Halil
3.Riza
1.Gani
2.Ali
3.Gani
1.Azim
1.Hysen
2.Firdus
1.Teufik
2.Jusuf
3.Mehmed
4.Ismail
5.Muhtar
1.Hajrudin
2.Fahrudin
1.Alen
2.Nexhat
1.Haris
1.Haver
2.Bajazit
1.Shyqyri
1.Rexhep
2.Haxhi Ali beg
2.Haxhi Mehmet beg
1.Mahmud beg
1.Ibrahim beg
2.Sadik beg
1.Selim
2.Hamza
3.Abdullah
4.Zejnel
5.Mahmud
1.Beqir
1.Xhevid
2.Qemal
1.Hajrullah
1.Enver
2.Ahmed beg
1.Mustafa beg
1.Jusuf
2.Aqif beg
1.Fadil
2.Skënder
1.Gëzim
2.Besnik
1.Ymer
2.Beqir
2.Teufik
3.Ali
4.Hivzi
5.Hilmi
3.Halid
1.Edmond
1.Sajmir
1.Rubin
1.Arben
1.Endrit
2.Ardian
1.Orest
3.Artan
4.Alban
3.Haxhi Murat beg-1.Rifat beg
4.Hasan beg
1.Sulejman beg
2.Tahir beg
1.Riza
2.Hasan
3.Fetah
1.Sadullah
2.Ruzhdi
3.Zija
2.Rifat
2.Xhemal
4.Ahmed
1.Murat
5.Abaz beg
1.Mahmud beg
2.Said beg
3.Zyber beg
1.Osman
2.Asim
1.Selman
2.Shyqyri
3.Iljas
1.Said
1.Ilir
1.Iljas
6.Osman Beg
7.Salih beg
1.Islam beg
1.Salo
2.Halil
4.Isa
3.Mustafa beg

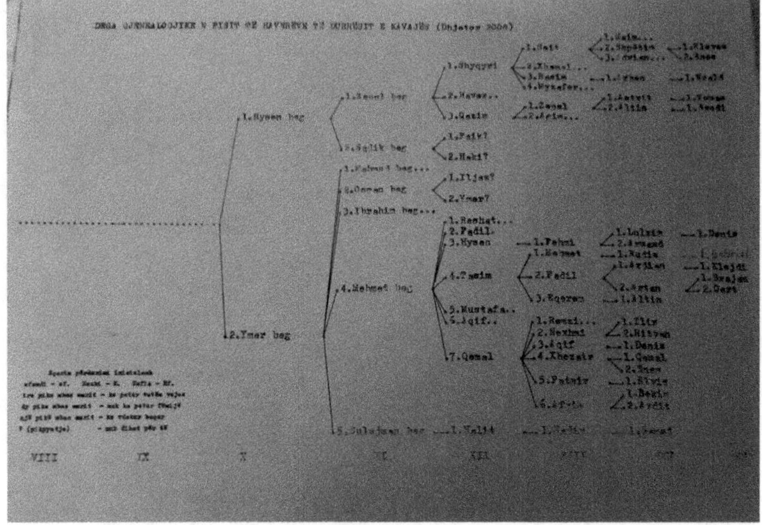

Durres and Kavaje branches of the Haveric family tree

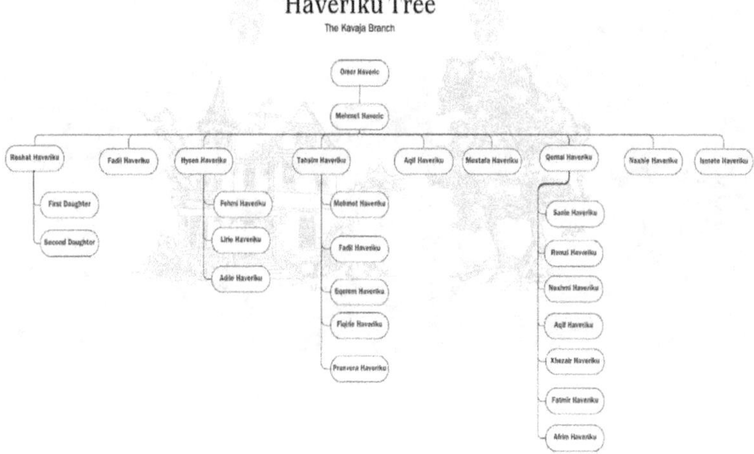

The Kavaje branch of the Haveriku family tree by Haverikus in Kavaja

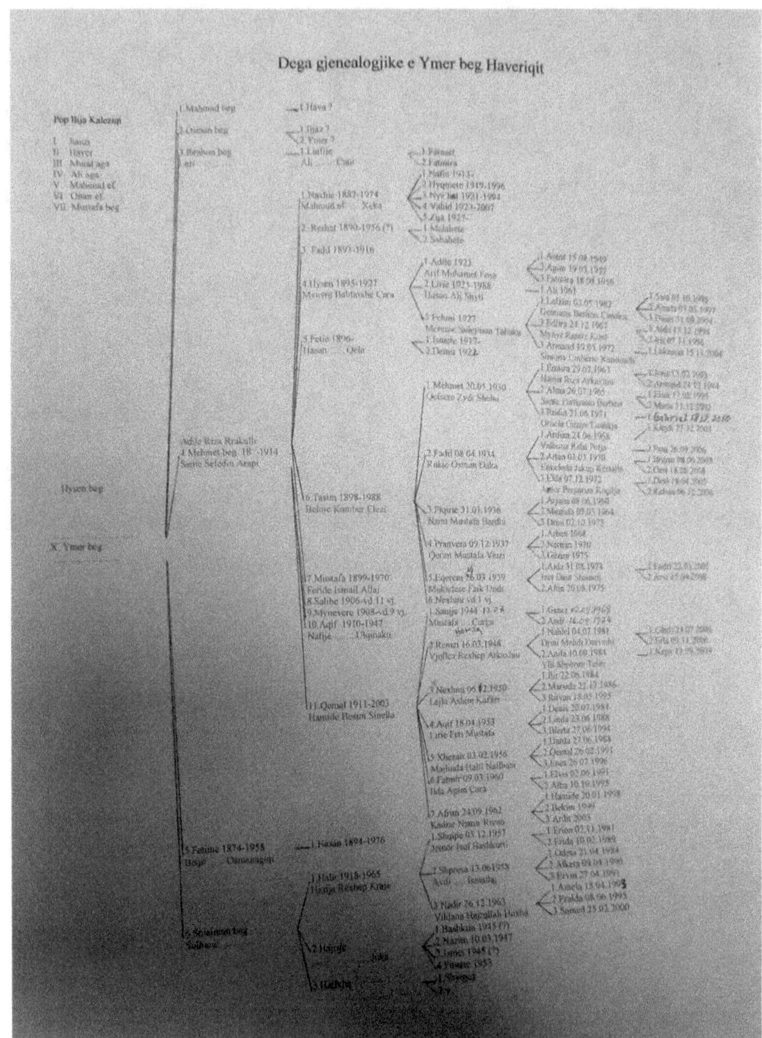

Branch of Ymer Bey Haveric

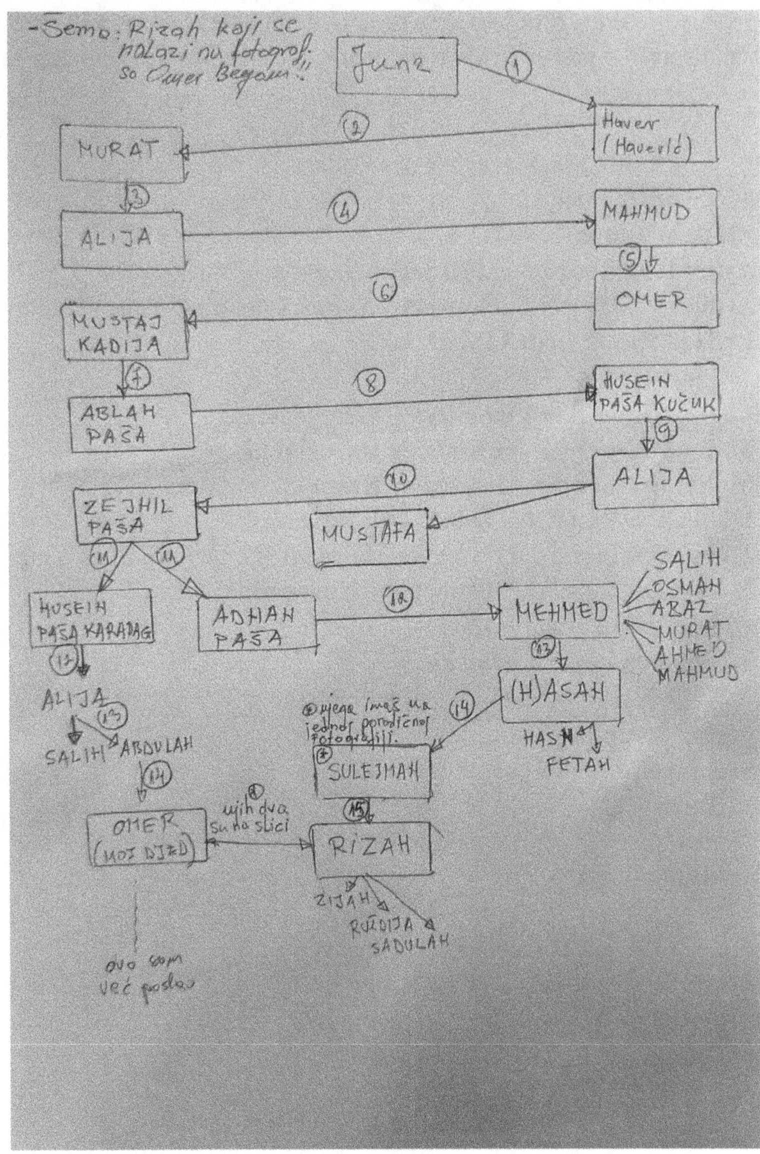

Family tree made by Enver Backovic in Sarajevo, Bosnia

A few more brunches need to be added to the Haveric family tree and some of names (from top down – ancestors to descendants – *paternal lines*) from it are:

- **Tahir bey Haveric's** descendants:

Mehmet Haveric
Ali Rıza Tanbay's sons:
Aydın Rıza Tanbay and **Erdogan Tanbay**
Aydin's son **Haver Tanbay – Haver's** sons **Dogan** and **Yunus Tanbay**
Erdogan's son **Cem Tanbay**

- **Omer (i.e. Ymer) bey's** descendants:

Mahmut Ymer (i.e. Omer) bey Haveriqi his brother, **Osman Mahmut Ymer (i.e. Omer) bey Haveriqi** sons are:
1. **Ibrahim Ymer (i.e. Omer) bey Haveriqi**
2. **Osman Ymer (i.e. Omer) bey Haveriqi** his sons **Ilijaz** and **Ymer**
3. **Mehmet Ymer (i.e. Omer) bey Haveriqi**
4. **Sulejman bey (i.e. Omer)**
5. **Mehmed bey (i.e. Omer)**

- **Salih bey's** son:

Suljo (Seljo) Salih bey Averic with sons:
1. **Ramo**
2. **Sacir**
3. **Muhammad**

- **Husein Haveric's** descendants:

Mustafa
Abdullah
Bekir

- **Miftar Haveric's** sons:

1. **Hafiz Halil's sons Teufik, Jusuf, Mehmed, Ismail and Muhtar/ Teufik's son Fahro/ Ismail's son Haris/ Muhtar's sons Almedin and Almir**
2. **Rizah**
3. **Ibrahim**
4. **Mustafa's sons Bajazit, Murat and Haver**
5. **Cazim**

- **Omer Haveriku**

Mehmed's sons:
Remzi, **Nexhmi**, **Aqif**, **Xhezair**, **Fatmir** and **Afrim Haveriku**

Rudin Mehmed Haveriku

Xhemal Shyqyri Haveriku

Nazim Haveriqi

- A few ancestors of different branches to be included:

Muhamed Haveric

Nazim Haveric

Reshat Adenise

Father of Murad and grandfather of Osman, **Haji Sulejman**

You may add your ancestral information in the last section of the book titled 'an addition to my family branch'.

The Noble Titles of the Haverics

From the arrival of the Ottomans in Montenegro and the Balkans, the Haverics hold their honorific tradition of the beys for 500 years. A publicist, Zelimir Rukavina, wrote in the article *Podgorica Muslims in the past* that 'Haverics are among several Muslim noble families' and that they were among 'the most prominent families in Podgorica'. Similarly, it is also written that in the second half of the 18th century, 'famous families in Podgorica were Osmanagics, Lacevics and Haverics'.[31] During the Ottoman period, the Haverics lived, worked and ruled in the Zeta region of Montenegro, which is between Podgorica and Lake Shkoder. Today, its largest part is the territory of the Municipality of Golubovci, which is within the capital city of Podgorica.[32] The highly appointed Haveric maintained fidelity to Islam and Turkish rule.

'Bey' is a Turkish word that means a nobleman, a title usually given to those who were representatives of the military order. Later, the term applied to those who were wealthy or had a reputation as chieftains. It is also an honorific traditionally applied to people with 'special lineages' to the leaders or rulers of variously sized areas in Central Asia, South Asia, Southeast Europe and the Middle East by the Ottomans. The feminine equivalent title was 'begum'. The word 'begum' for the wives was added to husbands' names, signifying their marriage relationship (e.g. Selim-begum, 'Selimbegovica' or Hamza-begum 'Hamzabegovica'). The regions or provinces where beys ruled or administered were called *beylik*. Depending on the size and importance of the beylik, it roughly meant 'governorate' or 'region', which is the equivalent of a county, duchy, grand duchy or principality in Europe.

The honorific title 'bey' is somewhat equivalent to the title of 'lord' in the United Kingdom, which is not always transferable but similar to the way the titles 'sir' and 'mister' are used in the English language.[33] 'Distinguished persons and their sons' as well as 'high government officials' could become beys, which was one of two conventional designations as indefinite as 'esquire' has come to be in the United Kingdom.[34] Early Muslim families of ancient beliefs, most notably Bogomils, were 'role models' for other families to spread Islam. The Ottomans granted them high posts, especially if they held large blocks of land or were keen to maintain rule on their behalf. This is because, at the beginning, the Ottomans were hesitant to give high posts to Christians until the 17th century but later this changed.[35]

The Ottomans introduced completely new honours, titles and styles for the Ottoman Sultan. The general rule is that the honorific title is used with first names and not with surnames or last names. Next to Muslim names there were added titles, honorary titles for offices, positions and ranks testifying to their belonging to the nobility.[36] In accordance with the Turkish concept of personal nobility, these titles were based on merit, so not inherited by their descendants. The greatest title was *Pasha*, which was a military or civil title awarded to high-ranking civil servants like ministers and governor in the Western world, and the title was not transmitted to descendants. This does not mean these titles were not held within the same family for several generations, but if so, only on a personal basis as a tradition.[37] The title of bey was given to honourable people or the elite among the Bosniaks under the Ottomans in Montenegro, Bosnia, Albania, Macedonia and surrounding areas.

The Haveric family has a noble tradition. They enjoyed respect, especially from the local urban people and authorities who were aware of their merit. During the Ottoman Empire, many Haverics held honorific titles and posts in military, civil and religious professions. One Haveric was a *Musir* (field marshal), while several held the rank of *Pasha*, which was given to high-ranking military or civil dignitaries for their contribution. There was one Haveric with the title *Miralay* (colonel) and another with the tile *Binbası* (major), several were *Zabits* (commanders of the town), a *Kaptan* (captain) and two were *Katibs* (a scribe or vizier's secretary), one *Bashqatip* (chief secretary of the court) and two *Kaymakams* (administrators of district kazas, customs officers), one or two *Konsolosars* (consul) and one recorded as *Agha* (an honorific title for a civilian or officer) or other dignitaries.

Several Haveric beys were *Kadis* (Muslim judge, an expert in the Sharia law but also an administrator of the region). A few families were appointed by the sultan on the recommendation of the highest religious officials and were in effect civil servants. Other religious titles held by Haverics, like by some other families, were *Shaikh* or *Imam* (Islamic Sufi leader or high cleric), *Hafiz* (one who knows the Qur'an by heart) and *Hoja* (Muslim cleric). *Effendi* (literally, master, a man of high education or social standing owner, dignitary) was a designation common not only in Southeast Europe, but in other parts of the world. Several Haverics held these titles after being educated in Islamic studies in Istanbul and being appointed as religious leaders. During this time, they enjoyed respect from the community and government because of their religious education, which was highly regarded. Although the roles of the Haveric women were less known, they enjoy respect within family circles. In Ottoman time and afterwards, *Kaduna* meant a Muslim woman of noble birth, a distinguished woman or similar.

In the Kingdom of Montenegro, a few Haverics were royal *senators*, several were influential representatives in other fields of the kingdoms, while a few were *perjanici* (royal flag bearers), the officers in the honorary units of the Montenegrin royalty.[38] In the Albanian Kingdom, there were a couple secretaries, including *Bashqatip* in the court of King Zog. In the Republic of Turkiye, one Haveric was a general and another held a high position in the Turkish Department of Police. In 1934, Republican Turkish authorities, under Act No. 2590, abolished titles and appellations such as effendi, bey and pasha.[39]

The Turkish *Defters* (a type of tax register and land cadastre in the Ottoman Empire), as important sources of demographic, property and statistical data, mainly included tax payers (*rayah*), but did not list the Muslim population exempt from taxes, such as nobles, ulema, dervishes and their followers, former military personnel and elders; that is, 'the civil population that was exempt from paying taxes'.[40] These were the reasons why the Haveric beys probably were not recorded in the Ottoman *Defters*. While the title of bey continued in the kingdoms of Montenegro and Albania, it gradually lost its significance. While the honorific title 'bey' has not been used in Bosnia and Herzegovina, Albania and Turkiye since the mid-20th century, the title of 'bey' was kept only as a tradition by some descendants.

Podgorica and *Zabits* (Commanders)

When the Ottomans came to Podgorica in 1472-74, they built a military fortress at the mouth of the Ribnica and Moraca rivers. In 1496, Montenegro became an integral part of the Ottoman Empire (*T. Devlet-i Osmaniye*) and from 1499 it was annexed to the Sandjak of Shkoder. The city of Podgorica became the seat of state authorities where the entire religious educational and cultural life took place. Ottoman authorities were particularly involved in the urban development of society. The state took care of the construction and maintenance of roads, bridges, embankments and caravan routes, creating ideal conditions for the development of trade. Under Ottoman rule in 1477, they built a fortification around Podgorica, called 'Depedogen'. During construction of the fortress, a series of oriental streets and houses were created, which would later be better known as *Stara Varos* (old town of Podgorica). A valuable record of the appearance of Podgorica and its inhabitants was left by Evlija Celebija, a famous Turkish travel writer. Celebija visited Podgorica in 1660 and on that occasion noted this in his *Sayahatname* (Travel Book):

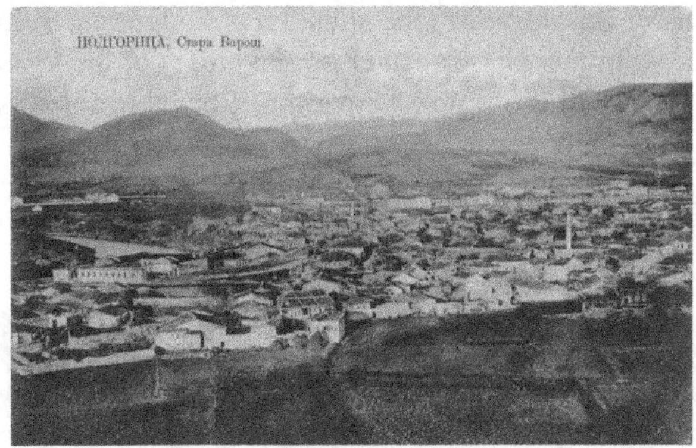

Podgorica

It [Podgorica] has a quadrangular fortress built of stone. It was equipped with strong towers, loopholes and battlements. It had one gate, and it lay on a sharp cliff surrounded by armour. The army was also stationed in the fortress. It housed the city commander and seven hundred brave soldiers. There were about 300 houses in the fortress. There was also a mosque, wheat barns, ammunition storage, cannons and cisterns…

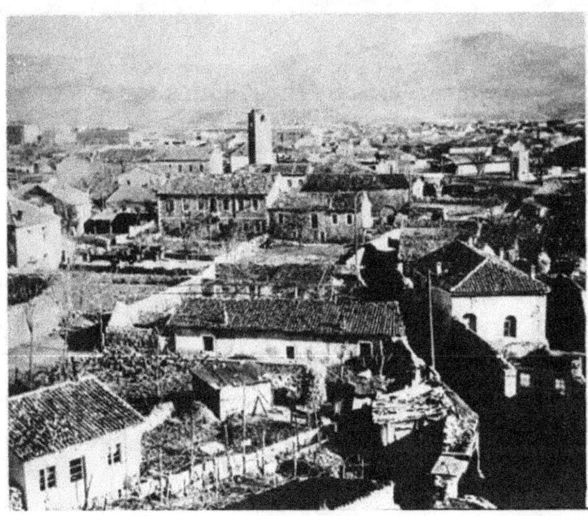

Podgorica, Stara Varos (old town of Podgorica)

A settlement was nestled in the old town of Podgorica, from the top of the caves to the Ribnica River, so the pillars of the houses were several metres in the water. Above the Ribnica River was built a bridge of the same name. About fifty meters below on the riverbank were the butcher, blacksmith and tanner shops. A part of Podgorica was named *Tabhana* ('Tabakhana') after the tanner shops.[41]

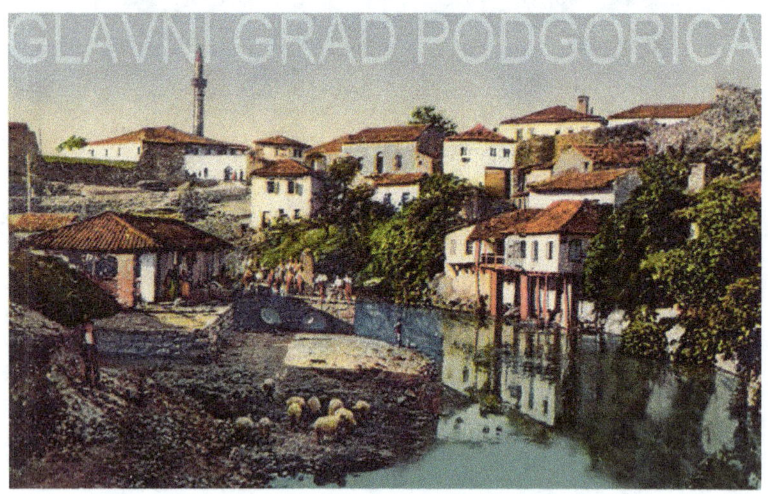

Stara Varos by the Ribnica River

Podgorica as an open urban settlement was gradually developed. During urbanisation it was predominantly inhabited by a Muslim population with several mosques and other Islamic institutions as part of the multi-religious life. So, Podgorica should not be attributed exclusively to an Islamic character. From the beginning of the Ottoman administration, there was a large Christian population too. In this small area, residents lived in harmony as good neighbours. The streets of the area were surrounded by fig, lemon and olive trees.

Beside *kadis* (judges), a key role in the law and order of the city was the *zabits* (or zabtiye, military commanders of the town, officers) and *ajans* from the ranks of 'well-chosen persons'. The *zabit* – 'a commander of the government authority' – commanded the city, while the *kadi* (Islamic judge) had jurisdiction not only in the city, but in the administrative region.[42] The Turkish word *zaptiye* was used to refer to the Ottoman Empire's gendarmerie, which derived from the Arabic word *dhaabet*, meaning 'officer'.

The imperial *berats* (Sultan's decree on appointment) were entrusted to the position of *zabit* with headquarters in old Podgorica. It is said that power in Podgorica rested on several families, including the Haveric family, who held the positions of *zabit* and *kadi*. Given the position of *zabit* was hereditary and passed from father to son or a close relative, Haverics held that position for several generations. According to the genealogy of the Haveric family in Montenegro, Albania and Bosnia, there were ten *zabits*, the first of which was **Haver**. The family tradition also held that '**Haver** was a friend of the Ottoman envoys and that he was also appreciated by other Muslim brotherhoods from those areas'.

After **Haver**, a *zabit* was **Alija bey**, then the beys of the family Haveric who also performed the function of *zabits*, recorded in the genealogical family tree, including **Murat**, **Alija**, **Mahmud**, **Omer**, **Mustaj Kadi**, **Alija**, **Edhem** and **Osman**. **Husain Pasha Kucuk**'s son, **Alija bey**, who was considered a learned man and the seventh in the chain of *zabits* among the Haveric family, developed an inter-ethnic understanding and tolerance in Podgorica. Several Haveric leaders of the town also emphasised common social interests and similar cultures above religious differences.[43] Such mutual respect contributed to urbanisation of the town, and for Muslims, it was an Islamic style of architecture, which was greatly developed under Ottoman rule.

In a part of Podgorica, Islamic-oriental urban planning was the most evident on the left bank of the Ribnica River.[44] It was reflected in Podgorica's *cardak* (*čardak*) towers (house's upper floor), which retained the essential features of urban life with the Mediterranean influence. In their lower parts that of courtyard, they had a garden and well, while their interior had a bathroom, *minderluk* or divan (long, cushioned seat), and a section with a straw bed and mattress. Those *cardak* towers had deeply dug foundations, usually built with the first part of stone and the upper parts made of oak wood.[45] The *cardak* opened its doors when 'the people of that part of the city used to come for *muhabat* (conversation), and when a visitor or traveller came to stay for a while'.[46] Friends from different cultural-religious backgrounds were traditionally welcomed.

At the beginning of Islamic architectural development, there were three *cardak* towers, one of which was built by the Haveric family among a few wealthier families in Podgorica.[47] The Haveric's tower along with two others built by other families had observation rooms for the protection of the headquarters.[48] Perhaps, it was **Zejnil Pasha** Haveric, a high military officer of the Sultan, who built the *cardak* tower, which was among the first of its kind in Podgorica. Tradition said, at the top of the tower, he had a well-kept garden. His house was in the centre of the fortress. He came to Podgorica every year to visit his family. When he finished his military mission, he sold that house.[49]

A further distinctive Islamic building type in Podgorica were the houses in the style of villas. A Muslim villa in an oriental style built in 1630 in *Stara Varos* (old town of Podgorica), where urban life began, was owned by the wealthy bey's Haveric family. The **Haveric villa** was a nice residential building of that time, which had several rooms and *verndah* (open-sided roofed structure). Under a ground floor, a storage area was in the basement. Sometimes, the lower part of the house was rented to a Montenegrin to run a café. During the war between 1876 and 1878, the *Basibozuks*, who were irregular Albanian soldiers in the Ottoman army, left their belongings in the café when they went to Shkoder. Their belongings were picked up and sold by the café proprietor to buy the house from the Haveric, who had moved to Anatolia. Local people believe there is a record in the tax records, including the former ownership of the house in the Cetinje archive.

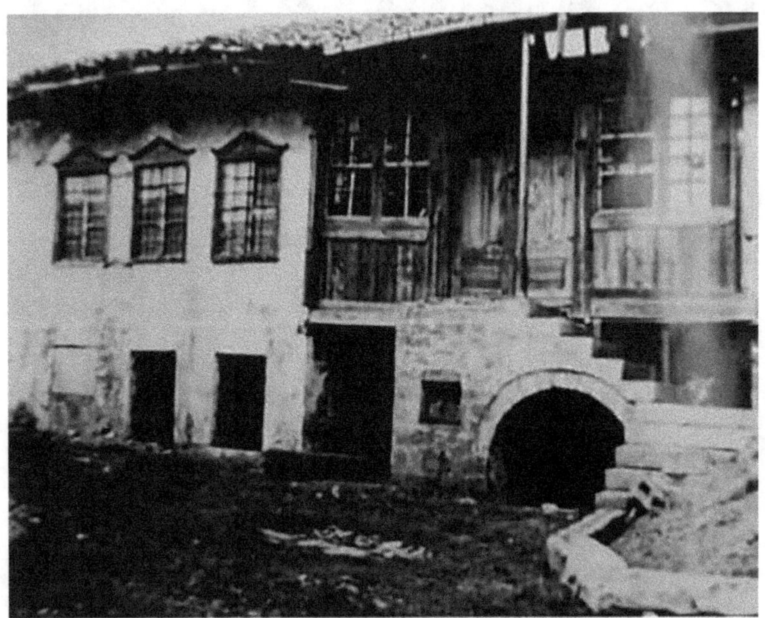

Remnants of the house of the Haveric bey in Stara Varos (old town of Podgorica)

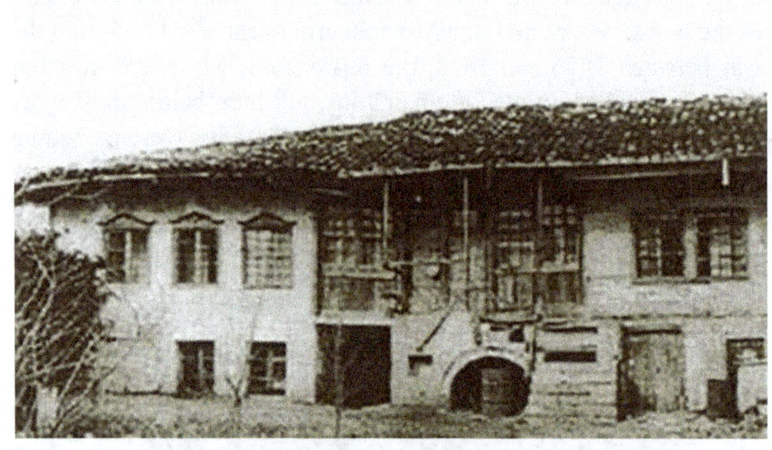

Remnants of the house of the Haveric bey in Stara Varos (old town of Podgorica)

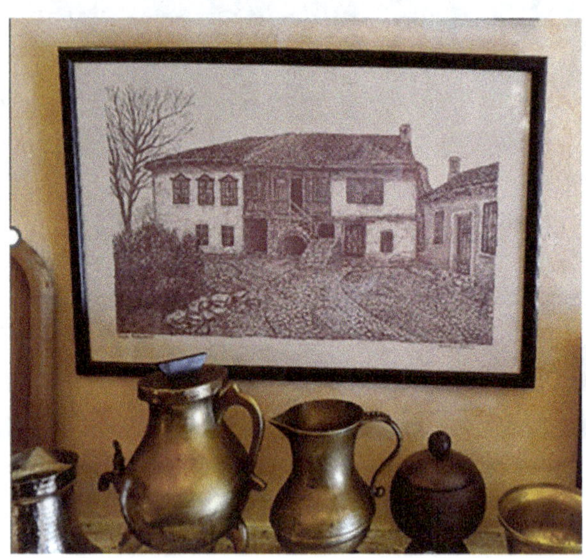

House of the Haveric bey in Stara Varos; an inspiration for painting

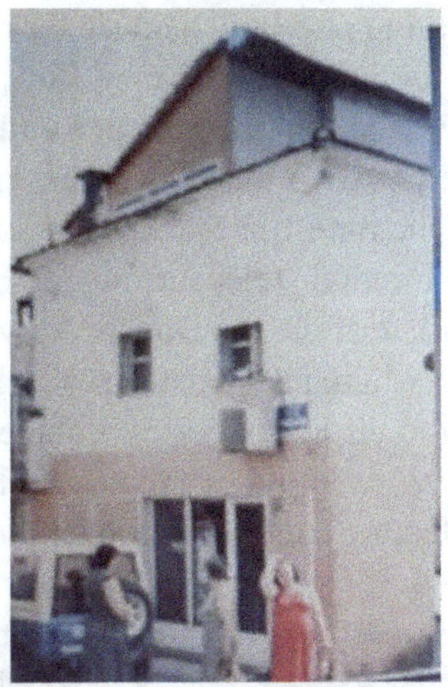

Jusuf bey and Ismail bey house in Podgorica, Stara Varos, 2007

In Podgorica, **Husein Pasha Karadag** had four sons: **Jusuf bey**, **Alija bey**, **Muslija bey** and **Jakup bey**. They were engaged in 'commercial work, butchering… His son **Jusuf bey** Haveric [and his son **Ismail**] lived in the two-story house'. It was built more than 100 years ago, said Agim, and continued:

> Entering a narrow street, where cars can barely walk, after you have passed the clock tower and walk just a little, without going to the old Doganjska Mosque, there is an alley on the left. Facing back there, on the right there is a large two-story house, now a small addition has been partially made on top of it. So, the house is built in the corner. That building, it is said, used to be a bank, which was previously called *Hazna* (Tabla). Down under the floor, they were filled up to the top with earth, maybe to prevent a fire or something else. The kitchen and the living room downstairs were filled with dirt, that is, the entire lower floor.[50]

Husein Pasha Karadag also built a house for his son **Jakub bey** in Stara Varos, which the heirs of **Mehmed bey** and **Omer bey** have preserved to this day. The son of **Redzep**, **Fuad** and next to it a son, **Enver**, still use the house, a legacy of their ancestors. The house is said to be one of the oldest in Stara Varos and Podgorica. It was made of stone in an oriental style, surrounded by walls with a large courtyard. It was built near the old Doganjska Mosque in the central alley of Stara Varos, where also existed several Haverics' houses.[51] In 1966, school textbooks in Podgorica included a depiction of this Haverics' house as an example of Islamic architecture.[52] Near the house was a water feature called 'the fountain of **Jakub bey**'.[53]

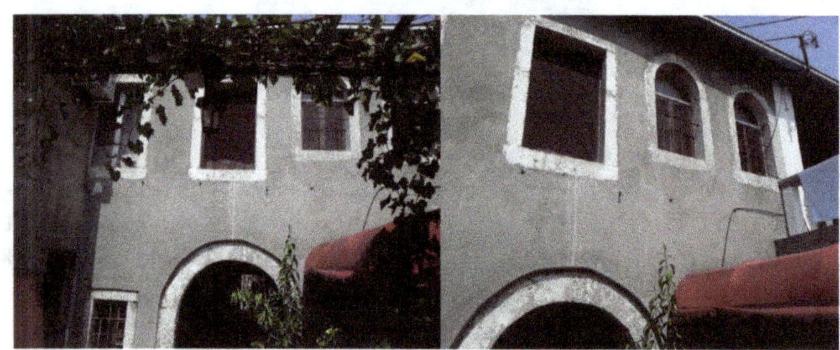

House of Haveric family in old Podgorica

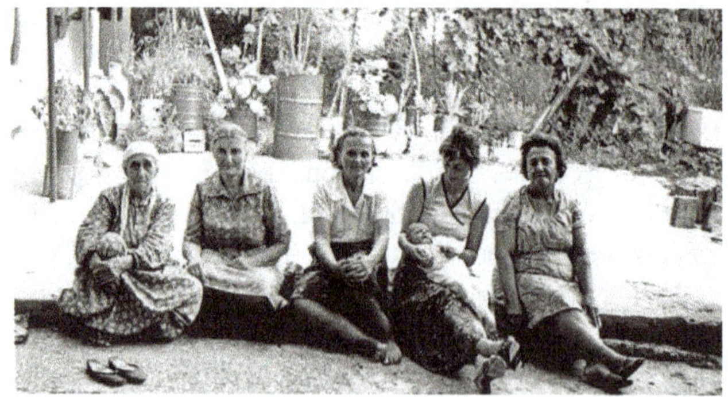

In the yard of the house

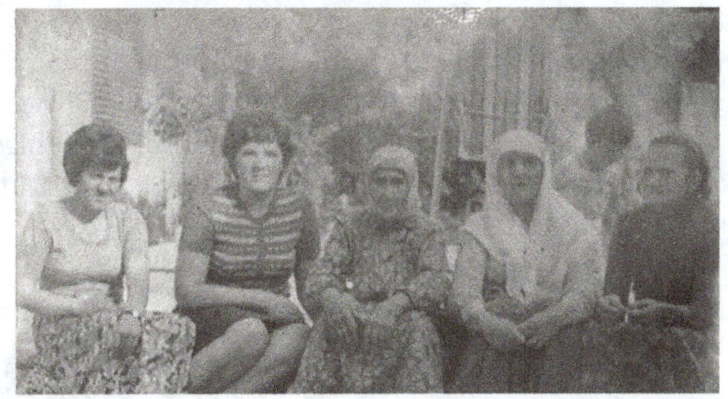

In the yard of the house

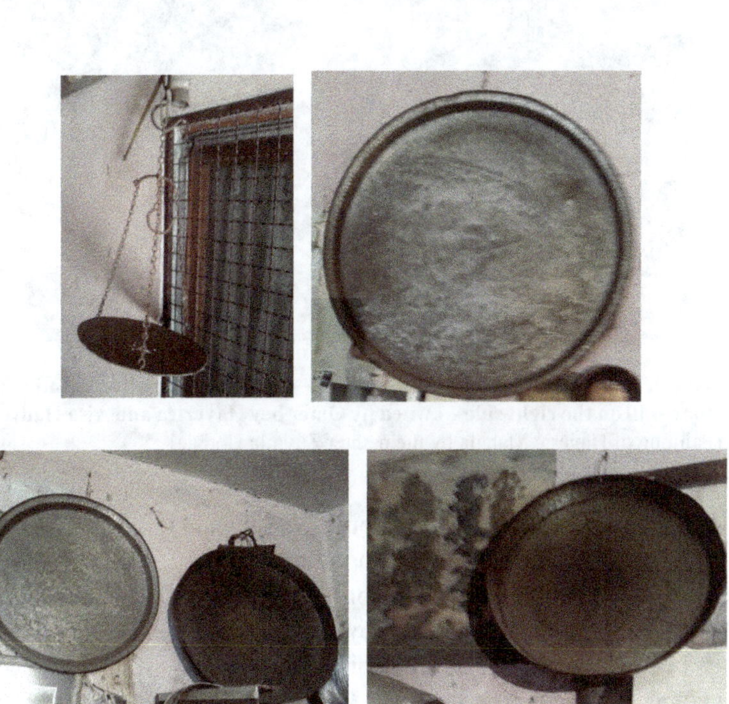

Scales and old pans used by Haveric women

In the attic of the house, copper buckets (*bolandža, kantar*) and several pans (*tepsija*) used by the old Haverics were placed. One part of the courtyard had a garden with flowers and partially covered with vines, and the other part was used for family meetings and welcoming friends of all religions and cultures, especially during Eid holidays.

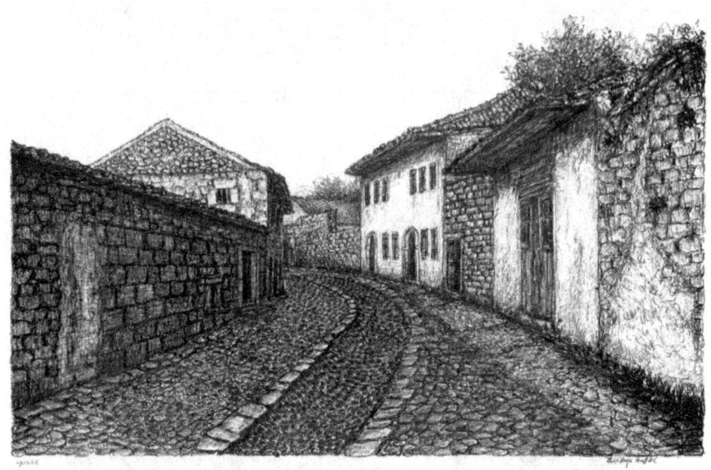

Haveric Mahala (street) in old Podgorica – with a two-store house and a long stone wall on the right side – owned by Omer bey Haverica and Aisa Hadrovic
(Painting of Haveric Mahala by the painter Zuvdija Hodzic)

One of the beautiful Haverics' houses was bought from the Orthodox Christian priest Prota Zahari Popovic, and when he died, his sons sold it to Omer Alibalic.[54] Another example of a large house in Stara Varos owned by **Omer bey**, a wealthy merchant. Because of its beauty, the house was an inspiration to painters who depicted its splendor of the time. There was **Omer's mahala** (street), probably according to the address where Omer bey lived.[55] Other streets bore names after the brotherhoods (families) that inhabited them or first founded them, and some families also bore an unofficial name of the mosque.[56] For example, the name of the street that led to that mosque was also lovingly called the **'Haveric's mahala'** because several Haveric families lived in that part of the town, or the old Doganja Mosque was fondly called the **'Haveric Mosque'** because of its imams from the Haveric family.

Among the landlord families were the Haveric.[57] It is also evident in the list of '*Muslim land (house) owners from Podgorica (February 23, 1879)*'. The following linkages of the Haverics were mentioned: **Mustafa**, **Abaz**, **Zejnel**, **Ibrahim**, **Jakup**, **Suljo**, **Islam**, **Mahmut bey**, **Zuber bey**, **Hasan Bey** and **Jusuf bey**.[58] Haverics' *begovat* was firmly and permanently tied to their home territory, possessions and privileges (*beyli*). In 1880, it was also recorded that **Ibrahim bey Haveric** had '229 sheep in the Podgorica captaincy' on his block of land.[59] From the city of Podgorica to Lake Shkoder, **Ibrahim bey** and other Haverics had their own land in Zeta, describing its size as 'how many days a year there were as many plows for ploughing'. Haverics had houses and shops not only in Podgorica but in Danilovgrad and Bar.[60]

The toponym, '**Crnjaka Haverica**' ('mulberry tree of the Haverics' beys') is reminiscent of the former residence of the Haverics in Stara Varos, until the liberation from the Turks.[61] The area from the Vezir bridge to the old town on the right bank of Moraca (where the sports centre is today) was called '**Haverica meadows**' ('Haveric livade'). These meadows were where the Turkish army camped.[62]

On the right bank of the Moraca River in the central part of Podgorica, the Haveric family as well as Zlaticanin and Milonjic families had their own land.[63] It was the land of Kruska Glavica (Krusevac), where King Nikola built a castle in 1891, after the Montenegrin liberation of Podgorica from the Ottomans. The king chose this location because of its peaceful and panoramic view. To build a castle on that site, the King exchanged land owned by those families for other land of their choice. The Milonjics chose land in Spuz, while the Zlaticanins and the 'Bey family of Haverica' chose new land in Stara Varos.[64] This castle served as a winter residential palace for the Petriovic royal family. The royal castle later became Krusevac Hospital and today on that site is a church, museum and the US Embassy.[65] On the right side of the photo, a minaret belonging to the old Doganja Mosque can be seen.

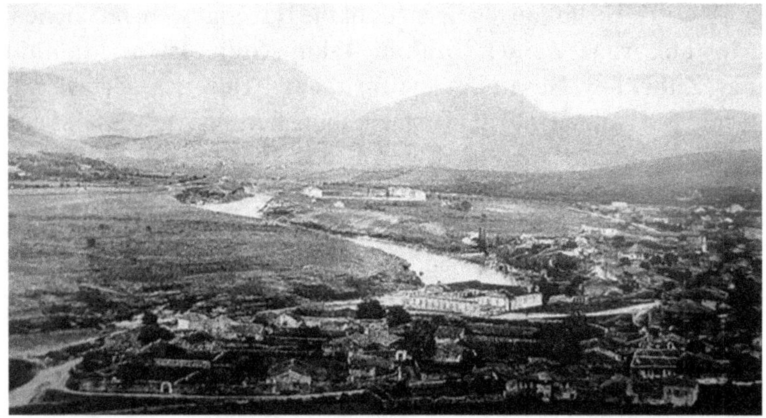

Lanad on the bank of the Moraca River where the King's castle was built

In the beginning of the 17th century, Mariano Bolizza (Marin Bolica), a nobleman and writer from the Republic of Venice recorded that 'around Podgorica there was a spacious and beautiful plain, 60 miles long and 30 miles wide. There are 17 beautiful and fertile villages in it, where the more prominent 'Turks' (Bosniaks) from Podgorica spend most of the year enjoying themselves'. This area was inhabited by the Haverics for centuries. **Omer Abdulah bey** had land 45 kilometres long along the Zeta Valley, all the way to the mouth of Lake Shkoder.[66] There are toponyms from around the Lake Shkoder, such as **Averic (Haveric) žar**, which means 'a locality with reed and sedge plants', reflecting the Haverics' bygone era.[67]

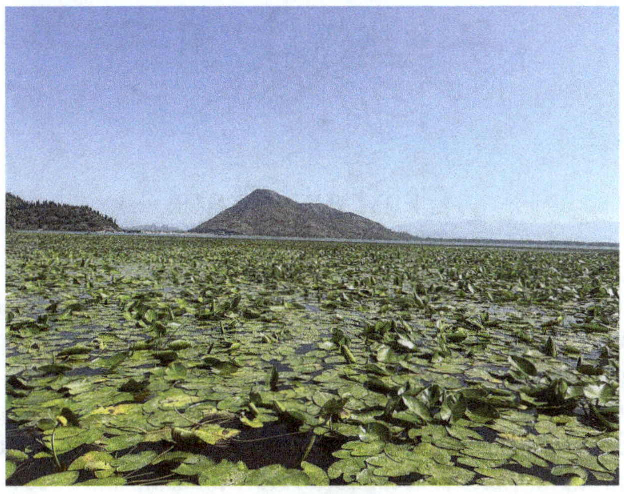

The Shkoder Lake

Haverics had not only the estate and influence in ruling administration in Podgorica, but Tuzi, Spuz, Zabljak, Cetinje and Bar. They had large estates, endowments and influence in the government in Zeta, between Podgorica and Lake Shkoder, including Golubovci with the settlements of Mahala, Berislavci and Goricani.[68] **Husein Pasha Karadag** used his son **Alija bey** to manage large land holdings in Zeta, especially in Golubovci, Mahala, Berislavci and Goricani, until the agrarian reforms during the Kingdom of Yugoslavia, when they were confiscated and handed over to serfs, who cultivated it, peasants and landless people. The owners of the land, the descendants of **Alija bey**, continued to live in Podgorica and engaged in trade. **Husein Pasha Karadag** also granted his son **Jusuf bey** land holdings in Stari Bar and Shkoder Krajina, simply known as 'Krajina' (a geographical region in southeastern Montenegro stretching from the southern coast of Lake Shkoder to the mountain of Rumija), which were preserved for a long time, partly even today, because Jusuf bey's descendants lived on that land.[69]

Craft and Trade

Montenegrin cities, most notably Podgorica, under Turkish rule not only had administrative or judicial functions and religious institutions, nor were they exclusively military strongholds. Their importance was far greater. Cities were producers of material goods, as well as gathering places and markets for surplus agricultural products. They were also centres of craftsmanship and trade (*esnafs*, guilds) in which Muslim and Christian crafters and merchants commonly contributed to economic life.[70] Podgorica's location also enabled the trading connection of Shkoder with Herzegovina. Trading was profitable because around Podgorica there were settlements on the hills, mostly Orthodox Christian population, who came to the city for trade with Muslim merchants.[71]

The Haverics, like other Muslim families from Stara Varos, worked in trade and craft businesses. In Stara Varos, on the left bank of the Ribnica River, fish, grain, flour, sugar, livestock, leather, wool, salt, olives, oil and handicraft items were traded in numerous shops. At the same time, numerous crafts were developed in that area, including millers, tanners, butchers, tailors, shoemakers, goldsmiths, masons and blacksmiths. These crafts created a colourful life and gave a special charm to this part of Stara Varos.

Water mills, which were placed along the four rivers – the Ribnica, Zeta, Moraca and Sitnica, often changed hands, and some mills were owned by several families. Danilo Burzan, a journalist and publicist, wrote in *Podgorica toponyms and heritage* that in 1884 the Podgorica Captaincy had 22 water mills. He noted, 'One of the oldest water mills on the Ribnica River in Podgorica was owned by **Mahmud bey** Haveric', who then 'in 1860 sold it for 1,400 *groschi*'. His mill, like other mills, supplied the markets, bakeries and shops of Podgorica and its surroundings.[72]

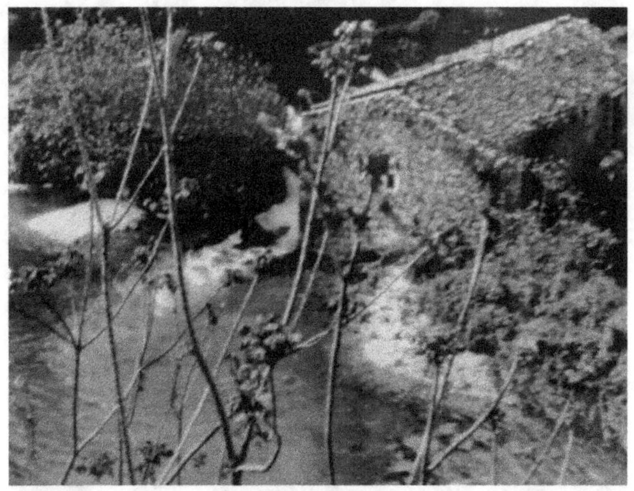

A water mill on the Ribnica River

During the 17th century, the powerful guild of Tabhana craftsmen built a bridge over the Ribnica River, which was named after the tanners (*tabaci*), who used to wash the cattle's skins, converting it into leather under the bridge.[73] The word *tạbhana* is Arabic/ Persian and means 'tannery workshop, tannery'. For Adnan Cirgic, the word 'tabana' originates from the Turkish word, *tabakhan* – a tanner. Leather export was a traditional 'specialty of the people of Podgorica'. Podgorica was written about in Kotor in 1612 as a 'big and trading city', when there was a considerable number of respectable Muslim families who worked in the *tabhanas*.

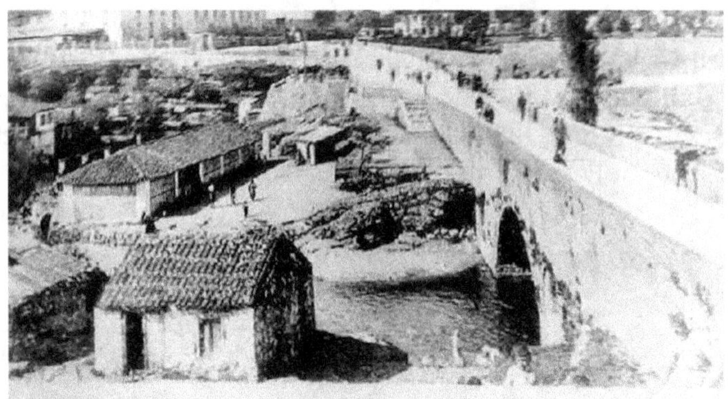

Tabacki Bridge

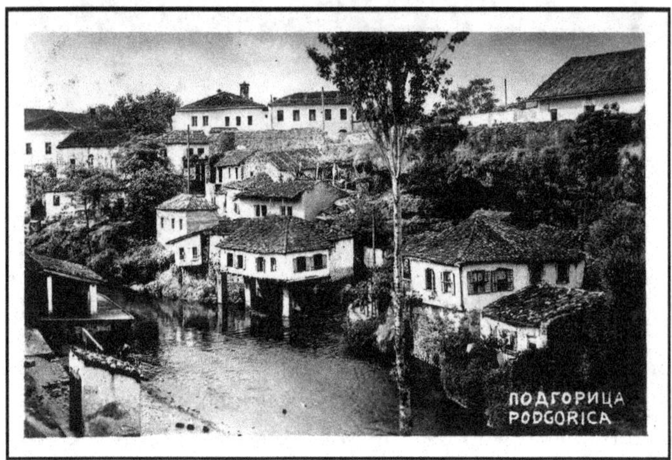

Tabhana

Haveric traders were traditionally prominent in trade with leather, wool and livestock in Montenegro. They also exported it in surrounding countries. By the 1830s, Podgorica merchants annually exported five wagons of wool, 100,000 lamb and goat skins, and 20,000 sheep. Almost the entire import and export of goods from Podgorica took place via Shkoder in ships called *ondre*. At one time, wool was the most important export product of Podgorica, especially for the nobles in Venice. The sale of thoroughbred Arabian horses was also popular on the Adriatic coast. Cattle belonging to Muslims from Podgorica were also brought to the island of Kotor for sale.

The establishment of mills and milling had special importance in the development of Podgorica and neighbouring towns. The old millers of Podgorica remember that once 'sacks of white, domestic corn and wheat from Bjelopavlici, Zeta, Malesia came down to the mills of Podgorica, and the flour went up the steep path', and they milled 'for the whole day as long as there was enough'.

Old Haveric traders, **Ibrahim bey**, **Selim bey**, **Abdullah bey**, **Tahir bey**, **Hamza bey**, **Zejnil bey**, **Mahmut bey** and **Bajram bey**, just to mention a few, were wealthy residents who contributed to the economic life of Podgorica. **Mahmut bey** and his brothers had textile shops not only in Podgorica but also in the city of Danilovgrad. At the end of the 19th century and the beginning of the 20th century, **Abdullah Dulja bey** often travelled from Podgorica to Istanbul for trade in leather, having successful business contacts with Turkish trading partners. During his business dealings in Istanbul, he met and collaborated with numerous Bosniak merchants. However, at the end of the first decade of the 20th century, he moved from Podgorica to live in Albania for a while where he continued to do his business and settled in Trebinje (Bosnia and Herzegovina) with his son, **Hajrulah**.

Other Haverics from Podgorica, probably more affluent, such as **Omer bey** and **Rizah bey**, went to study and trade in bigger centres like Vienna and Istanbul. Some Haveric merchants also brought their goods to Dubrovnik, left them in a depot and from there they were shipped to Ancona.[74] They traded with Shkoder, Istanbul and Dubrovnik, where they had docks in the port of Gruz where they kept raw goat leather for sale.

Not only in Podgorica, but in Bar, Niksic and Danilovgrad, Haverics ran shops. In particular, the old town of Bar underwent dynamic development and significant trading in which the Haverics were involved. An old woman from the town of Bar recalled the shops and stores in Stari Bar:

> ... Down the street from here, the first was a joiner's shop, and he sold groceries to the shop. There were the shops of **Haveric** among others, such as a shoemaker, a tinsmith, a textile shop, a barbershop, a bakery, a shoemaker, a tavern and a teahouse, a tavern where there was also *rakija* [brandy]... Nearby was the Islamic Community Commission and the Municipality next to a tailor's shop, another cafe and a shop which sold newspapers and cigars by the piece...[75]

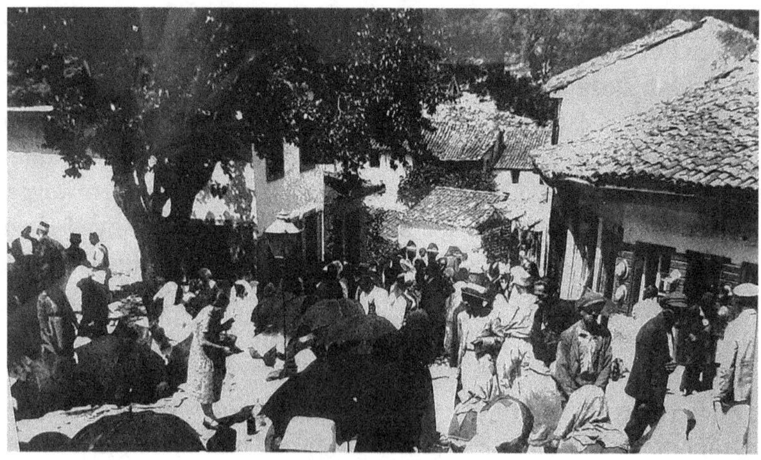

The old city of Bar

Members of the Haveric family were successful in their businesses in Bar. They were traditionally wealthy landowners. They had olive and livestock farms producing olive oil, milk and cheese. Trading documents stated, during Zejnel Bey's time, between 1786 and 1798, several merchants from Bar were selling olive oil in Sarajevo.[76] In Bar, Haverics established several shops and exported goods to Croatia and Albania. In the article titled 'History in a different way' (*Istorija na drugačiji način)*, it is written that the Haveric brothers had, in addition to other assets, a large shop (store) of colonial and manufactured goods in Stari Bar before the Second World War. The shops were called **'Braca Haveric'** ('**Brothers Haveric'**).

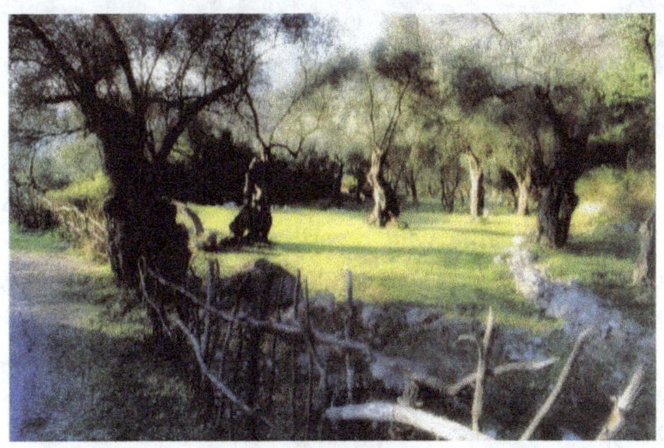

Olives in Bar

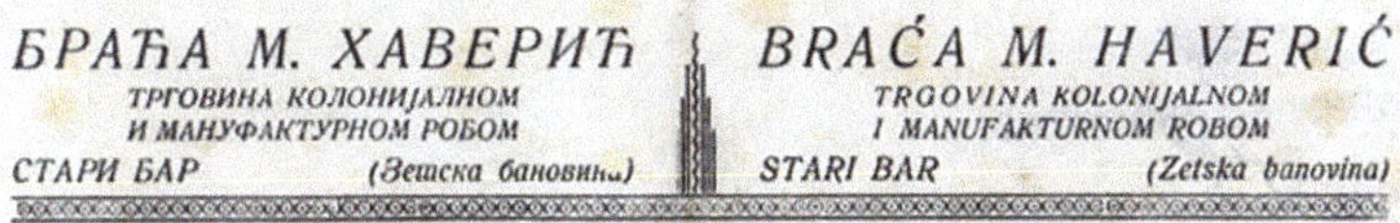

Brothers M. Haveric Shop: colonial goods (mixed goods and textiles), Old Bar

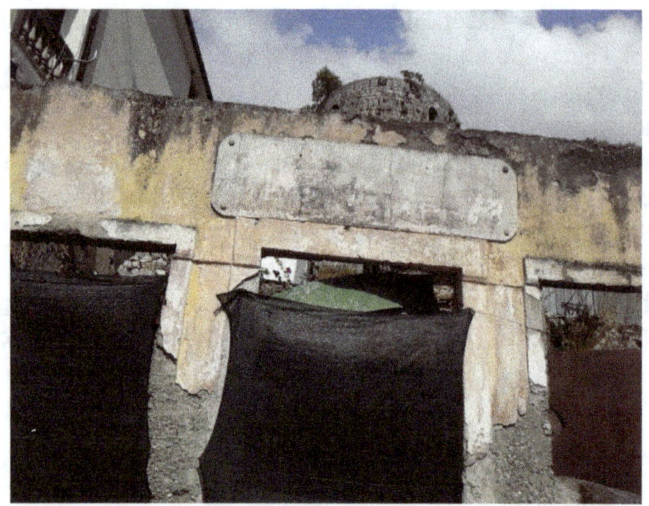

Remains of the shop, Cazim Haveric 1930s in Stari Bar

Many successful Haveric merchants lived and worked in Albania. Some of them became well regarded in their trading field. That tradition was preserved towards modern time. Like in Montenegro, most notably in Bar, they established their company called **'Vllazen Haveriq' ('Brothers Haveric')** for selling cars in Durres. The company name testifies to their attachment to the family, family business and the image traditionally used in the market. There was also a building company called **'Hveriku brothers'** in Kavaja. In Sarajevo, Bosnia, a successful tailor shop was fondly called 'Montenegrin Embassy of Haverics and friends'.

Mosques and Imams

In the immediate vicinity of the fortress where Muslims lived in Stara Varos, Skender Caus built a mosque in 1474. The mosque was called old Dogan Mosque (*Starodoganjska Mosque* or Skender Caus Mosque, or Ejnehancaus Mosque) because it was maintained by merchants and crafters who had their shops in its surroundings. The word 'Doganjaska' came after the Albanian word *doganja* or *dogana* (shop, workshop) because Albanians were also part of the Muslim community. Local Montenegrin and Albanian Muslim merchants and crafters cooperated with the ulema to support religious life in Podgorica. It was the only mosque in the town until 1582 when the large Glavatovic Mosque was built.

After Glavatovic Mosque, other mosques were built in Podgorica in subsequent periods: the main ones were the Hadrovic and Drac mosques, which no longer exist today, and the Osmanagic Mosque. In the wider area of Podgorica, there were also mosques on Medun, Golubovci, Goricani and Berislavci.[77] Haveric's imams in Podgorica were instrumental among the ulama to perform religious services. They were also key religious figures in Bar.

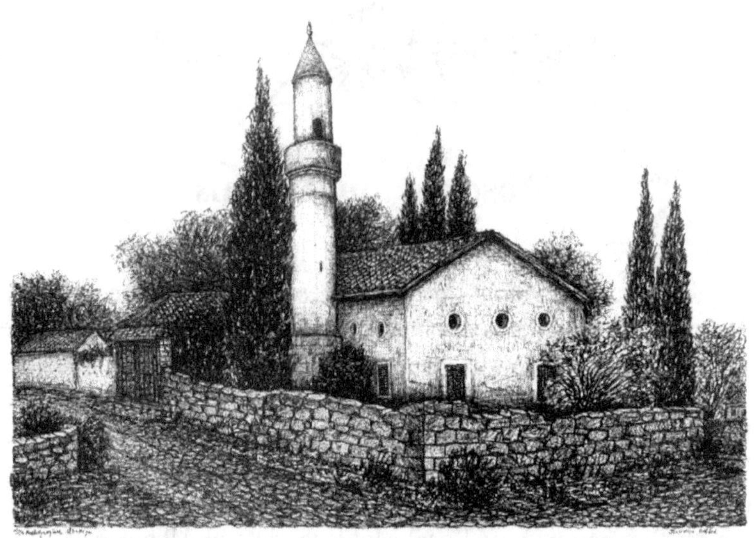

Starodoganjska Mosque (i.e. Skender-Caus Mosque) by the painter Zuvdija Hodzic

In Podgorica, next to the mosque, was the Skender Caus *Tekke* (a Sufi monastery), built before the mosque. Even one part of Stara Varos was named Tekke (Tecija) after it. There is little information about the dervish order from the end of the 15th century. According to the Turkish defter from 1523, two water mills belonged to this *waqf* of tekke Podgorica (*Vakuf-i zaviye-i Caus Iskender, der nefs-i Podgorica*) for its maintenance. The *waqf* also owned part of the fishing area within the boundaries of the mill on the Sitnica River.

Being religiously educated in Islam, the Muslim leaders had great merit and significance at that time as they educated the local Muslim population. This is what made the Haverics, who included several imams, 'among the famous ulema families'.[78] They were considered among the most literate families in the community. Those who were closest to the Haveric family used to refer to a traditional saying that the 'Haverics were born with a pencil', signifying their orientation to literature and writing. There is another saying among the people of old Podgorica that 'everything that happened during the time of the Turks in Zeta was written by Haverics'.[79] Of all the Muslim families in Podgorica, the Haverics were 'most distinguished by their work in literature and science'.[80]

The Haverics performed religious services and spiritual teaching as imams, hafiz and Sufis, kadis, scribes and *waqfs*. Their work was intrinsically linked with mosques, *madrasa* (Islamic schools) and courts. For instance, some community members fondly called the old Dogan Mosque the **'Haveric Mosque'** because several Haveric imams performed religious services there, including **imam Becir bey**, **imam Sulejman bey** and **hafiz Halil Haveric.** The title 'effendi' was held be **Becir**, **Mahmud**, **Omer**, **Mustafa**, **Miftar** and **Halil** among others who also performed religious service. Those who went to the *Hajj* (pilgrimage) to Mecca were **Haji Ali bey** and **Haji Husein bey**, because their names were preceded by 'Haji'. They are from the eighth and ninth generations of the Haveric family.

The Haverics, as an old Muslim family, contributed to the promotion of fraternal harmony and respect within the community, as well as interfaith tolerance in the wider society. For them, it was in accordance with Islamic teachings that 'a person is either your brother in faith or your equal in humanity'. In Montenegro, numerous kinship, fraternal, tribal and friendship ties among various families were evident in many positive deeds.[81] Members of the Haveric family often reconciled conflicting groups or communities and helped maintain social harmony and solidarity. They also expressed their loyalty to the authorities, who felt they respected the needs and characteristics of the Podgorica Muslims and wider Montenegrin region.

Religious tolerance, which they also promoted, was noticed by Muslim families towards the followers of other religions. This was evident not only in times of peace, but in turbulent times. Several historical accounts describe how they tried to solve issues through wisdom not by force, including protecting the lives and possessions of non-Muslim neighbours. With other Muslims, they promoted Islamic virtues without imposing their beliefs. For instance, in the 1850s, 'nobody forced a Christian Orthodox woman married to a Muslim to convert to Islam'.[82]

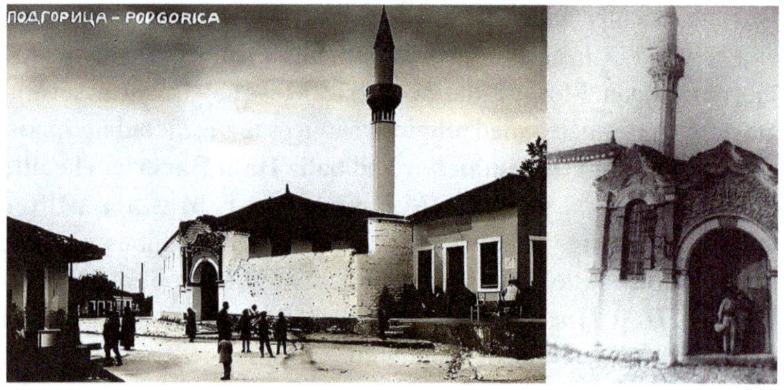

Glavatovic Mosque

Haji Sulejman bey Haveric was born in 1867 in Podgorica. After finishing primary school and madrasa, he (apparently) went on to further study in Cairo, Egypt. From 1919, he was appointed in Podgorica as a state imam, then, by decree of Ulema *majlis* (court) from Skopje, he was assigned as an imam of the registrar in Dinosa in the municipality of Tuzi in 1933. For some time, **Sulejman bey** was an imam in the main mosque in Podgorica, the Glavatovic Mosque.[83] Because of his reputation, he was also chosen as the imam of the old Dogan Mosque. It was said that **Sulejman bey** was also a capable merchant.

A story was preserved about Imam **Sulejman bey** Haveric. It was said he was a 'handsome man and wore white clothes'. When he was young and single, he appeared in a song by those who admired him. At that time, the girls were covered, but this did not stop them from looking at boys when they crossed the street. Even the scarf helped her to see him secretly. The story continued:

> There was a wedding in Podgorica in the neighboring 'Ashik Mahalla' ('Lovers' Mahala') where was carrying the flag while singing and dancing to get the bride. Like others, **Sulejman bey** attended the wedding party to see bride and bridegroom. Some young women climbed over the wall, or among the figs and plums trees from where they could see him at the wedding whom they admired. They wear scarfs to cover themselves and to see him at the wedding. They also put a ladder to climb to the top of the wall, because the walls were high. Watching the weddings over the walls, one of girls injured her finger, hardly to recovered it. Apparently, she said to her friend that her finger will be healed only if **Sulejman bey** come to her. And then the song came out:

There is an injured finger
Sulejman Haveric didn't see me
The finger will not recover until **Sulejman** sees it.

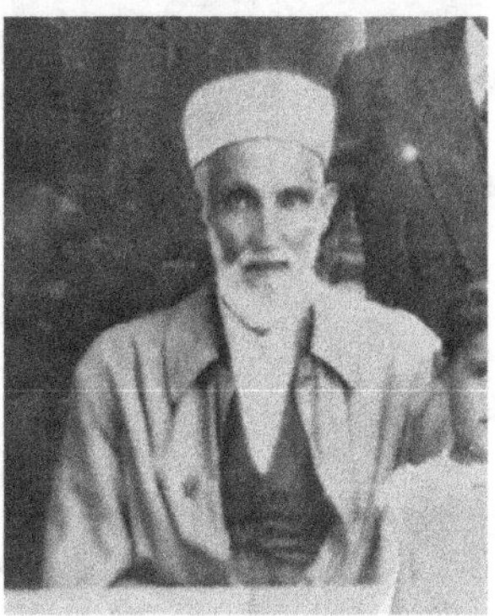

Imam Sulejman bey Haveric

Rifat Haveric remembered that his grandfather, **Sulejman bey**, 'taught him a verse from the Qur'an as a child, placing him on his lap'.[84]

Effendi Becir (Bekir) Haveric, an imam in the old Doganja Mosque, was also a teacher in madrasa as well as a dervish and calligrapher. He was a respectful alim in the Montenegrin Islamic community. In his manuscript written in Arabic he noted that he gained the book *Kitab Sarh Tariqa Bibarika* ('The explanation of Bariqa Sufi Order') during his journey from Podgorica to Albania.

This document written in 1262h. (i.e. 15 July 1845) states that **Becir** Haveric worked as an imam in the old Doganjska Mosque in the old city of Podgorica and that he had a student from the castle of Zabljak. This manuscript was initially preserved by a librarian of the *waqf* in the city of Skoplje, Macedonia.[85]

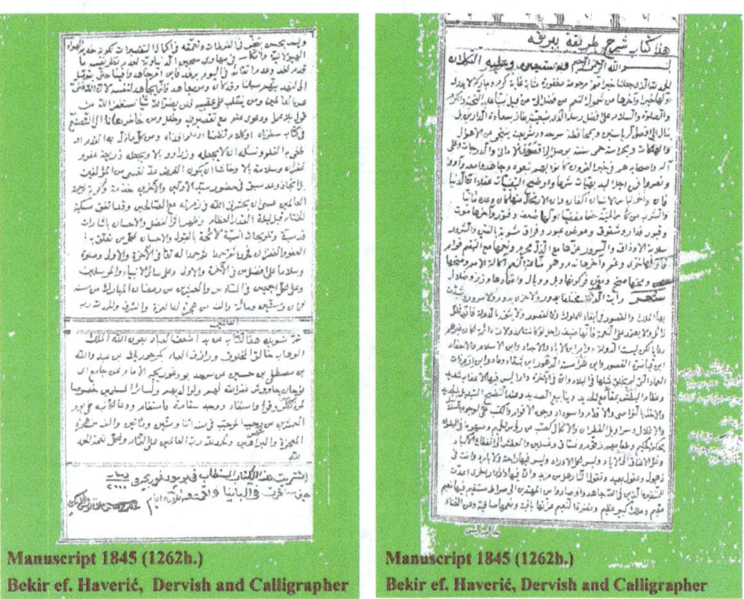
هذا كتاب شرح طريقة بريقه

Manuscript 1845 (1262h.)
Bekir ef. Haverić, Dervish and Calligrapher

Manuscript 1845 (1262h.)
Bekir ef. Haverić, Dervish and Calligrapher

Kitabu Sharh Tariqat Bariqa
(it is written Babriqa or Bibriqa) lit. A book explaining the sparkle method

Page one

In the name of Allah, the Most Merciful and Compassion

Wa bi-Hi na'stain wa alayhi tuklan (We ask for help only from him and trust only from him.) Praise be to Allah, who has made us the best, forgiven (*maghfur*), merciful (*marhum*), attained the most generous rewards, and blessed us. Because of the grace of the Prophet, upon whom the best greetings and the range of blessings are bestowed, a person does not know whether the first ones or the last ones are better. Peace and blessings be upon the most virtuous Prophet, to whom the happiness of two worlds (this world and the hereafter) can be achieved by following him, and even by following the secrets of the limits of Sharia, one can attain the two most unattainable positions and be safe from fears, destructions. Those who come under the protection of his Sunnah are under the safest shield, greatest degree. It is one of the clearest facts, both religiously and mentally (*badihi* and *yaqini*), that the world is mortal and the last garment a person will wear is a shroud. Exodus from this world is God's promise for the future, and drinking from the bowl of death is an irreversible end. Its beginning is weakness and helplessness, its end is death and the grave. It is a place of transition and separation that humiliates a person, where pleasure and joy are taken away, its beginning is humiliation and its end is regret and deprivation of blessings, it is a sin to rely on it, a sin and misguidance to trust it. I have seen many different people, some turn constantly, some continue unhappily, they have built mansions and palaces, but there is no eternity for them, the state (*dawla*) cannot be trusted because it is temporary, this providence (*nimat*) cannot be trusted either, it is also a traveling guest. If these were permanent, the others would also be permanent. But they are not permanent, so is the state. Where are the fathers and grandfathers, where are the children and grandchildren, where are the palaces of the Kisras, where are the heroes who jump on people like lions, where are the buildings of the people of Ad, where are the buildings of the people of Ad who live in the city of Iram, the like of which has not been created among the towns and is full of high buildings, and where is the abode of the Hereafter, where there will be painful torment, Sledgehammers made of iron, springs made of pus, the rebuilding of the skin every time it falls off, being caught by the feet and necks (forehead), the faces of some people being pitch black, chains and iron rings being prepared for them, trousers made of tar, boiling water pouring from their heads and tearing their stomachs to pieces. It will be by the judgment of *al-Hakim* (All-Wise Allah). Their food there will be the tree of oleander, and their drink will be hard and black pus, their lungs will tear apart due to thirst, their hands and heads will be subjugated, there will be neither comfort nor coolness for them there, and you will be in confusion, and the fire of hell will be more intense (hal min mazid). There is another home there prepared for the pious. They strive in the way of Allah and are on the straight path, where they enjoy permanent blessings, incomprehensible possessions and fresh happiness. The glory of this land is eternal, its blessings are clear.

Page two

The beauty of this work is not in its depth in eliminating deficiencies or in its beauty in balancing excesses, but in its ability to be the servant of forms (*hayula*/surat: the original state of the universe) and to show the human soul what it has prepared for tomorrow (the afterlife) by turning away from the prison of this world. Whatever a person does is his own; Allah Almighty is independent of what he does. Whoever turns back cannot do any harm to Allah, so we repent to our Lord (*istighfar*) from the word without action, and we seek refuge in Allah from the claim of having knowledge even though it contains many flaws and confusion. Whoever calls us to artificiality and pretence because of the book we wrote, the words we preach, or the knowledge we express, we pray to God not to impose this burden on us. We pray that He will forgive us, otherwise isolating ourselves from believers is not the purpose. On the contrary, doing something in the service of the Prophet, means receiving the mercy of Allah, the Most Merciful. May Allah gather me together with the righteous. I completed this book before the holy night of Power, so that the virtue and benevolence associated with the work was revealed by these sacred signs, it would be accepted and everyone connected with this work would be forgiven. Praise be to Him at the beginning and at the end, Praise be to Him again and praise again, blessings and peace be upon the most virtuous person (pbuh) in the afterlife and in the world, and peace be upon all other prophets and messengers. The 26th night of Ramadan of the year 1168 *Hijri* has been completed. All glory and honor belong to Allah. Praise be to the Lord of the worlds.

The writing of this book was completed by the hand of the weakest of His servants (Bekir Havrik b. Abdullah b. Mustafa b. Huseyin), with the help of Allah, the Creator of all creatures, the provider of the servants. (This person) from *Sarhad* (city) Podgorica Mosque imam, that is, *nawhan* (*turhan*) *chavush*, may God forgive all the sins of them, their parents and other Muslims, especially those who look at this book, read it and benefit from it, find healing and direction in the book, May He forgive those who found it and prayed to the author of the book on the 20th of Rajab, 1262 Hijri. Thank God for giving me the opportunity to complete the book. Praise be to Him for His every blessing.

I bought this beautiful book in Podgorica for 2000 dinars during my trip to Albania where I stayed for three days.

(Bakr- Bekir Huriyek or Bakrhavrik)[86]

Becir's manuscript contains the names of his father, grandfather and great-grandfather as a contribution to the genealogy of the Haveric family. He also mentioned several of his direct descendants: **Bekir Haveric** son of **Abdullah**, son of **Mustafa**, son of **Husein** from Podgorica.

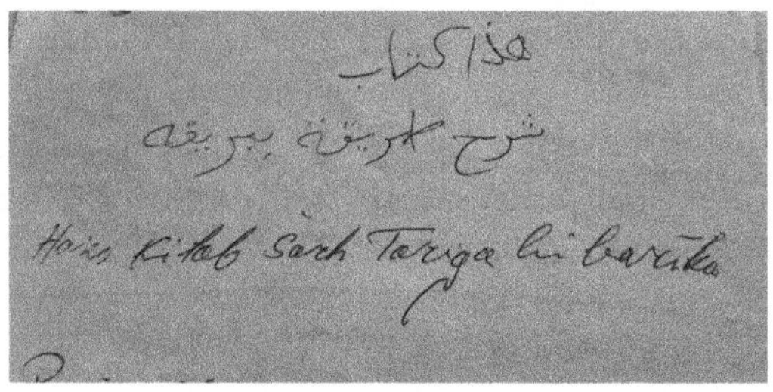

A copied of title from Bekir's manuscript

Another manuscript by **Becir** Haveric mentioned the scribe Alivodic from Zabljak Fortress, who 'signed himself as a student of **Becir** Effendi'.[87] Historian Zvezdan Folic said that Omer Mustafa Agha Alivodic was a student of **Becir** Effendi Haveric in the

Podgorica madrasa, which confirmed this Haveric was a teacher in the Podgorica madrasa.

Becir bey was young, handsome and described as an 'Arab boy', probably more because of his knowledge of Arabic. He was mentioned in the verses:[88]

Grown yellow quince,
Near the loved girl,
There is young boy walking,
Becir bey Haveric

Hafiz Hysen Jusuf bey Haveriq was born in Podgorica at the beginning of the 1860s. He graduated from a madrasa in Sarajevo and became a *hafiz*. He came to Shkoder where he gave religious lessons. Although he was blind, he knew the Qur'an well. They call him Hafiz 'Gurrahi' (after his short, deep tone), because he recited the Qur'an with an interesting accent.

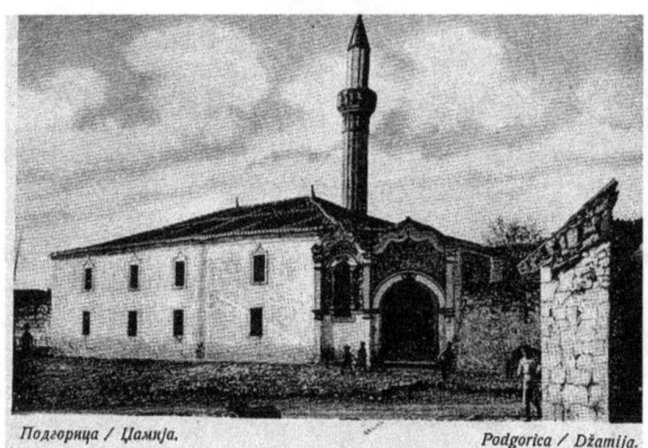

The Glavatovic Mosque

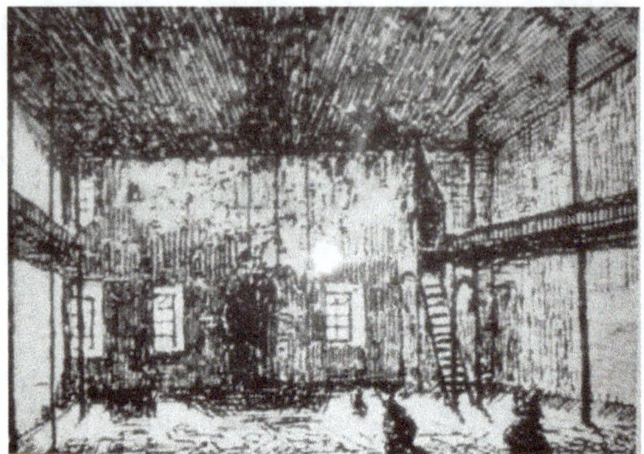

Forgotten interior of the Glavatovic Mosque

Osman bey Haveric, from father M. Murad (son of Haji Sulejman), was born in 1884 in Podgorica, graduated from the old madrasa, passing an exam before the kadi h. h. Sarkic in 1915 in Stari Bar under Sharia administration. He worked as a *mualim* (Islamic teacher). He served as imam in the mosques in Goricani and Vladne near Tuzi. From 1915 to 1918, he was imam of 7 divisions in Podgorica.[89]

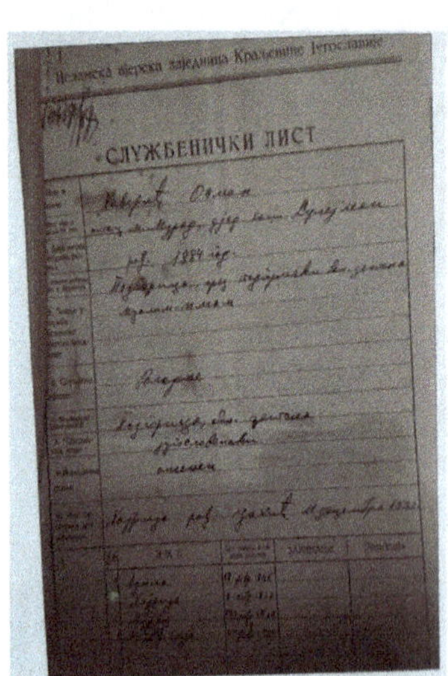

СЛУЖБЕНИЧКИ ЛИСТ

Islamic Community of the Kingdom of Yugoslavia
Osman Haveric was a *mualim;* he spoke 'Yugoslavian' and Arabic
He was husband of Hajrija (Jahic) Haveric and they had four children.

Imam Jusuf, Muhtar Effendi, Hafiz Bey and **Hafiz Halil Effendi Haveric** performed religious services in several mosques and also taught religious education in neighbouring towns.

Hafiz bey Haveric from Podgorica served as imam in the main mosque in Glavatovic Mosque in 1906. He advocated for the religious rights of Podgorica's Muslims and corresponded with the authorities of the Zeta region, receiving a 'guaranty of the Muslim religious freedoms and rights by His Royal Highness Prince (later the king) Nikola I Petrovic-Njegos'.[90]

Jusuf Haveric, a son of **Husein** Karadag Pasha, was an imam. His son, **Hafiz Miftar Effendi Haveric**, was born in 1870 in Podgorica, completed Arabic-Turkish education in Vucitrn, Kosovo, then studied in Podgorica and Istanbul. **Hafiz Miftar bey** was sometimes mentioned in literature as Hafiz Muhtar Haveric.[91] He served in Niksic, Leskovac, Tudemil, Dobra Voda and Gorani. His first appointment in 1895 was in Haji Ismail's Mosque in Grudska Mahala in Niksic, built in 1807. In several *madrasas*, he taught Turkish and Arabic.[92] He was a Muslim community leader in Bar among various religious representatives. As a Muslim leader, **Hafiz Miftar bey** complained to the king's administration in Podgorica. He said, 'If the King approved us the Sheria Law and religious freedom why than he doesn't let us to bury deceased Muslims in less than 24 hours after their death'.[93]

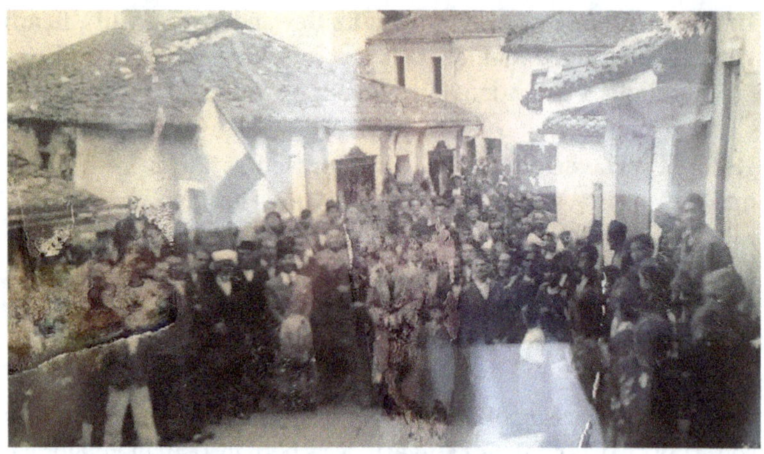

Hfz Muhtar Haveric (under flag with a fez hat ahmediya) at a public gathering in Bar

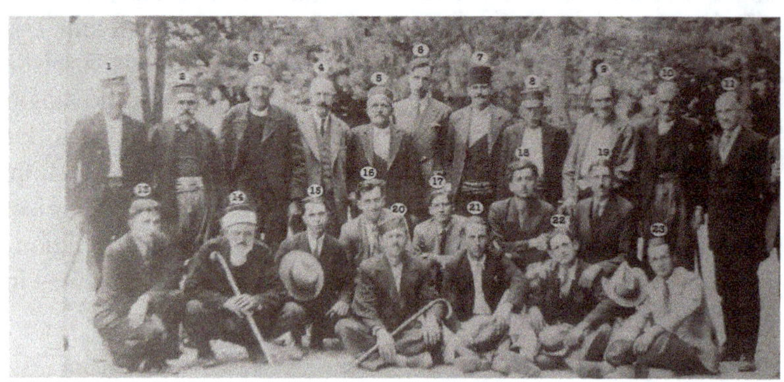

Hfz Muhtar Haveric sitting with a walking stick (left, no 14) with a prominent group of Bar representatives of various cultures and religions at a public gathering

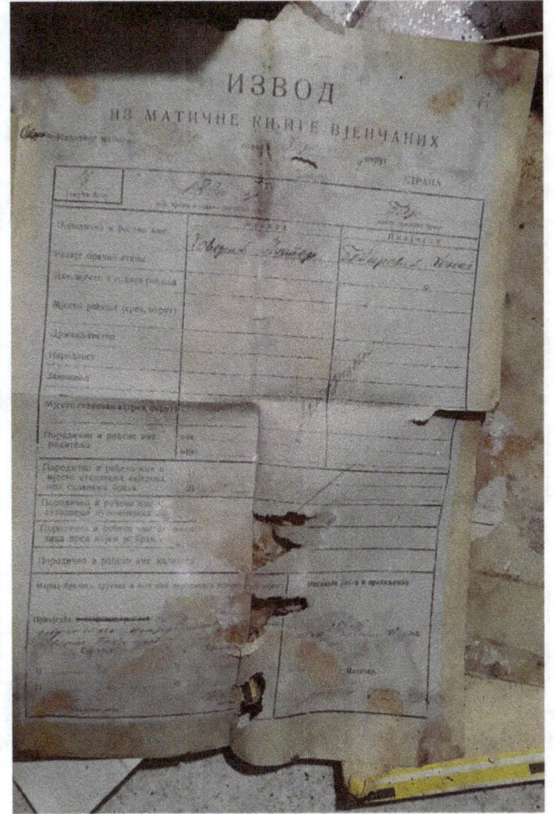
ИЗВОД
ИЗ МАТИЧНЕ КЊИГЕ ВЈЕНЧАНИХ

Muhtar (Miftar) Haveric's marriage certificate

Imams of Omerbasic Mosque in Old Bar from 1880 to 1953:
Muhtar Haveric and Hafiz Halih Haveric were listed (Islamic community Bar)

Hafiz Halil bey Haveric was born in 1900 in Podgorica to father **Muhtar (Miftar)**. He bore the nickname 'Medo'. He was educated in Istanbul and Shkoder, where he graduated from the Epar Madrasa. His studies in Shkoder lasted six years. In addition to his mother tongue, he spoke Arabic, Turkish and Albanian. **Hafiz Halil** served as imam in the old Dogan Mosque in Podgorica.[94] He was also an appointed imam in the Klezna, Mikulici, Zaljevo and Omerbasica mosques in Stari Bar as well as the Skanjevica Mosque and a nearby tekke. The regional waqf commission in Stari Bar had two schools and **Hafiz Halil** was also a *mualim* (teacher) appointed by the commission's decision in 1933.[95]

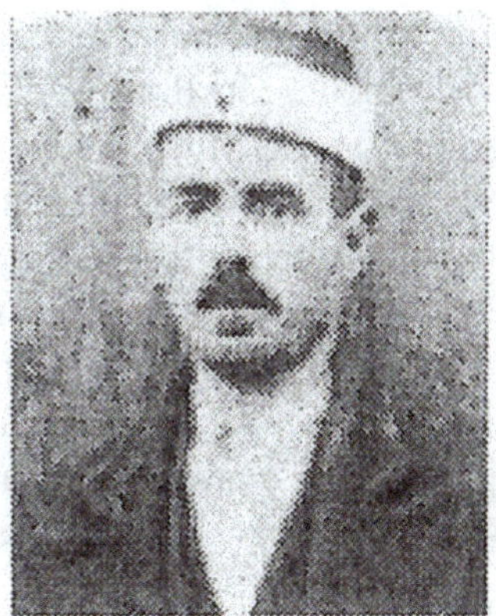

Effendi Halil Haveric

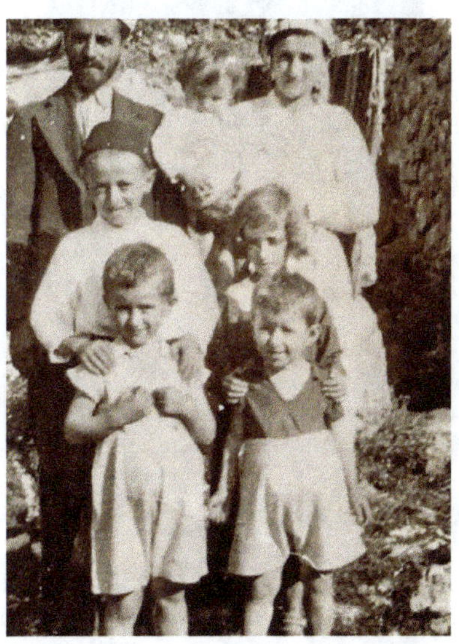

Father Halil and Mother Havaja. The children are: first row, on the right, the little boy in a white shirt is Ismail, next to him in the first row is his son Mehmed, who was killed in Sarajevo in 1967. In the second row, the boy with the fez is the son, Teufik. The girl next to him is a daughter, Rukija. In the mother's arms is the little daughter Baflija (Hajrija), 1938.

Like his father, **Hafiz Halil** was upright, fair and respected by representatives of all religions, Muslims, Catholics and Orthodox. In his time, being a hafiz in the Muslim community meant a lot. In 1974, **Halil** went on Hajj. He was sent from Careva Mosque in Sarajevo and travelled by bus to Mecca. In the Skanjevica Mosque and a tekke, Halil also performed the religious service there. **Hafiz Halil** together with **Ismail** Haveric co-authored a book *Namaz-Salat: Why and how to pray*, which, after the first edition in 1972, saw almost 20 editions. It was available in many countries of the world, especially among Bosnian Muslim communities (i.e. the Bosniak Diaspora).

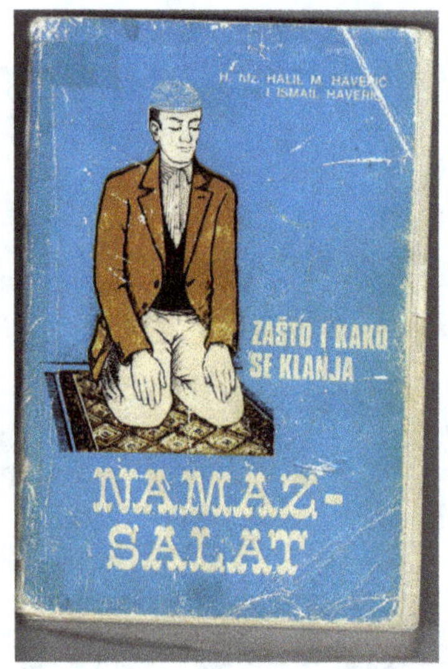

Book by coauthors Hafiz Halil and Ismail Haveric

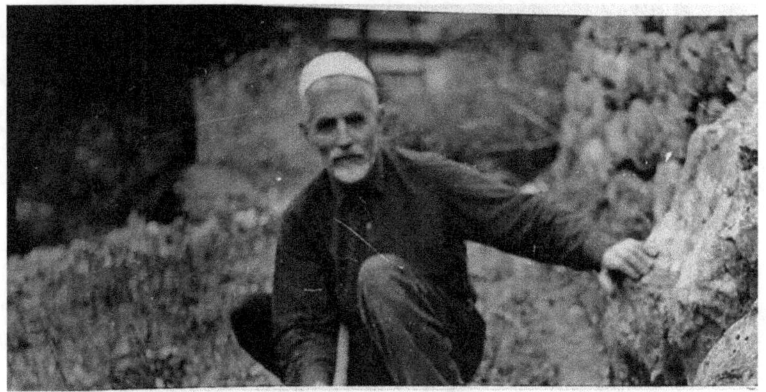

Halil in his olive and cattle farm

His son, **Dr Muhtar**, recalled:

> As a young boy, I had a fez on my head when I went to the mosque with **Halil**. He was responsible and serious at work as well as had a clear and sensitive voice. He took care of every spoken letter or accent. In his free time, he was engaged in olive growing, agriculture, cows, goats and sheep.[96]

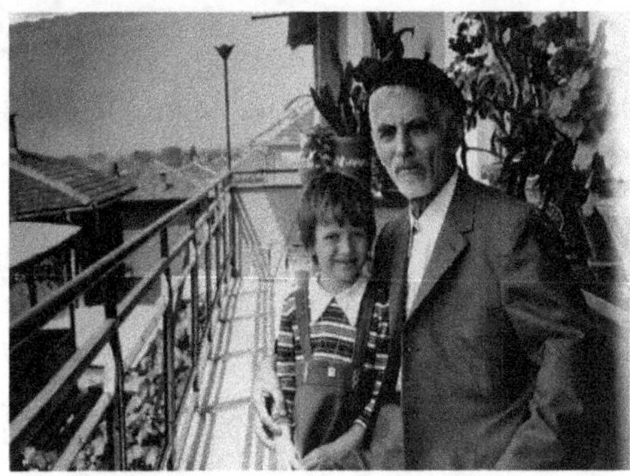

Halil with grandson, Haris

Halil had a grey beard, he wore a French cap at home and a *fez* in public.[97] When there was an earthquake in Bar, a large stone wall collapsed and fell on Halil's feet. Two family members and a neighbour moved the stone from Halil's feet. Since then, Haji Halil was disabled and used a walking stick, but soon after he died at the age of 80.[98]

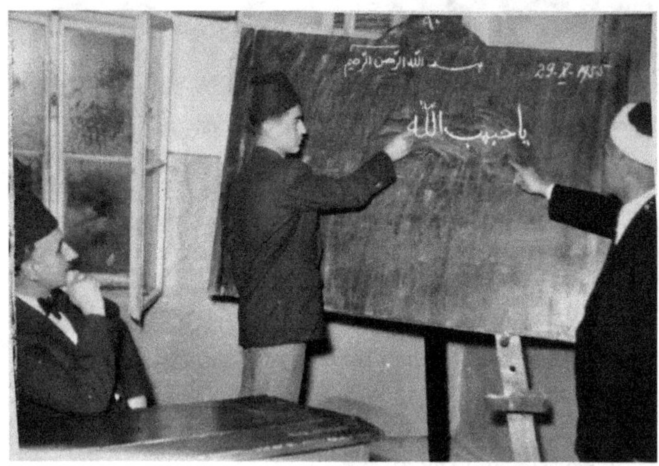

Ismail Haveric in the Gazi Husrev bey Madrasa, Sarajevo, 1955

It is also worth mentioning that, in 1942, **Nijazi Haveriku** in the *Culture of Islam Review* wrote a notable article entitled 'Why we have a barren pen'.[99]

Hasan Tahsin Haveriku (1893-1964), in the views of several Islamic scholars in Albania, deserves special attention. His mother was **Fatimija (Fatima)** (1874-1958), **Ymer bey** Haverik's daughter, born in 1874 in Podgorica, and father was Becir Osmanagic. They all came from Podgorica together and initially stayed in Shkoder. Becir soon passed away when Hasan was a year and a half old.

Fatima spent her life caring for her son. With the sacrifice, needle in hand, sewing, she made a living, raised him and supported the boy through school. **Hasan** retained his mother's surname all his life. **Hasan** was mentioned by surname as Haveric in his documents and by various authors. When he was sent to a *madrasa*, the mother and son moved to Tirana. She died in 1958. **Hasan** graduated from the Military Academy in Istanbul in 1914, but he wasn't interested to be employed within military service, so he opted for education as he obtained qualification in the religious culture.[100] **Hasan** realised that knowledge is essential to the Islamic tradition and the Qur'an inspires Muslims to pursue knowledge, ponder God's signs in creation and reflect on the instructions given in its holy text. He dedicated all his life to the Islamic faith, spirituality, teaching and calligraphy.

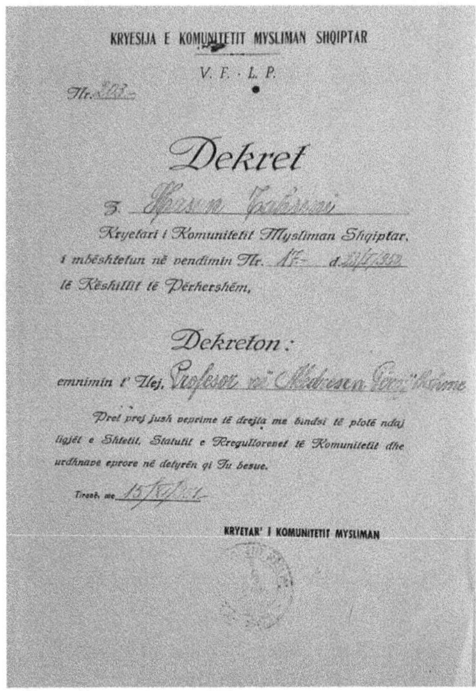

KRYESIJA E KOMUNITETIT MYSLIMAN SHQIPTAR

V. F. - L. P.

Nr. [illegible]

Dekret

Z. Hasan Tahsini

Kryetari i Komunitetit Mysliman Shqiptar, i mbështetun në vendimin Nr. [illegible] d. [illegible] të Këshillit të Përhershëm,

Dekreton:

emnimin t' Uej, Profesor në Medresen [illegible]

Pret prej jush veprime të drejta me bindsi të plotë ndaj ligjët e Shtetit, Statutit e Rregullorenet të Komunitetit dhe urdhnave eprore në detyrën qi Ju besue.

Tiranë, me 15/[illegible]

KRYETAR' I KOMUNITETIT MYSLIMAN

Hasan Tahsin Haveriku

PROCLAMATION
Mr Hasan Tahsini
Head of the Albanian Muslim Community, supports the decision Nr. 17 date 28-1-1950 of the Permanent Advice Committee.

Decree

In the Name of Professor of General Madrassa
I expect from you fair actions with full obedience to the law of the State, the Statute of the Community Regulations and superior orders in the task entrusted to you.

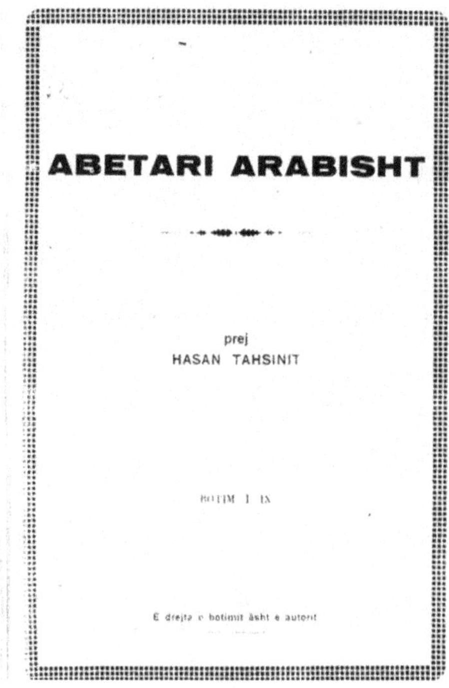

ABETARI ARABISHT

prej
HASAN TAHSINIT

BOTIM I IX

E drejta e botimit âsht e autorit

'Arabic Primer'
(a small introductory book on a subject)
Hasan Tahsin Haveriku
Printing contractor Ismail Mai' Osmani – Tirana

Hasan Tahsin worked as a teacher in a madrasa where he taught not only religious studies but also general subjects, such as history, mathematics and others. His first job was at the 'Dervish Bey school' in the Paruruce, near Shkoder. He was appointed a teacher of faith.[101] In 1934, with the death of the director, his work began in the dormitories – a school for boys and girls in Tirana. With the closure of this school, he was appointed a professor at the 'General Madrasa' in Tirana, where he taught geography, the Arabic language and theology. He was literate in Albanian, Turkish, Arabic and Persian.[102] He was an artist making calligraphy. His *levhes* (calligraphic writings and designs) can still be found in some houses in Shkoder today. In 1930, he was appointed director of the madrasa, which operated for only two years. He performed Hajj, then was chosen to be Sheik of the Tijani Order (Tijani Tariqa), a dervish order that was founded in Shkodra in 1920.

Hasan Tahsin is the author of several titles in the magazines *Zani i nalta* and *Kultura Islame*. He is the author of the *Sufar* in Arabic, as well as *The Basic Pillars of the Tidžani Order*, published in 1941 in Tirana. Most of his works have been lost, as well as a translation of the Qur'an in the Albanian co-authored by **Hasan Tahsin** Haveriku, Hasan Sharofi and Junuz Buljaj. **Hasan Tahsin** Haveriku's most notable works are *The Great Prophet of Islam, Hazrat Muhammed* and *Gratitude to the Great Prophet*. He wrote the prose *As Time Passes, As Science Rises and Advances*, and *That's How the Wits of the Hadiths are Discovered.*[103]

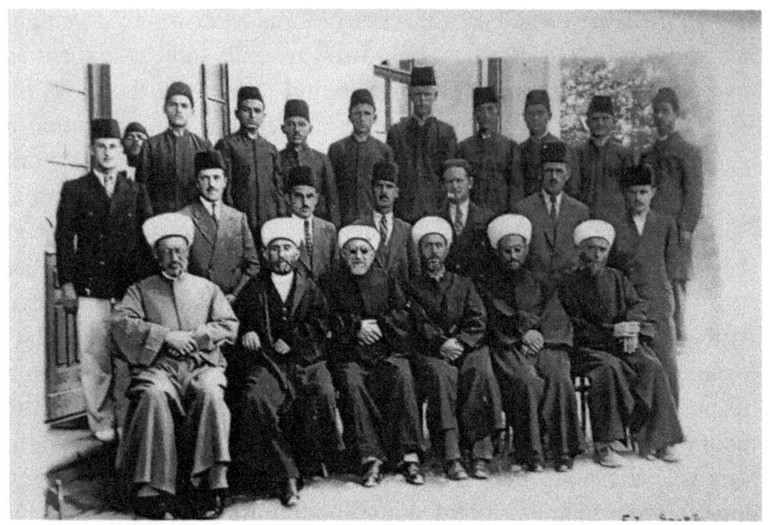

Alims in Tirana (the first from left in grey jacket in the middle row) in front of madrasa

At the beginning of 1946, the Presidency of the Albanian Muslim Community decided to create a commission for the translation of the Qur'an into the Albanian language. This commission consisted of Hafiz Ismet Dibra, chairman; Prof Sadik Bega, member; Prof Haki Sharofi, member; Prof Jonuz Bulej, member; and **Hasan Tahsin**, secretary. However, during a meeting with Enver Hoxha, the President of the Muslim Community, Hafiz Musa Haxhi Aliu, asked him for a letter for the publication of the Holy Book, the translation of which had been worked on for a long time. Enver Hoxha advised the Chief Mufti not to stop the translation, but added its publication should be postponed until 'better times', since, as the Chief Mufti knew, the situation with paper in the country was serious, so the government could not help him in this matter.

Hasan Tahsin's contribution to the translation of the Qur'an from Arabic to Albanian is worthy information. He should be regarded as one of Islamic pioneers in the early translation of the Qur'an to European language. In his time, the communist system in Albania after the Second World War undertook violent interventions in the life of the Albanian Muslim community, including sequestration of property, control over the budget, banning literature, strict restriction and control over the madrasa. The communist policy strengthened harsh propaganda through the press, radio, forms of education, cinema, theatre and variety shows, parts of school readings and education with contempt for religion. Soon, among the confiscated books are *Ya'sini* (Arabic and Albanian), the Qur'an, Mevludi, *Libri i se falmes*, as well as magazines published by the Muslim community, *Zani i Naltë* and *Islamic Culture*.[104]

Muslim scholars, ulema and Sufis experienced shocking events during the communist regime. Many of the most influential leaders and scholars were spied on, shot, convicted and exiled by State Security, who also produced false witnesses in mock trials and sowed a general atmosphere of terror. Among those who were sentenced to prison was **Hasan Tahsin**.[105]

Hasan Tahsin was among several decisive opponents of communism and ready to take any action against totalitarian Enver Hoxha's regime, advocating freedom of religion.[106] Under the government oppression against religious practices, in 1947, he was arrested along with several other professors of the madrasa – due to political 'motives' and sentenced to 5 years of forced labour. In 1948, the sentence was reduced to two years. In 1951, the mentor was re-appointed a professor at the 'General Madrasah' until 1960, when this school was closed.[107]

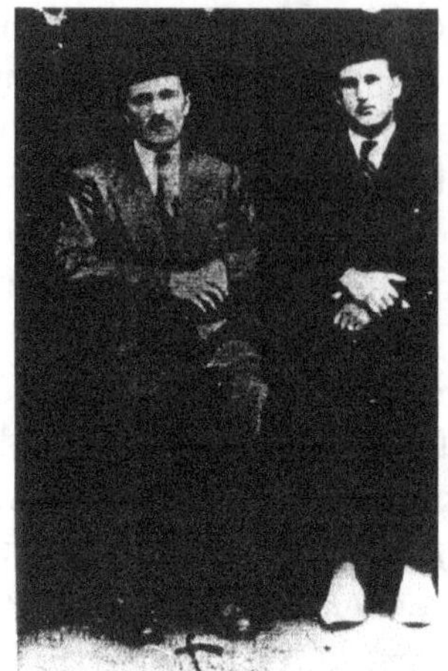

Hasan Tahsin Haveric, left

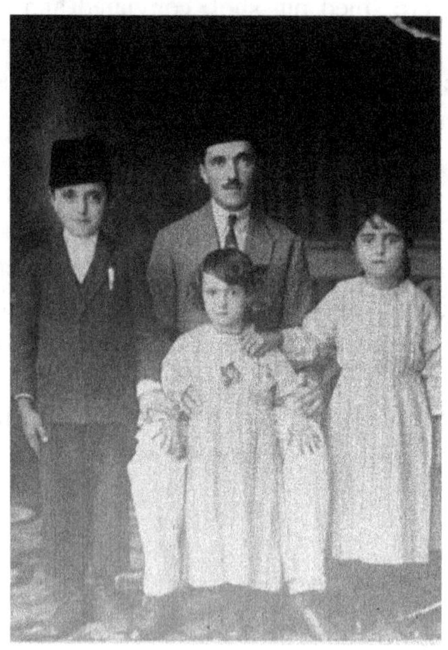

Hasan Tahsin Haveric with his children

Hasan Tahsin was a pious man, with a muscular body. He was married, had children and was always taking care of his family. He was known as a leader of the Islamic community with progressive thoughts. He passed away at the age of 70. On the day of his death, it was said, 'The last cultured and progressive religious person died. He respected religious practices of other religions'. For instance, one of his friends said, 'I am Orthodox Christian but when Hasan Tahsin was speaking, my friend and I stood up'. A street in the city is named after him; a government ordered to use the name Tahsini for his second name, 'Tahsin'.[108]

In scholarly works, **Hasan Tahsini**'s literal creativity was highlighted as an extraordinary contribution. His sensitive spirit found its expression sometimes with almost poetic translations. He expressed in high tones of glorification and hymns, dedicated to unique graces of the Prophet. His ecstatic feelings about Islam are conveyed to the reader through the compression of attributes and literary figures – 'the dough of the rosary, the soul of all creation, the source of everything, the path of truth, the treasure of life and the river of hope'. Some of his poems are in the schemes of *ilahi*, containing 16 couplet stanzas with couplet quatrains and beautiful rhymes.

In his work, *The basic pillars of the Tixhani Tariqat*, he opens with 'Praise' from the well-known cleric and leader of the sect Tixani, Qazim Hoxhes. Sheh Qazim. The most positive considerations and evaluations for the work are successfully carried out by the 'indefatigable author' and 'willing friend', filling a vital need for the brothers of his Tijani. He made a noble commitment, guided by high religious ideals, to continue his honourable mission. He doesn't do anything else, except live according to prophetic sayings: 'The best teaching is the knowledge that a Muslim teaches and then teaches it to his Muslim brother' and to 'learn from others and spread knowledge in writing'. Tahsin was an example of a great educator, who tried to give his help for the benefit of man in general and the nation in particular.

Hasan Tahsin Haveriku's legacy is mentioned in works by several authors, such as Nathalie Clayer in the work titled *The Tijaniyya: Reformism and Islamic Revival in Interwar Albania* (2009), Sheik Faik Hoja in *Shaykh of the Tidjani Tarikah in Albania* (2007), Sacir Smajlovic in *Forum Bosniak Muslims, Through History* (2006), Bajro Agovic in *Mosques in Montenegro* (2001) as well as three academics of the University of Shkoder: Faik Luli, Islam Dizdari and Nedzimi Bushati in the work titled *Ne kujmim te brezave* (Generations for remembrance).

It is worth emphasising that his work on the translation of the Qur'an from Arabic to Albanian represents a great contribution to religious education and culture at that time in Europe. Sheikh Faik Hodja said:

> **Hasan Tahsin** Haveric was an extremely learned scholar who was a professor at a madrasa in Tirana and then a Sufi of the Tijani Order (Tijani Tariqa, dervish order), a dervish order that was founded in Shkodra in 1920. During the weakening of the Ottoman rule, which was followed by the period of modernization, the Tijani Tariqa gained in popularity and began to spread along with other Sufi orders and for a time participated in the plurality of cultural and religious life. This dervish order produced several influential Islamic intellectuals and imams including **Hasan Tahsin** Haveriku.[109]

Hasan Tahsin Haveriku was also mentioned in the 'Muslim Forum of Albania'. **Nexhmi Haveriku**, a vice president and organiser of proceedings for the Forum, greeted the participants in his opening speech. **Aqif Haveriku**, chairman of the Municipal Council of

Kavaja, also welcomed the proceedings of the symposium and announced the decision taken by this council to announce the Honorary Citizen of Kavaje of former mufti Muhamed Hoxha. At the Forum it was said:

> I take this opportunity to thank the organizers activity: 'Muslim Forum of Albania' and the sponsorship of the six **Haveriku brothers**, for everyone in Shkoder we have extraordinary respect, for the activities they have done for the benefit of Islam. God reward them with good things in this world and with Paradise other.

In a summary of the speech:

> With the same faith in the Creator, with depth of thought, with a rich spiritual world, with high a linguistic and culture, they paid respect to older group of the Muslim intelligentsia of Shkodra such as **Hasan Tahsin Haveriku**. The characteristic of this group is the harmonisation of work in the field of secular education with their engagement in the learning process in the field of faith, and the enrichment of religious literature with translations, adaptations and writing texts, with contributions to the magazines 'Zani i Naltë', 'Islamic Culture, Njeriu'. In the years 1940-44, Albanian libraries were enriched with new poetic collections, translations, the publication of a number of alims, including **Hasan Tahsin Haverikut.**[110]

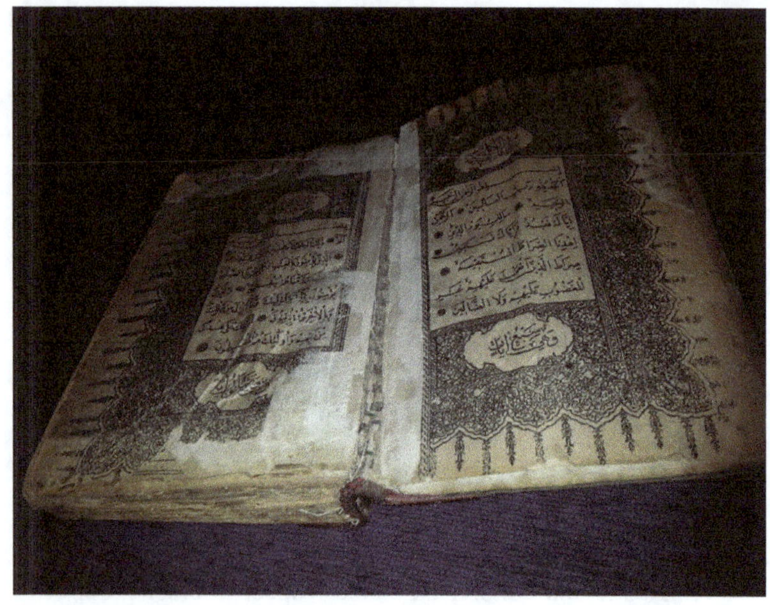

A copy of the old Qur'an kept by Suco Haveric in Sarajevo

A Story of *Eid* (Bayram) in Podgorica

A story of the Eid holiday in Podgorica, with reference to his father **Hamza Ibrahim bey**, was written by his son, **Kemal** Haveric. It reflects Hamza bey's kindness to local residents by expressing his gratitude, strong community bonds and values like compassion, unity and generosity.

I

Put od kuće do njegove terzijske radnje Hamzabega je vodio pored Šaćiragine bakalnice.

Nije to bio jedini put iz Stare u Novu varoš,ali je obično tim putem išao.Kad god bi tuda prošao,vidio bi Šaćiragu kako stoji na vratima svoje bakalnice kao da nekoga očekuje,i u mimohodu pozdravivši se s njim,produžio.

Stojeći na vratima,Šaćiraga je dugo gledao za Hamzabegom i divio mu se.Činilo mu se da ljepšeg starijeg a urednijeg čovjeka nije bilo u Staroj varoši:ovisok,sa crvenim fesom na glavi,brkovi i kosa sijedi,krupne crne oči iznad kojih vise debele,crne vjeđe.Na njemu kao nebo plave čohane čakšire i vezeni džamadan,ispod kojeg se nazirao crveni, vuneni pas-"trabulus".

Hamzabeg je rijetko navraćao u bakalnicu.To je obično činio pred Bajram da naruči veću količinu brašna,šećera i druge robe koju je dijelio najsiromašnijim porodicama.

Uoči Bajrama je,pa je Šaćiraga napunio svoju radnjicu vrećama punim brašna i glavama šećera,te se jedva kreće između njih.Spotiče se, ali mu to ništa ne smeta,jer je siguran da će mu se radnjica brzo isprazniti.

Gleda u vreće brašna i glave šećera,zadovoljno trlja ruke očekujući Hamzabega i druge mušterije."Biće pazara"-pomisli.

Bilo je bogatijih Podgoričana od Hamzabega,ali su bili rijetki oni kao on,koji su saosjećali sa sirotinjom koje je bilo mnogo u Staroj varoši a naročito u Tabhani,a nisu željeli da im se zna da je pomažu.

"Bog mu đecu sačuva'.Vazda mu Bog da' đe čujo i ne čujo".

Sirotinja nije krila.Blagosiljala ga je i zahvaljivala mu kad god bi neko spomenuo Hamzabegovo ime.

During *Eid* (Bayram) in Podgorica

Hamza Ibrahim bey's path from the house to his *terzi* shop led past the grocery store of Sacir Agha. It was not the only way from Stara to Nova Varos in Podgorica, but he usually went that way. Whenever he passed it by, he would see the Sacir Aga standing at the door of his shop as if he was waiting for him, and in passing he always said 'hello' (*salaam*) to him.

Standing at the door, Sacir Agha looked after **Hamza bey** for a long time and admired him. It seemed to him that there was no more handsome and neat old man in Stara Varoš: a tall man with a red fez on his head, a moustache and grey hair, large black eyes above which hung black eyebrows. On him, like the bright sky, was worn a blue cochineal *caksir* (traditional baggy pants) and an embroidered *jamadan* (sleeveless embroidered jacket), under which was a red, woolly belt *trabulus* (wide traditional belt).

Hamza bey rarely visited the grocery store. When he did, he usually went before the *Eid* (Muslim festival) to order a larger quantity of flour, sugar and other goods which he distributed to the poorest families.

It is in the front of the ponds, so Sacir Agha has filled his shop with bags full of flour and sugar dices, so he could barely move between them. He stumbled upon them but didn't bother him because he was sure that his store would be emptied quickly.

He looked at the bags of flour and sugar, contentedly rubbing his hands, expecting **Hamza bey** and other customers. 'There would be a purchasing' – he thought.

There were richer Podgorica people than **Hamza bey**, but there were only a few people like him, who sympathised with the many poor people in Stara Varoš, especially in area around Tabhana Street. He did not want that his deed needs to be noticed.

About **Hamza bey**'s charity, they would rather say, 'May God take care of his child, always, God grant him the best reward whether he heard or not'. The poor people did not hide their appreciation. They blessed him and thanked him whenever someone mentioned Hamza bey's name.[111]

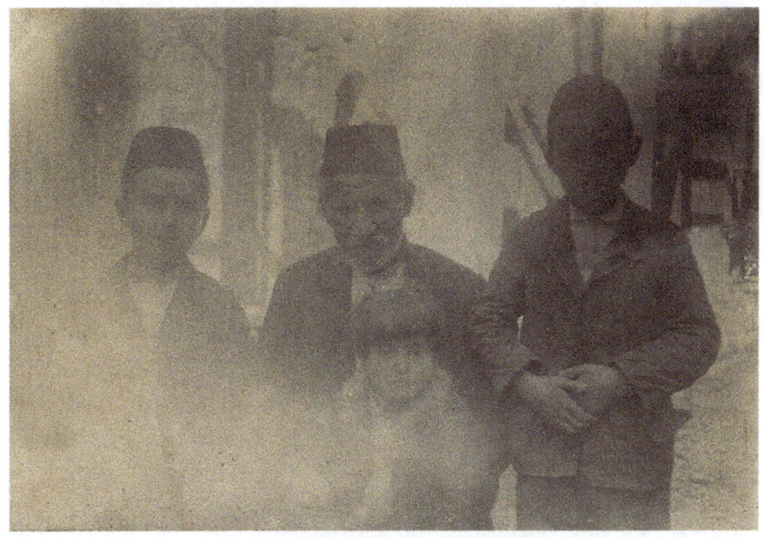

Hamza bey with children, late 1920s

A Story on the Bridge

Bahrija Haveric Bibezic remembered an old story that Selim bey Haveric told her:

> A young Montenegrin Christian Orthodox, after he sold a bunch of wood, went along the bank of the Ribnica River to buy rice, flour and sugar with the money he earned. However, going over the bridge, the money fell out of his hands into the Ribnica River. He remained in tears…
>
> Shortly after, **Selim bey** Haveric met him on the bridge and took pity on the young man because of his awkward moments. He helped him by giving him bags of rice, flour and sugar from his pantry and brought him to the town of Danilovgrad. The boy later went to study at a military academy in Russia and became an officer in the Russian army.
>
> After some time, there were Russian Turkish conflicts in which the Montenegrin Russian officer was fighting against the Turks. The Russian army captured several Bosniaks, among whom was Selim bey. When that officer recognized him, he wanted to release Selim bey as for his good deed in the past. However, **Selim bey** said: 'I don't want to be free without my friends'. And so, as a sign of a gratitude for the help he received from **Selim bey**, this Montenegrin reciprocated by releasing Selim bey with his friends. He even paid for their trip back to Podgorica.[112]

An Anecdote about Turkish Costumes

An anecdote was found about a Montenegrin woman named Mara and Turkish collectors of tax, in which Bey Haveric in Podgorica was mentioned shielding her against the Turks. He supported this oppressed non-Muslim woman.

> The Turkish *haraclija* (collector of tax or tribute) were taking a *kharac* (tax, tribute, a tax on land held by non-Muslims) from the sales of heavy wood at the Podgorica market. They were so heartless that they wanted at any price to take everything the local non-Muslims brought to the market for sale. Such was the case with a certain woman named Mara.
>
> On market day, Mara went to Podgorica with a load of wood on his back. She was waiting in the fields to sell firewood, but before the buyer came a *haraclija* (a collector of tax or tribute) said:
>
> Give me a quarter, woman.
>
> Mara ceded the fourth part of her burden, and with the rest she remained waiting for the buyer. It took a while, and other tax collectors came.
>
> Give me a quarter.

I gave already one, she said!

But Turks did not even want to hear it, instead they took another quarter of the remaining wood.

Soon after these came the third, again asking for a quarter of Mara's wood.

I have already paid twice for that damned scammer of yours, she defended herself.

That is what you said! We do not know about it, they said. God willing, then, Mara said, I will give you proof," then she threw a thunderbolt from the tree and hit the Turk on the head, and he fell, covered in blood.

The Turks were appalled as they were attacked by Mara and wanted to punish her. **Bey Averic** protected Mara and asked her, "Why did you hit him, hillbill?"

I wish I had a Turkish "proof" because nothing else helps me to get rid of hem.

The story pointed to the courage and resourcefulness of Mara. However, the story also hints at the difficult life of our women, who had to come from distant villages at night. They sat with wood on their backs to earn some money.[113]

Cemetery (*Mezarlık*) and two Pashas Graves (*Nishans*)

Muslim *niches* are special guideposts, sources of information about the past. *Nišani* (B. grobnje; T. *mezarlar*), as memorial forms of architecture, enable a reconstruction of the forgotten past. The first cemetery (*mezarlık*) where the oldest Havericas were buried was called the 'Turkish Cemetery on Pobrezje'. Today, this area is neglected with damaged inscriptions and Islamic symbols.[114] Located outside the city walls, for a long time until the 1970s, it was the only active cemetery for the Muslims of Stara Varos, with a total area of 24,200 square metres. Its silent removal began immediately after the end of the Second World War.[115]

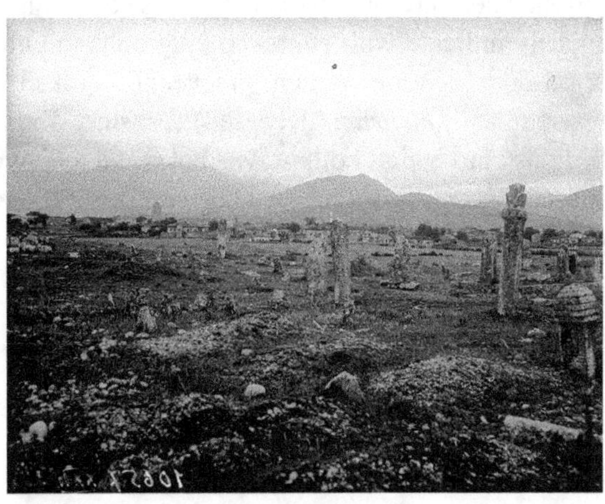

The old 'Turkish cemetery in Pobrezje', Podgorica, where members of the family were buried, including Alija bey and Abdulah bey

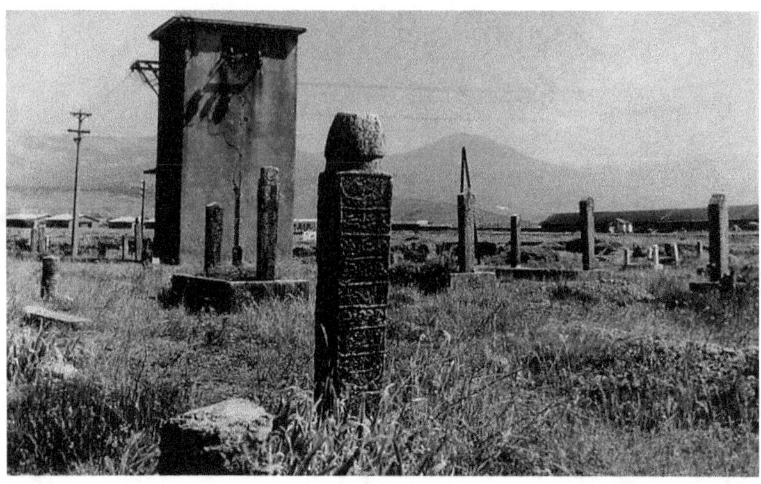

The old 'Turkish cemetery in Pobrezje', Podgorica, where members of the Haveric and Mandic were buried

On the road from Podgorica to a small town of Tuzi is an old *Nizam cemetery* (Military *Mezarlık*) near *Nizam Mosque* (Soldier's Mosque). By its shape and writing, it dates to the era of the Ottoman administration. There are two *nishans* (graves) of ruling Haverics, which primarily indicate with engraved epigraphs in Ottoman and Arabic script, on which are written '*mehrum* (deceased) Havar…' [kadi and pasha], and '*mehrum* (deceased)…Pasha…Ibn Haveriki'. The inscriptions clarify that both graves belonged to Haverics, one for a pasha and another a kadi.[116] They are humble and almost unnoticed symbols of dignity and remembrance of the time.

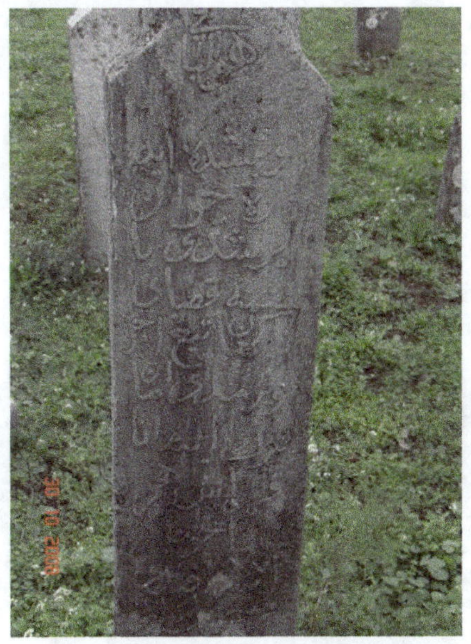

Mezar with an Osmanli inscription:
He (*Allah*) is eternal
***Mehrum* (deceased) Kadi Havar...**

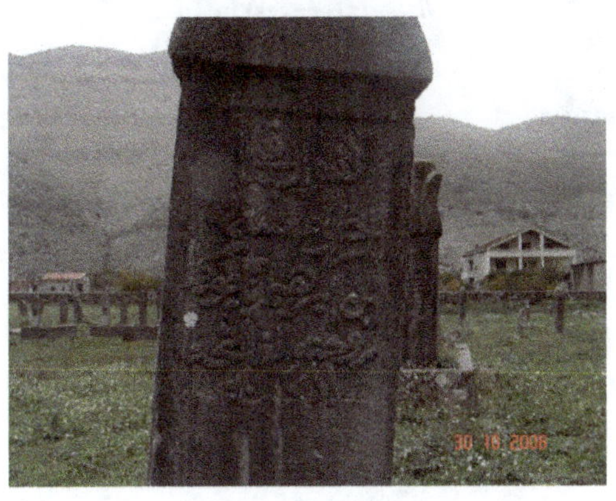

Mezar with an Arabic inscription:
He (*Allah*) is eternal
***Mehrum* (deceased)...Pasha...Ibn Haveriki**

Beside these two *nishans* of Haveric's pashas is another couple of *nishans* bearing the surname Haveric, one of which is probably the wife of Senator **Dervis bey** Haveric.

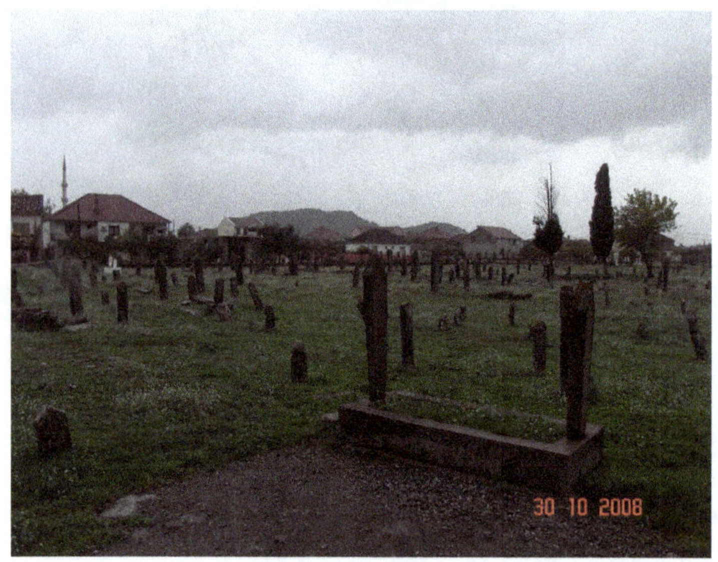

***Nishans* (graves) in Tuzi**

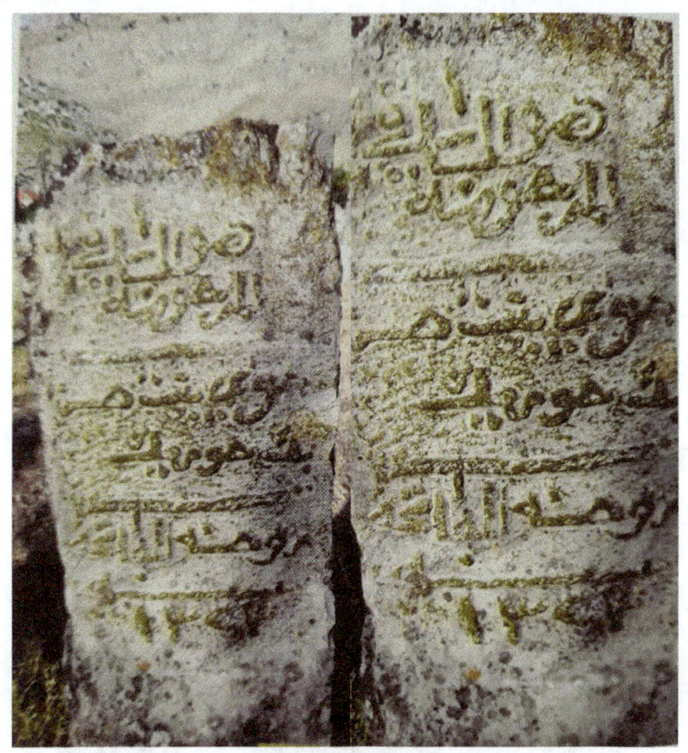

Deceased Hava, daughter of Hasan bey Haveric
For her soul, *Fatiha*
Year 1323h [i.e. 1905]

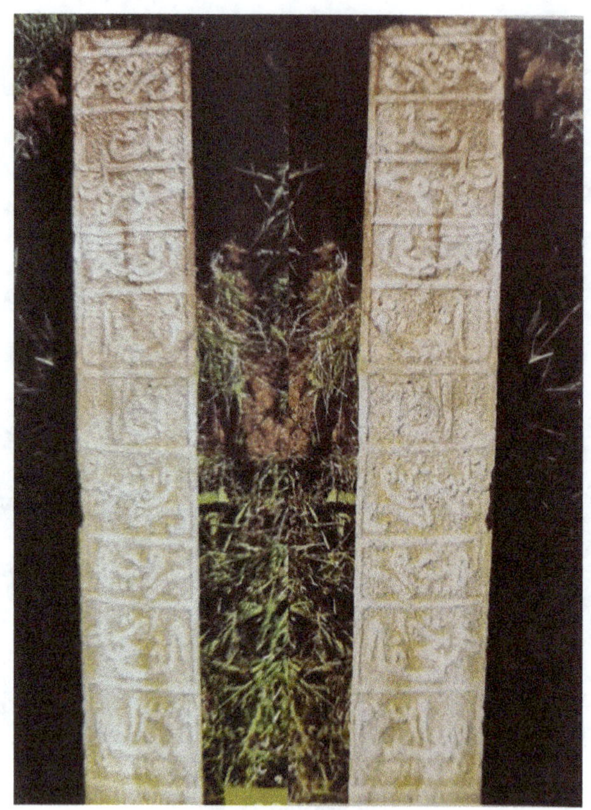

Wife of Dervis bey Haveric
(daughter) Zejnelja age Dervisevic
For her soul *Fatiha*
Year 1329h. [1911]

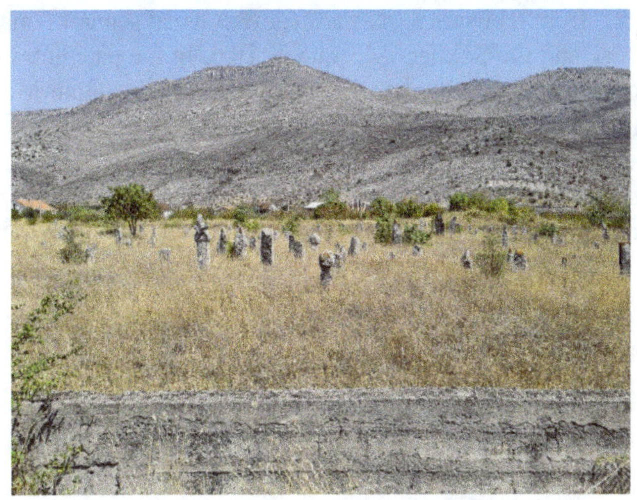

Old Nizams graves near the town of Tuzi

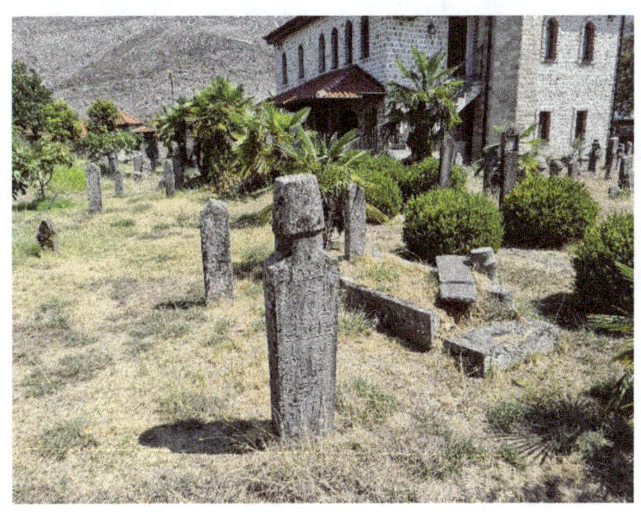

Martyrs' cemetery and Soldiers Mosque in Tuzi[117]

Not far from Haveric's *mezars* (grave) is a separate martyrs' cemetery and the Soldiers Mosque in Tuzi. In the gate entrance of the mosque, it is written: 'After the burial of the Sultan Mehmed Fatih's soldiers, a barracks and a mosque were built. Here [also] rest: *sehids* (martyrs) and leading people who died before 1911; 400 Ottoman martyrs of the 1911 cholera Epidemic; martyrs of the Balkan War of 1912'.

Kadis (*Judges*)

The term *kadi* refers to judges who preside over matters in accordance with Sharia (Islamic law). During the Ottoman Empire, the *kadi* (Islamic judge) became a crucial part of the central authority. In hierarchy, the court and kadi who presided over it were among the most important administrative institutions and offices in the Ottoman cities, including Podgorica. Kadis were appointed by the Sultan's *divan* (Imperial council). Within the Ottoman's provincial administrative system, known as the *timar* system, the *kadi* served as an important check on the power of the military class.[118] The supervision of the actions of administrative and military officials was under the authority of the *kadi*.[119]

An important figure of the central government was a *kadi*.[120] Despite the unquestioned authority of the sultan, *kadis* possessed a degree of autonomy in their rulings.[121] Kadi maintained jurisdiction and as a conciliator promoted tolerance in matters of civil and religious dispute among residents. He exercised judicial functions, such as legal regulations of marriage and divorce, mediation, guardianship over orphans and minors, distribution of inheritance and leaving names in inheritance, as well as other types of legal proceedings.[122] This basic principle was interpreted by Islamic jurists with the stance: 'We are ordered not to endanger them (non-Muslims) and what they have accepted as their religion'.

The Shkoder Sandjak, which included Montenegro, was divided into *kadiluks* (an administrative division of the Ottoman Empire) and *nahiya* (a regional or local type of administrative division that usually consists of several villages or sometimes smaller towns). A *kadiluk* is a judicial and administrative area or district. More *nahiyas* made up a *kadiluk* and more *kadiluk* created a *sandjak* (historical and geopolitical region in the Balkans). The *kadis*, after the *sandjakbeys* (Ottoman military and administrative officials who governed a Sandjak), were the most influential figures in the cities under Turkish rule. At the head of the *kadiluk* stood the *kajmekan* (administrator), *kadi* and *muselim* (executive). The *kadi* also had his *subash* (an Ottoman gubernatorial). In their work, they were assisted by a jury, made up of respectable personalities, usually called 'proper Muslims'. In Podgorica, the *kadi* was assisted by a jury composed of prominent people, mostly but not exclusively Muslims.[123] From 1756 to 1835, with certain interruptions, the Podgorica *kadiluk* with the cities of Podgorica, Spuz and Zabljak, was part of the Bosnian *Eyalet*. During that, time there was a kadi in Spuz. *Nahiya* belonged to the Podgorica *kadiluk*, as well as Medun, Bjelopavlici, Pipera and Hota.[124] One of the most important *kazas*, as an administrative centre, was Podgorica.[125]

In the Podgorica chronicles, it was said that, during the time of Ottoman rule, the Haverics worked in the judiciary.[126] In history, several Haverics were *kadis* in Montenegro and one in Albania. A few of them studied law in Istanbul. From the end of the 17th century and at the beginning of the 18th century, Haveric *kadis* were among the main elders in Podgorica.

The first and most famous Kadi in the Haveric family was **Mustaj Kadi**, who lived in the 17th century (around 1695). The Sultan's *divan* gave him the right to adjudicate a *kadiluk*. 'He lived in Podgorica, and often travelled to Cetinje'. At that time, **Mustaj Kadi Haveric** was also the *zabit* of Podgorica, governing Podgorica and its surroundings, including Ceklici, in Katunska *nahiya*, which was made up of nine villages. He was described by the Montenegrin chronologist Ilija Zlaticanin as a 'literate and prudent man'. Other sources write that he was 'a very interesting and layered character'. Because of his peaceful stance and Islamic integrity, he enjoyed great respect.

Mustaj Kadi was in charge of jurisprudence not only in Podgorica but also its surrounding area. In his time, two local tribes, Rovcani and Moracani, rebelled against the Turks. When he found out about this rebellion, the vizier of Shkoder ordered the *kadi*, who was recognised as 'a hero and military leader, to gather enough troops to punish the rebels most severely, the kadi carried out the order'. When **Mustaj Kadi** came with the army to a place where both tribes could be seen, he stopped the army and thought. 'You could see that he was a smart man because this is what he did', said Ilja Zlaticanin. Kadi immediately ordered the army to return. When one of the officers asked him the reason, the *kadi* replied: 'I was sent by the vizier to punish them most severely, and I will prove to the vizier that I cannot punish them more than God punished them, because they live in that abandoned area, separated from the whole world so that they know neither God nor men'. 'Kadija did a great job, no blood was lost, that is why we included him in the list of famous Podgorica residents, as he really deserved it', said Ilija Zlaticanin.[127]

It was not surprising that **Mustaj Kadi** appeared in the celebrated Montenegrin epic poem, *The Mountain Wreath*, by Petar Petrovic Njegos. Knowing about **Mustaj Kadi** in history, Njegos used his name and title in a conversation in the poem. He mentioned '**Mustaj Kadi** as a member of the enemy (Bosniak Muslims) side was given a significant place in the epic'.[128] Among some Christian Orthodox radicals was the opinion that two religions cannot exist next to each other in Montenegro. In *Ontology of Islam* ('Ontologija Islama') Muhic explained that their fictional interpretation of 'Muslim betrayal of ancestral Orthodox faith and their myth of the

Turkish slavery' created a *carte blanche* ('freedom to act upon their interpretation') to take revenge against Bosniak Muslims without any reason.[129]

However, being firm in his attitude, **Mustaj Kadi** answered the radicals that 'it is impossible for Muslims to submit to Christians'.[130] **Mustaj Kadi** believed they were 'sticking a thorn in the healthy leg'. He believed that 'one day of worship is better than four years of baptism'. He also said those who stick a thorn in the leg would also throw people into unconsciousness or drunkenness.[131] Thus, just because of maintaining his Islamic identity, **Mustaj Kadi** was seen by radicals as a blind follower of Prophet Muhammad. In the *Mountain Wreath*, **Mustaj Kadi** maintained:

What are you talking about?
Are you in your right mind?
You are sticking a thorn in a healthy leg!
Why are you burdening the only true religion [ie.e. Islam][132]

A famous author, Miroslav Krleza, said *The Mountain Wreath* was 'an anti-Turkish song'. Hadziabdic pointed out that the poem was an epic synthesis of classics, oral epics and an 'Ottomanophobic' literary tradition. Njegos's Ottomanophobic writing produced an image of the enemy not only as a foreigner conqueror, but also in the internal other, i.e. Muslims who became the 'instrument' of the conqueror's rule.[133]

Others highlighted the most picturesque parts of *The Mountain Wreath* were verses about Istanbul in the foreground, which are the most beautiful in the Njegos' apotheosis of Islam. This referred to the description of *Stambol* (Istanbul) put in the mouth of Mustaj Kadi. So, one of the eight small towns with which the Montenegrins were conducting reconciliation negotiations, that is, under the guise of calming some heads, while everyone was suffering and watching them surrender. **Mustaj Kadi**'s speech to the Montenegrin leaders was the most extensive, intense and impressive in the entire painful dialogue in which they participated, more or less dominating the Muslim representatives.[134]

In this poetry, **Mustaj Kadi** is known for his love of stories about the *huris* (beautiful women) and Istanbul, and above all his rousing speech about his Muslim religion.

Alhamdulillah, they are two hundred years old
since we accepted Pasha's faith,
we stand in *Deen* (or *Din* faith or way of life)
O Stambole, earthly joy,
a cup of honey, more mountainous than sugar,
the sweet bath of human life,
where fairies bathe in sherbet;
O Stambole, the palace of the saints,
eastern powers and sanctuaries, -
God just comes out of you

A hundred times in my youth
at dawn he rushed from the guard
to your flow clear and lovely,
through which you see your face
more beautiful sun, dawn and moon.
I looked at the sky, at the sea
your towers and sharp minarets,
from which they ascended to heaven
at dawn, in the wonderful silence,
thousands of holy voices,
calling upon heaven the name of the Almighty,
on earth the name of a beloved Prophet.
What faith do you measure against this?[135]

As they passed by the Montenegrin Assembly, **Mustaj Kadi** also appeared in the poem by asking the boys to sing wedding songs, instead of military songs, so the leaders were not offended. He first started singing"

Don't cry mother for beautiful Fatima.
She was married but not buried.
The rose did not fall from its branch
but she was moved to her garden.
Suljo will take care of Fatima
as the apple of his dear eye.
Fatima is a wonderful figure,
. and her eyes are like two bright stars.
Her face is like a rosy morning.
A wreath of the Morning Star shines beneath her hair.
Her mouth is shaped like a coin.
Her lips burn the colour of a rose.
White sparks shine here and there between them
snow bracelets made of small pearls.
Her throat is like pure white ivory,
her white hands like the wings of a swan.
The morning star sails above the flowers,
and silver oars row with the Star.
Bless the pillow on which she rests![136]

Havérics are mentioned in other epic poetry. For instance, a Haveric *kadi* is mentioned in an epic poem called the *Battle with Kuči*:

Battle with Kuci (1739)

Pasha of Shkoder stood up,
after him an army of fifteen thousand,
of Pasha tabor erected white tents
on the land towards Podgorica;

From there Pasha is writing a book,
and he went to fortified Kuče

I [Pasha] want to have two hundred cash,
and more than a hundred oxen…
'If you are willing, Pasha,
we will give you a treasure of two hundred cash
and more than a hundred oxen'

Then said **Haveric Kadi**:
'What are you asking them, Pasha?
they won't be given to you,
instead, defeat their army'

Then, the Pasha says a word:
'My Podgorica servants,
how many Kuchach on weapons?'
And, **Haveric Kadi** says to him:
'There are thousands of raffles, Pasha'.[137]

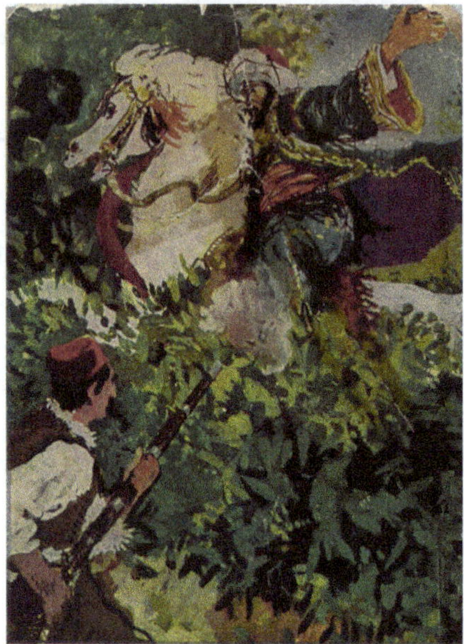

Old drawing based on an epic poem

According to Andrija Jovicevic, the Haveric family had *kadis* **Velija Kadi** and **Becir bey Kadi**. In his stories, Ilija Zlaticanin mentioned two *kadis*, **Osman Bey** and **Ahmet bey Haverić**. **Zuber bey** Haveric was also recorded as a *kadi*, after acquiring legal studies and work experience in Istanbul. These *kadis* tried to solve issues in a peaceful manner. For instance, when Jusa Mucin Krnic (~1874), a military leader and politician, appointed him to the position as the commander of the town of Kuce. **Zuber bey Haverić**'s duties were to solve the problems between the feuding tribes in Kuce and restore peace. **Osman bey Haverić**, a kadi, was said to have been an appointed administrator, a *katib* (vizier's secretary) for a time in Shkodra. On one occasion, **Osman bey**, who dealt with vizier letters and followed his decisions, became known for saving the life of a good fighter named Jusuf Abdiomerovic. Jusuf Abdiomerovic did not obey the vizier's rules and sentenced to be hung. The vizier accepted **Osman bey**'s pledge to save his life by warning Jusuf to obey the rules, but also 'knowing that it [was] good to have alive a brave soldier who will obey his rule'.[138]

In Podgorica, in the mid-19th century until the liberation of Podgorica from the Turks, there was a *majlis* (court) in the then house of Lekic, which had seven members, including Haverics. The members of court received a sultan *ferman* to operate a Sharia jurisdiction in the city.[139] There was also an Orthodox representative in that local court and legal decisions were made unanimously.

There was also an anecdote preserved by author Jevrem Brkovic: One girl narrated how she learned about self-defence. If you 'the hero' move to 'threaten' me, you will be the loser. The girl said, 'When I was young, **Haveric Kadi** taught me, if someone attacked "to shoot" to defend myself'.[140]

Waqifs (*Benefactors*)

The institution of *waqf* (an Islamic charitable endowment, foundation), which serves religious, cultural and generally humanitarian purposes, had a significant role not only in the construction of mosques, but also in various buildings of general importance for Muslims and non-Muslims. The Haveric *waqfs* (benefactors) founded their endowments since the development and flowering of Ottoman rule. Like other endowments, the Haverić's endowments for buildings and olive farms were created from their bequest. It testifies to the rich past.

During his service at the *Porte* (a headquarters of the Ottoman Empire), **Zejnil Pasha Haveric**, with consent from the sultan, visited Podgorica, his birthplace. During one of his stays in Podgorica, **Zejnil Pasha** dedicated *waqf* for a tower (*cardak*) and a bridge on the Ribnica River called the **'Haveric Bridge'**. He also tried to implement a water supply system for the Cijevina River in Podgorica following the example of Diocletian's water supply system, but this project failed. However, 'this famous man did not spare the effort and money to do a good deed while he was challenged to serve the Ottoman Empire overseers', said Ilija Zlaticanin.

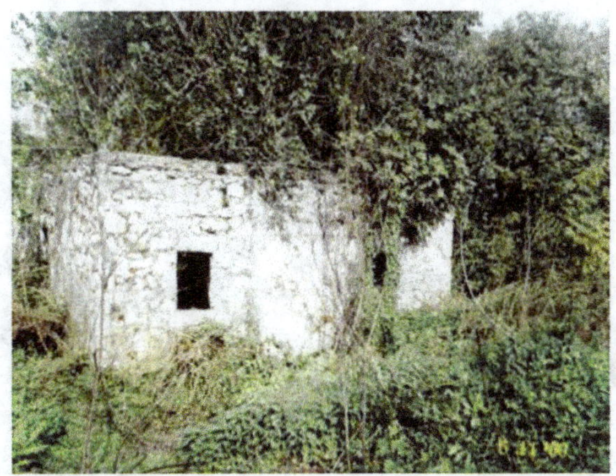

The remains of the Haveric Mosque in Goricani

From Golubovci, the Lower Zeta municipality, 800 metres from the main road on the right, there was a Haveric Mosque in the village of Goricani. It was the *waqf* foundations by Husein Pasha Karadag Haveric in Goricani (Golubovci). This *mahala* type of mosque had the ground dimensions of 11 x 7 metres. The *waqf* of Haveric Mosque owned eleven acres of land in this municipality. Nearby was a large cemetery in the mosque harem.[141] Long ago, some Haverics as imams also performed religious services there. The remains of this Haveric Mosque still exist today.[142]

Bajro Agovic stated 'the Haveric Mosque in Goricani, on the banks of the Moraca River, was destroyed during the Second World War' and added:

> Muslims, except for one family, moved to Shkodra … the mosque has been left to decay since then… As there were no Muslims in the nearby neighbourhood, because after 1912 they mostly moved to Shkoder, Bosnia and Herzegovina and Turkiye. The perimeter walls of the mosque remain, although with visible damage and cracks. Only its *mihrab* remained completely preserved.[143]

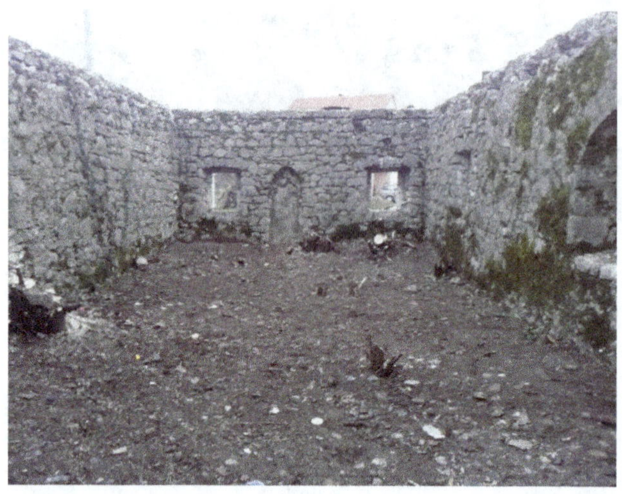

The remains of Haveric Mosque in Goricani, Golubovci – a *mihrab* in the middle

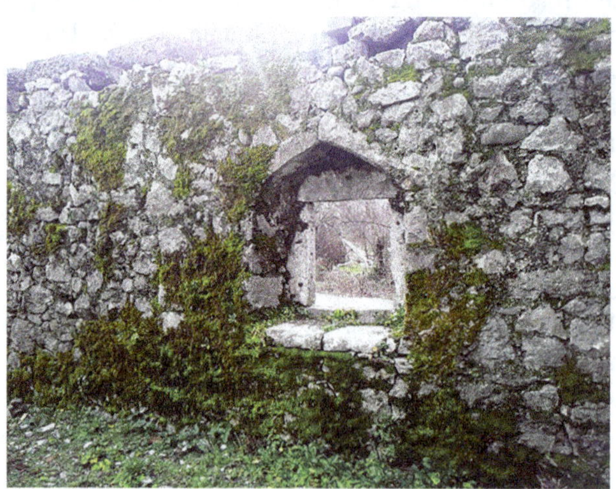

Side window of Haveric Mosque in Goricani, Golubovci

Pavle S. Radusinovic in the *Population and Settlements of the Zetska Ravnica from the oldest time to the modern period* (Stanovnistvo i naselja Zetske ravnice od najstarijeg doba do novog doba) mentioned the village of Berislavci, which had a mosque and was home to several brotherhoods, including Haverić. Haverics were landowners and *waqifs* there. The author said:

> In Turkish times, Muslims had a religious school for their children in the *mejtef* (basic Islamic school) near the mosque located in the middle of the village. The mosque was demolished in 1927, but its remains are still visible. There were no shops in Goricani… Nearby there was a big house with a tower, until the last decades of the 19th century where lived a certain 'Turkish Effendi' who supposedly protected residents from attackers.

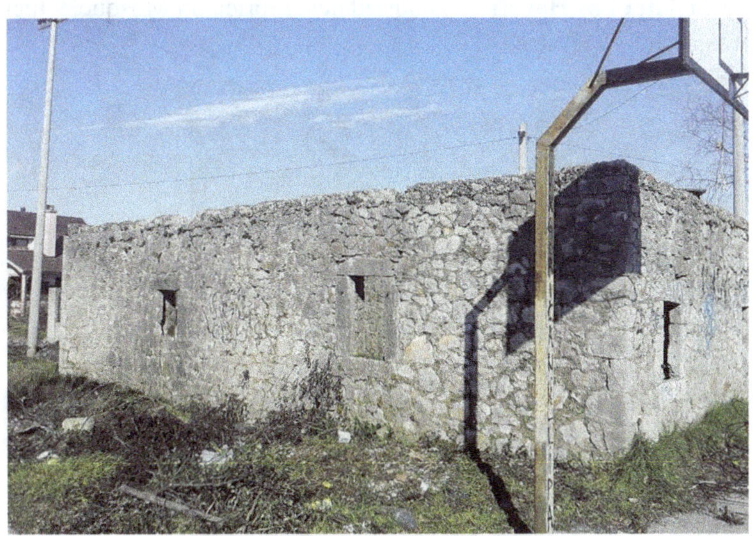

Haveric Mosque, Goricani, Golubovci

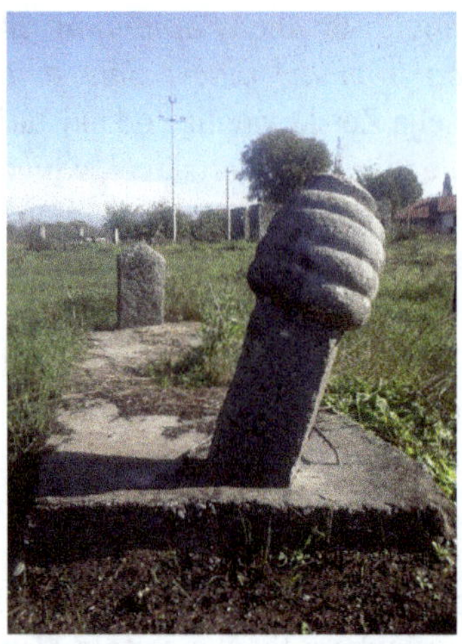

A grave near Haveric Mosque in Goricani, Golubovci

Salih Alija bey Haveric was buried near Goricanin Mosque, which was built by Haverics.

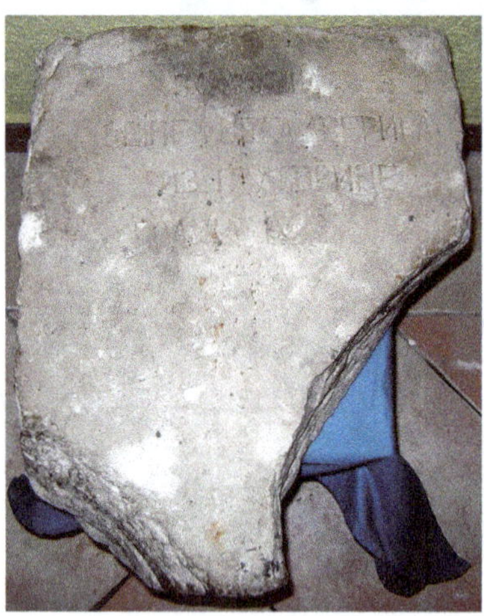

The rest of the stone on which the name Zeinel bay Haverica from Podgorica is carved

About 1000 metres of the road of the Muslim settlement of Brbot used to be valves that regulated the flow of water to the castle. Until 1992-1995, there was a plaque on which was written **'Zejnel bey Haverica's waqf'**.[144] The plaque was damaged but pieces have been preserved by **Isamil Halil bey** Haveric.[145]

The viaduct (aqueduct) of 17 larger arches of different spans, which rest on the same number of massive columns, a masterpiece of its kind in Montenegro, is where the **Zejnel bey**'s *waqf* was. The **Zejnel bey Haveric** water foundation is one of the most known Bar *waqf*. The date of creation of this foundation was apparently 'between 1786 and 1798' after **Zejnel bey** moved from Podgorica to Bar.[146] He bequeathed an amount of money with which to finance the works of bringing water from a cave that was located near several villages of Turčina to the town of Bar. Until then, the town and fortress did not have flowing water, but the population was supplied from cisterns and the nearby Bunar River. The water was brought through pipes that were originally made of earthen junta, which were replaced by iron pipes starting in 1905. It is also known that in 1901 **Zejnel bey** Haverić's *waqf* had a capital of 4,743 fiorins and 83 coins, as well as 926 olive roots, the value of which was then estimated at around 8,000 fiorins.[147] According to the *Book of Waqf* of 1922, the 'Haveric Water Foundation' had an income of 31,834.60 dinars.[148]

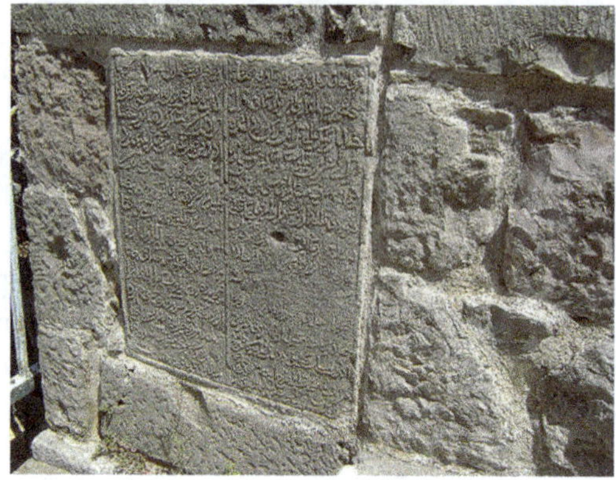

An old inscription

On one of the five public fountains inside the fortress, not far from Orta Mosque, where the remains of ceramic pipes were also found, there was a carved stone tablet with an inscription in Arabic. This inscription originates from a fountain whose remains were excavated in front of the church of St. Nicholas in Stari. From the text, we learn that 'the fountain was built by *silah-sor* (swordsman) **Zejnul** Abidin (Zeyn-ül-âbidîn) in 1756 (1169 according to the Islamic calendar)'. This text was once translated by Bosniak scholar Mehmed Mujezinović.

Papovic in *Examples of Philanthropy in Montenegro* ('Primjeri filantropije u Crnoj Gori') noted 'the **Zejnel bey** Haveric's water foundation was created when this merchant from Podgorica moved to Bar and bequeathed money for the construction of a water supply system in Bar'. Benefactor **Zejnel bey** Haveric was an educated and enterprising man, who worked tirelessly to improve his new homeland and the lives of the Muslim and non-Muslim residents of the town. At that time, the town of Bar (and the fortress of Bar) did not have enough flowing water, except in Podgrad (the lower town) in the Bunar River and one wheel (fountain) called 'Knez bunar'. Although the waters were clear, they were weak. **Zejnel bey** Haveric, seeing the scarcity of water, bequeathed a sum of money, to be given at interest until it grew, so water could be brought from the cave located in several villages of Turcine in the hill of Mukoval – an hour and a half away from Bar. Water was brought to the town of Bar through a part of the town called Brbot. Along the road through the town, and up to Bar and the fortress, several taps were left. On the way from the spring in Mukoval to Bar, a rock stood in the way, over 50 metres high and over 100 metres long. A legend preceded the water supply:[149]

> Tradition says that this rock obstructed the water supply and that because of this, **Zejnel bey** went forty mornings to that rock and prayed the morning prayer, begging Allah, if He may bless him and grant him peace to dissolve the rock (*Fajr* prayer or *Sabah* namaz). On the fortieth morning he prayed, and then he began to study as usual and fell asleep while studying. In the meantime, *Allah* answered his benevolent supplication and when he awoke, he saw the rock broken apart. Water started to flow… Afterwards, wooden pipes were laid along the created crack through the rock and the water flowed to Bar…

Papovic asserted that 'this water supply infrastructure was completely brought in from the end of the 18th century'. **Zejnel bey** Haveric not only established the water supply through the viaduct in the old Bar but also gave a special endowment for its maintenance. About 100 metres further, on the right side of the road, there was also a stone-walled building in which there were valves that regulated the flow of water into the fortress.[150]

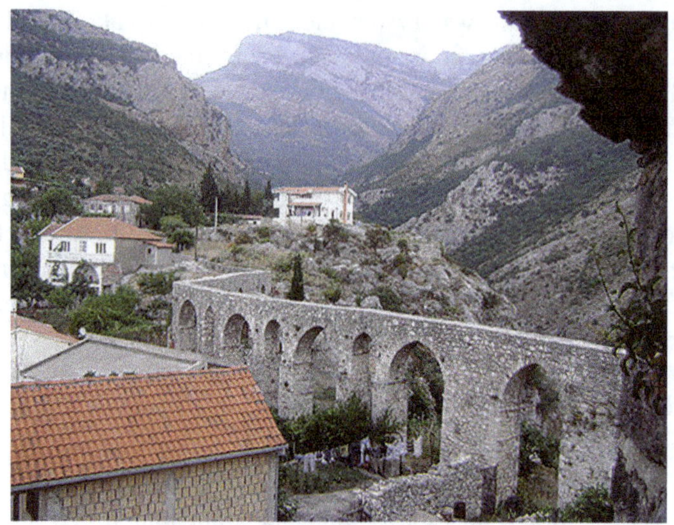

Waqf **of Zejnel Bey Hverica**

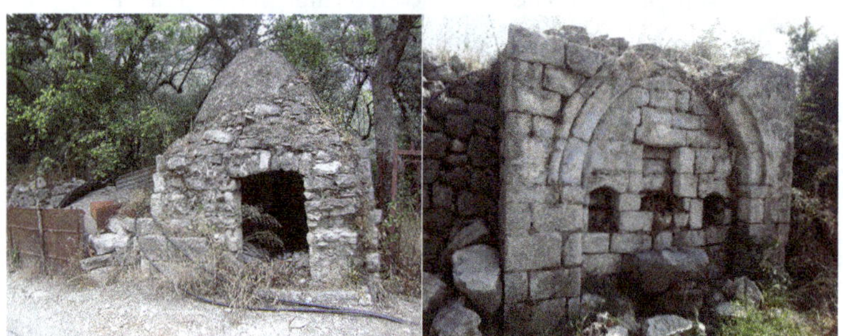

The remains of Zejnel Bey's *waqf*

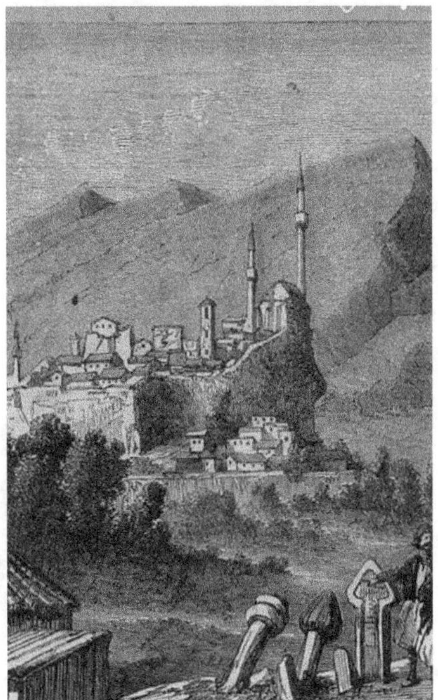

Historia Krajes 1874 Vue d'Antivari

In the fortress was a mosque, which was located at today's *baruthana* (munition storage) and about a hundred metres down from the fortification was another mosque. The mosque inside the walls was maintained by **Zeynel bey**'s *waqf*. Apparently, it became a *baruthana* during the time of King Nikola.[151]

Together with his wife, **Zejnel bey** helped preserve other *waqfs*. They donated olive trees for the maintenance of the mosque of Sultan Murat III (Orta, 'middle') built in 1595 and for the maintenance of other buildings in Bar until they were demolished. Reportedly, the Sultan Murat III Mosque had around its foundation 163 olive roots bequeathed by: Mahmut Januzovic, wife of **Zejnel bey** Haveric; then some *kajmekam* from Asia, and Murat Kapetanović, Smail

Etemagin and Sulejman Tomaš. While two roots were used for various needs of the mosque, after their demolition in 1881, the olive oil was sold and money received. In 1901, on the account of this *waqf*, there were 42,103 *groschi* and 18 *paras*.

The *waqf* of the Ahmed bey Mosque had 466 olive roots bequeathed by **Zejnel bey** Haveric and his wife, Osman Sulejmanovic, Haji Etem, Asan Tahiri, Adem Karaduzovic, Sulejman agha Tomas, Asan aga Skanjevic and two unknown persons.[152]

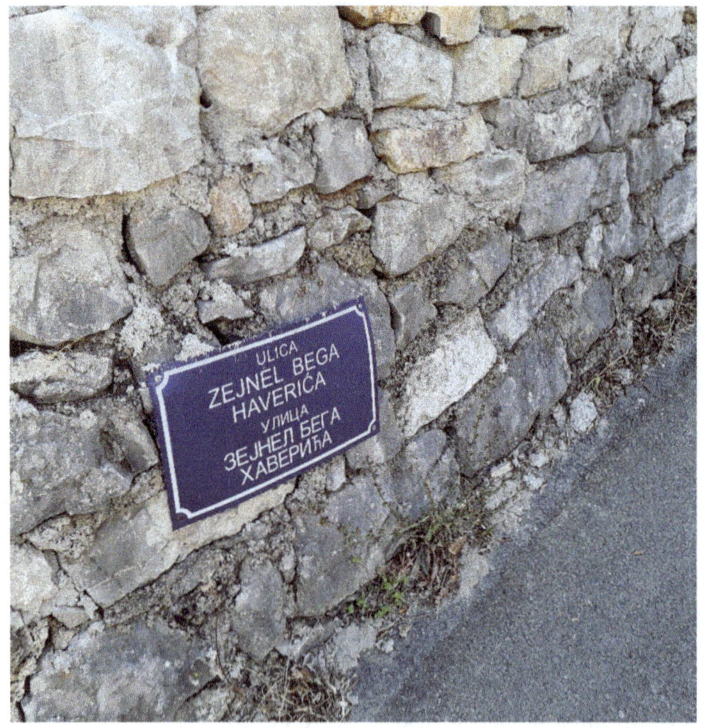

Zejnel bey Street

At a session held in 2009, the Assembly of Bar passed the decision on the determination of street names in Stari Bar. According to Article 1, the street in Stari Bar, 'which starts behind the cathedral in Gretva and extends to the Velembusi settlement' is a given name of '**Zejnel bey Street**', in memory of this great benefactor.[153]

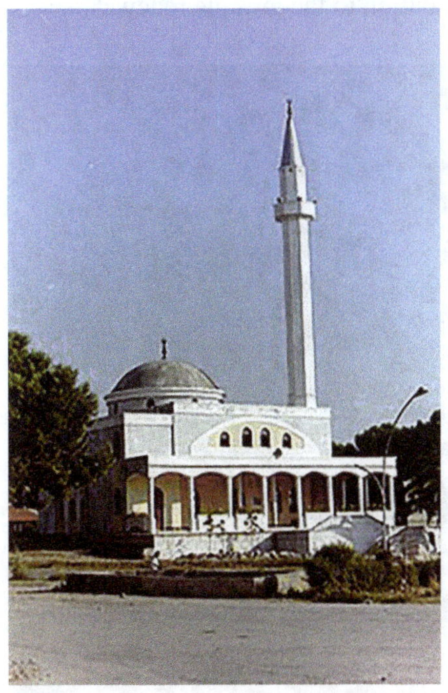

The Kubelie Mosque or Kapllan Beu Mosque (Xhamia e Kubelies), Kavaje

The old Mosque (Xhamija e Vjeter) in Kavaje was renewed by the **Haveriku brothers**, having originally been built in 1735 under the Ottomans by Kapllan Pasha. The mosque stood on the main street of the city, about 70 metres to the east of the current one. The Kubelie Mosque had been described as a 'grand, beautiful building, with a dome and a peristyle [with] marble facades rise under the cypress trees with their Byzantine columns and their Arabian arches'. After being destroyed by Communists in the 1970s, the new mosque has a simple style and is made of concrete and painted white, while the original mosque was an Ottoman stone building with beautifully coloured decorations inside.[154] On its memorial plaque is written '**Haveriku**' as a symbol of the Haveriku brothers for their contribution to the mosque renewal.

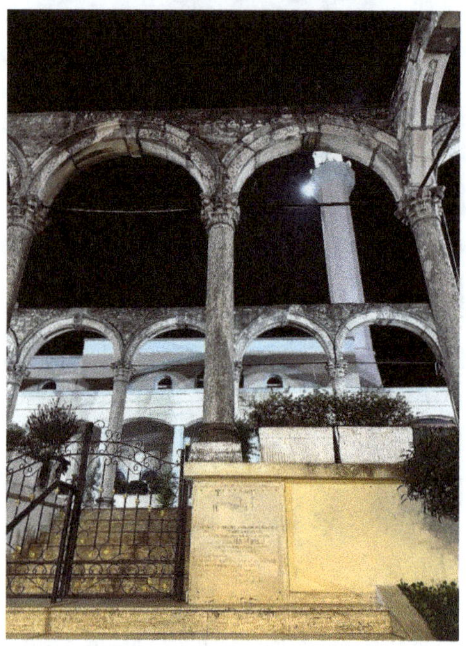

The old Mosque (Xhamija e Vjeter) in Kavaje

In the name of Allah, and with Allah guidance, the brothers **Remzi**, **Nexhmi**, **Aqif**, **Xhezair**, **Fatmir** and **Afrim Haveriku** built the extension of the square in front of the mosque with columns and arches. Altin and Dyrmishi brothers also helped with digging and transporting the soil for free. Blerim Arapi provided a free supply of marble for the mosaic.
November 7, 2003

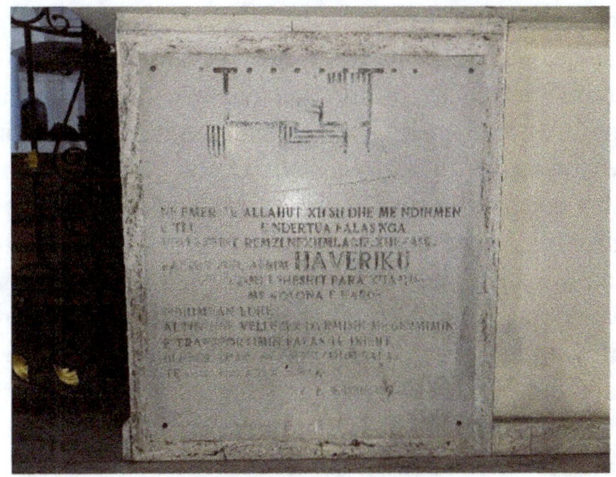

A plaque: Haveriku

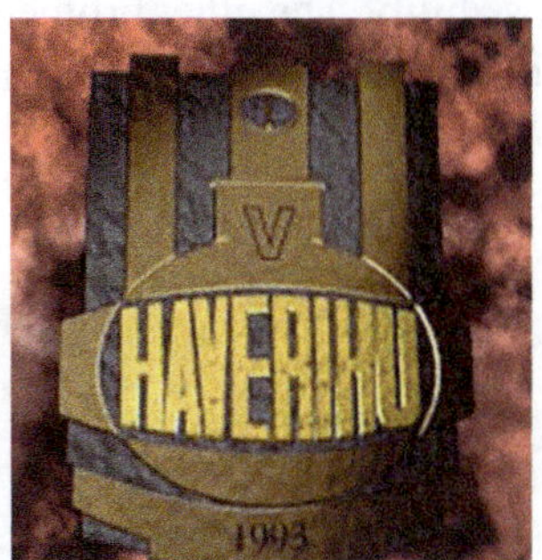

A banner: Vellezerit Haveriku

The **Haveriku** brothers asphalted roads, gave financial aid to low-income families and supported Muslim pilgrims to Mecca. During the Kosovo war, in March 1997, they sheltered many families of Kosovar refugees in Kavaje. They supported the progress of their local community and the country. For these social virtues, they became well-respected by the people of Kavaja.[155]

The **Haveriku brothers ('Vellezerit Haveriku')** in Kavaje: **Remzi**, **Nexhmi**, **Aqif**, **Xhezair**, **Fatmir** and **Afrim** created a construction company in the 1990s. They worked hard for several years, constructing two buildings in Kavaja, and several reconstructions. They established a site of inert materials extraction in Sinaballaj, near the Shkumbini River. To protect the land in which their site was established from constants river floods, they also planted a lot of trees. This area still exists nowadays, providing both a pleasant place to walk and enjoy the nature, and a measure to protect the area when there are river floods. the brothers managed to work and create a good life... **Nexhmi** and **Remzi** have always been an active part of the Muslim community in Kavaja and beyond, giving their contribution every time they had the possibility. The other brothers, **Xhezair** and **Afrim**, still work on the daily jobs that the construction company has.[156]

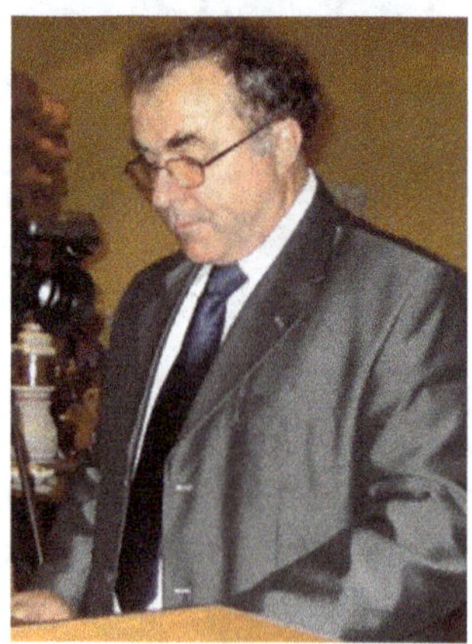

Nexhmi Haveriku

Nexhmi Haveriku (Vice President of the Muslim Forum of Albania) recalled one of the grandest celebrations of the Prophet's birthday, Mevlud, held in Shkoder in 1935:

> A group of students from the Tirana Madrasa attended the ceremony organised by the late Salih Efendi, the Mufti of Shkodra and the Prefecture of Kosovo, and it was performed in the square of the 'Fusha e Çele' Mosque. The minaret of the mosque was festivity connected to the Kumanore of the Franciscan Church of Shkoder, with an electric light that read 'Welcome, Resul i Pritun'. The Municipal Band played music and then the mufti delivered an excellent speech on the life of the Prophet, he also mentioned many opinions of foreign writers and scholars, non-Muslims, about the life of Muhammad. After that, parts of the Qur'an were recited by a Hafiz with an 'angelic voice'. When Mevlud began to be sung, each of attendee sang a certain part. *Salavats* at the end of each part were sung by a group of children. It was followed by sharing sweets and lemonade. At that occasion, a participant in one of five groups was **Nazim Haveriqi.**[157]

Pashas, Commanders and Other Officials

From the early Ottoman period, the authenticated Muslim population (*Bosniaks*) of the Balkans experienced the pejorative Asiatic name 'Turks' by non-Muslims as an identification with the state and the sultan they served. They were powerful, as long as the power and privileges of a great empire stood behind them, and this lasted for several centuries.[158] One of the earliest examples was **Alija Murat Agha Haveric**, later a *zabit* in Podgorica, who was born at the start of the 17th century. He worked for the Ottoman administration from which he received the title 'Agha'.

Podgorica was the military-administrative seat of the Ottoman government. In the beginning, talented and capable young men went to Istanbul for education. In the Ottoman military schools, besides military skills, many languages were taught such as Turkish, Arabic, Persian and French, as well as subjects such as mathematics, physics, history, geography, drawing, calligraphy and gymnastics. In Podgorica, however, only later would there be *meikteb idadiyya* ('preparatory military schools', 'higher gymnasiums', four-grade schools where they acquired the basics for schooling in the Constantinople Military Academy). Over time, some Bosniaks completed their education in *idadies* and obtained higher titles, such as pashas (generals), in Istanbul and reached high posts in the Ottoman Empire. In his chronicle of Podgorica as a multi-ethnic milieu, Ilija Zlaticanin wrote about the human merits and greatness of 'Muslim champions'. He noted:

> Knowing that our people in Podgorica and Montenegro have always been tough and strong-tempered, always

> striving for freedom and something new – that is why I set out to find out how many pashas Podgorica gave to Turkish Empire while it was under its government until 1879.
>
> And, I found that there were a number of pashas [i.e. 23? He said] to whom the Turkish sultans presented those great decorations. Inquiring about pashas, I unintentionally came across a very interesting branch of the history of Podgorica...
>
> Great and famous people and heroes worked in Podgorica. And what stands out the most, if we look through the history of Podgorica, we will see not only about its 'champions', but also about ordinary citizens in general – that they were all rebellious, tough, energetic people, and that they always strived for freedom...

Even if the number of pashas in Zlaticanin's work is exaggerated, modern historiography has revealed and shed light on that part of the almost forgotten past. Danilo Burzan wrote that 'old Podgorica gave as many as 18 pashas'. Zlaticanin and Stanic said, 'Haverics gave a lot of good heroes and outstanding people'. Zelimir Rukavina also pointed out that, next to Haverics, 'the Osmanagic family and several other prominent families gave a large number of famous people to Turkiye and Montenegro'.[159] Memic also stated that 'among wealthy Montenegrin landowners there were several Haveric pashas'.[160]

Several historians and chroniclers wrote there were at least seven pashas from the Haveric family holding the highest official title of honour in the Ottoman Empire; however, these sources are still sketchy. From the 'Haveric family **Ablah Pasha Haveric** was the first *pasha* in the service of the Ottoman

Empire'. He was the son of Mustaj Kadi and probably educated in Istanbul. According to family tradition, with his authority, '**Ablah Pasha**, as a highly respected Muslim from Podgorica and a native of that region, ordered to be kept the *kamilovka* (an Eastern Orthodox clerical hat) and the gospel', 'knowing that there is no compulsion in religion, and with that Islamic principle fulfilled his rule to preserve and nurture interfaith tolerance'.[161] Such a tradition was continued by other pashes from the Haveric family.

In the beginning of the 18th century, mention is made of **Husein Pasha Haveric**, who was of small stature, so he was nicknamed 'Kucuk', which in Turkish means 'small; of shorter stature'. **Husein Pasha Kucuk** participated in the Turkish rule of Montenegro, then fought on foreign battlefields.

A few years after the Assembly of Montenegrins elected Danilo I Njegos as a bishop in 1697, there was conflict between non-Muslim Montenegrins and the Ottoman Turks. In their war, it was said that. in 1702. the Ottoman army captured the bishop in Lower Zeta. This war against the Ottomans, which turned into Danilo's bloodshed against local Muslim population (Bosniaks), is well known in history as *Istraga Poturica* ('Investigation of Turkicised' or 'Inquisition of the Turkicised' people'), which also has interpretations in terms of its date and features. One of interpretations said **Husein Pasha Kucuk** was highly praised for his efforts to stop the attack and restore peace between the parties. Historian Andrija Jovicevic and Ilija Zlaticanin wrote that 'in 1702 **Husein Pasha Kucuk Haveric** and a few other Bosniaks helped to save the life of Bishop Danilo I Njegos', who was then imprisoned in Shkoder. Husen Pasha Kucuk was mentioned as trying to solve the situation peacefully by releasing the bishop. A few articles mentioned Kucuk Pasha, including the article: 'Distinguished Podgorica Muslims from the

Haveric Family: Husein Pasha Kucuk', Zeta, n.d. Page 6. Issue 16, Podgorica:

Ова братства дали су паше: Хусен пашу који је био од великог утицаја да се Владика Данило не објеси већ да се за новац откупи. Како је Хусен био малена раста прозват је Кучук (мали) Хусен паша. У рату Турска са Русијом имао је под своју команду један дио војске. Једнога окршаја на Одесу ту је Кучук погинуо и још седам Хаверића.

Husein Pasha Kucuk mentioned in a newspaper *Zeta,* n.d. Page 6. Issue 16, Podgorica

The bishop was imprisoned for his inhuman attack on Muslims and 'put up for ransom'. Over time, the Muslim defence of this notorious reality was portrayed in the epic tradition as a hero who acted ethically. It was said that **Husein Pasha Kucuk** was influential and, with the collected pledge of gold ducats, helped to save Bishop Danilo. The epic verse about that event states:

Three thousand gold *ducats*…

The 'Turks' [*Bosniaks*] came and brought him [Bishop Danilo] alive,
One [Montenegrin] group met with the 'Turks' [*Bosniaks*],
They gave ducats [in return] received and the bishop,
[Then] They returned safely to Cetinje…

Ilija Zlaticanin wrote that **Bajram bey** and **Hamza (Amzo) Salih bey** Haveric passed on the tradition of their ancestors saying how **Husein Kucuk Pasha** Haveric saved the life of Bishop Danilo in *akçse* (*asprams*), silver coins, which was the chief monetary unit of the Ottoman Empire:

> Bishop Danilo was caught in Zeta and that he was put on buyouts. The buyout was rather in *asprams*, because the values in *groses* were very large. The bishop's capture was because the Vizier Mahmud Busatlija wanted to be blamed the secret collusion of the Montenegrins to kill the local 'Turks' (*Bosniaks*). When the Vizier reported this case to the sultan and he was severely reprimanded for not hanging the bishop.[162]

Safet-beg Basagic also scripted that, in 1702, Bishop Danilo wrote that once he 'was ransomed from Podgorica ... the Montenegrins did not attack the Turks', then 'the Turks remained healthy and the majority started to accept even more Turkish rule and religion, because they were being inspired by the pasha [perhaps by **Husein Kucuk Pasha Haveric**] from Podgorica...'[163]

In the meantime, another local event occurred. It was when the Turkish Osman Pasha 'Turkusha' (derogatory term for Turk) from Asia wanted to attack Seoca tower in old Podgorica, Husein pasha Osmanagic, 'two pashas of Haveric, and the famous *kadija* Haveric also went to defend it'. Together, Krnics, Osmanagics and Haverics took out *yatagans* (sabers) and said: 'Great Turkus, you have to cut us down first and then set fire to Seoča tower'. Then, 'Turkuh' (Turk) asked the most famous Podgorica fencers for the reason 'why they are ready to pay for that tower with their heads'. The Seoca (old Podgorica) residents answered him, 'we want to protect it, as we are the Dukljans (Montenegrins)'.[164]

In 1710-1711, the war between the Turks and Russia (the Pruth River Campaign) was fought, in which the Russians were defeated on the Pruth River (present-day Ukraine). The Ottoman army was led by the Grand Vizier Baltacı Mehmet Pasha and the empire was ruled by Sultan Ahmed III (reigned 1703-1730). According to the *Podgorica Chronicle*, **Husein Pasha Kucuk Haveric** commanded a part of the army in the Ottoman campaign in 1710. They crossed the Danube River and headed for the northern shores of the Black Sea. The Tatars were also involved in the war. During the engagement, the Ottoman forces surrounded and cut off the large Russian army. However, on that battlefield, battles took place almost continuously. In a battle near Odessa, **Husein Pasha Kucuk** was killed along with seven more Haverics who also died in those battles.[165]

After **Husein (Kucuk) Pasha Haveric**, in Istanbul, came a *pasha* named **Zejnil bey** Haveric in the imperial court holding the rank of Marshal, whom the Sultan allowed to go to Podgorica, his birthplace, every year.[166] He was a son of **Alija bey**, a *zabit* of Podgorica and grandson of **Husein Pasha** Kucuk. In the 18th century, **Zeinil Pasha** served as a military official in Istanbul, where he was promoted to the rank of *pasha*, becoming an influential Porta military leader. He was the 'sultan's high military adviser in Constantinople'.[167] It was said, during his service at the Porte, **Zejnil Pasha** once 'travelled to Egypt for medical treatment'. When the war of the Ottomans against the Russians was over, the Ottoman Empire as part of its territorial expansion reached Persia. **'Zeinil Pasha** died in the battle of the Ottomans near the city of Bukhara in Persia'.[168]

Zejnil Pasha had a daughter who, according to folk tradition, was married to the famous hero from the town of Spuz, Zotovic bey (d. 1772). He also had two sons, **Adnan** and **Husein Karadag**, who were *pashas*. While there is some information about Husein Pasha, only tradition has passed down through the generations that

Adnan Pasha had a son who was born, lived and died in Anadolia. However, there is no specific information about **Adnan Pasha** and his son, but it is assumed they settled in other areas of the empire or died somewhere on the battlefields fighting in the multinational army of the Ottomans.

The second son of Zejnil Pasha, **Husein Pasha Karadag**, was the fifth *pasha* from the Haveric family. In Turkish military chronicles, he was famous as a military leader. He was regarded 'among the twenty best generals of the Turkish empire of his time'. 'Among the Turkish military elite, he was known as **Hussein Pasha Karadag**'.[169] Husein Pasha Karadag had larger land holdings in Zeta, especially in Golubovci, Mahala, Berislavci and Goricani, where the old Haveric's *waqfs* were established. Most of the land was inherited by his eldest son. About Husein Pasha Karadag, **Ismail Halil bey Haveric** wrote his remark:

> **Husein Pasha Karadag** is our (my) direct ancestor. He had four sons: **Jakub bey**, **Jusuf bey** is my great-grandfather, **Muslija** and **Alija**. Since then, there are records of the male heirs of Haveric in these areas: Montenegro, Bosnia and Herzegovina (Sarajevo, Trebinje and Prijedor) and Albania (Tirana, Shkoder, Durres, Valon), where they fled from Podgorica to save their lives. **Husein pasha Karadag** is the father of our great-grandfather, **Jusuf bey**.[170]

Historical records also showed **Izmail Pasha Haveric**. At the end of 1852, Omer Pasha Latas launched an attack on Montenegro in three places. He tried to separate Brdo from Montenegro. While Osman Pasha was operating in the region of Moraca, the army under the command of Omer Pasha Latas crossed the Zeta River and headed for the Ljesavan region. Dervish Pasha attacked Grahovo and **Izmail Pasha** advanced towards Ostrog Monastery in Montenegro.[171] **Izmail Pasha Haveric** and his brother **Dulo Haveric** were mentioned in a letter, dated August 27, 1887, from Mita Bakic, a diplomat from the Montenegrin Embassy in Constantinople to the Secretary of the Ministry of Foreign Affairs, Mitro Plamenac, Emirgan (Emirgijan):

> Dear Mitar,
>
> **Izmail (or Ismail) Pasha Haveric** from Podgorica understood that His Highness was pleased to appoint his brother **Dulo bey Haveric** (later a member of the Municipality of Danilovgrad) as an *adjutant* (a military officer who acts as an administrative assistant to a senior officer) for one of his sons. Because of this, **Izmail Pasha** wrote me a letter, asking me to submit to His Highness his most humble gratitude for that proof of trust and favour, which he showed towards a member of his family. Hec said, please, submit this gratitude to His Highness, either through Duke (Vojvoda) Radonjic, or personally – in the way which you see that is the better.[172]

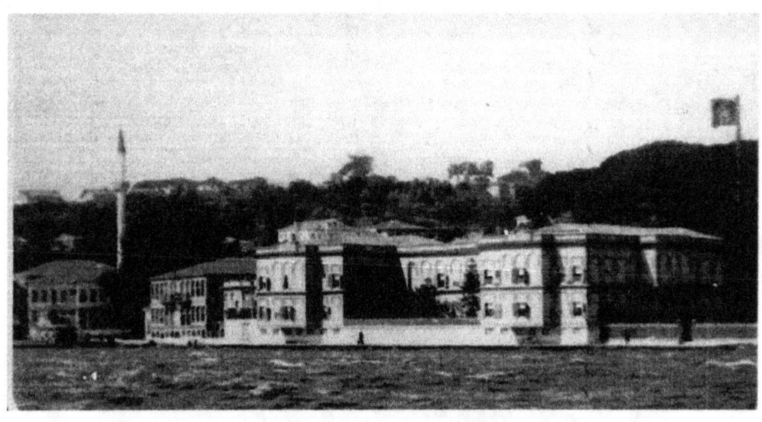

Castle Emirgijan, Istanbul

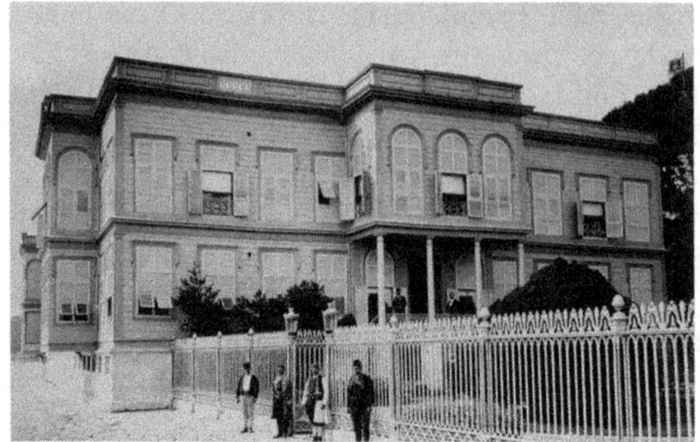

Castle Emirgijan, Istanbul[173]

Edward Tanbay Haveric (Erdogan Veysi Tanbay) recalled:

> During the last years of the Ottoman Empire, my grandfather **Mehmet bey Haveric** was the Chief Commandant of the Ottoman's ruling not only of Montenegro but also part of Dalmatia (Croatia). He held a senior rank, ***Binbası*** (Major).

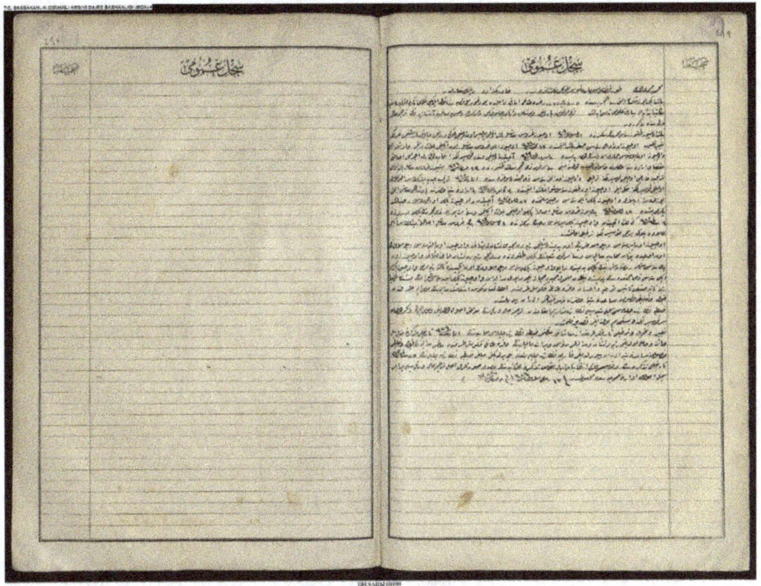

A letter honouring Mahmud Hamdi-effendi Haveric by the sultan's decree with medals

MAHMUT HAMDİ EFENDİ (1286/1870)

Tuz Kazası Rusumat Memur-ı sabıkı Mehmet Bey'i' mahdumudur. Haver Beyzade denmekle müteariftir.
Bin iki yüz seksen altı sene-i Hicriyesi'n'e, sene-i Maliye 1285 (1870) Karadağ Emareti dahilinde Podgoriçe Kasabası'n'a tevellüt eylediği Nüfus Tezkire-i Osmaniyesi'n'e mukayyettir.
Mekatib-i ibtidaiyede mebadi-i ulûmu tederrüs ederek Türkçe okuyup yazdığı ve Boşnak ve Arnavutça söylediği ve Fransızca ve Sırp lisanlarına âşina idiği tercüme-i hâl varakasında mezkurdur.

Bin üç yüz dokuz senesi Muharreminin sekizinde 1 Ağustos sene 1307 (14 Ağustos 1891) üç yüz kuruş mauallieyoğlu Polis on üçüncü bölük dördüncü çavuşluğunun beşinci neferliğine tayin kılınıp üç yüz on üç senesi Saferinin altısında 17 Temmuz sene 1311 (30 Ağustos 1892) üç yüz elli kuruş mauallin İkinci bölük birinci çavuşluğuna terfi ve üç yüz on beş senesi Cemaziyelevvelinin on yedisinde 2 Teşrinievvel sene 1313 (14 Ekim 1897) açıktan üçüncü sınıf komiserliğine intihap olunarak icra-yı asaleti mukteza-yı irade-i seniyye-i hazret-i hilafet-penahiden olmasına mebni sene-i merkume Zilhiccesinin dokuzunda 19 Nisan sene 1316 (1 Mayıs 1898) beş yüz kuruş mauallieyoğlu Tertip Harici Üçüncü Komiserliği'n' terfi ve üç yüz on altı senesi Zilkadesi gurresinde 1 Mart sene 1315 (13 Mart 1899) tertib-i cedid Beşiktaş Altı Numara Üçüncü Komiserliği'n' nakil ile üç yüz on dokuz senesi Şevvalinin›n'n altısında 3 Kânunusani sene 1317 (16 Ocak 1902) bâ-irade-i seniyye-i hazret-i padişahi maaşı altı yüz kuruşa iblağ ve üç yüz yirmi iki senesi Recebi selhinde 27 Eylül sene 1320 (10 Ekim 1904) açıktan ve üç yüz yirmi üç senesi Recebinin yirmi beşinde 12 Eylül sene 1321 (25 Eylül 1905) yedi yüz kuruş mauallisaleten yirmi üçüncü bölük İkinci ve sene-i mezbure Zilhiccesinin yirmi dördünde 6 Şubat sene 1321 (19 Şubat 1906) kezalik açıktan ve üç yüz yirmi beş senesi Recebinin sekizinde 4 Ağustos sene 1323 (17 Ağustos 1907) bin kuruş mauallisaleten Beşiktaş İkinci İlâve Bölüğü Birinci Komiserliği'n' terfi olunmuştur.

Üç yüz on beş senesi Rebiülahirinin on yedisinde (15 Eylül 1897) beşinci rütbedine Mecidî Nişan-ı zîşanı ve üç yüz on altı senesi Rebiülevvelinin on üçünde (1 Ağustos 1898) Yunan Muharebe Madalyası ve sene-i merkume Şabanının yirmi dokuzunda (12 Ocak 1899) dördüncü

rütbeden Nişan-ı âli-i Osmanî ve üç yüz on yedi senesi şehr-i Ramazan-ı şerifinin yirmi yedisinde (29 Ocak 1900) rabi ve üç yüz yirmi senesi Rebiülevvelinin on ikisinde (19 Haziran 1902) salise rütbeleri ve üç yüz yirmi iki senesi Zilkadesinin yedisinde (13 Ocak 1905) Nikel'd'n mamul Hamidiye Hicaz Demiryolu Madalyası ve üç yüz yirmi beş senesi Şevvalinin beşinde (11 Kasım 1907) terfian rütbe-i saniye sınıf-ı sanisi tevcih ve ihsan ve Karadağ hükumeti tarafındah ita kılınan Gümüş İstikamet Madalyası'n'n mumailiyh tarafından kaualle ta'lîki hususuna müsaade-i seniyye-i hazret-i hilafet-penahi erzan buyurulmuştur.
Zabtiye Nezaret-i Celilesi Sicil Şubesi›y'e Nezaret-i müşarünileyha makamından tercüme-i hâl varakasının muvafık-ı usul olduğu ve mumaileyhin zikr olunan serkomiserliğinde müstahdem bulunduğu tasdik kılınmıştır.
Tayin ve tahvil ve terfii tarihleriyle miktar-ı maaşatını mutazammın Zabtiye Nezaret-i Celilesi Muhasebesi'n'n 1 Mart sene 1324 (14 Mart 1908) tarihli müzekkere-i müzeyyelesiyle haiz ve hamil olduğu rütbe ve nişan ve madalyalar ruus ve berat-ı âlilerinin ve Karadağ Hükümeti tarafından muta madalyanın kaualle ta'liki hususuna müsaade-i seniyye erzan buyurulduğu Hariciye Nezaret-i Celilesi'n'en bildirildiğini mübelliğ Zabtiye Nezaret-i Celilesi'n'n 25 Şubat sene 1315 tarihli tezkiresinin ve komiserlik intihabnameleriyle Nüfus Tezkire-i Osmaniyesi'n'n musaddak suretleri asıl tercüme-i hâl varakasıyla beraber Sicill-i Ahval İdare-i Umumiyesi'n'e mahfuzdur.
Fi 17 Rebiülevvel sene 1324 fi 5 Nisan sene 1322 (10 Mart 1909)

MAHMUT HAMDİ EFENDİ (1286/1870)

Mahmud Hamdi Effendi, by the Ottoman sultan's decree, was issued the *Honourable Order of Medjidie of the fifth degree and nickel medal of the Hijaz Railway of Hamidi* by the sultan and a *Silver Medal for Meritorious Service* by the Government of Montenegro. A letter honouring letter details:

> **Mahmud Hamdi Effendi** is the son of a former customs officer of the *kaza* (an administrative region) of Tuzi **Mehmet bey**. He is known as **Haveric**. In the birth certificate of the Ottoman State, it is written that he was born in the year 1286 Hijri, i.e. 1285 financial year, in Podgorica *kasaba* (a small town), part of the Principality of Montenegro. The biography states that he attended elementary (religious) studies, that he is literate in 'Turkish, speaks Bosnian and Albanian, and is fluent in Albanian and Serbian'. On the eighth of Muharram one thousand three hundred and nine, i.e. On August 1, 1307, with a salary of three hundred groschi, he was appointed as the fifth soldier assigned to the fourth unit of the thirteenth company of the Beyoğlu police.
>
> On July 17, 1311, in the sixth safera (thousand), three hundred and thirteen, he was promoted to the position of first *chaush* [equivalent of 'sergeant'] of the twelfth company with a salary of three hundred and fifty *groschi*. In addition, on the seventeenth of *Jamazija'l'evvel* (one thousand three hundred and fifteen), i.e. On the 2nd of *Tešrini-Evvela* in 1313, he was elected to the position of commissar of the third class, which he would perform remotely. However, due to the necessity to perform (the service) personally in accordance with the *irade-i senia* [imperial decree] issued by Hazrat Padishah,

the protector of the caliphate, the said person is on the ninth of *Zi'l'Hijja* of the mentioned year, i.e. On April 19, 1316, he was promoted to a position in the Third Commissariat for Foreign Ordinances in Beyoglu with a salary of 50 grosz. On the first zi'l'ka'd' (one thousand three hundred and sixteen), on March 1, 1315, he was transferred to the Third Commissariat under number six, in Beşiktaş, where, on the basis of the *irade-i senija* issued by hz. of Padishahasht ševval (one thousand) three hundred and nineteen, that is, on the 3rd of Kanunisani 1317, the salary was increased to the sixth *groschi*. On the last day of the month of Rajab (one thousand) three hundred and twenty-two, i.e. On September 22, 1320, he was appointed to the position of second commissar of the twenty-third company, which he will carry out at a distance, and on the twenty-fifth *regjeb* (thousand) three hundred and twenty-third, i.e. September 12, 1321, in person.

On the twenty-fourth of *Zi'l'Hijja* of the mentioned year, that is, on February 6, 1321, he also performed his duties remotely. On August 4, 1323, he was promoted to the position of first commissar of the supplementary company in Beşiktaş, with a salary of one thousand grosz, which he would perform personally. They were assigned to him on the seventeenth *Rabi'u'-ahira* (one thousand) in the three hundred and fifteenth year of the *Honorable Oreden Medjidija of the fifth degree*, in the thirteenth of Rabi'u'-Evvel (one thousand) of the sixteenth year, the medal for the **Greek-Turkish war**, on the twenty-ninth of Shaban of the said year the exalted *Order of Osmania of the Fourth Degree,* then on the twenty-seventh of the honorable of the month of Ramadan (one thousand) three hundred seventeen and fourteenth and on the twelfth of *Rabi'u'-Ewvel* (one thousand) of the three hundred and twentieth year the third rank, on the seventh of *Zi'l'Ka'd'* (one thousand) three hundred and twenty-first nickel *medal of the Hijaz Railway of Hamidi,* and on the fifth of *Shawwal* (one thousand) in the year three hundred and twenty-five, he was promoted to the second rank of the second class.

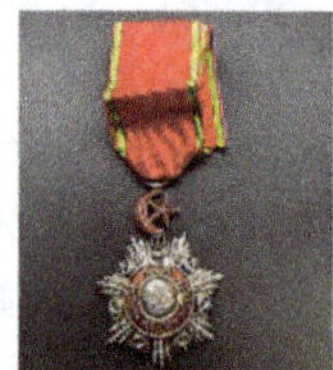

Honourable Order of Medjidie of the fifth degree

Order of Medjidie of the fifth degree was a military and civilian order of the Ottoman Empire. The Order was often conferred on non-Turkish nationals. The Order was issued in considerable numbers by Sultan Abdulmecid as a reward for distinguished service to members of the British Army, Royal Navy and French Army who came to the aid of the Ottoman Empire during the Crimean War against Russia and to British recipients for later service in Egypt and/or the Sudan.[174]

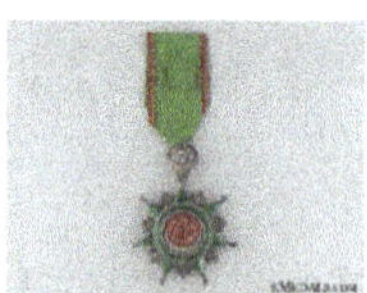

Order of Osmania of the Fourth Degree, Silver/Enamelled

The Order of Osmania became the second highest order in the Empire. This Order was awarded to foreign and national personnel, within civil and military realms, for extraordinary services for the sultan.[175]

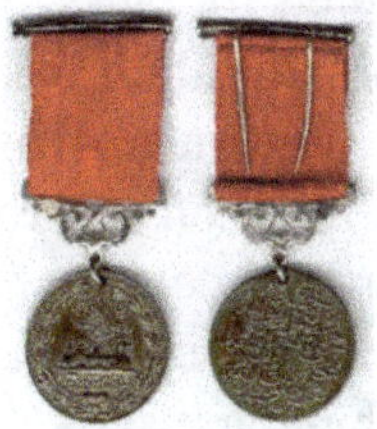

Medal of the Hijaz Railway

This medal, which was awarded **Mahmud Hamdi Effendi**, was endowed to those who donated funds to the Hejaz Railway. The railway was intended to facilitate Hajj. Its main branch connected the Ottoman railway networks in Istanbul and ran from Damascus to the holy city of Medina through Hejaz (Saudi Arabia) with an additional branch line added to the port of Haifa. Being an important part of Sultan Abdulhamid II's policy, the railway attracted donations from Muslims all over the world after calls for help with finance and it was decided to reward donors. 'The medal was a visible symbol of their piety' and was made and dated to his silver jubilee year in 1900.[176]

Mahmud Hamdi Effendi also received a *Silver Medal for Meritorious Service* awarded by the Government of Montenegro, and by the Hon. the Caliph (Padishah) was given permission to hang it around his neck. It has been confirmed from the home branch of the famous Ministry of Gendarmerie and the ministry mentioned above that his biography is acceptable and he was employed in the mentioned main commissariat. In the Office for the Register of the Status of Civil Servants, an official act has been preserved with the attached document from the Accounting of the famous Ministry of Gendarmerie dated March 1, 1324. This contains the dates of appointment, transfer and promotion, as well as salary amounts, then a certified copy of the certificate issued by the famous Ministry of Gendarmerie on February 25, 1315. The certificate states he has official letters and high berets for ranks, orders and medals, that the illustrious Ministry of Foreign Affairs has stated the medal awarded by the Government of Montenegro has been accepted and the Padishah has obtained permission to wear it around his neck. The original also includes certified copies of the certificate of election to the post of commissioner, certified copy of the birth certificate of the Ottoman State and a biography.[177]

Besides *pashas* in this period, the role of *zabits* was also significant. For instance, **Osman bey** Haveric served two *pashas*, Mahmud and Mustafa. From the end of the 18th and early 19th century, **Osman bey** Haveric is mentioned as a *katib* (scriber, secretary) in the service of the vizier of Shkoder, Mahmud Pasha Busatlija (1779-1796). **Osman bey Haveric** is also said to have been appointed *zabit* in Shkoder for a time. In 1827, the Montenegrin Bishop Peter I wrote to Mustafa Pasha, telling him that he had heard that **Osman bey Haveric** had forwarded him an accusatory letter. This letter said Peter I had allegedly sent to the Christians in Ljeskopolje wanting 'to cause confusion and slaughter the Turks of all three cities (Zabljak, Spuz and Podgorica) and the Christians from Zeta and surrounding places will attack those cities'. Apparently Peter I justified this by saying, 'My intention is opposite and difficult for me, because I don't want to fight with anyone'.[178]

Zabits **Alija agha**, **Mehmed bey** and **Edhem bey** Haveric were the commanders of Podgorica. They were influential figures and **Edhem bey** was said to have been an excellent 'diplomat' in resolving local disputes. He was considered by the locals to be 'among the most educated citizens of Podgorica'. He contributed to the peacemaking, bridgebuilding and even fraternising among confronted families, groups or communities.[179] At the beginning of the 19th century, the Montenegrin government tried to maintain peace between neighbours. In this sense, Bishop Petar I Petrovic addressed 'the leading men, Mustafa-Pasha and **Dervis bey Haveric'**. The letter followed international visits, negotiations and diplomatic correspondence involving major powers such as Russia, Moldova, England and France. The authorities from Albania were also involved. Branko Pavičević recorded the address of Bishop Peter I in 1813:

> After the meeting on the Crnojevic River, the bishop sent a message to Mustafa Pasha, expressing his wish that the situation on the border calm down as soon as possible and that 'we live in friendship and neighbourhood'. In the bishop's message, it was also emphasized that a similar agreement was reached with the captain of the city of Bar at a meeting held in the town of Sutomore. At the same time, the bishop announced the order to the Montenegrins to live in peace with the Turks and that anyone who would try to 'perpetrate any evil or trouble against the Ottoman subjects would be severely punished'. The bishop once again informed Mustafa Pasha about his desire to restore order on the border as soon as possible, and then sent a similar message to **Dervis bey Haveric**.

The next year, Vizier Mustafa Pasha Busatlija (1797-1860) broke away from the sultan and went with Bosnian captain Gradascevic (-1834) to Kosovo. That fight lasted for 7 months. Being between two fires, Podgorica cancelled its loyalty to Gradascevic and Busatli to be free. During the rebellion of the Bushatlis from Shkoder against the central Turkish authorities in 1828, the Podgorica Muslims immediately convened a National Assembly on Glavica, a locality on an elevation south of the Tabacki bridge, and 'declared a certain republic'. They elected a 12-member government. President Jusuf-aga Alivodic (Alivojvoica) was at the head of the government and the 12 Muslim *aldermen* were from the **Haveric**, Osmanagic, Decevic, Adzialijagic and Prasakovic families. There was also Lisicic, one of the Christian representatives. These 12 Podgorica representatives, with the president at their head, sat every day holding sessions in Glavatovic Mosque – 'they ruled a large area of Zeta, judged, reconciled blood feuds and maintained public order'.

At the beginning of the 19th century, **Tahir bey Haveric** came to the position of a Podgorica *zabit.*[180] From 1814 to 1832, **Tahir bey Haveric** was an important feature, as can be seen in the correspondence from the beginning of the Russo-Turkish war (1828-9). In 1829, Bishop Petar I Petrovic, in the capacity of a Montenegrin bishop and Russian knight, addressed the 'Podgorica commander, governor **Tahir bey Haveric**' in a letter:

> Learning about the arrival of few armies with the *bayraks* (banners with crescent and star) from Shkoder to your cities nearby our border in the time when there is no war among us, I was surprised what was going on and I sent my confident man, abbot Mojsej, with letters to them into the Highlands to take care avoiding any further clash with your side, and everybody to stay in peace. Approaching the Russo-Turkish war, the Petar I Petrovic firstly begged **Tahir bey Haveric,** commander of Podgorica, for cooperation, referring to 'common Slavic … folks although from the two confessions'. In his friendly letter, to a friend **Tahir bey Haveric**, said to write in and for peace… 'It is better for both of us to cooperate for good sake, not for bad… My best wishes for your health!

In his address, the bishop also expressed his desire for good neighbourliness and respect. In this sense, a historian, Branko Pavicevic, noted influential messages to **Tahir bey Haveric** and other Bosniak-Muslims. For **Tahir bey Haveric** and 'his gentlemen from Podgorica … it would be best for us and for you to work on how to live in a more beautiful and peaceful neighbourhood'. By his letter, the bishop was aware of the importance of his relations with the inhabitants of the Turkish territories. He left the impression of a true neighbour, 'whose word is hard, and inter-neighbourly cooperation and solidarity in times of trouble are great'.[181]

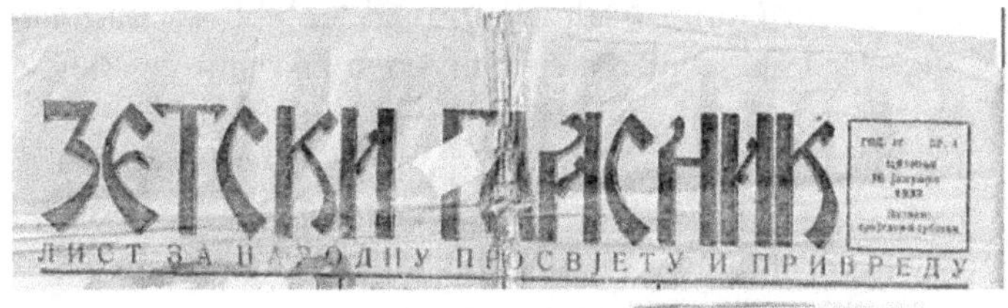

ЗЕТСКИ ГЛАСНИК

ЛИСТ ЗА НАРОДНУ ПРОСВЈЕТУ И ПРИВРЕДУ

Zetski glasnik, 16. januara 1932, s. 2
Crnogorski državni arhiv br. 99/1828

An article in a newspaper *Zetski Glas*, 1932

The newspaper *Zetski Glasnik* published an article in 1932 outlining the time of war between Russia and Turkiye plus the letter Petar I Petrovic sent to Tahir bey Haveric.

In 1829, Peter Petrovic I, the Bishop of Montenegro and Cavalier of Russia, sent a letter with friendly greetings and concerns to the honourable Mustafa Pasha, the Vizier of Shkoder and all Arbania (Albania):

> I understand that **Tahir Bey Haveric** and some other Turks from Podgorica, Spuz and Zabljak want to take my ponds near Gornje Malo Blato [and Golubovci] on the Shkoder Lake, which are on my land and in my valley, left from antiquity, of which I have ancient books. The land includes all the borders around. I wonder how they can take a pond in my water and in my land, which was left to me from Ivan bey Crnojevic's books, including 'one from your grandfather Sulejman Pasha'. For that reason, I am asking you, as the great emperor and the true judge, to tell **Tahir bey** and his followers to get over that business, or to send your two boys, who can read Turkish and speak our language, to look at the ponds and the borders and check mine and Tahir bey's books. I don't ask for anything from others and I don't want fights. **Tahir bey**'s followers threaten to attack my people on my ponds, although I pay tax, like on all my lands to the Montenegrin *kuluk* (feudal tax given to Ottomans in the form of personal labour or servanthood) of Sinaj, tax from everything for his tribute. I love peace and friendship in the neighbourhood with everyone. For that reason, I am asking you again, to answer me about this matter so that I know if the said Turks will get away with such an attack, or if you will not send your men, so that the court can see how it will be right without any

regrets or quarrels. Wishing you good health and long life.[182]

Branko Pavicevic interprets that the disputes between the Montenegrins and inhabitants of the Shkoder's Pashalik as mentioned were being exhausted, related to the resolution of property-legal disputes, which also connected to disagreements over vessels on the lake, the establishment of property rights on some lots along the boundary line or around lake pond ownership. However, adhering to the practice of not disrupting border traffic in times of peace, Mustafa Pasha harshly reprimanded the bishop for restricting the export of certain items to Albanian markets, recalling his order by which all Montenegrin merchants were given the freedom to purchase all goods at the Shkoder and other Pashalik markets. The bishop, in fact, had in mind the possibility that the Turkish authorities in Shkoder and Podgorica, using the freedom of commercial traffic, would start winning over the leaders of the bordering tribes.

—

Владика се држао схватања да у односима с житељима турских територија остави утисак тачног сусједа, чија је ријеч тврда, а комшијска сарадња и солидарност на муци велика. На такав начин поступао је и у току руско-турског рата, поручујући Тахир-бегу Аверићу и "свој господи од Подгорице": да би "за нас и за вас најбоље било да радимо како ћемо љепше и мирније на комшилуку живјети".

Milan Jovicevic in *Barjaktars and the banner act in Montenegro* (*Barjaktari i barjaktarstvo u Crnoj Gori*) wrote that spontaneous and serious military actions sometimes took place, despite the bishop's will and without his consent. So, Peter I, fearing the consequences of openly supporting the rebellion in Leskopolje, tried to prevent it. However, a considerable number of Montenegrins were already actively involved in the Leskopolje riots. The bishop tried to excuse himself from it. 'To the accusations of **Tahir bey** Haveric of

Podgorica and Mehmed captain of Spuz, the bishop justified that it was all against his will…'.[183]

When there was an attack in Podgorica by the Turks against the Orthodox Christians, **Hasan bey Haveric** in Zeta acted nobly. Ilija Pelicic writes: "When Jusa Mucin was killed in 1874, two *krk-serdars* (commanders in the Ottoman military unit), Beco Dekovic and Asan Begovic, came to Berislavci, where the Haverica family lived, with 200 men to kill the Serbs there. After seeing their intention, **Hasan bey** Haveric said in defence: 'there are no Serbs here'. At the same time, he gave the sign to the Serbs 'to escape from the village across [Malo] Blato in Montenegro'.[184] For his good deed, **Hasan bey** Haveric is well remembered in Zeta for saving the life of Orthodox Christians. When he married, he invited many people from Podgorica and Zeta. The entire village from Berislavac, where he lived, attended the ceremony. Everyone brought him bread and pastry as a sign of respect. Monk Stevan was his bride's brother-in-law too. Later the King Nikola wanted to appoint **Hasan bey** Haveric as the commander of the Muslims in Zeta, especially because he saved people of the town of Zecane from the massacre in 1874, but he chose to move to Turkish part of the Ottoman Empire.[185]

Ali bey Haveric, from the city of Prijedor, was mentioned in 'Fragments from the History of the Bosnian Uprising of 1875 and 1876'. In historical records, this is among the first mentions of Haveric in Bosnia and Herzegovina. It was during an uprising led by the Serbs against the Ottoman Empire, first in Herzegovina, from where it spread into Bosnia and Raska (Serbia). The war broke out in the summer of 1875 and lasted in some regions up to the beginning of 1878. It happened at a similar time as the Bulgarian uprising of 1876 and coincided with the Serbian-Turkish wars (1876-1878).[186]

Until 1878, Podgorica was under Ottoman rule, established as a Turkish town. When the great powers at the Berlin Congress in 1878 redrew the map of the Balkans, Podgorica was liberated the following year. The Turkish government left it and the Montenegrin government entered the city. Subsequently, general revival in the state and society began.[187] A significant part of the Muslim population served in the Montenegrin army. They also held high officer positions; there was one duke, several commanders and several holders of military ranks. There were also royal orderlies at the court in Cetinje. Even during the time of Prince Danilo, their participation in the Montenegrin army was regulated, with special coats of arms on their caps.[188]

Together with the Senate and Guard at the Assembly of Heads in October 1831, the *perjanici*, the bodyguard and royal flag bearers, were formed. They got their name from specific caps with feathers. The *perjanici* were bodyguards and an elite police squad with permanent headquarters in Cetinje. In addition to the function of guarding the Montenegrin ruler, the *perjanici* also took care of the security of the Senate and, independently or together with the Guard, the perpetrators of crimes were caught and punished.[189]

From time of the Prince Danilo (-1860), members of the Muslim faith were also hired *perjanici*.[190] *Perjanici* were hired for protection and as personal escorts, but also for ceremonial purposes to show their beauty and reputation in front of representatives of other countries.[191] For the elite guard of King Nikola, the Muslims were also engaged as members of the *perjanici*.[192] Several Haverics were *perjanici*, the officers of honorary units of the Montenegrin prince and king. It was because the highest leaders from the ranks of the *perjanici* were young men chosen mainly from those families that had some influence on the historical scene.[193]

In 1897, Prince Nikola decided to designate a detachment of 80 soldiers to be sent to Crete on a peacekeeping mission. With that decision, the prince confirmed his 'commitment to peace and the protection of people without distinction'. The detachment spent two years and 10 days in Crete. '**Zejnel bey** Haveric, a high military official [pasha] at the sultan's court, escorted the soldiers from Bar to this honourable task and warmly greeted them. Upon their return, the prince awarded the detachment with the *Order of military commitment*'.[194]

In 1911, **Aqif Ahmet bey Haveric** took part in the **Battle of Deçiq** ('Decic War'). He was born in 1854. He was for a long time a customs officer in Tuzi, then he held a civil office. He married three times: first with Aisha Mehacevic, second with the daughter of Ibrahim bey Osmanagic, and last with Man Dude's daughter. His son, **Yusuf**, was born in 1896. His other sons were **Ahmed**, **Omer**, **Halid** and **Teufik**. With his son **Yusuf bey**, **Aqif bey** went to war serving in the Ottoman Empire. '[The father and son] were brave, wore uniforms, carried armed … pistols and rifles…' They both fought with the Turks against the Montenegrins. 'They were known [for] this in Podgorica as well'. After the Balkan War, in 1913, **Aqif bey** went to Turkiye and was appointed as a clerk in the Turkish consulate in Trabazon, a city on the Black Sea.[195] There are some indications that **Aqif bey** left Albania after being appointed as a secretary of King Faruk I in Cairo.[196] It is also known that the king had staff, including 30 bodyguards, originally from Albania.

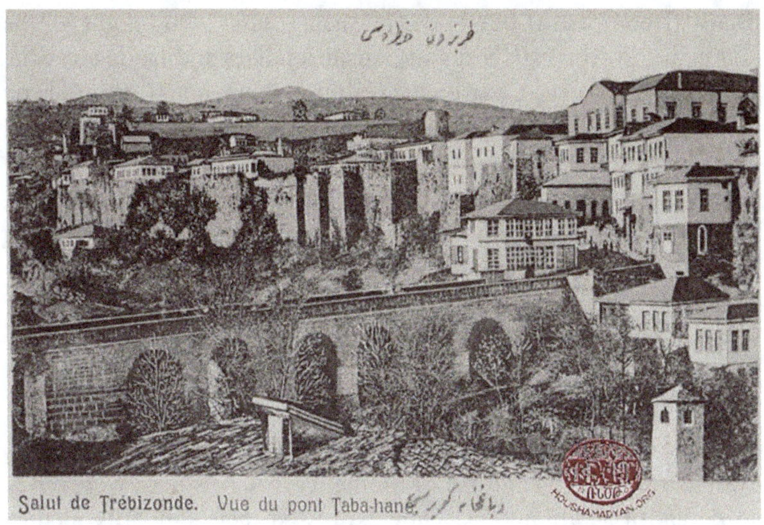

The city of Trabazon, on the Black Sea coast of northeast Turkiye

In 1914, wealthy beys and Muslim leaders, who wanted to preserve their property and influence under the new government, unfortunately did not reflect the mood of the Muslim population in the newly acquired areas. This is how a smaller group of Muslims wrote to King Nikola on January 14, 1914:

> Fortunately, this is the second new year since your powerful protection and freedom have been watching over your faithful and loyal Muslims here, whom you have always honoured with your high favour. So, we would like to, on this occasion, along with the New Year greetings, offer your majesty deep gratitude for the unfettered to our just protection, praying to God for your precious health, that you may live many more to the happy and proud of our exalted Home, our dear Montenegro and all of Serbia. In front of the Muslims: **Becir agha Haveric**, Mufti Delevic, Hilmi bey Kajabegovic.[197]

Beqir (Becir) Jusuf bey Haveric was a soldier who fought for the Ottomans in April 1915 against Anzac soldiers and landed at what is now called Anzac Cove on the Gallipoli Peninsula (Çanakkale on the Dardanelle Straits). For the battle, it was said 'the sea was filled with black hats, so fierce was the fight'. In the battle, **Beqir bey** received several wounds. **Tahir Pasha**, who had supported him, died, so **Beqir bey**, who had no money left in his pocket, came to Shkoder and **Ismail bey**. In the meantime, his relatives **Ethem bey** and **Zejnel bey** passed away. Then, **Beqir** returned to Istanbul for several years where he passed away in his 30s.[198]

During the annexation of Bosnia and Herzegovina by the Austro-Hungarian monarchy, the Montenegrin Bosniaks and Albanians, as well as a significant number of Montenegrin Christians, were ready to defend it as volunteers. They expressed their solidarity against the Austro-Hungarian occupation of the Bosnia and Herzegovina population. At that time, a special delegation of Bosniaks from Podgorica visited King Nikola and expressed their readiness to be actively involved in the defence of Bosnia and to prevent the expansion of the Austro-Hungarian monarchy.[199]

In January 1916, after the defeat of Serbia, Montenegro was occupied by the Austro-Hungary monarchy. The Austro-Hungarian occupation of Montenegro was during the First World War. The occupation lasted from the beginning of 1916 until autumn 1918. During that period, the Austro-Hungarian occupation government in Montenegro was organised as the Military General Administration in Montenegro (German: *Militar-Generalgouvernement in Montenegro*). During the First World War, **Osman Haveric** was recruited as an imam of the 7th division in Podgorica.[200]

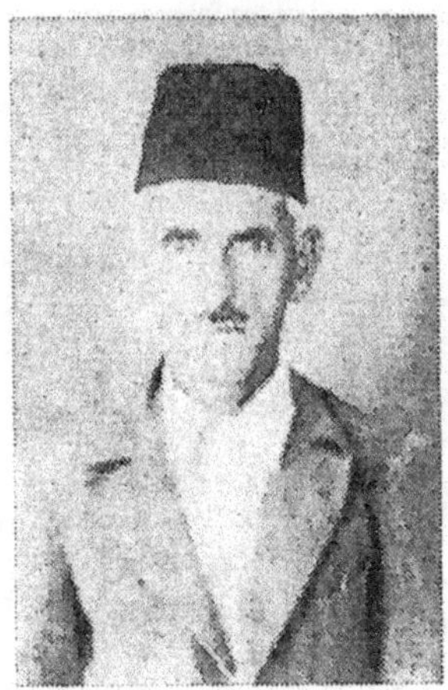

Imam Osman Haveric

In 1908, Prince Nikola ordered the formation of a battalion of Muslims and assigned the *elders* (leaders) to those conscripted and their duties. The Muslims in Podgorica were resolute in their intention to join the ranks of the Montenegrin army. More than 500 soldiers attended the meeting of the Podgorica Muslim battalion in 1908. The dilemmas surrounding the commander and standard-bearer in the Podgorica Muslim battalion were resolved. An elder for the Donja Varos area in Podgorica selected to be the officer in charge was **Smail Jusuf bey Haveric.**[201]

The framework of Montenegrin efforts against the Austro-Hungarian occupation carried out armed actions against the Austro-Hungarian gendarmerie members.[202] **Ismail bey Haveric** fought the Austro-Hungary army for Bosnia holding a rank of captain. He was an adjutant of King Nikola.[203] According to archival information, **Smail Haveric** lost his life in 1916 fighting in the Austro-Hungarian army.[204]

Anhang.

Ergänzungen zu den Verlustlisten Nr. 396–400.

Offiziere.

Mannschaft.

Berichtigungen zu den Verlustlisten Nr. 396–400.

Offiziere.

Mannschaft.

Ergänzungen und Berichtigungen zu den Verlustlisten Nr. 396–400.

Offiziere.

Mannschaft.

Smail Haveric in the loss list of 1916 against the Austro-Hungarian army Alphabetical list No. LXXIX of names listed in loss lists 396 to 400[205]

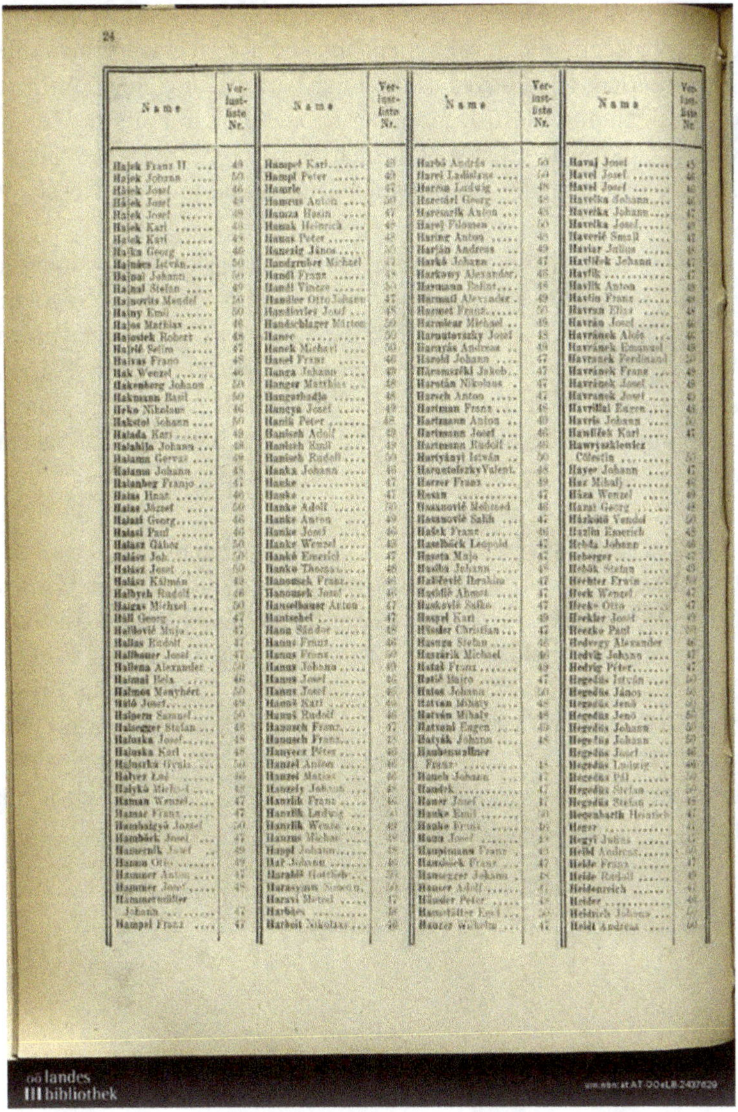

24

Name	Verlust-liste Nr.	Name	Verlust-liste Nr.	Name	Verlust-liste Nr.	Name	Verlust-liste Nr.
Hajek Franz II	48	Hampel Karl	49	Harbó András	50	Havaj Josef	48
Hajek Johann	50	Hampl Peter	49	Harci Ladislaus	50	Havel Josef	46
Hájek Josef	46	Hamrle	47	Harcsa Ludwig	48	Havel Josef	46
Hájek Josef	48	Hamrus Anton	50	Harcsárl Georg	48	Havelka Johann	46
Hajek Josef	48	Hamza Hasin	47	Harcsarik Anton	48	Havelka Johann	47
Hajek Karl	48	Hanak Heinrich	49	Harej Filomen	50	Havelka Josef	49
Hajek Karl	48	Hanas Peter	48	Haring Anton	48	Haverić Smail	47
Hajka Georg	46	Hanezig János	50	Harján Andreas	49	Haviar Julius	46
Hajnács István	50	Handgruber Michael	47	Harkó Johann	47	Havlíček Johann	47
Hajnal Johann	50	Handl Franz	48	Harkawy Alexander	48	Havlík	47
Hajnal Stefan	49	Handl Vincenz	50	Harmann Bálint	48	Havlík Anton	48
Hajnovits Mendel	50	Handler Otto Johann	47	Harmati Alexander	49	Havlin Franz	49
Hajny Emil	50	Handlerler Josef	48	Harmet Franz	50	Havran Elias	48
Hajos Mathias	48	Handschlager Márton	50	Harmlear Michael	46	Havrán Josef	46
Hajostek Robert	48	Hanec	50	Harnatovszky Josef	48	Havránek Alois	46
Hajrić Selim	47	Hanek Michael	50	Harayás Andreas	49	Havránek Emanuel	48
Haivas Franz	48	Hanel Franz	46	Harold Johann	47	Havranek Ferdinand	50
Hak Wenzel	46	Hanga Johann	49	Háromszéki Jakob	47	Havránek Franz	49
Hakenberg Johann	50	Hanger Matthias	48	Harstán Nikolaus	47	Havránek Josef	49
Hakmann Basil	50	Hangarhadja	48	Harsch Anton	47	Havranek Josef	49
Hako Nikolaus	46	Haneya Josef	49	Hartman Franz	48	Havrillai Eugen	48
Hakstol Johann	50	Hanik Peter	48	Hartmann Anton	49	Havris Johann	50
Halada Karl	49	Hanisch Adolf	49	Hartmann Josef	46	Hawlíček Karl	47
Halabila Johann	48	Hanisch Emil	48	Hartmann Rudolf	46	Hawryszkiewicz Cölestin	50
Halama Gervas	49	Hanisch Rudolf	50	Hartyányi István	50	Hayer Johann	47
Halama Johann	48	Hanka Johann	46	HaruntofszkyValent.	48	Haz Mihalj	49
Halanberg Franjo	47	Hanke	47	Harver Franz	49	Háza Wenzel	49
Halas Ignaz	46	Hanke	47	Hasan	47	Hazai Georg	48
Halas József	50	Hanke Adolf	50	Hasanović Mehmed	48	Házköši Vendel	50
Halasi Georg	46	Hanke Anton	49	Hasanović Salih	47	Hazlin Emerich	48
Halasi Paul	46	Hanke Josef	46	Hašek Franz	46	Hebda Johann	46
Halász Gábor	50	Hanke Wenzel	48	Haselböck Leopold	47	Heberger	47
Halász Joh.	50	Hankó Emerich	47	Haseta Mujo	47	Hebák Stefan	49
Halász Josef	50	Hanko Thomas	48	Haška Johann	48	Hechter Erwin	50
Halász Kálmán	49	Hanomak Franz	46	Hašimović Ibrahim	47	Heck Wenzel	47
Halbych Rudolf	48	Hanousek Josef	46	Hasičić Ahmet	47	Hecke Otto	47
Halgas Michael	50	Hanselbauer Anton	47	Hasković Safko	47	Heckler Josef	49
Hall Georg	47	Hantschel	47	Haspel Karl	49	Heczko Paul	50
Hallović Mujo	47	Hann Sándor	48	Hässler Christian	47	Hedvegy Alexander	46
Hallas Rudolf	47	Hanns Franz	46	Hasnga Stefan	46	Hedvig Johann	47
Hallbauer Josef	47	Hanus Franz	50	Hasrárik Michael	46	Hedvig Péter	47
Hallena Alexander	50	Hanus Johann	49	Hatal Franz	49	Hegedüs István	50
Halmai Bela	46	Hanus Josef	46	Hatić Haira	47	Hegedüs János	50
Halmos Menyhért	50	Hanus Josef	46	Hatos Johann	50	Hegedüs Jenő	50
Haló Josef	49	Hanuš Karl	46	Hatvan Mihály	48	Hegedüs Jenö	50
Halpern Samuel	50	Hanuš Rudolf	46	Hatván Mihaly	48	Hegedüs Johann	50
Halsegger Stefan	48	Hanusch Franz	47	Hatvani Eugen	49	Hegedüs Johann	50
Haluska Josef	48	Hanusch Franz	48	Hatyák Johann	48	Hegedüs Josef	48
Haluska Karl	48	Hanyecz Péter	46	Haubenwallner Franz	48	Hegedüs Ludwig	46
Halusrka Gyula	50	Hanzel Anton	46	Hauch Johann	47	Hegedüs Pál	50
Halyer Lai	46	Hanzel Mates	46	Haudek	47	Hegedüs Stefan	50
Halykó Michael	48	Hanzely Johann	48	Hauer Josef	47	Hegedüs Stefan	49
Haman Wenzel	47	Hanzlik Franz	46	Hauke Emil	50	Hegenbarth Heinrich	47
Hamar Franz	47	Hanzlik Ludwig	50	Hauke Franz	49	Heger	47
Hambalgyó József	50	Hanzlik Wenzel	49	Haun Josef	48	Hegyi Julius	47
Hambück Josef	47	Hanzus Michael	50	Hauptmann Franz	49	Heibl Andreas	50
Hamernik Josef	49	Happl Johann	48	Hausbeck Franz	47	Heide Franz	47
Hamm Otto	49	Har Johann	46	Hausegger Johann	48	Heide Rudolf	49
Hammer Anton	47	Harald Gottlieb	50	Hauser Adolf	47	Heidenreich	47
Hammer Josef	48	Harasymiw Simeon	50	Häusler Peter	48	Heider	48
Hammerwöllner Johann	47	Haravi Metod	47	Haustätter Emil	50	Heidrich Johann	50
Hampel Franz	47	Harbács	48	Hauzer Wilhelm	47	Heidt Andreas	50
		Harbeit Nikolaus	48				

Smail Haveric in the loss list of 1916 against the Austro-Hungarian army
Alphabetical list No. LXXIX of the names listed in loss lists 396 to 400[206]

The First World War and occupation of Montenegro interrupted the country's economic development and social movements, including in Podgorica. The horrors of the First World War claimed millions of victims plus destroyed material and cultural assets. In the whirlwind of war, great state formations disappeared – the Austro-Hungarian monarchy, the Ottoman Empire and Imperial Russia.[207]

At that time, the Montenegrin Muslims, Bosniaks, helped numerous refugees who fled to Montenegro from Bosnia and Herzegovina and Boka Kotorska. In all the Montenegrin towns where they lived, Muslims actively helped the refugees. For example, in 1915 in Danilovgrad, **Mahmut Haveric** and **Tahir Haveric** were among other officers and soldiers of the 'Muslim faith' who gave financial contributions to the *Red Cross Committee* to help refugees.[208]

Ali Riza (Tanbay) bey Haveric, born in 1880 in Shkoder, was sent to Istanbul to the Sultan's schools and then he studied at the *Harbiye* Military Academy. Then, he was sent to the famous military school in Germany. He held the rank of colonel (*Miralay*). During the First World War when Turkiye lost the war against the allies, the British army caught him in Egypt and imprisoned him in Malta for four years. At the end of war, he used to say, 'If you are going to be a prisoner, be a prisoner of the British…' His excellent English was learnt in Malta.[209] He lived in Turkiye.

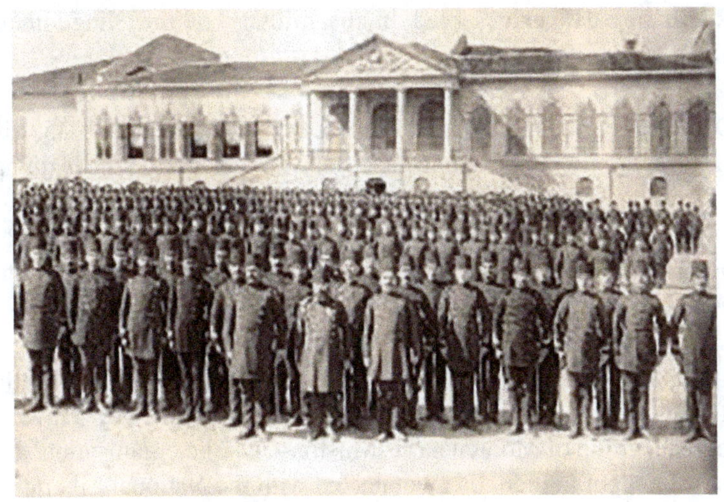

Turkish Military Academy (Mekteb-i Ulum-u Harbiye), Pangaltı, Istanbul.
(Turkish Military Academy Collection)

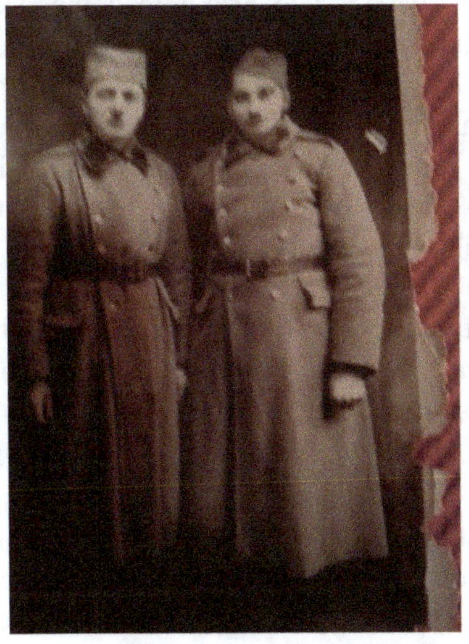

Rizo Haveric (right)

Rizah bey Haveric served in the military of the Kingdom of Yugoslavia.

During the Second World War, between 1941 and 1945, the Haveric family included anti-fascists, who took part in the National Liberation Front against the occupiers and dictatorship. Some of them were recognised as national heroes, such as **Dzavid Hamza bey Haveric**, **Aqif Mehmed bey Haveriku** and **Dr Hilmi Teufik bey Haveri**.

In 1942 and 1943 when Podgorica was under occupation by the Italians, Chetniks and Germans, **Omer Abdulah bey Haveric** joined a group of Montenegrin 'Muslim-Catholic organisation' and their freedom fighters then connected with the National Liberation Front. He knew the Muslims in Montenegro had neither their own state nor party since 1918. He was also aware that, in 1918, the Muslims of Podgorica were robbed to the 'bare skin' and it could be repeated in 1940s.[210] He also joined the Albanian freedom fighters.[211] In the Albanian provinces, which remained outside the borders of the Kingdom of Albania, a revival of demands for the use of the Albanian red and black flag was recorded. In 1942, this request by the representatives of Podgorica and its surroundings was addressed to the official Tirana. In the long letter, which besides Albanian signatures, it bore the names of the Bosniak representatives of Podgorica, including **Omer Abdulah bey**. It was mentioned that many people of Podgorica warmly invoked their support to Albanians.[212] After the war, **Omer Abdulah bey** was broken by the sufferings of war and illness. In 1942, he broke his hip and spent a long time recovering with a walking stick.[213]

In the mid-1950s, Dr Murat Backovic was present at the meeting when an official Turkish delegation visited Podgorica. The members of the delegation told him 'there is an ancestor of the Haveric family who has a rank of general in Turkish army'.[214]

The Kingdom of Montenegro

After the crumbling of the Ottoman power in the Balkans, the change of borders, the establishment of new governments of the Kingdom of Montenegro and the Yugoslavian Kingdom, followed by the Federative Republic of Yugoslavia, the social and cultural changes and influence of the new government took roles. The 20th century wars that continued in the Balkans, the First World War, and later in the Second World War, created great turbulence and changes in the Balkan countries. Since the withdrawal of the Ottomans from those areas, Muslims loyal to the new government resisted the previous Turkish rule, while others chose to remain within the Ottoman Empire by immigrating to Albania or Turkiye. There were also the King's contradictory and extremely polarised positions. The first was his apologetically based stance on the epic of heroism of Montenegro, and the second was his attitude towards Muslims with political mimicry and demagogy to encourage their emigration.[215]

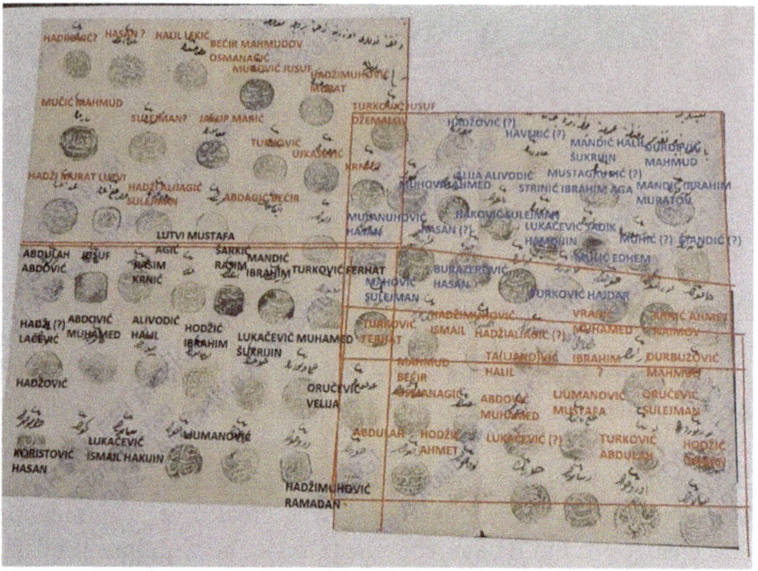

Seals of Podgorica leaders and dignitaries who spoke out against the Ottoman authorities on behalf of the residents. The surname Haveric is marked in blue, among others. The seals date to before the entry of the Montenegrin army into Podgorica[216]

After the fall of Ottoman rule in Montenegro, those Muslims of Podgorica, who remained immediately after the surrender of Podgorica by Montenegrin army in 1879, did not want to leave their homes, but they also were not too willing to obey the state decrees of the new authorities. However, in the middle of the year, there was massive resistance by the Muslims of Podgorica and Zeta, which resulted in the arrest of 13 Muslims from Podgorica, including **Hasan bey Haveric**. Subsequently, they were taken to the prison in Zabljak Crnojevic. The person who ordered the arrest must undoubtedly have been Becir bey Osmanagic. They were blamed for opposing the authorities by doing it in a 'Turkish way'. The Ottoman Government also reacted to the arrest, which, through its officials, worked to collect data on the treatment of the

Muslim population in the regions, which it was obliged to hand over to Montenegro. A verbal note of protest was sent through the Montenegrin embassy in Istanbul, pointing to the pressures that the Montenegrin government exerted on the Muslim community in Podgorica, including the search of private houses for hidden ammunition, as well as the 'arrest of Podgorica leaders', and demanding their release. According to the telegram of the Minister of Internal Affairs dated July 31, 1879, addressed to the court in Podgorica, referred to Becir bey Osmanagic, the arrested citizens of Podgorica were released, since allegedly it was established there was a 'misunderstanding between them and the authorities in Podgorica'. It was stated they will be registered voluntarily, as it was clarified that the population census 'will not prevent them from leaving Montenegro in the future' (within two years) without any burdens or further obligations towards it.[217]

Soon another large-scale arrest operation was quickly carried out, based on the translation of incriminating letters from the Ottoman-Turkish language, as well as information by captured conspirator Ibro Bedovic. The people arrested soon found themselves in prison or under police surveillance on suspicion of treason and military intelligence work, including **Acif Haveric**. A good number of suspects and arrestees faced serious charges for supporting armed Malisors (local tribe) and sending intelligence information to Osman Pasha.[218] At one point, the investigation took the form of a 'witch hunt' because almost every respectable Muslim in Podgorica was suspicious of the new authorities. Many prominent citizens of Podgorica were under suspicion, such as *kadis*, *hajis*, *muderis*, *imams*, *hafiz*, *beys* and *agas* and among them **Mulla Dervis Haveric**. One of the suspects was imprisoned during the interrogation before Becir bey's commission only because he said in the courtroom that 'he knew nothing about the whole case, that he was innocent and that imprisoned innocent people were suffering because of a fabricated guilt'. Due to the reaction of the Minister of

Internal Affairs, he was released from prison and the next day went to Cetinje to have an informative interview with him.[219]

The Special Commission of Judges, headed by Becir bey Osmanagic, which was entrusted with the entire case, worked quickly and in just a few weeks passed difficult verdicts. Some were sentenced to death and a few, such as **Acif Haveric**, were sentenced to life imprisonment.[220]

In 1879, a deputation of Muslims from Podgorica, after accepting a new rule, came to Cetinje, to express their 'devotion to Prince Nikola' and acknowledge 'his fairness'. In that deputation of Muslims from Podgorica were 'all the first agas and beys' led by Becir bey Osmanagic. **Ibrahim bey Haveric** was also in the deputation that the Montenegrin prince received at a formal audience. The occasion was reflected by interfaith tolerance. A Muslim leader, Becir bey Osmanagic, gave a special speech to the 'Shining Crown, Lord of Montenegro and the Hills', Prince Nikola, expressing the loyalty of Muslims to him, his government and the state. He said:

> Faithfully devoted your new subjects of the Muslim faith…under your mighty auspices…We pray to you, to shade us with the shadow of your mighty wings. God and you, Master. Long live to you.

In turn, the Montenegrin prince replied to the Muslim delegation:

> 'To be known, I and my authorities, will not discriminate you among my subjects based on [Christian] religion. My justice and my love are equal for all who deserve it by their loyalty and their civic virtues'. Then, the deputation stayed in Cetinje for four days. On the last day of its stay, a festive lunch was arranged in a large inn in Cetinje near the prince headquarters.[221]

On that occasion, the twinning of Osmanagic and Martinovic took place as a sign of a close relationship. However, some Muslims of Podgorica were still suspicious of the new Montenegrin government, which is also shown by the fact they refused the order of the Ministry of Internal Affairs on the mandatory census.[222]

In 1880, there was also a reaction after the Muslim ulema was summoned to the District Court, where was explained the need for their children to be educated in schools. Hafiz Hasan Lacevic declared: 'If our sultan wanted it like that, we would not listen to him, even if we were to be burned in the fire'. Shortly after, the Muslims allegedly sent several representatives, among them **Dervis bey Haveric**, later a member of the High Court representative of the authorities for Podgorica[223] ,declaring that 'they did not want to enrol their children in Montenegrin schools under unequal conditions'.[224] The ban on wearing the fez and obligation to wear Montenegrin caps, the loss of feudal incomes that they received from their serfs on the estate, Montenegrin radicalism and their inability to fit into the state of their [Montenegrin] two-century-old opponents were the reasons for the dissatisfaction of local Muslims.[225]

In 1881, a 'Serbian reading room' was founded in Podgorica, which at that time had only 25 regular and four honorary members. Considering that half the citizens were of the Islamic faith, the founders of the reading room decided to 'enter into a good social life' with them and wanted to cultivate cordial relations with their co-citizens, as they interpreted, 'of the same blood'. Thus, they invited Muslims and Catholics to get involved in the reading room's work. At the assembly convened in 1881, with the presence of Montenegrin Governor, 'a number of respected Muslims' were invited and among them was **Mulla Medo Haveric**. Out of the 48 members at that time, 15 Muslims were on their board. Ten years later, in addition to 53 donors of the Orthodox faith for the construction of a new reading room building in Podgorica, there were also 57 Muslim donors. This development was in agreement with official state policy, which claimed that everything the state has had and could serve its citizens, all its institutions and all its schools were equally at the service of every Montenegrin without distinction. 'No one has more rights, not even an Orthodox Montenegrin, than a Muslim or Roman Catholic Montenegrin', and all of them are masters together.[226]

In 1881, initially, ten representatives were included in the government, including **Dervis bey Haveric**, headed by Governor Marko Mijanov.[227] The Senate represented the highest administrative and judicial power in the country. At its head was the president with the vice-president then 14 senators. Almost every *nahiya* and tribe was represented in the Royal Senate.[228] Andrija Jovičevic also wrote that 'the first Muslim Senator in the state of Montenegro was **Dervis bey Haveric**'.

The Podgorica Captain Becir bey Osmanagic, on behalf of the Economic Society, which included members of all religions, welcomed the healthy arrival of Prince Nikola to Petrograd in MUD, August 1882. The Haverics were mentioned in these lines.

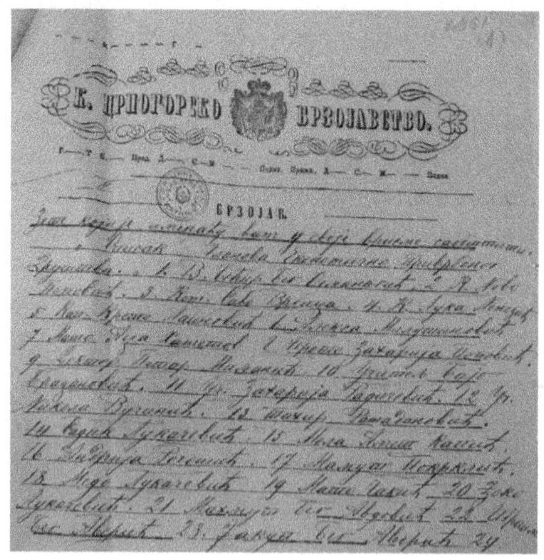
К. ЦРНОГОРСКО БРЗОЈАВСТВО.

БРЗОЈАВ.

Ibrahim bey (H) Averic was mentioned[229]

Mula Medo (H) Averic and **Jusuf bey (H) Averic** were mentioned in the letter 1882[230]

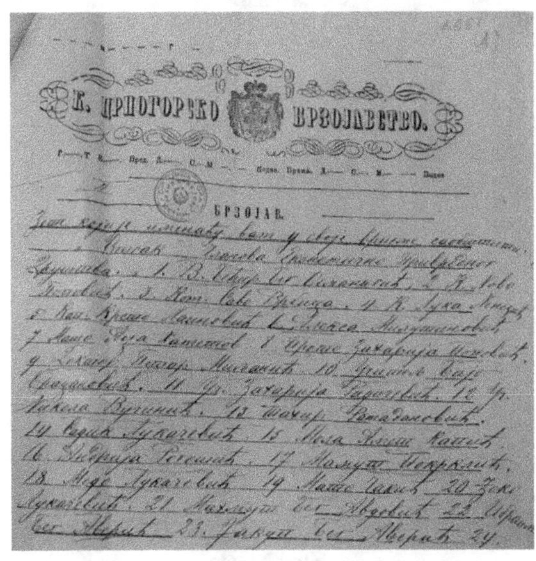

К. ЦРНОГОРСКО БРЗОЈАВСТВО.

БРЗОЈАВ.

Jakub bey (H) Averic was mentioned in 1882[231]

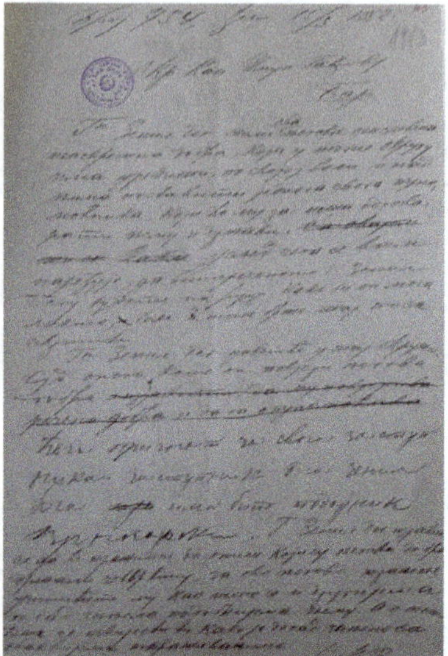

Order to the Captain of Bar to enable **Zejnel bey** to manage his goods in 1882[232]

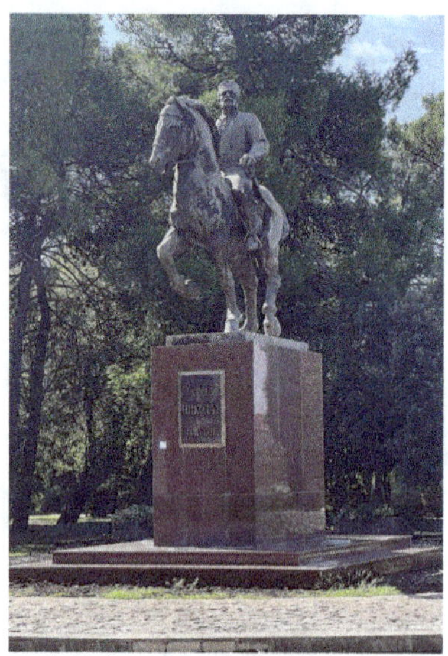

King Nikola

King Nikola (prince 1860-1910; king 1910-1918) had Muslim dukes, senators, teachers, *perjanici* (royal flag bearers) and other civil servants in his closest service, respecting 'all the laws and customs of the Islamic religion'. As a sign of respect and tolerance towards Muslims, he decorated several Montenegrin Muslims with the *Order of Danilo*, including members of the **'Bey's family of Haveric'**.[233] He considered Muslims 'people of his own blood'.[234] At that time, the Haverics were among the honorary *perjanici* at the court of King Nikola. They were respected and trusted by the Montenegrin authorities.

> During the rule of Montenegro, the Haveric family maintained close relations with the royal house and personally with King Nikola and Duke Mirko Petrovic. They supported state authorities and its army materially and financially.[235]

Members of the Haveric family were on the list of legal voters from the municipality of Podgorica for the election of a deputy for 1905. The election was held November 14, 1905, at the local primary school in Podgorica. The data is from the office of the municipal administration on November 9, 1905. According to that list, as many as 17 of them were Haverics. They were '**Afis, Amza, Afis O.**, **Duljo**, **Ethem**, **Zejnel**, **Zuber**, **Ibro**, **Jakup**, **Mano M.**, **Mahmut**, **Medo, Seljo I.**, **Seit**, **Smajo**, **Selim** and **Sulejman**'.[236] In 1908, the newspaper *Glas Crnogoraca* ('Voice of Montenegrins') mentioned that **Suljo Haveric** 'contributed to the children's hospital' as a sign of his loyalty.[237]

On March 26, 1910, the Podgorica Muslims held a large gathering on the premises of the local school for the celebration of Prince Nikola's jubilee. At this meeting, a special committee was chosen, comprising several Muslim representatives, including **Hamza bey Haveric**, 'to express thankfulness for the celebrated prince's jubilee'. Under the chairmanship of Commander Selim Bibezic, his son Omer, a local teacher, gave an inspired speech:

> I cannot describe the glory, happiness and greatness of the reign of our exalted ruler because even the best pens of scholars can scarcely do this. We Muslims, as faithful subjects, must admit that no nation in the world has enjoyed as many benefits as we have in the past 32 years, under the rule of the glorious ruler, the prince. In his name, under his protection, we have preserved our faith, honour and property, so we enjoy and will enjoy significant privileges. [Cheering] All this for his health.[238]

In 1911, one Muslim representative in Podgorica wrote: 'There are no similar examples that any ruler in one country has ever given such rights to non-believers, like the King, the ruler, to us Muslims'. At the same time, the alleged ingratitude and insincerity of some Muslims regarding the alleged desecration of a mosque in Podgorica was criticised. However, several *hajis* and *kadis*, as well as beys **Said Haveric**, **Duljo Averic** and **Suljo Averic**, reacted to the allegation. They made a joint statement in which they emphasised: 'We have always and will always fulfill our duties as subjects and citizens towards the Throne and the Motherland with the highest motives and the highest loyalty'.[239] Among those who disagreed this was **Smail bey Haveric**. Although he was 'appointed as an officer by the King, he decided to emigrate to the Turkish Empire'.[240] Soon it was announced in the newspaper, *Glas of Montenegro*, that 'By the grace of God, Nikola I, ordered that the resignation of the officer of the national army **Smail bey Haveric**, which he submitted to the state service, be accepted'.[241]

Around that time, there was also a historical trace about several Havérics. *Dacia (Montenegro) Records for 1913 of the Podgorica Captaincy* ('Zapisnik Dacije za 1913 godinu Kapetanije Podgoricke') mentioned '**Ibrahim Beg** (H) Averic', **Temo** (H)Averic, **Sulo** (H) Averic, **Malo Murat** (H)Averic and **Jakub bey** (H)Averic.[242] This was a time when new circumstances would challenge the domestic population and its government.

In 1918, Serbia occupied Montenegro and abolished its statehood. The decision of the Podgorica Assembly of November 26, 1918, on the unification of Montenegro with Serbia was a prelude to the declaration of a joint state, the Kingdom of Serbs, Croats and Slovenes. Work on the unification of Montenegro and Serbia intensified during the entry of French, English, American, Italian and Serbian troops into Montenegro. Consequently, Montenegrin King Nikola, who emigrated from the country in 1916, was overthrown.[243]

Fadil Alija Haveric made a note relating to the King of the Serbs, Croats and Slovenes, and the King of Yugoslavia:

> Close relations were also established with the royal house of Karadordevic, namely, the grandson of King Nikola II. The King of Yugoslavia Aleksandar, as a prince, often stayed in Podgorica. During his enthronement, the **Haverics** gave King Alexander a golden sabre encrusted with pearls and precious stones as a gift.[244]

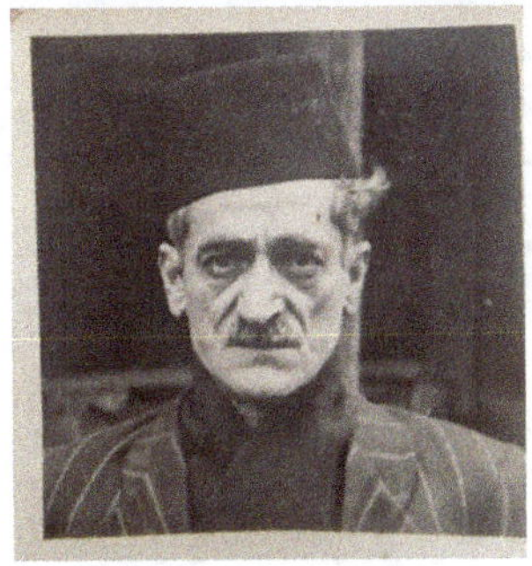

Bajram bey Haveric

In difficult period of the Kingdom of Yugoslavia, progressive ideas and workers' rights, regardless of the ethno-national and religious differences, were held by members of the tanners, merchants and tailors union. Among these Montenegrin social activists were the Montenegrin Mufti Murtez ef. Karaduzovic and some scholars. At that time, **Bajram bey** and **Osman bey Haveric** from Podgorica were among the first members of the 'Terzijsko-Krojacka branch and strike committee'.[245]

Emigration (*Muhajirluk* or *Muhacirlik*)

From the rule of the Ottoman Empire to the Second World War, numerous members of the Haveric family moved to Turkiye, Albania, Bosnia and Herzegovina and Italy. It was mainly in four periods: 1) During the Ottomans' rule; 2) After the Congress of Berlin; 3) During the First World War; and 4) During the Second World War. Muslims as a minority never attacked others or took revenge, but they were often exposed to difficult trials. These wars and the fate of the *muhajirluk* ('emigration') left a deep mark on the Muslim people, because it caused long-term traumatic consequences. These difficult times were also experienced by non-Muslim people.

Many aspects of life were 'changed overnight'. Being traditionally a bey family, the Haverics who previously held high posts in the Ottoman Empire and Montenegrin Kingdom plus their descendants faced new realities. There were varied individual and family struggles for survival and destinies.[246] In the memories of older generations of Haverics, who experienced direct attacks on their land, people, home and forced exodus, they were accustomed to saying, 'Time before the attacks and time after the attacks'. This statement is in accord what Muhic highlighted, 'being a Muslim in the Balkans was not always easy, even though Bosniaks and Albanians are European autochthonous inhabitants'.[247] The fates of exoduses with heavy circumstances testified the direction and fortune from which the Haverics arrived.[248] Those who left Montenegro were challenged to rebuild their life, face new challenges and hardship, adjust themselves to new environments, preserve their tradition and contribute to new homelands.

Several Haverics came to the Turkish part of the Ottoman Empire, appointed by the last Ottoman sultans and during the rule of the general and new statesman Kemal Pasha Ataturk. Most of them never returned to their homeland. **Kadi Hasan bey** was among the first to move to Anatolia, perhaps Istanbul, but it was unknown whether he returned to his homeland. The first of several **Haverics** came to the Shkoder Sandjak as they were appointed by the Ottomans in service of the vizier during the rule of the Busatlins. Later, some Haverics came from Podgorica in 1875, settling in Shkoder, Tirana, Durres and Kavaja.[249] **Agim** Haveri narrated:

> My father, **Gani bey**, told me about the history of the family branch. Today, many descendants with the surname Haveri and Haverik live in Albania. My great-grandfather and grandfather came from Podgorica in 1875. They settled in Durres, where they established their businesses. During the Albanian monarchy, we changed the 'Slavic ending of the surname'. So, it is known that 'Haveri' and 'Haveriku' are actually Havercs. I also have the Haveric family tree that shows our generations since the 15th century.[250]

The earliest *muhajir* (refugee) families from Podgorica who flocked to Albania were during and after crumbling of the Ottoman Empire. They became Albanians in accordance with their new homeland. They Albanianised their names by removing the Slavic suffix 'ic'. The earliest mentioned families are: Alivoda (Alivodovic), the Bajri family which was once called Muxhiq (Muhic), Mandia (Mandic), Osmani (Osmanagic), **Haveri (Haveric)**, Baci (Backovic), Uruci (Urucevic), Bebeziq (Bibezic), Sykaj (Suknic), Juka (Jukniq), Llukaqi (Lukacevic), Halluni (Hallunovic), Striniq (Strinic) and many more.[251]

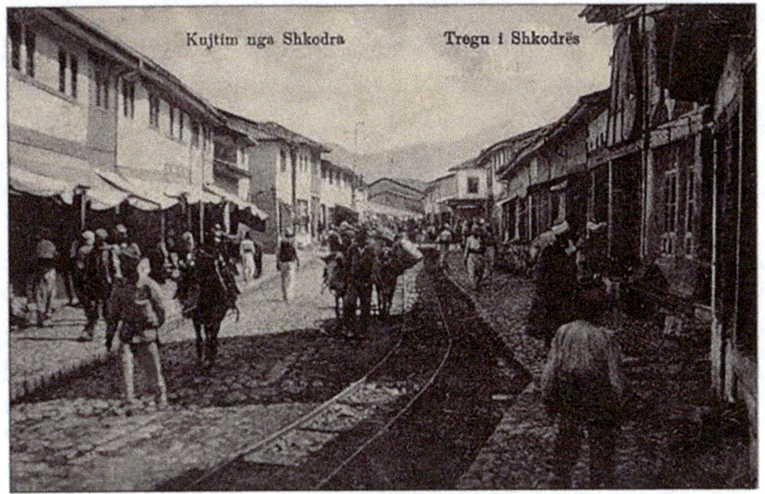

Shkoder

By the decision of the Congress of Berlin, the Ottoman army had to withdraw from Montenegro. Immediately after the fall of Bar on January 10, 1878, into Montenegrin hands, numerous Bosniaks took refuge in Shkoder. When the Berlin Congress ended the war, they asked Prince Nikola to allow them to return to Bar, but he did not allow them. Then, Ottoman Sultan Abdulhamid II, because of their bravery during the defence of Bar, allowed the Bosniaks to settle in Kucuk Cekmedza in Istanbul and sent ships to Shkodra to pick them up. However, under foreign pressure, Prince Nikola let 198 Bosniak families return to Bar at the end of May 1879.[252]

The year following the Congress of Berlin, with the entry of the Montenegrin army, Podgorica was freed from the Turks. By then 8,000 Muslims lived in the territory of the former *kaza* of Podgorica. With the entry of the Montenegrin army, the Muslim populations of Spuz, Zabljak Crnojevic and Ljeskopolje were displaced *en masse*. In the same year, this migration affected only a part of the Muslims from Podgorica and Zeta. British data stated the Montenegrin army did not find around 600 families from Podgorica, but they retreated with the Ottoman army to Shkoder.[253] The exodus of *muhadjirs* (emigrants) was further initiated in the same year after Haji Lojo's revolt against the Austro-Hungarian occupation. They sailed for Anatolia, Albania and Dubrovnik.[254] Others found a temporary safe haven in Macedonia.

Pavle S. Radusinovic in *Stanovnistvo i naselja Zetske ravnice od najstarijeg doba do novog doba* ('Population and Settlements of the Zetska Ravnica from the Oldest Age to the New Age') mentioned several emigrant families who moved out during the liberation from the Turks, among whom were members of the **Haveric** family.[255] From 1879, they left Montenegro for Shkoder when many other Muslim families also emigrated.

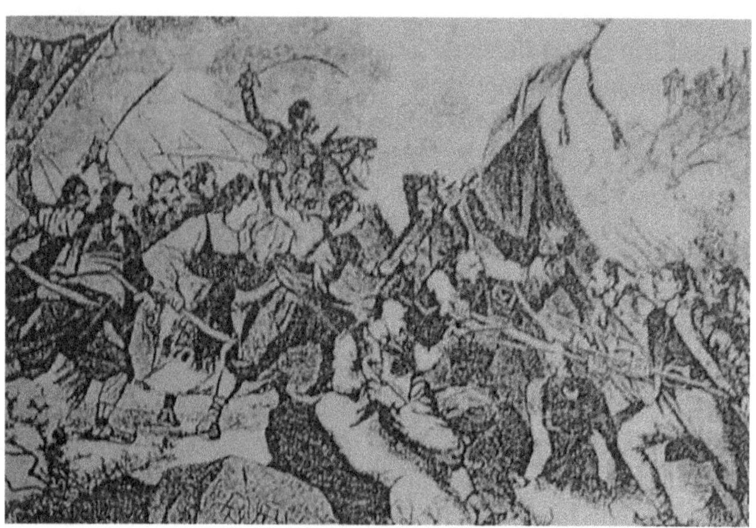

Battle near Podgorica, painting by Ferdo Kikerec

On the eve of the handover of Podgorica to the Montenegrins in 1879, more than a quarter of the Muslim population of Podgorica emigrated to Shkoder, Durres, Kavaja, Elbasan and Tirana. **Abla Haveriku** recalled, 'our parents of a bunch of **Haverikus in Kavaje** have always tried to tell stories about our family, and learning to appreciate every possibility that we now have'. Remarking about her family, whose great-grandfather was **Mehmet bey**, she said:

> In 1879, 4 members of the Haveric (Haveriqi) family moved from Podgorica in the cities of Shkoder, Kavaja, Durres and Peqin. **Mehmet bey** together with his brother and two of his cousins were nominated in administrative position from the Ottoman Empire in customs duty, court and prefecture. They came alone and later got married and created their life in the respective cities in which they moved into. Unfortunately, we have not closely kept in touch with other Haveriku family members leaving in other cities. From what we know, the Haveriku family in Durres are direct descendants of the members that came from Podgorica. **Haveriku** family members now living in Tirana, are mostly members who moved from Shkodër and Durres. In my father's knowledge during the King Zog monarchy, some surnames were changed removing the extension of 'ic'. The family members in Shkodra kept the surname **Haveri**, while the ones living in Durres and Kavaje changed their surname into **Haveriku**.[256]

According to data from the Ministry of Internal Affairs, by the end of 1880, 50 Muslim families had moved out of Podgorica.[257] Between 1881 and 1912, the reason for the migration from Montenegro was that they did not agree with the new ruler.

In particular, the 20th century was regarded by many Bosniak scholars as the most difficult period in history.[258] The largest organised departure for Turkiye was recorded during the first years of the 20th century, when a caravan of nearly 2,000 wagons and carriages was formed – 'they left the city for three days and three nights'. Many *muhajirs* 'were weeping and screaming while departing to foreign world'.[259] During their flight, many died on the way from *komitas* and disease. Thus, numerous families vanished from these areas, and once they settled in new countries, many changed their surnames and 'disappeared'. Many Haverics migrated to Sarajevo, Trebinje, Prijedor, Shkoder, Tirana, Durres, Kavaja and a few to Valone plus Istanbul, Izmir, Ankara and other parts of Turkiye, such as Preveza.[260]

Archival documents in the State Archives of Montenegro in Cetinje stated that several Muslim families moved from Podgorica to different European parts of the Ottoman Empire in 1909. Some of them settled in districts called 'Bosniak areas'.[261] **Seljo Averic** and a few other families received passports to move to Preveza, a coastal settlement in Epirus, on the coast of the Ionian Sea, which at the end of the First Balkan War in 1912 was annexed to Greece. The emigration of Muslims took place according to the established procedure. When the expatriate received a release from Commander Selim Bibezić and confirmation from the captain's court that they did not owe any state duties, the president of the Podgorica municipality submitted a document to the Passport Department of the Ministry of Foreign Affairs in Cetinje in which he recommended that the expatriate be issued a passport 'for the purpose of resettlement'. Acts on the emigration of Muslims from Podgorica during 1909 have been preserved.[262]

The document of family emigration stated, '**Seljo Salihov Averic** from Podgorica; the Mohammedan religion; born in Podgorica; 40 years old medium-tall stature; cheeks plain, hair black; eyes black; mouth and nose ordinary; by profession a cafe owner; moustache small black; burned on left cheek; married status; intends to move from Montenegro to Preveza-Turkey'. He moved with his family to Preveza in 1909.[263]

For emigration, **Seljo** Averic took with him nine family members:
1) Mother **Mera** (unknown age)
2) Wife **Hava** (30)
3) Sister **Dzefa** (40)
4) Son **Ramo** (16)
5) Son **Sacir** (8)
6) Son **Muhammad** (2)
7) Daughter **Secer Nurija** (10)
8) Daughter **Gondža** (7)
9) Daughter **Havuša** (4)

To receive a passport, **Averic** submitted the discharge papers from Battalion Commander Selim Bibezic, as well as the confirmation from the captain's court that 'he does not owe any state duties, and it is referred to the Ministry'. It was in 'Podgorica, July 30, 1909, the President of the Municipality of St. Markovic DACG-Cetinje, MID, Passport Department, fasc. 5, number 1051'.[264]

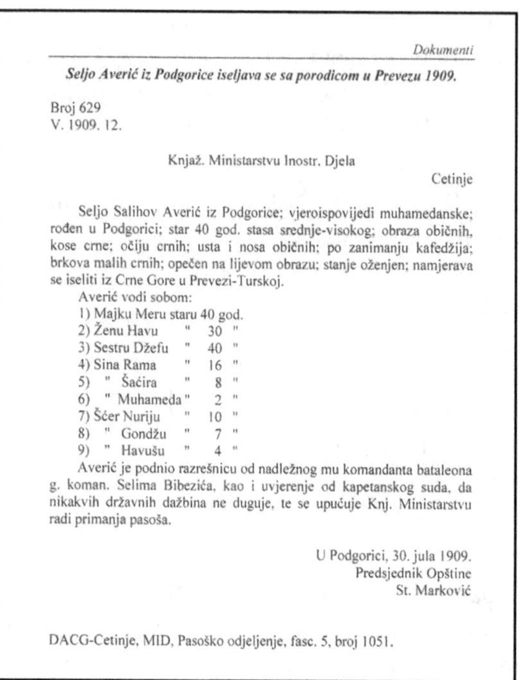

Dokumenti

Seljo Averić iz Podgorice iseljava se sa porodicom u Prevezu 1909.

Broj 629
V. 1909. 12.

Knjaž. Ministarstvu Inostr. Djela

Cetinje

Seljo Salihov Averić iz Podgorice; vjeroispovijedi muhamedanske; rođen u Podgorici; star 40 god. stasa srednje-visokog; obraza običnih, kose crne; očiju crnih; usta i nosa običnih; po zanimanju kafedžija; brkova malih crnih; opečen na lijevom obrazu; stanje oženjen; namjerava se iseliti iz Crne Gore u Prevezi-Turskoj.

Averić vodi sobom:
1) Majku Meru staru 40 god.
2) Ženu Havu " 30 "
3) Sestru Džefu " 40 "
4) Sina Rama " 16 "
5) " Šaćira " 8 "
6) " Muhameda " 2 "
7) Šćer Nuriju " 10 "
8) " Gondžu " 7 "
9) " Havušu " 4 "

Averić je podnio razrešnicu od nadležnog mu komandanta bataleona g. koman. Selima Bibezića, kao i uvjerenje od kapetanskog suda, da nikakvih državnih dažbina ne duguje, te se upućuje Knj. Ministarstvu radi primanja pasoša.

U Podgorici, 30. jula 1909.
Predsjednik Opštine
St. Marković

DACG-Cetinje, MID, Pasoško odjeljenje, fasc. 5, broj 1051.

Haveric family, emigration document, 1909

Further information about **Seljo Haveric**, his wife **Mera**, his sister **Dzefa**, his three sons and three daughters is unavailable. Perhaps the family assimilated into the new environment.

Following the Balkan wars, the Muslims were exposed to a difficult period. As a consequence of the Balkan wars in 1912 and 1913, many Bosniaks took refuge in surrounding countries, including Macedonia.[265] By 1914, Lazar Roganovic found 44 surnames of Muslim families who emigrated from Montenegro. Among the families who immigrated to Shkodra and other Albanian cities were the **Haverics**. According to archival data from Albania, their presence had been visible for several generations in several

Albanian cities. Jovicevic recorded statistics on 'settled families of Muslims from Podgorica', including Haveric, from the end of the 19th century and the beginning of the 20th century. According to his [uncompleted] data, the **Haverics** lived in Montenegro, Bosnia and Herzegovina and Albania according to: 'Podgorica 6 families; Sarajevo 7 families; Shkodra 6 families, and Durres 1 family of Haveric'. However, according to Haveric family records, the number of their families was much larger, including those who moved to Turkiye.

In these and following periods, the Muslims of Montenegro, including the Haverics, emigrated in three directions. The first was through Tuzi-Shkoder or Trebinje-Sarajevo. The second direction was by ship sent by Turkish authorities. Those who escaped to Albania and Bosnia during the rampage were often stopped at crossings and faced ambushes. On the way to Shkoder, those who survived would say 'They may have been killed because of the gold they were carrying with them – God saved them from overtaking'. The third were those who went to Turkiye, for which the Turkish authorities planned to settle them not only in cities but remote areas across the sea. They were the so-called people who 'go over the sea'. These Muslim refugees unwillingly left their wealth in Podgorica to their Orthodox servants.[266] Those *muhadjirs* who emigrated to Turkiye were 'the national memento [remembering] of our lost lands', stated the Turkish general and stateman, Mustafa Kemal Ataturk.[267]

Some displacement data from the period includes:

> **Adlije Ismail bey Haveriqi** was born in Shkoder around 1914 and died at seven years old, shortly after his mother's passing, 'burning with longing and love for her ...'

Ahmet H. Mehmet bey Haveriqi was born at the beginning of the 20th century in Podgorica. He was the second of the boys. With his second *Boshnjake* (Bosniak) wife, they had two sons, **Mustafa** and **Aqif**, and two daughters, **Qamile** and **Mahije** …

Ahmet Aqif bey Haveriqi was born in Shkoder around 1913 and 1914. He died very young around 1918 …

Islam Salih bey Haveriq was born in Podgorica in 1875. He moved to Shkoder around 1918. His sons were **Salih**, **Halil**, **Enver** and **Isaja (Isa) Islam bey** born in Shkoder.

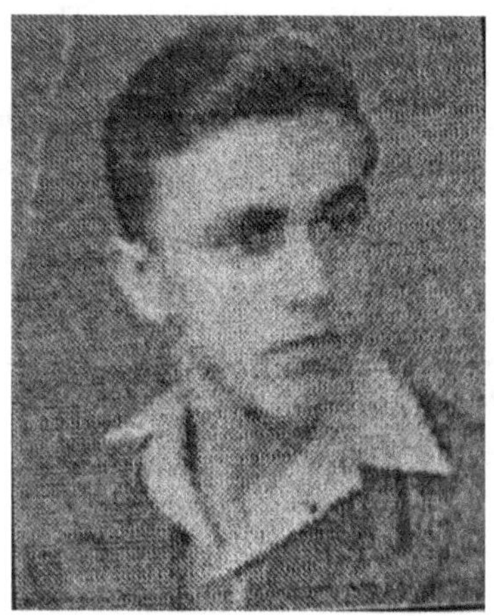

Isaja (Isa) Islam bey Haveriq, Shkoder

During and after the First World War, numerous departures of almost entire Haveric families to Albania, Bosnia and Turkiye were recorded. They were under pressure due to an atmosphere of fear and insecurity.[268] After the expulsion by the *komita* rebels, they usually settled in safer places in the immediate vicinity, most notably in Albanian cities that 'belonged to the Ottoman vilayet', so within the Turkish realm. For instance, among them were the brothers **Zuber** and **Said Haveric**, who emigrated to Shkoder in 1918.[269] For those who moved further for reasons of security or the need for sustenance, they were mostly directed towards urban areas such as Trebinje and Sarajevo.[270]

At that time, there was also an increased influx of migrants to Herzegovina who would settle in Trebinje. Among several Haveric families were, for instance, those of **Hamza bey**, **Osman bey, Selim bey**, **Tahir bey** and **Zejnil bey**. Some of them lived in Resul bey's house in Trebinje, which was built in 1794 on the bank of the Trebisnjica River. It was one of the most important local family monuments and a summer house in the Ottoman architecture style. In this house, the Haverics found a temporary safe haven. They lived, worked and some children were born.[271]

Osman bey Haveric, from father **Selim bey**, came to Trebinje. He had inherited a tannery shop with warehouses in Podgorica where he kept raw and dry lamb, sheep, calf, beef, rabbit and fox skins. He helped his father to dry and sell the skins in Podgorica. That fur was prized and popular, especially among the beys' costumes such as fur collars. **Osman bey**, together with his father and brothers, left Podgorica after the First World War and moved to the town of Trebinje, Bosnia and Herzegovina, together with some of his relatives. He continued his trading activities in Trebinje and frequently travelled to Dubrovnik, Croatia.

Nazira Hamza bey Haveric Kerni (Krnic), who was born in Trebinje, recalled the family exodus:

> My *babo* [father], **Hamza Ibrahim bey**, heard that there was going to be an attack and robbery by the armed gangs (*komite*) and went to King Nikola to protect his family because the King was his friend. The King was

also a godfather of his child after a cut strand of hair from **Hamza bey's** child. He told **Hamza bey**, 'Nobody will do anything to you'. 'You will be protected'. However, soon the situation got out of control of the King and the family must have taken refuge.

In the meantime, a horde of 100 Serbian *komitas* from Montenegro entered our house and robbed it. **Hamza bey**, who always dressed beautifully in the national costume, was surrounded by *komitas* with 5 bayonets. They took off his costume and dressed him in dirty *komit*'s clothes. Our family had a horse, *ata*, so the *komitas* took his horse, along with women's jewellery, a collection of *fezzes*, gold rings and sacks of gold. The *komitas* told *babo* that they would rape the women the next day. It was awful and unbearable to hear, so **Hamza bey**, who saw the situation as very bad for the family, could not stand it, so he took his family and fled...

They came first to Danilovgrad near Podgorica where he and his brothers had a three-story house and a store with manufactory. His father, **Ibrahim bey**, told **Hamza bey** and his sons that their house may also be looted by the same gangs.

Hamza bey 'went back and forth', running away with family from the *komitas*, searching for safety and peace. From Danilovgrad he went to Trebinje (Herzegovina). There, for a while, he established a tailor shop. A son, **Kemal**, and a daughter, **Nazira**, were born there.

Nazira remembered when she came to that house: 'The Bey's House' in Trebinje where I was left was like a 'museum'. It was a two-storey house. The hill is above the Trebisnjica River. Its water flowed under it and passing under a bridge. 'It looked cool'. After some time, **Hamza bey** came to Shkoder. When they were getting ready to go to Shkoder, he had to get his passport. **Hamza bey** did not stay long in Shkoder, maybe only two or three months. It was difficult to stay longer. Thus, he stayed a little with his daughter, **Hatidza**, and a little with his cousin, **Fiko** Haveric.

Hamza Ibrahim bey, as a *muhadjir*, faced a lot of struggles. His wife **Zejnepa (Zepa) Omercahic** passed away and his children, **Hatidza**, **Dzavid, Nazira and Kemal** were separated across three countries, Montenegro, Albania and Bosnia.

Son Kemal, father Hamza bey Haveric, daughter Nazira and son Dzavid (left to right)

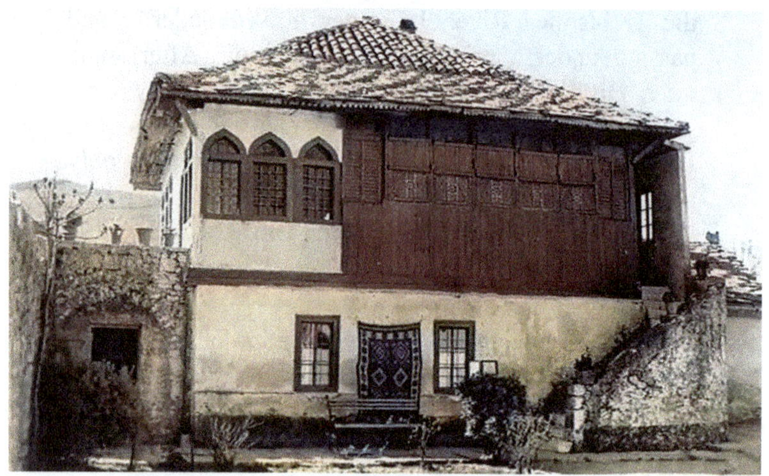

Bey's House in Trebinje, Bosnia and Herzegovina

Some relatives in Albania tried to help their relatives from Podgorica, as this story explained:

> In a letter from **Ali bey Haveriq**, the son of **Ismail bey**, addressed to his brother, **Gani bey**, wrote about the situation of **Hamza bey**. He asks **Gani bey**, who is in Tirana, to inquire about finding a job for **Dzavid**, the elder son of **Hamza bey**, who is about 13 years old while keep him in their house giving him shelter and food. He praises the boy, saying that he is a smart and very good boy, and even gives him ideas to set him up with a job. They are sharing this letter, where **Ali bey** insisted on finding a way to help **Dzavid**.
>
> **Hamza bey** did not stay long in Shkoder. Only **Dzavid** remained there. **Hamza bey** went to Trebinje where his son **Kemal** and daughter **Nazira** were born. He later visited to Tuzi by himself, hoping to return with his family, but there he died of jaundice, leaving his children

orphans. When he passed away, **Hamza bey** was about 60 years old. Life brought him a lot of suffering. Did he die in Tuzi like his wife? Their graves are unknown.

Nazira was only three years old. She was taken by his uncle, **Mahmud**, to Sarajevo. There **Mahmud** and two brothers **Abdullah** and **Zenel** lived in one house. For a while **Kemal** was taken to the family home and stayed in a home for orphans upon recommendation by the *Reis-ul-Ulama* (chief of the ulama) Dzemaludin Causevic while **Nazira** completed her four-year primary school in Sarajevo and returned to Albania to her sister **Hatidza** who was already married to Ahmed Keraj (Krnic) in Shkoder.

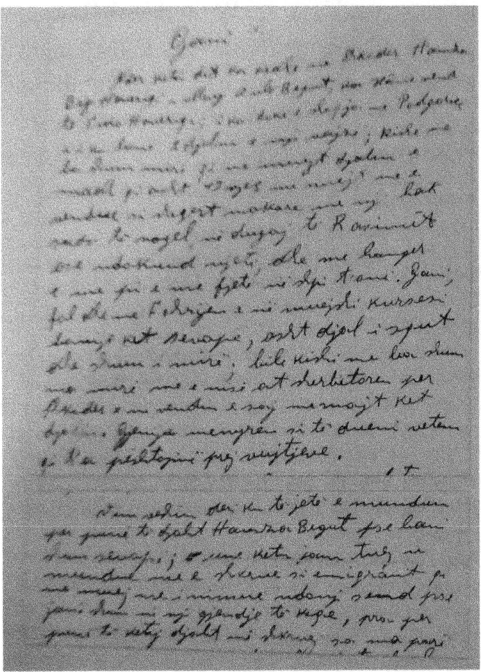

Story in the letter

In Montenegro, there was evidence at every step of the mass withdrawal of the population, so there are also testimonies that 'wherever one came across, dead bodies lay, which no one had to bury, and people ate tree bark....'[272] About the difficulties of the time she experienced, **Envera Haveric Kalmar** recalled how they overnight were left without a roof:

> It was a holy month of Ramadan when her family cleaned the house in Podgorica, made it nice and tidy, prepared a halal meal for *iftar* and invited family relatives and some friends. It was the time when joy should knock at the door. However, there was a noise raising from a distance. These were wild Serbian *komitas* coming close to their house. It was during the *iftar* when all family members and friends were sitting around a table. We suddenly became scared, left the table and served *iftar*. We quickly picked up some necessities, took carriage for Albania spent the last money to run away. We wanted to take refuge in a safe place – our families were separated by emigration and soon we saw ourselves as *muhajirs* without an address.[273]

Fear of the Serbian *komitas* was evident in the narration by Nazira Haveric Kerni:

> ....**Selim bey**'s wife (called 'Selimbegovca' or Selim begum) told me that we had houses and shops in the town of Danilovgrad, so my grandfather [**Ibrahim bey**] asked his sons, 'Why are you building in Danilovgrad, it is a *Vlach* ['Slavic Orthodox Christian villager'] own?' Soon the town will all be robbed, deserted by the Serbian *komitas*.

Zejnil bey, a son of **Ibrahim bey**, was a merchant, who escaped from Podgorica between 1914 and 1918. He married **Camila** Lukacevic. Zejnil bey's wife managed to take the gold with them when they escaped from Podgorica. After a short stay in Albania, they first came to Trebinje in Bosnia and Herzegovina. As they migrated from place to place, their children were born in various countries and towns. In Montenegro, **Fahrija (Faka)** was born in 1918 in Podgorica, daughter **Magbula** was born in 1920 in Shkoder, Albania, while their sons **Enver** in 1923 in Trebinje, **Semsudin (Semso)** in 1925 in Bihac and daughter Hava in 1932 in Visegrad in Bosnia and Herzegovina. Zejnil bey came to Sarajevo in the 1930s and from there he was thinking of going to Istanbul. However, his wife said not to go to Istanbul and they decided to stay in Sarajevo.[274]

Velija Haveric (Veli bey) also said, 'It was unbearable in Podgorica, the small shops were 'desolate and in misery' and 'we were in panic'. **Veli Bey** also said, 'We collected rugs so they could sleep with them on their way to Albania and Trebinje. It was painful to live the country of our origin'.[275] In 1918, **Velija's** brave mother, **Nurija Haveric** née Vranić, together with her children, left Podgorica and went to Trebinje to live with her brothers. In 1917, when he was 9 years old, his father, **Selim bey**, passed away. He lived in Trebinje for 10 years. He was trained for the tannery trade and worked as a tanner-merchant. In 1928, Veli bey's father and his family left Trebinje and came to Sarajevo, where he lived and worked for the rest of his life.[276]

From the memories of **Cazim bey Haveric**, it is possible to understand his displacement process.

> I [**Cazim**] escaped the war from Podgorica to Albania in 1918. I travelled in a carriage with a few clothes, which I carried with me. It was about a 60-kilometre drive from Podgorica to Shkoder. I was only seven years old when I left my hometown and came to Shkoder. There, I lived for almost two years. In 1919, I left Albania on an

> Italian ship which, I think, was called *Baron Bruck* for Durbovnik. It used to be a transport ship until its owner decided that the ship should carry passengers.
>
> The sailing trip lasted ten hours. After sailing, the ship anchored in the port of Gruž in Dubrovnik. That Italian ship had about 50 beds and among the passengers, there were also Bosniaks. From the Haveric family, the ship passengers were **Abdullah (Dulja) bey** and his son **Hajrulah (Hajro)**... After arriving in Dubrovnik, we stayed for a few days in the Petka Hotel, thinking about the way to Sarajevo....

Numerous families from Podgorica left their homeland as emigrants settling in Durres, and since then they participated in the development of the city where they continued the rest of their lives. In the article titled 'Durreses and Italians: A story of coexistence' (*Dračani i Italijani: priča o suživotu*), it is said that in the years between 1928 and 1934, in cooperation with Italian experts, they worked on a construction project to build the port. In the same period, the city's regulation plan was also designed, which is attributed to Italian architects and the Bosniak Albanians. Referring to Mahmut bey's book, before 1939, the Municipality building, the National Bank, the power plant and 'villas of the wealthiest families in Durres, such as Shijak, Fanny, Vokopola, Margerita, Koja, Delliallisi, Rexha, Manushi, **Haveriku** and others, were built in Durres'.

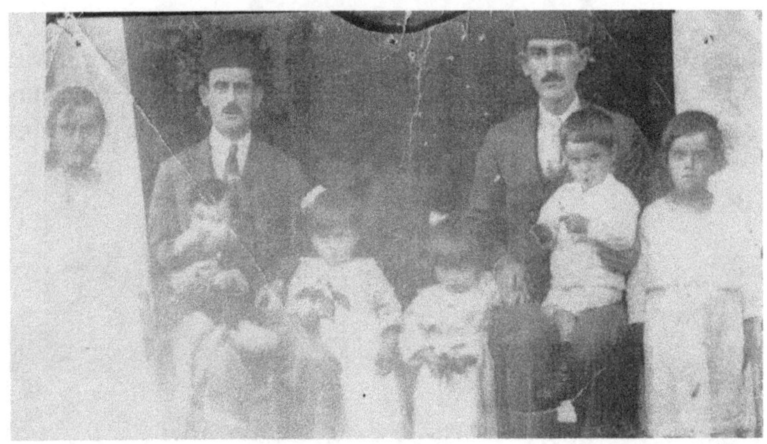

Haverics in Albania

The number of emigrants increased even more during and after the Second World War. It is recorded that approximately 600 Muslim families existed in Podgorica until the beginning of the Second World War, when almost two-thirds of them moved to Shkoder.[277] They relied on support from their relatives in Shkoder, who migrated there in the previous periods. Of the Muslim families who emigrated from Podgorica and its surroundings, 47 families chose to live in Shkoder and its surroundings, including the **Haveric** family. When Podgorica was occupied by the Italian army then by Germany, from 1941, the Haverics moved to Albania.[278]

Fear of a Chetnik invasion was increasingly present among the Muslim population. Many families set off across the Cijevina River to Tuzi and Albania. About 90% of the families went to Tuzi and Shkoder, leaving their possessions behind to save their lives. In Tuzi and Shkoder, they were inaccessible to Chetnik retaliation and could more safely join the resistance, the National Liberation Front. A small number of Muslim families remained in Podgorica. Some of their members were persecuted or killed by members of the 'Black Hand', which consisted mainly of young men from Podgorica families.[279] It caused a new exodus of Muslims. Like in time of the First World War, some **Haverics** settled temporarily, while most stayed permanently in Albania. Others left for Turkiye, while a significant number permanently moved to Bosnia with a stop in Albania.[280]

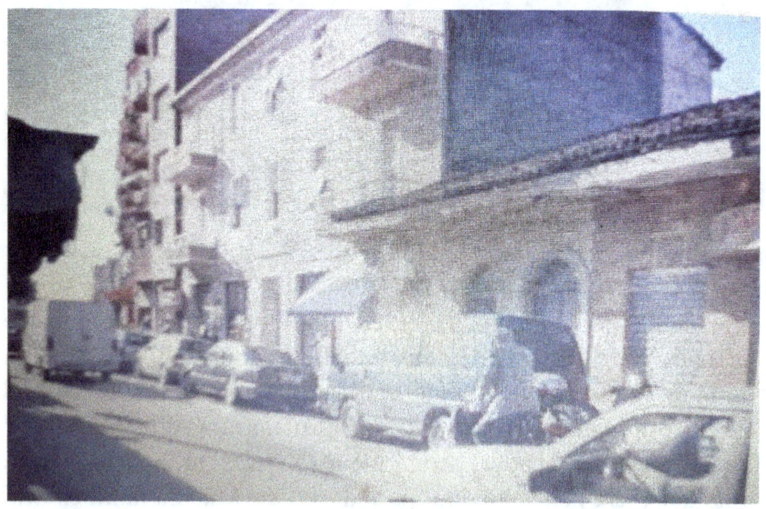

The street where Sulejman's family lived, Shkoder

Among the Haverics who took refuge in Albania during the Second World War was **Sulejman bey**, his wife and their son **Hasan (Cano)**. Prior to the war, **Sulejman's** son, **Fetah (Feto) Haveric**, was in the partisans fighting against the occupation in Podgorica.

> The Chetniks came and said that 'if they did not bring **Fetah** to them within 24 hours, they would kill them all'. They all rushed to flee to Albania by bus. Arriving in Shkoder, they lived in the lower floor of the house. In Shkoder, they got food on vouchers for bread and cheese and occasionally meat.[281]

In Shkoder, **Hasan** worked as a tailor. **Hasan's** two sons and two daughters – **Rifat (Rifo)**, **Semsudin (Dino)**, **Zineta (Dinka)** and **Munevera (Vera)** – were born in Albania. In Podgorica, together with **Rizo**, he ran shops. In Albania, they had the opportunity to obtain Albanian citizenship, which they did not want. Another Haveric lived in Shkoder, who lived near the stadium, not far from them. The family lived in Shkoder until 1957.

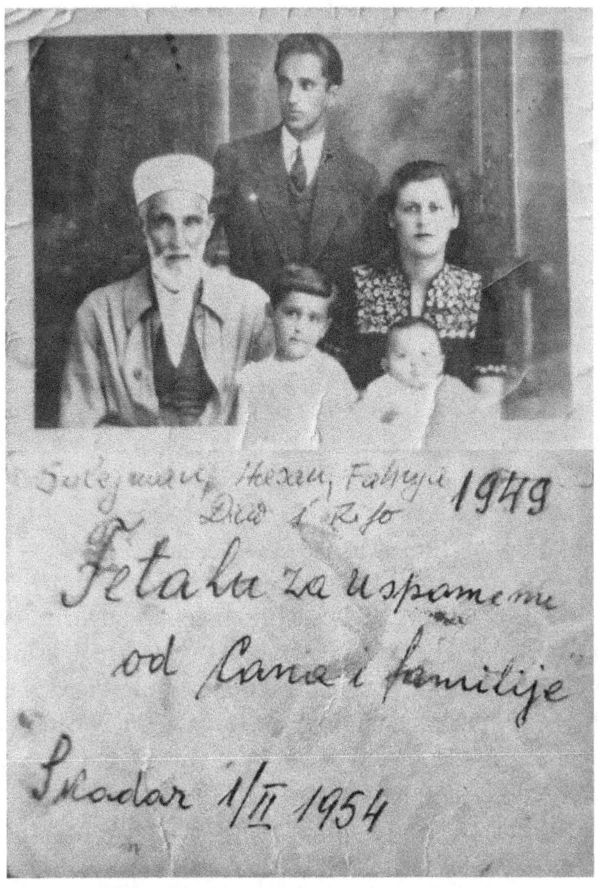

Sulejman Bey with family in Shkoder, 1949 –
Sulejman, Hasan, Fahrija, Dino and Zijo

When the family first tried to return home to Stara Varos, Podgorica, the Chetniks returned them. Their house was taken by the rebels. Then, they came to Sarajevo and their 6-member family found accommodation at two addresses. Half of the family lived at one and the other half at another address in Sarajevo. The house of **Hasan (Cano)** and **Rizah bey** in Podgorica won their lawsuit in court. They believed they would receive decent compensation, but the value of the payment was ironically 'the value of two televisions'.[282]

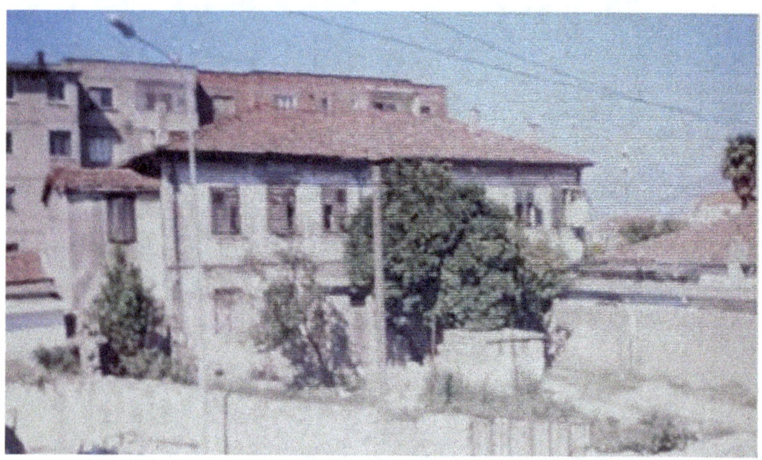

Ismail bey house in Shkoder

Hamza Salih bey dealt in the textile trade in Podgorica. With his brothers, he had three stores in Podgorica, one store in Danilovgrad and another in Kokota on the outskirts of Podgorica. Their trade flourished until the occupation in 1941. In 1941, when Podgorica was bombed, the entire **Hamza bey** family and other family members fled to Shkoder. **Hamza Salih bey** and **Omer Abdulah bey** left for Shkoder and returned in 1945. In the meantime, their land was stolen. Nevertheless, **Hamza Salih bey** with his family returned to Podgorica, where they re-built their life. However,

Hamza Salih bey's daughter stayed in Albania. For a long time she could not manage to visit her relatives in her homeland because of restricted border passage from both sides, Albania and Yugoslavia. It was said that Enver Hoxha made the border crossing so tough that 'even chicken couldn't cross it'.[283]

Bahrija Haveric Bibezic, whose great-grandfather **Haji Mehmed bey** was the chief of Stara Varos, recalled:

> Our family was good with our neighbours. Our father and they drank, ate, smoked and talked together. One day, my father complained to his Vlach neighbour that he heard the Muslims would be robbed by the *komitas* in Podgorica.
>
> That neighbour said there would be no war, swearing that it would have nothing to do with them. However, in 24 hours, some Podgorica Muslims were robbed and some killed.

After all, she said:

> Haverics were bey's family, but God will grant them [again] *begovat* ['nobility'], *Inshallah.* The beys, that's what they called them. Did anyone reward them? ...[284]

Bahrija's daughter, **Hazera Haveric Repisti**, told her fragmented memories:

> I have lived in Shkoder for sixty-five years. I haven't seen Podgorica for forty-five years. I changed my last name to Repushti. I had problems with the police, as just because I changed my last name. There was a lot

of misunderstanding. Our family was separated. That's why I didn't see my father, mother, or brother when they died. It was hard to be a *jabandzija* (foreigner). In Albania is where my grandfather Sulejman bey, whom we all called 'babo', died.[285]

We have not forgotten the 'naski' (our 'nashke' authentic language Montenegrin, 'Bosnakian') language. Babo [my grandfather] always said don't forget to speak 'naski'. I cried when I listened to our songs in 'naski', I cried...[286]

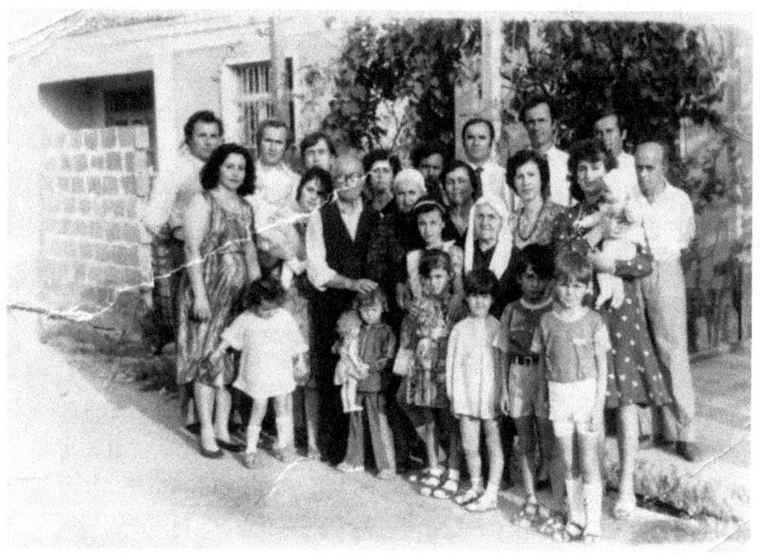

Abla Haveriku's grandparents, their children, nieces and nephews, 1991

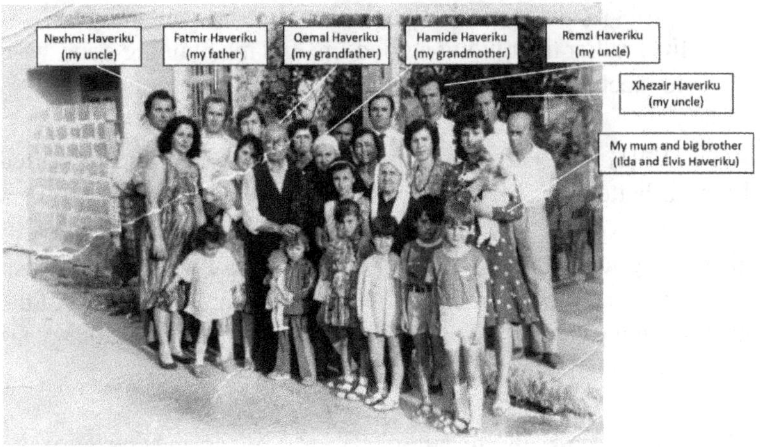

About the Haveric family in Kavaja, Albania, **Abla Haveriku** narrated:

> The **Haveriku** family in Kavaja has lived a difficult life during the communism period of 1946 to 1991. Since the brother of my grandfather, **Aqif**, a national hero, was executed during the regime, all the family members were persecuted, leading to various difficulties. My grandfather, together with his children, were not allowed to study in university or work in meaningful positions.
>
> Similar to our family, my father tells me that even Haveriku members in Durres had similar problems. Their persecution came mostly due to the fact that they previously were wealthy families or had family members who were educated outside Albania. During that time, well-educated people were negatively targeted by the regime. In our opinion, these difficulties in life have also had a negative impact on the connections between **Haveriku** members in different cities in Albania, leading

> to loss of connections. People were mostly struggling to live, rather than living a good life and maintaining good connections.

After 1991, the Haveriku family members in Kavaja started living a better life. My father **Fatmir Haveriku** and his brothers started working in constructions, owning a construction company, also trying to give a good contribution to the city. The 'Haveriku Brothers' construction firm also helped with renovating a part of the mosque in the centre of Kavaja. The Haveriku family in Kavaja has always been linked with Islam as a religion.

My father, **Fatmir**, also had the chance to graduate in law school and become a lawyer. Nowadays, for my generation finishing university seems like quite a normal thing, but at that time (especially after having been prohibited from going to university) that was quite a big accomplishment. We have been raised, hearing so many sad stories about forbidden possibilities, learning the importance of a good education and advocating for our rights.[287]

Scattered Information

Ahmet Myftar Bey Haveriqi may have been born in Podgrica before 1900; that is, before they moved to Bar (Montenegro) or Leskovac. He died young, probably around 15-16 years old, in **Leskovac (Serbia)**.

Ali Mustafa bey Haveriqi – 'little is known about him, except that he has the title 'Bey', as well as his father'. He performed a pilgrimage to Mecca, Hajj. He had three sons: **Hysen**, **Mehmet** and **Mustafa**.

Ahmet bey had two sons – **Mustafa** and **Aqif** – who were born in 1854 and two daughters – **Qamile** and **Mahije**.

Edmund Haveri's father **Yumer bey** migrated to Albania in 1954, when there were already a number of Haverics in Shkoder, Kavaja and Durres.

Agim Qazim Haverik was born in Durres. He graduated from a high school for biochemistry in Tirana. Most of the time, he worked as an educator in the district of Durres, such as Rrushkull-Xhafzotaj Freme, in the Vorroza of Kavaje, while the last 6 years in the schools D'lip Tabaku and Mother Teresa as a school principal. He was a former member of the Durres leadership for education problems.

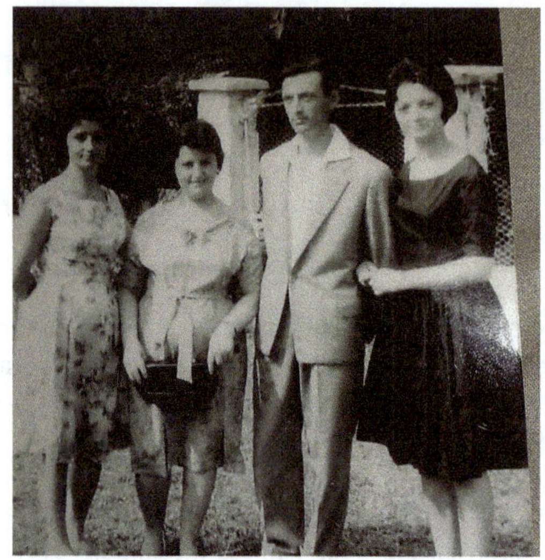

Meri Haveri in Shkoder

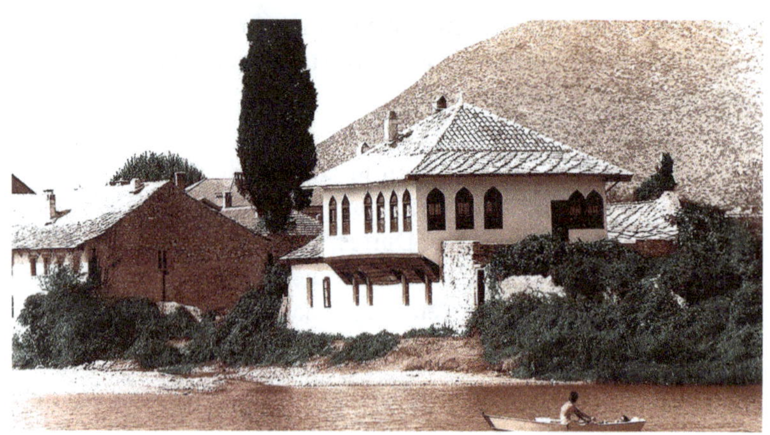

Bey's house, Trebinje

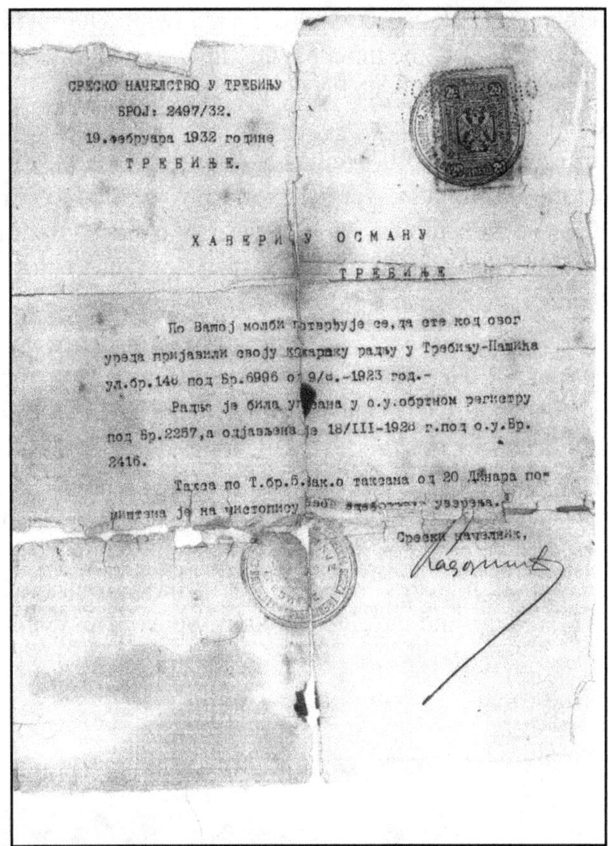

СРЕСКО НАЧЕЛСТВО У ТРЕБИЊУ
БРОЈ: 2497/32.
19. фебруара 1932 године
Т Р Е Б И Њ Е.

Х А В Е Р И Ћ У О С М А Н У
Т Р Е Б И Њ Е

По Вашој молби потврђује се, да сте код овог уреда пријавили своју кожарску радњу у Требињу-Пашића ул.бр.148 под Бр.6996 од 9/6.-1923 год.-

Радња је била уписана у о.у.обртном регистру под Бр.2257, а одјављена је 18/III-1928 г.под о.у.Бр. 2416.

Такса по Т.бр.5.Зак.о таксама од 20 Динара поништена је на чистопису [illegible] уверења.

Срески начелник,

Osman Bey Haveric's registration of the leather business in 1923 in Pasica Street, Trebinje, Bosnia and Herzegovina, which was deregistered in 1928

In 1923, **Osman bey** was issued a decision by the Trebinje County Court for registration of a tannery shop in Pasic Street. During his life in Trebinje, **Osman bey** often travelled to Dubrovnik (Croatia), where he brought hides by train wagons from Trebinje. The trading partner was mainly the Dalmatian group ('Dalmatinska društvo') with which he and the other Haverics had fruitful cooperation. He successfully traded with Dubrovnik entrepreneurs of the time, having numerous Dalmatians and other Croats among his business partners. They were good business partners, so on one occasion **Osman bey** entrusted them with keeping a larger monetary value that these Dalmatian partners correctly returned to him. When he passed away in 1928, his shop was closed. It was said that young **Osman bey** died from tuberculosis. He never married and didn't have children.

The *Leotar* sporting club brought a special vitality to Trebinje, which at that time had about 3,000 residents. **Murat Tahir bey Haveric** played for the first team of the *Leotara Soccer Club* in 1925. That year, after the precondition of a few matches played in Dubrovnik, this club was officially registered and joined the 'Football Sub-Association of Sarajevo', thereby gaining the right to compete in all matches. The club got its name from the highest hill above Trebinje and the club's colours were red and white.[288]

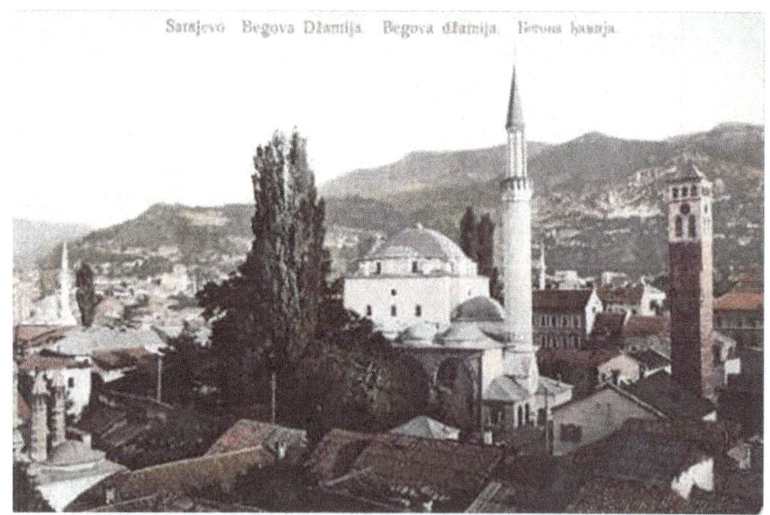

Sarajevo, the old city

Podgorica Muslims are a characteristic group which almost completely migrated to Bosnia and settled in Sarajevo. During the first years after the Second World War, there were about 2,800 of them. With an increase of about 4,200 citizens, it is estimated there were about 7,000 Sarajevo citizens in the city. Out of 114 fraternities registered in Podgorica before 1912, after the Second World War, 88 were in Sarajevo.[289]

It was primarily a result of the Second World War that a second major wave of Haveric emigration to Bosnia and Herzegovina took place. Usually, the paths were through Shkoder and many of them settled permanently in Bosnia.[290] The Haverics were an urban family. They lived in the city of Podgorica and settled in the cities, such as Sarajevo, Tirana, Istanbul and so on. In Sarajevo, they lived mainly in the old and central parts of the city, from Bascarsija to Marijn Dvor at the addresses of Ferhadija, Titova, Cobanija, Tabhana, Kralja Tomislava and Bjelave streets and near the known place of the Eternal Flame.

In the central parts, they managed trade or craft shops and enriched the social-cultural life of the city. As the city developed, families also settled in new areas, bringing their descendants.

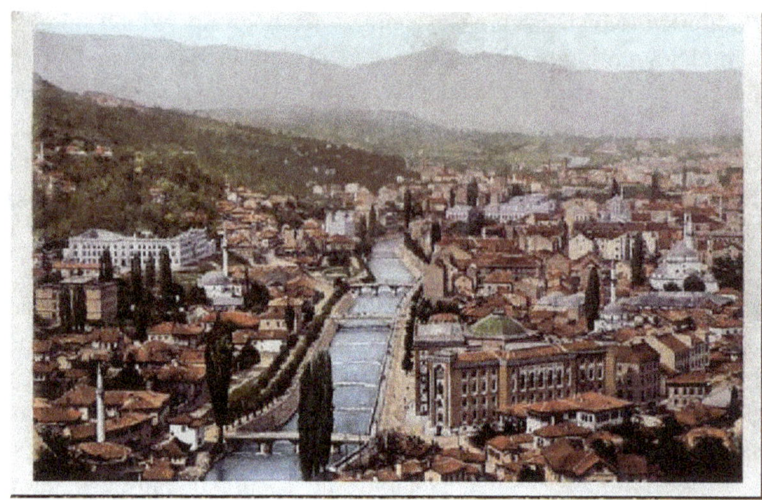

Sarajevo

Stories

Aqif Mehmet bey Haveriku (Aqif Averiku, Haveric) was born in Kavaje, Albania, in 1910. He completed the Military Academy for artillery in Italy. On the day of the graduation ceremony, **Aqif**, together with a group of Albanian officers, refused to take the oath in front of the Italian flag, with the axes of fascism. They declared before the high Italian military authorities: 'We take the oath, sitting on our knees, only in front of the flag of our Albanian nation'.

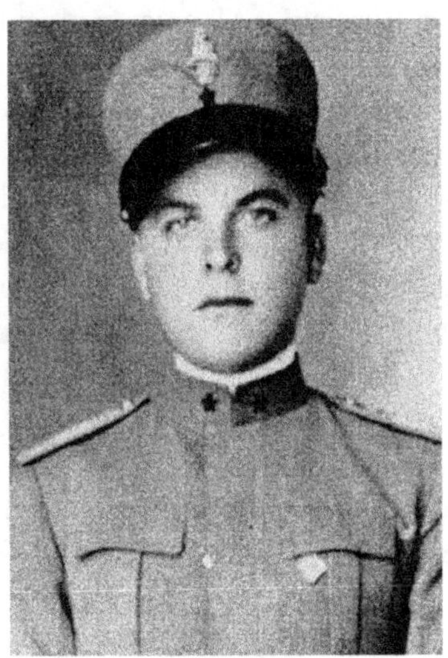

Aqif Haveriku

The heartbeat of my city Kavaja
Honorary Citizen

During the reign of King Zog I, **Aqif** committed himself to the work of strengthening and modernising the Albanian army. He worked as an officer in Kucove, Elbasan and Lezhe. He joined the group of nationalist patriots, where they fought against the Italian aggressors. In the first years of the war against fascism (1940-44), as a nationalist patriot, **Aqif** went to the mountain with a gun in hand in the Anti-Fascist National Liberation War Front. He believed in the idea put forward at the Peza Conference held on September 16, 1942, for the creation of a united front against the invaders 'without distinction of religion, region and idea'.

Since he was a loyal nationalist and patriot, he also refused to put the red star of the dictatorship on his cap: 'I am Albanian', he said, 'and not a Serb or a Russian'. 'Albanian nationalists did not accept the red star, the symbol of communism. They sought freedom and democracy', he said. Through the years 1944-46 of the Nationalist Organization Resistance Front, most activists from the Resistance Front were arrested in 1946 by the State Security and either shot or imprisoned. **Aqif** was arrested by the State Security and put in the Tirana prison, experiencing the most inhumane torture with the decision of the communist court to 'punish by firing squad'.

After a year of inhumane treatment in prison, he and a friend were sent to the fortress of Gjirokastra. Both were chained. **Aqif** refused to have his face covered with a scarf. The first gunmen's hand trembled because they were executing two innocent people. As they were threatened with death, they were replaced by another firing squad, shooting twenty-one bullets in **Aqif's** body…

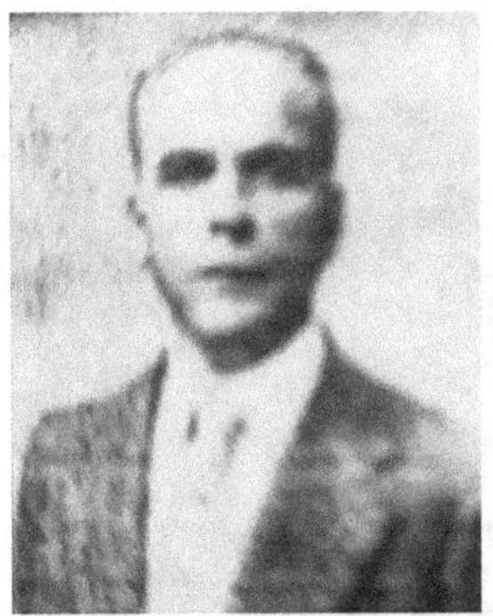

Aqif Haveriku

Aqif remains alive in the ranks of the Heroes of the Nation. A poet, Mehmet Tepelena, published some verses dedicated to **Aqif**:

Aqif Mehmed Haveriku

Twenty-one bullets hit his body
Twenty-one wounds on the Motherland!
Aqif Haveriku was exposed to the fire
Aqif Haveriku did not die, but he left!
(Mehmet Tepelena)

He was shot as an 'enemy of the people, who sought to overthrow the people's power by force'. The execution was in 1947. The whole nation mourned! **Aqif**, with the nationalists of the nation, had not committed treason. But the communist council decided the law. He is now in the list of honorary citizens in Kavaja.[291]

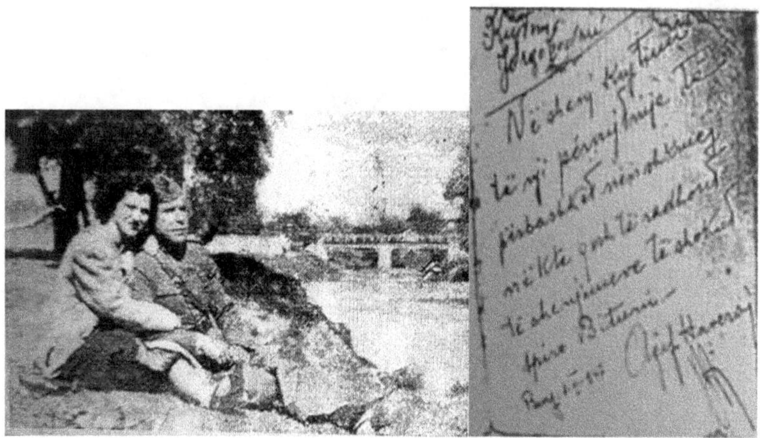

Aqif Haveriku and his wife Nafije

He married **Nafije Ulqinak**, but did not spend even a week with her before he was arrested. They kept him in prison for about nine months until they shot him in 1947. Sadly, **Aqif's** tragic fate also left behind his wife. His nice handwriting suggests he was a literate man. The patriotic Haverik family in Kavaja was hit hard by the communist dictatorship. In the democratic processes, the nephews (brother' sons) of **Aqif**, including Nexhmi Averiku, together with his brothers, were among those patriots who first moved forward with the protest for the overthrow of the dictatorship. After the victory of democracy, in 1993, the former president of the Republic, Sali Berisha, declared **Aqif** a 'Martyr of Democracy'.[292]

For their political motifs and fight for freedom, other members of the Haveriku family experienced difficulties from the totalitarian reign. For instance, the Archive of Victims of Communism listed **Mehmet Haveriku**, **Rudin Mehmed Haveriku** with residence in Kavaje, **Alma Mehmet Haveriku** with residence in Tirana and **Xhemal Shyqyri Haveriku** with residence in Durres.[293] Another victim of communism was **Fahrija (Ramadan) Haveriku**.[294]

Omer Abdulah bey Haveric (1887-1960) was born in Podgorica. He was educated at the commercial academy in Vienna, Austria. He spoke Bosnian, Turkish, Greek, Albanian, Italian and German. He was married twice. His first wife was **Aisa** Hadrovic from a distinguished bey family that possessed a great *waqf* in Sandjak. They had a daughter named **Hasija**. Later, he married **Mejrema (Mejra)** Mejra-Bajraktarevic who, next to Bosnian, also spoke Turkish, Greek and Italian. **Mejra** was a great-granddaughter of Ferhat bey, a flagbearer from Podgorica and daughter of Mustafa bey Bajraktarevica. **Omer** and **Mejra** had two sons, **Dzavit** and **Halit**, and a daughter, **Muvedeta (Deta)**. Mejra had two daughters, Hanifa and Hajrija, from her first marriage.[295]

Omer bey Haveric was interested in the cultural history of his people and always emphasised the authentic origin of the Bosnian Muslim people (*Bosniaks*), as well as the genealogy of the Haveric family, saying 'we are natives of the Balkans and that as Bogomils we accepted Islam long before the 15th century'. He was not only an intellectual and polyglot, but a successful merchant and landowner. **Omer bey** developed his commercial entrepreneurship not only in Podgorica, but also in different areas of the Balkans and beyond. He had trade relations with many foreign partners, which promoted his trading skills and knowledge of several foreign languages.[296]

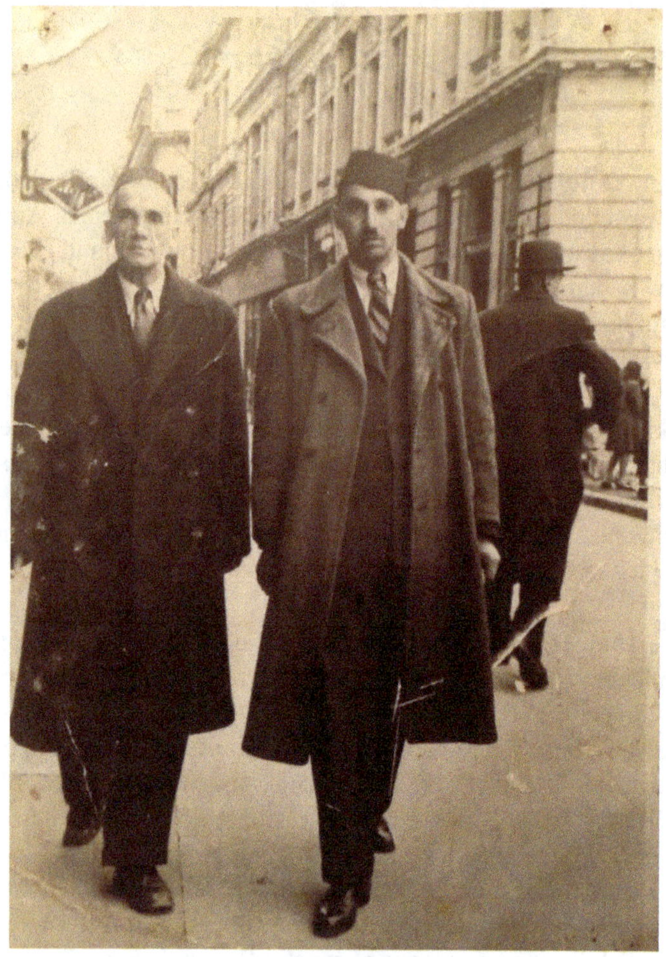

Omer bey and Rizah bey Haveric in Vienna, Austria, 1920

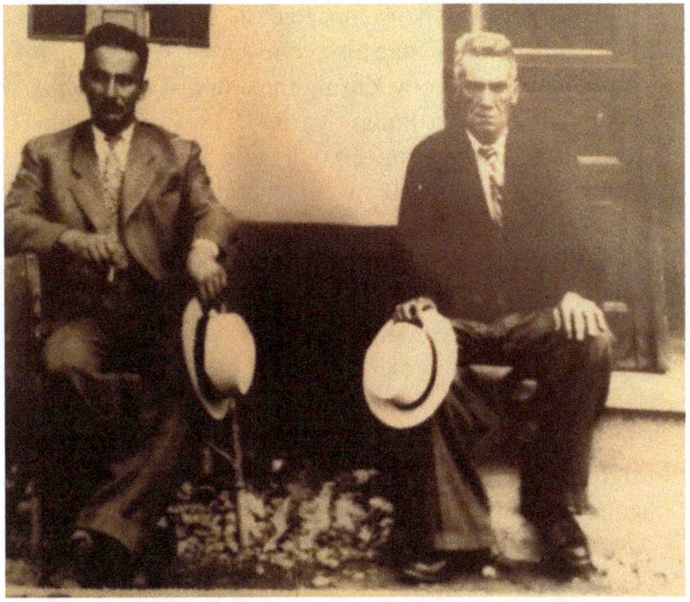

Omer bey Haveric (right) with Rizah bey Haveric partners in the late 1930s and early 1940s, Ancona or Bari, Italy

He imported large quantities of so-called colonial goods (mixed goods, textiles and fabrics). While the smaller part he distributed to Montenegro and Albania, the majority of goods he dispatched were to Serbia, Hungary, Romania, Bulgaria and Greece. Being always a stylish man, he wore a Panama hat in Italy.

> **Omer bey** Haveric had a large property in the Zeta Valley to the Lake Shkoder. He owned several shops and a publishing house. In 1924, during the agrarian reform implemented by the Kingdom of Serbs, Croats and Slovenes (1918–1929), 1,350,000 m^2 of orchards and vineyards in the part of Zeta Valley were taken from him.

> **Omer Bey**'s warehouse located in the port of Bar, goods and vehicles were also confiscated. According to **Omer bey**'s testimony, during the entry of the Serbian occupying army in Podgorica in 1918, it confiscated (read stolen) from him 60,000 gold coins (zlatnika) of 12.5 grams. Those were mainly the so-called French *napoleons* (after Napoleon, a French emperor and military commander) and the so-called *sorvana* (after Franz Josef, an Emperor of Austria and King of Hungary). The estimated value of that gold is in the current value of approx. 35-40 million USD.
>
> During the 22 years of the existence of the Kingdom of Yugoslavia, **Omer bey** was able to earn a great fortune again. In 1943, fleeing to Shkoder from the Chetnik *kama*, he took a 20-liter container of oil full of gold coins…[297]

Using professional calculations, his grandson, Dr Enver Backovic, an expert from the Faculty of Economics in Sarajevo, concluded: 'The sum is impressive, but the mathematics shows so!' Omer wrote the records for these amounts personally. 'This was told to me by **Dzavit**, son of **Omer bey**, who at the time was 17 years old and personally helped his father packing his things to flee to Shkodra, Albania'.

While young, **Omer bey** was active in cultural life in Podgorica. Along with the establishment of the cultural society *Čitaonice* ('Reading room') Muslim youth, artisans, merchants and workers founded the Muslim entertainment and singing association *Podgorica*, which included a choir and tambura orchestra. Ideas for the establishment of reading rooms were given by educated people, including ulema, and material resources were provided by rich merchants and landowners. Financial support was given by the wealthy merchant, **Omer bey Haveric**. At a similar time, **Omer bey** also 'founded his publishing house in the centre of Podgorica' whose print material, such as postcards, were distributed in different parts of the Balkans. Over the door of his large store was written his name in Latin and Cyrillic scripts as it was welcome to all residents.[298] After the war, he became frail and passed away in 1960. He was buried in the old Pobrezje Cemetery, Podgorica.[299]

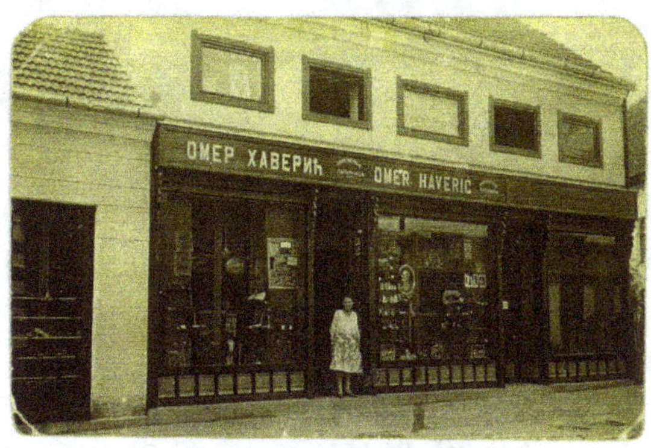

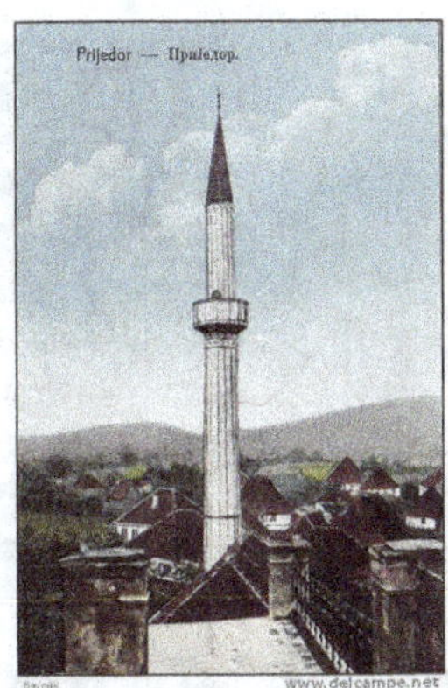

The shop belonging to Omer bey Haveric, Podgorica
Postcard of Prijedor Mosque, on the back is written 'Naklada (company) Omer Haveric', 1927/32

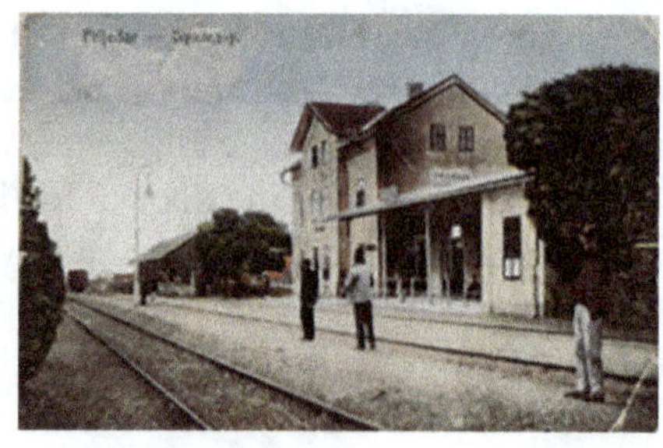

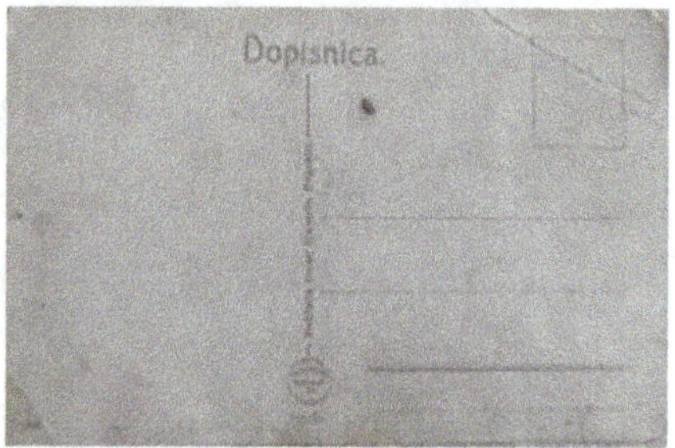

**A postcard of the railway in the city of Prijedor,
on the back is written 'Naklada (company) Omer Haveric'**

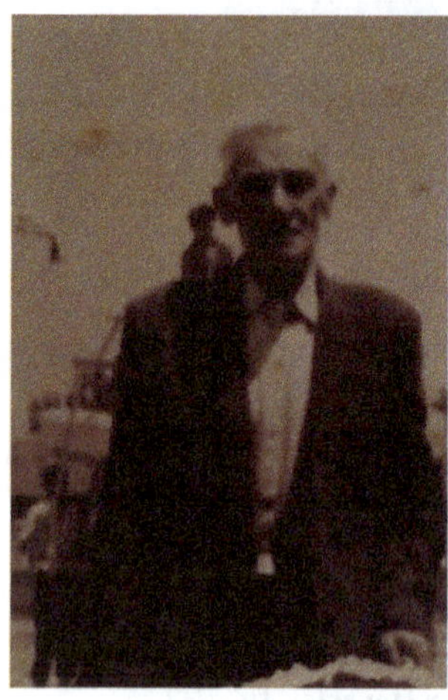

Omer bey Haveric in 1947-8

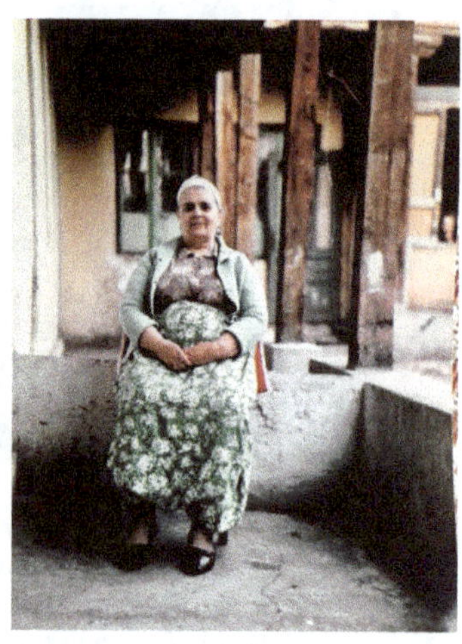

Mejra Bajraktarevic Haveric

Muvedeta Deta Haveric married Dr Murat Backovic, a prominent university professor, businessman and leading representative of an international Yugoslav company, 'Sipad'. He is mentioned in several books, including *Bosnian Muslims in Australia* by Dzavid Haveric.

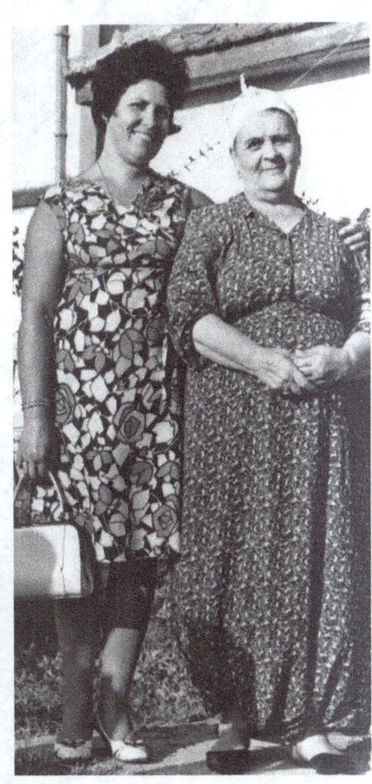

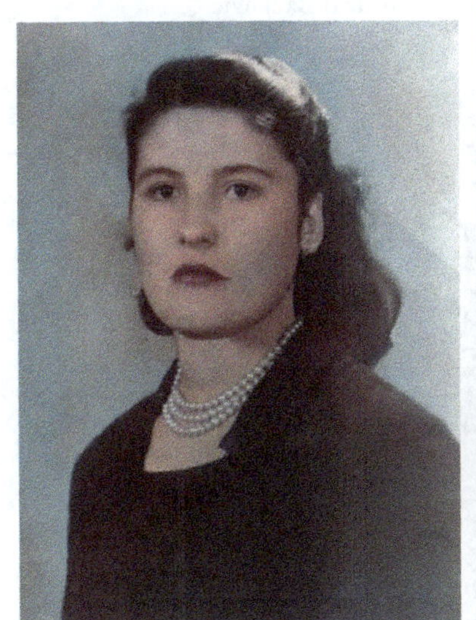

Muvedeta Deta Haveric
Deta with her mother Merjema, Omer bey's second wife

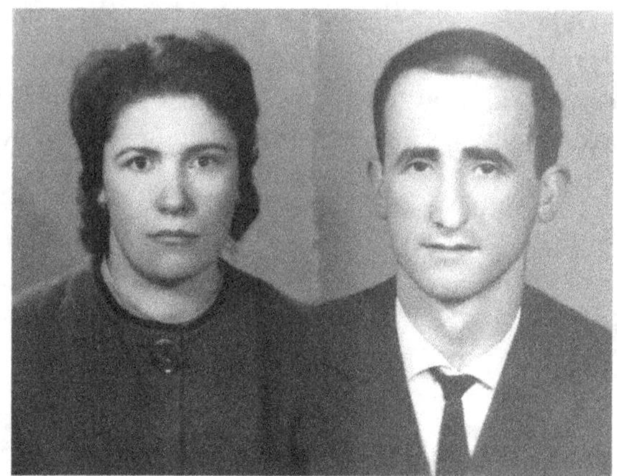

Deta Haveric Backovic and Murat Backovic

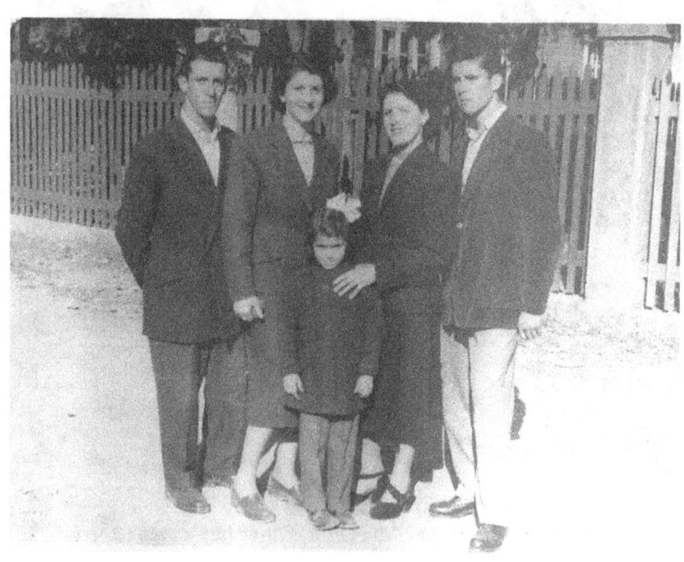

Dzavit, Hanifa (sister), Muvedeta (Deta) and Halit Haveric. The girl is a daughter of Hanifa and Serif Kabaši. (Serif Kabasi was a high officer of King Zog and the husband of Hanifa Haveric)

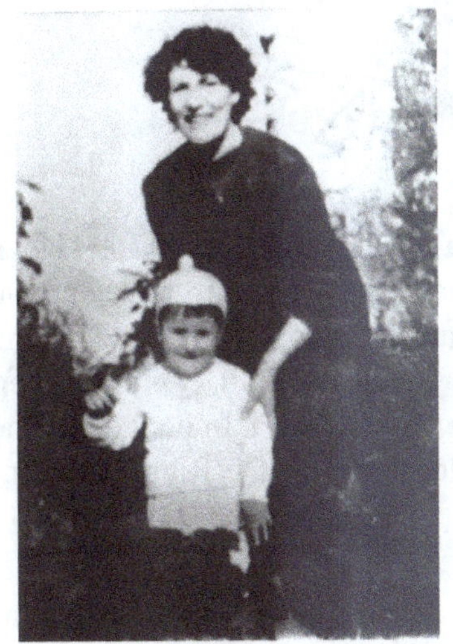

Zaim, Murat, Deta

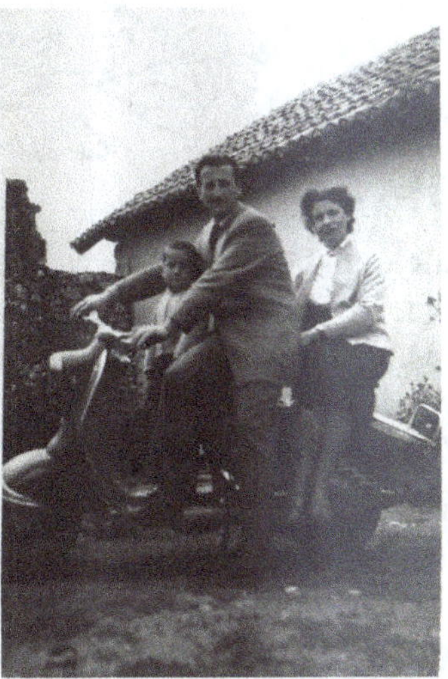

Zaim with his mother Deta

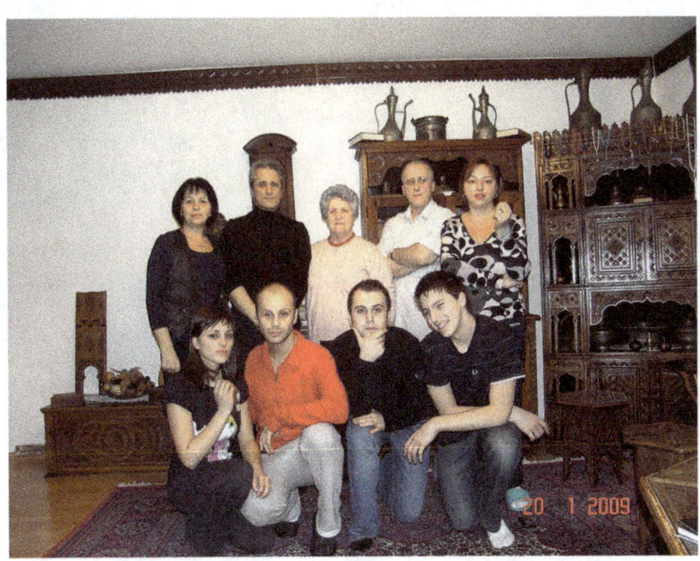

Deta with her sons, Zaiam and Enver, daughters-in-law, Sabina and Humica, and her grandchildren Adna, Deen, Faris and Adin

Sulejman bey, a son of **Hasan Kadi**, married **Hanifa** (Fife) Hadzic, originally from Spuz. After the marriage, **Sulejman bey** continued to work for some time as an imam in Dinose Mosque. They had several children: **Rizah**, **Hasan (Cano)**, **Fetah (Feto)**, **Zenepa (Zepe)**, **Sebilja**, **Mejrema (Mera)** and **Bahrija**. In Podgorica, they lived in a house near the shop, located near the Ribnica River, a branch of the Moraca River.

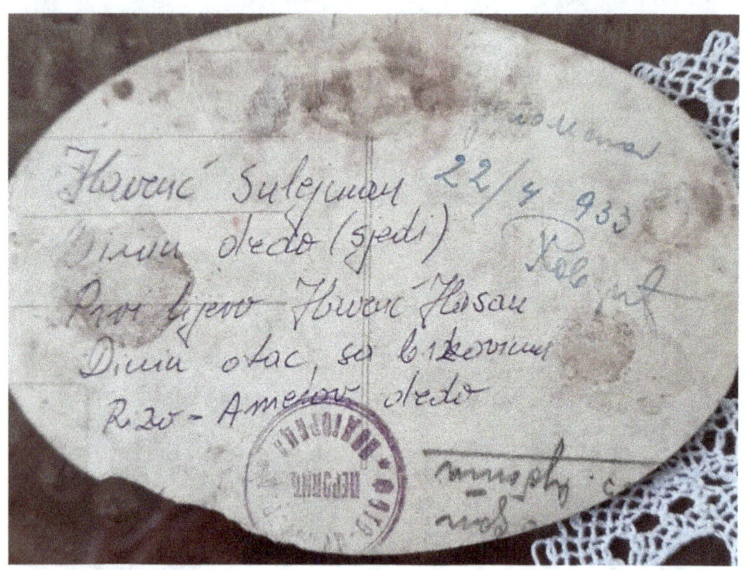

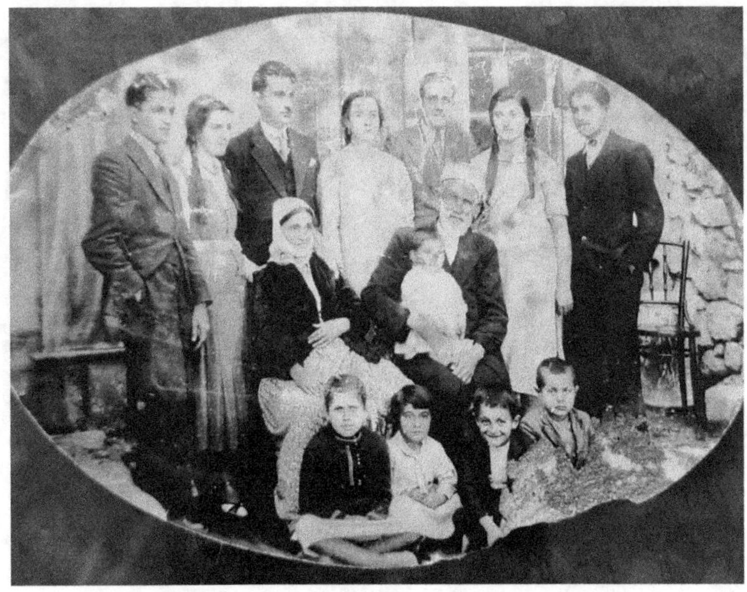

Sulejman Bey with family in Podgorica, 1933

Sitting on the chairs are:

Sulejman bey Haveric, his wife Hanifa and granddaughter Hazera (daughter of eldest son Rizah) on his lap

Top row from left to right:

Hasan (Cano), then unmarried, next to him an unknown woman, Rizah (Rizo) and next to him his wife Havusa (née Osmanagic), then a male friend whose name is unknown, next to him the youngest daughter of Sulejman bey, Bahria who later married Mustafa Bibezic, the other older daughters were married and are not in this picture, the last in the top row is the youngest son Fetah (Feto) then unmarried

Row of four children:

The smiling boy is Sadulah (Sado), Rizah's eldest son. On his left is sister Camila (Caka), Rizah's daughter. The children on the side are probably the grandchildren of Suleiman's older daughters Zejneb, Mejrema (Mera), Sebilja and Bahrija

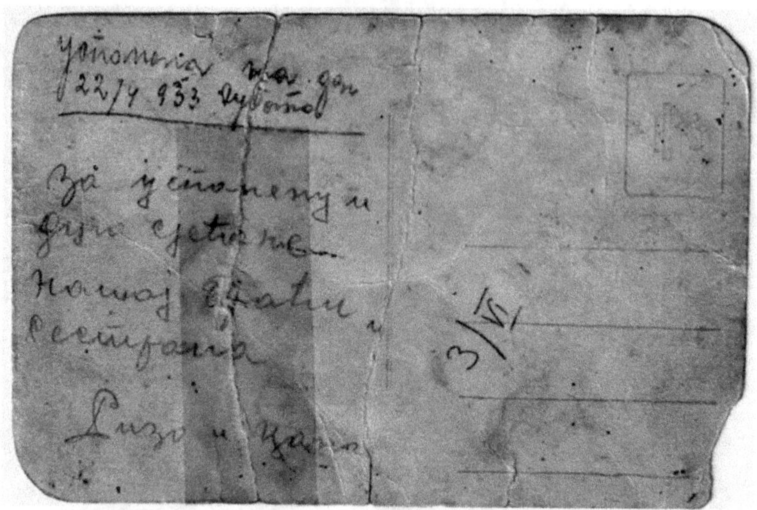

Rizo and Cano wrote on the back of the card: In memory and long remembrance of our brothers and sisters, 1933

Rizah (Rizo) Sulejman bey Haveric (1898-1978) lived in old Podgorica in a large house. His wife was **Havusa** Osmanagic and they had three sons, **Sadulah**, **Ruzdija** and **Zijad**, and three daughters, **Fadila, Camila** and **Hazera**. Not far away was the green wall of the old Podgorica where the house was located. When **Rizah** was a young boy:

> At that time, there was no washing machine in the house, so they hired a woman to fetch water and wash clothes in the Ribnice River. Jellusha (probably, Jelica) had a name. She loved **Rizah** and respected him, and he respected her, too. The house was near the river, close to go to wash clothes.

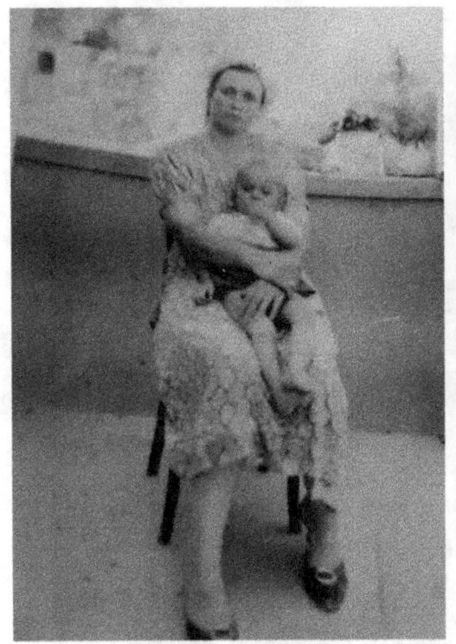

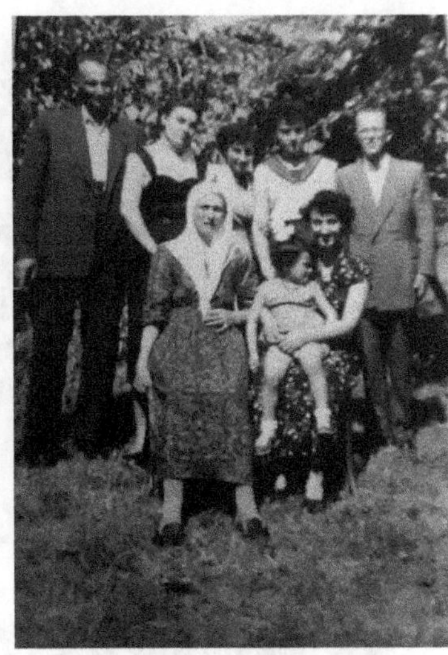

Rizo's wife Havusa with daughter
Rizah, Fadila, Hazera, Zijad and Hazera's husband, Ruzdija Repyshti. Rizahs's wife Havusa Osmanagic with daughter Camila and granddaughter Zana

Rizah bey was a successful merchant and manager of a store selling coffee, flour, textiles and so on. He was a learned man and spoke several languages. He was also mentioned by Mustafa Memic 'as a wealthy merchant from Podgorica'.[300] Before moving to Sarajevo, he also lived in Shkoder. He further developed his business together with his partner **Omer bey** Haveric. They both stayed in hotels in Budapest and Vienna for business purposes. **Rizah bey** often went by himself to the Bursa in Turkiye to import textiles from the East, probably from China.[301]

Singing and playing music were the notable activities of the singing association *Podgorica*, which lasted for almost 20 years. Among the members of this society was **Rizah bey Haveric**.[302]

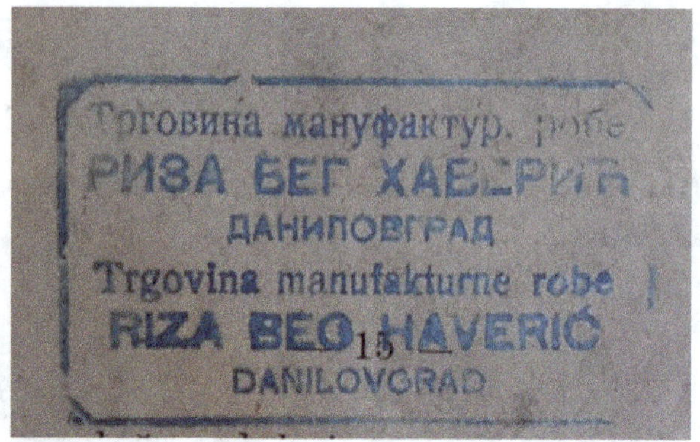

Rizah's trading shop in Danilovgrad, local newspaper advertisement

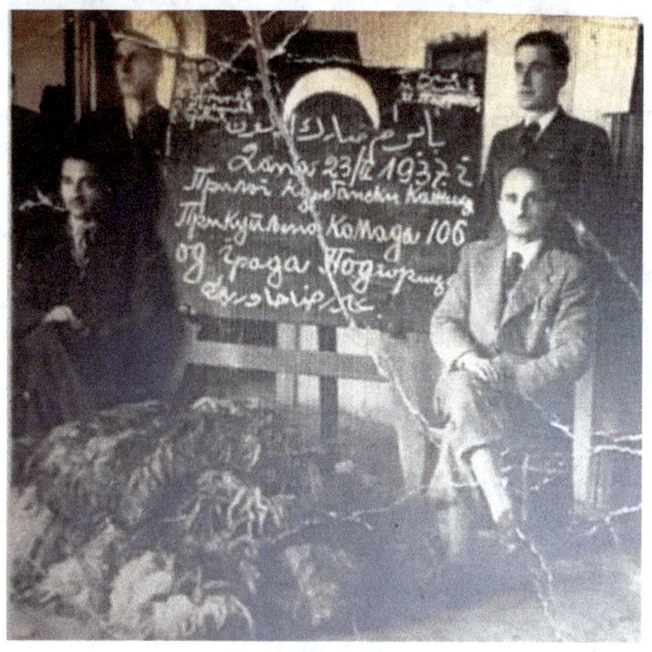

Bayram Mubarak Olsun 23.2. 1937
Contribution with the skins of sacrificial sheep
Collected 106 pieces [of sheepskin] from the city of Podgorica
Ali Rizah Haveric

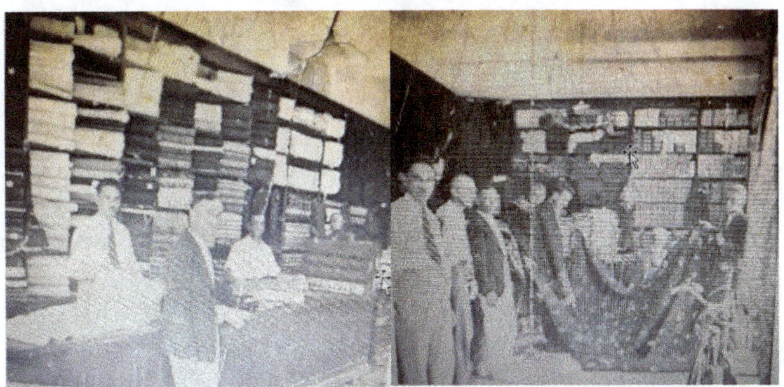

Textile store run by Omer bey and Rizah bey Haveric, Shkoder

Omer bey and **Rizah bey** owned a textile shop in Shkoder. In the mid-1940s, Rizah Bey managed the shop. Omer Bey was sick at that time; he was lying unwell at home. In 1943, Rizah bey and Omer bey invested a lot of money into purchasing textile goods in Italy and to transport it by two Italian ships. When the ships sailed near the Port of Durrse, the enemies torpedoed and sunk it. Although they insured the goods with insurance company *Banco di Napoli*, which also monitored the transport, the losses incurred were not reimbursed because, according to the contract, 'war causes were not covered by the insurance'.[303]

When the Second World War ended, **Rizah bey** returned to his native Podgorica to visit his relatives. There he learned about the tragic fate of his friend, Vaso Kalezic, a respectable resident of Danilovgrad and a café owner with whom he maintained fraternal relations and friendship. Vaso was interned in Albania because his son, Radovan, otherwise a judge, fought against the occupiers and was the first political commissar of liberated Danilovgrad in 1941. He asked **Rizah bey** to find his father's grave in Albania and, if necessary, renew it so that it would not be forgotten. Returning to Shkoder, **Rizah bey** searched for Vaso's grave in the military cemetery, which he managed to find in the overgrown grass with a crooked cross with almost erased words on it, 'Vaso Kalezic internee, died July 1942'. With tears in his eyes, he fulfilled his friend's son wish, cleaned the grave, pulled out the overgrown grass and straightened the crooked cross. Later, from his money, **Rizah bey** brought crafters and materials to build a modest grave for his friend as an act of kindness and respect. He also wrote the following lines:

Dear uncle Vaso
You are far from everyone,
But there is hope again,
From the cradle of your family
I am from Kalezic,
Blood cannot be water,
So, I visited my uncle
I give you your son's greetings…[304]

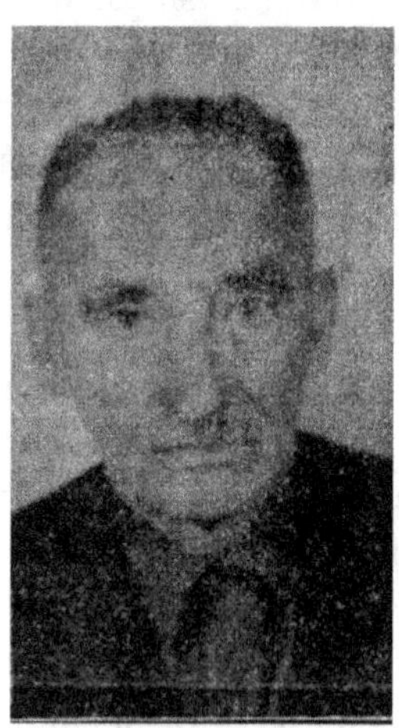

Rizah bey Haveric

Rizah bey spent the last years of his life in Sarajevo, where he earned a pension. **Rizah bey** was an interesting personality, a 'living lexicon about Montenegro, especially about his native Podgorica, its people, events and anecdotes'. He spent the days of his retirement with his family, relatives and friends where, as he said, he 'tied the ship to the shore after many stormy years'. As a pensioner, he always liked to move around, visiting friends and relatives, such as **Sefket** Haveric and his two workers at Sefket's tailor shop. Elderly **Rizah bey** came every morning and afternoon to tell them about the past times of Montenegro and his anecdotes. Before telling his stories, he often flipped through his old books to remind himself, so he wrote down what he needed on paper. Sometimes, he brought his little books to talk to all visitors who come to Sefket's tailor store. In the store, he also often recited a few poems, witticisms or jokes he wrote up until the last days of his life in 1978.[305] His wife, **Havusa**, passed away in 1960.

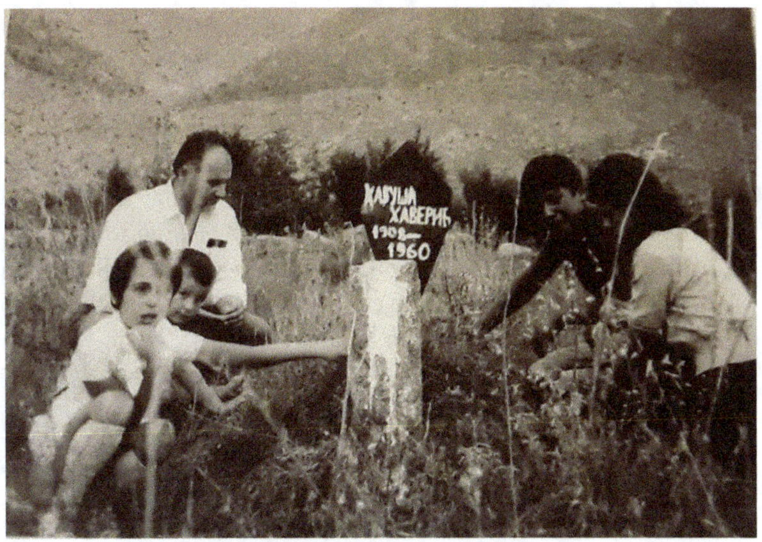

Havusa (Osmanagic) Haveric's grave

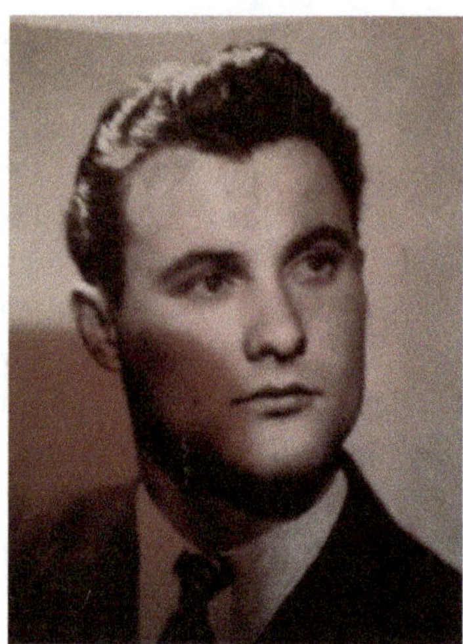

Sadulah Sado Haveric

Sadulah (Sado) Rizah bey Haveric left Podgorica for Albania and came to Sarajevo in 1946/7 to avoid military service in Albania. In Sarajevo, he met **Dzemal Tahir bey Haveric** and stayed for a while at his address. **Sado** was a dentist and married **Madzida** Rasidagic, a master of math and science, an assistant at the Faculty of Natural Sciences and Mathematics in Sarajevo. Their son **Amer was** a businessman in the US, who graduated from the Faculty of Economics, Sarajevo. He married **Alma** Ablakovic, who also graduated from the Faculty of Economics, Sarajevo. Sado and Madzida's daughter, **Amela** Haveric Imamovic, graduated (Mr.Ph) from the Faculty of Pharmacy in Sarajevo.[306]

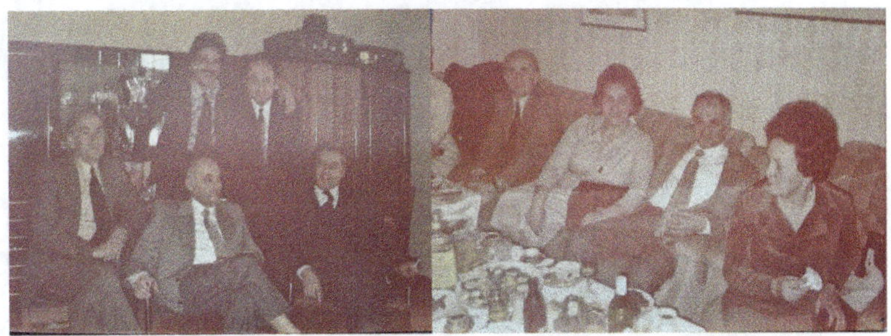

Becir, Sado, Ruzdija **Becir Zaganjor, Fadila, Sado and Madzida Haveric**

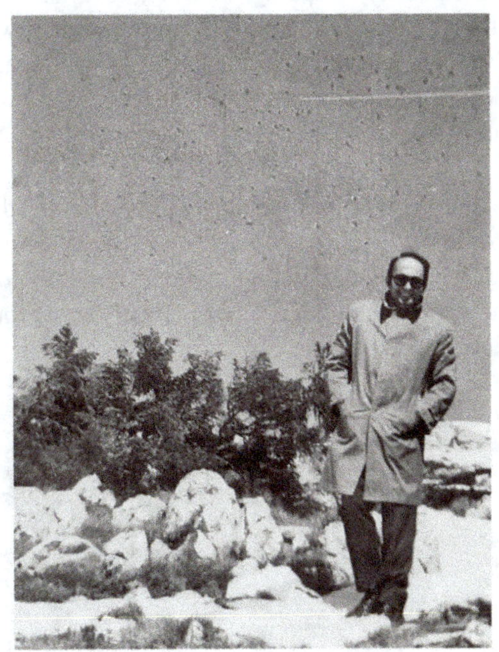

Ruzdija Haveric (Emir's photo)

Lejla Haveric Sejdic, a lawyer, and **Emir Haveric**, a professional photographer, wrote about their father, **Ruzdija (Ruzdo)**:

> In Ferhadija Street in the heart of Sarajevo our father, **Ruzdija**, worked as a manager in a large textile and cloth store 'Sarajevo Tekstil'. He loved to travel to Ljubljana, Opatija, Venice and Wienna.
>
> Although many memories have faded over the past thirty-two years, we have recalled fond moments and anecdotes. What we both remember most deeply is father's sincerity, empathy, nobility, care and endless love for us, his children. His presence and warmth have shaped us, and as parents today – Lejla, with two beautiful sons, and I, with an equally wonderful daughter – we try to be parents like he was to us.
>
> 'Love is probably the only thing in the world that doesn't need to be explained or looked for a reason' as wrote a well-known author, Meša Selimović. If one photograph can show the nature and soul of one person, it would be this picture of our father.[307]

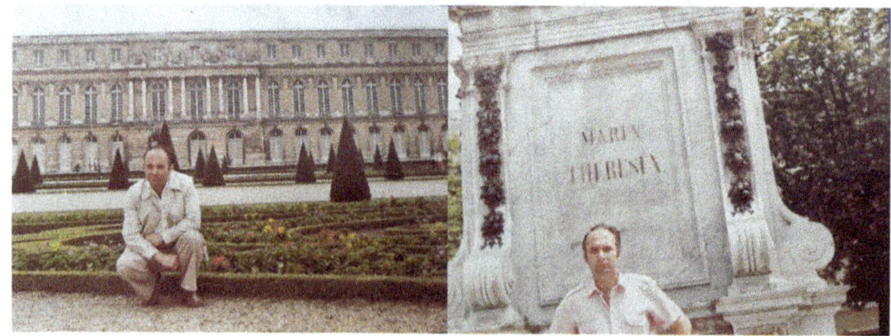

Ruzdija Haveric

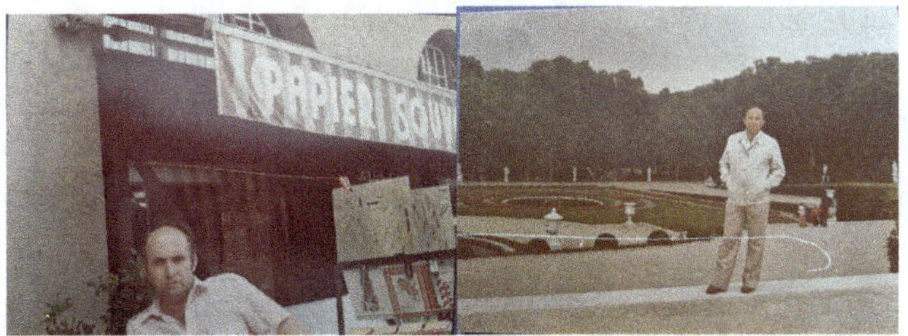

Ruzdija Haveric

Fadila Rizah bey Haveric and her brothers **Sadulah (Sado)**, **Ruzdija (Ruzdo)** and **Zijad (Zijo)** had two sisters, **Camila (Qamile)** and **Hazera**, in Albania. They were born in Podgorica. The sisters stayed in Albania in 1943. They stayed there because the Albanian President, Enver Hoxha, ordered that the borders must be closed. **Camila** (1926) came to Albania when she was 17 years old and **Hazera** (1930) was 13. **Camila** lived in Durres and **Hazera** in Shkodra. One married Sefket Ferovic in Durres and the other to Albanian Redzep Repisti in Shkodra.[308] After Enver Hoxha's death, when the open travel restriction between the Albanian and Yugoslavian borders were lifted, they came to Bosnia a couple of times. They cried with joy after meeting their brothers and sister in Sarajevo.[309]

Fadila Haveric Zaganjor, as a little girl in Podgorica narrated, 'I spilled water from the water jug when my father, **Suleiman bey**, was performing ablution, and when he finished it, he always thanks to me, "Allah has given you a reward in paradise"'.[310] **Fadila** gave a Bosnian dictionary to **Camila's** daughters from which they learned Bosnian.[311]

Fadila married Becir Zaganjor, a respected *alim* from Montenegro. They had two sons: **Nedzad**, a graduate engineer, and **Ramadan**, an Islamic teacher. Becir was the author of the first collection of *hadith* published in Bosnia and Herzegovina. It included 1,328 *hadiths* that he collected from Islamic newspaper articles and sermons in mosques. He carefully checked their authenticity and painstakingly printed it on a mimeograph ('stencil machine', sapirograf). Technically, it was a form of manual work.[312]

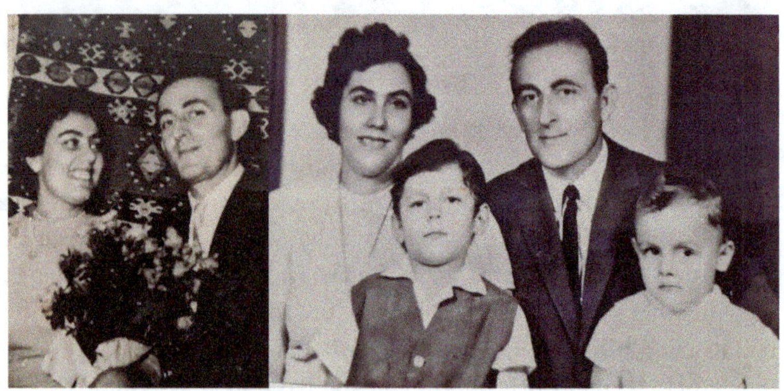

Fadila Haveric and Becir Zaganjor Fadila, Becir, Nedzad and Ramadan

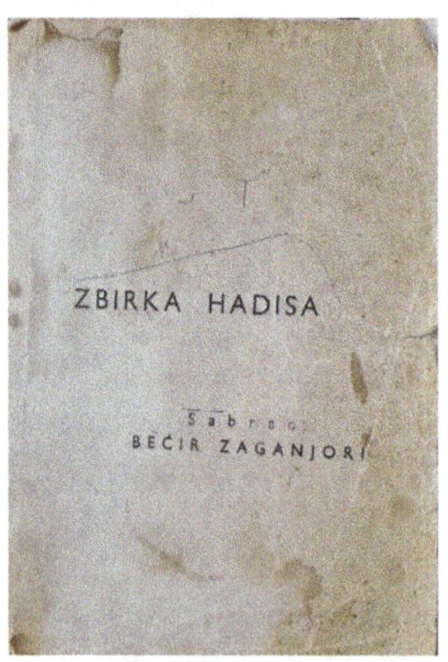

Collection of Hadiths, 1973

Camila (Qamile) Haveric was born in 1926. She married Sefket Ferovic, with whom she had two daughters, **Djana** and **Zana**. Djana Osmanagaj lived in Shkoder and her sister Zana Burgija lived in Durres. The sisters were told they are as beautiful as 'Miss Albania'.[313] Camila and Fadila' sister, **Hazera** Haveric, was born in 1930. She married Ruzdi Repyshti. They did not have children.

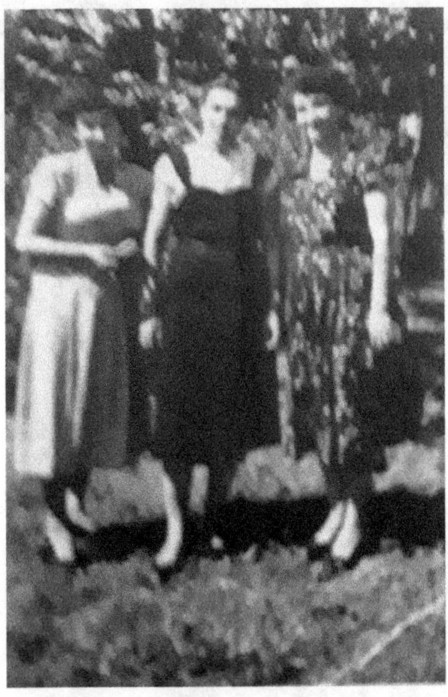

Haveric sisters: Camila (left), Fadila (middle) and Hazera (right)

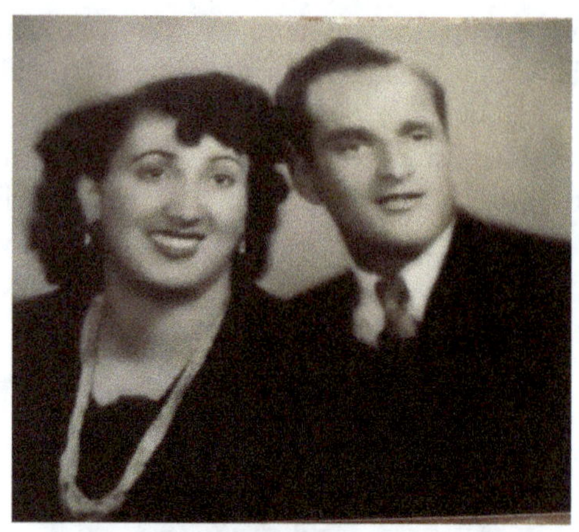

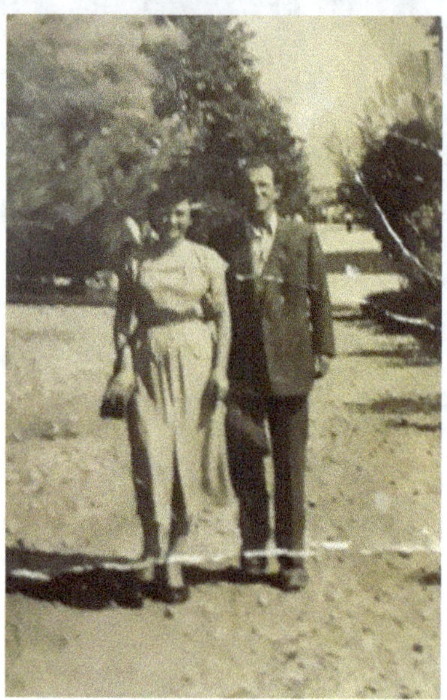

Hazera and her husband Ruzdija Repyshti in Shkoder

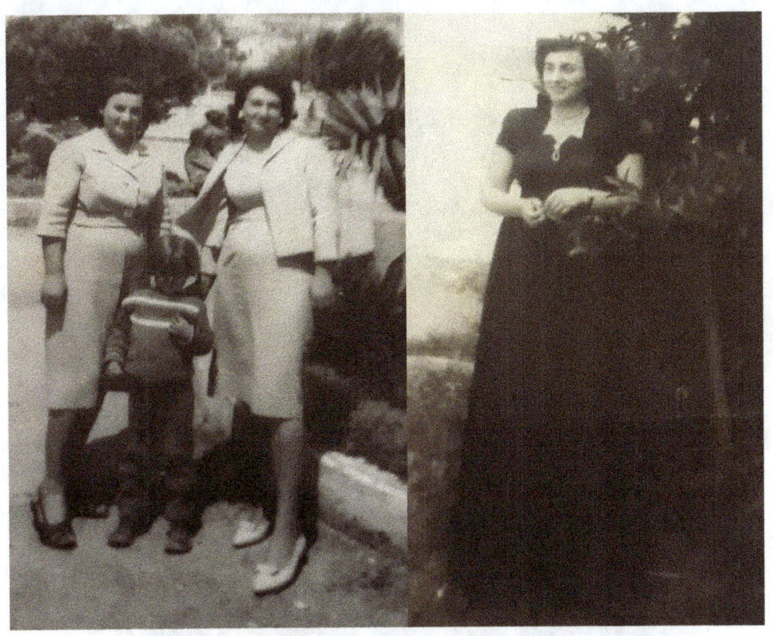

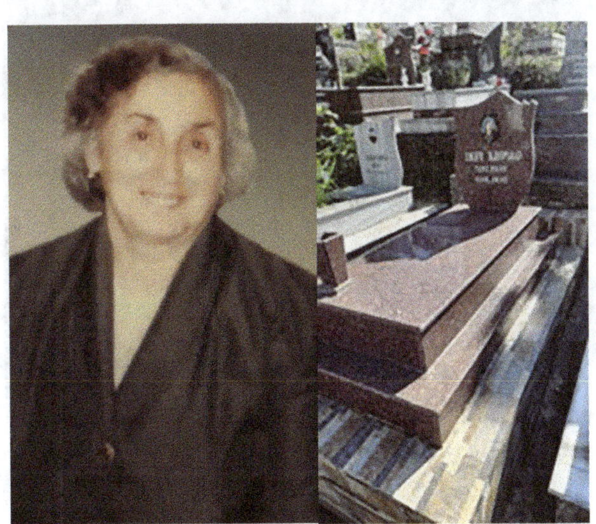

Qamile Haveric Feri (Camila Ferovic) **Qamile Feri's grave**

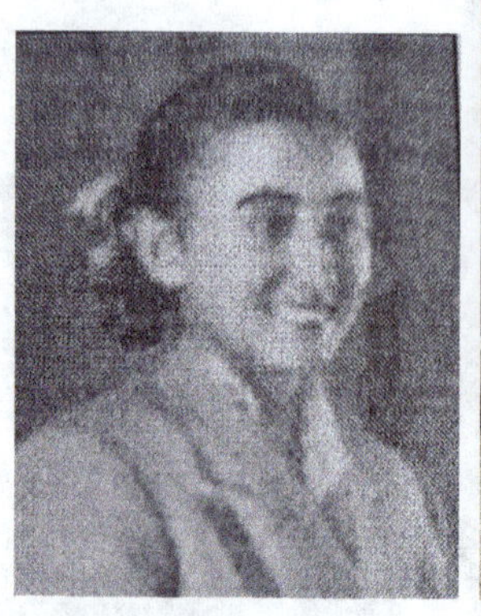

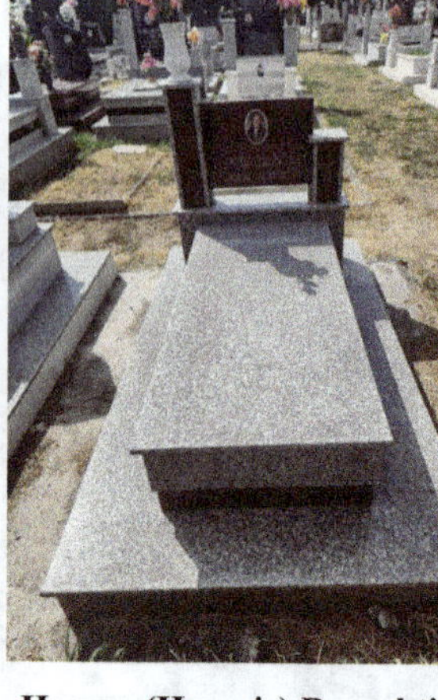

Hazera Haveric **Hazera (Haveric) Repyshti**

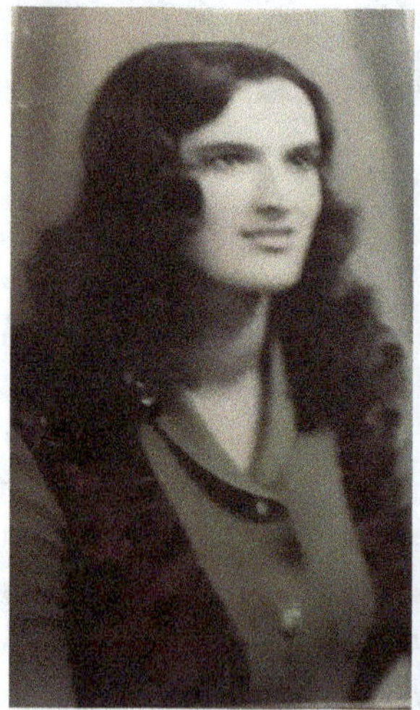

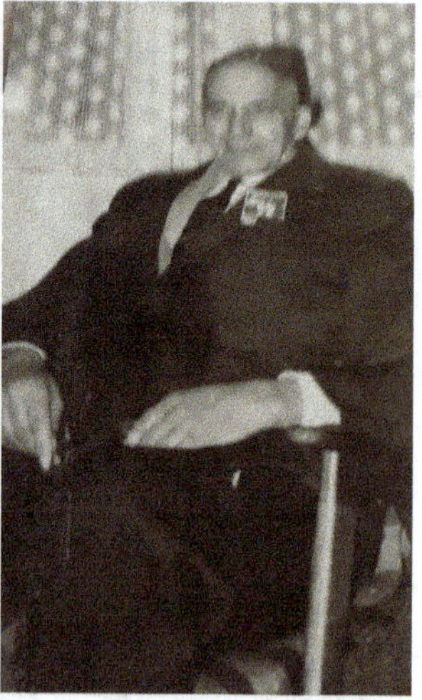

Djana Haveric Osmanagaj and her grandfather Rizo Haveric
Rizo and Havusa had two daughters and two granddaughters (Zana and Djana)

Hasan Sulejman bey Haveric was born in Podgorica and was named after great-grandfather **Hasan** who was a *kadi.* As a young man, **Hasan (Cano) Haveric** took part in the traditional performances of Gajret's (a cultural society established in 1903) choir celebrating cultural and religious holidays in the central Glavatovića Mosque for special events attended by numerous distinguished personalities and cultural representatives from other religions.[314] It was said, '*Gajret*'s choir was part of the same name cultural and educational society which had a number of established members, among whom was young **Hasan (Cano) Haveric**'.[315] Thus, like some other Haverics, he contributed to the local cultural life through choir singing in traditional Muslim costume.

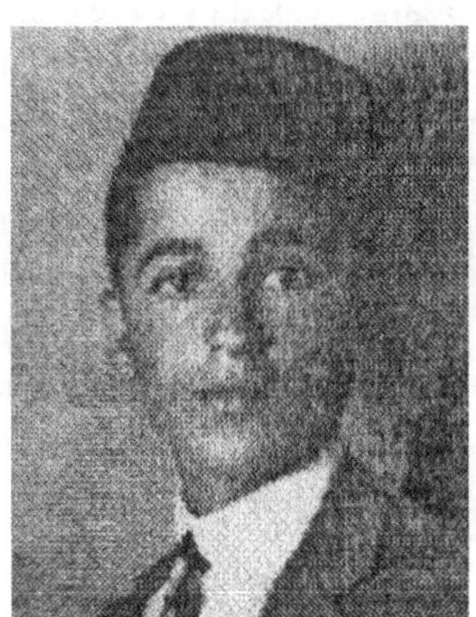

Hasan (Cano) Haveric

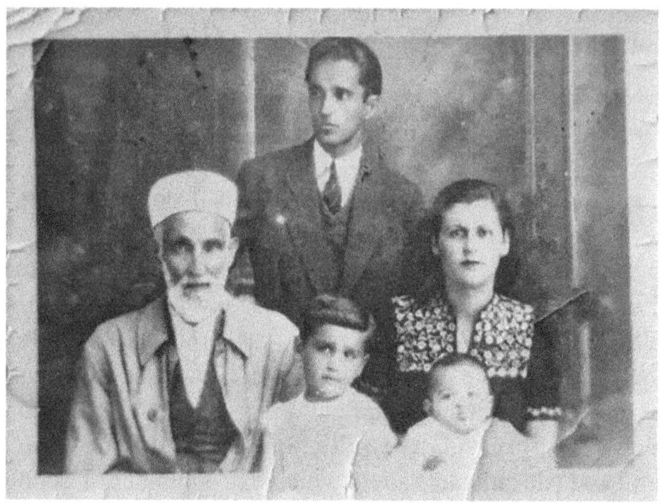

Sulejman bey, Hasan, Fahrija i Rifat Haveric, Shkoder, 1954

Hasan (Cano) married **Fahrija** in 1943, who was also born in Podgorica, and in the same year, they were expelled from Podgorica to Shkoder, Albania. They were the parents of **Semsudin**, **Rifat**, **Zineta** and **Munevera**, all born in Shkoder. **Hasan** worked as a tailor and **Fahrija** was a housewife and seamstress. In 1957, they moved from Shkodra to Sarajevo. In Ferhadija Street, Sarajevo, **Hasan** worked in a textile and men's clothing shop called 'Uzor'.[316] **Hasan** died in 1994 in Sarajevo, buried in curcica Mosque in the old city. **Fahrija** passed away in 2003 and was buried in the Bare Cemetery.

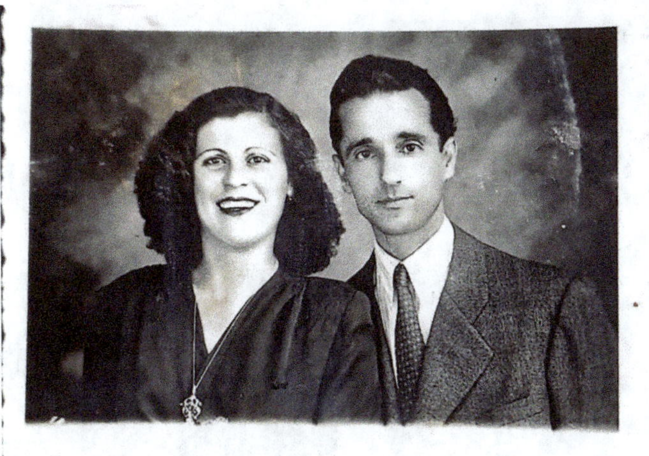

Fahrija with Hasan (Cano)

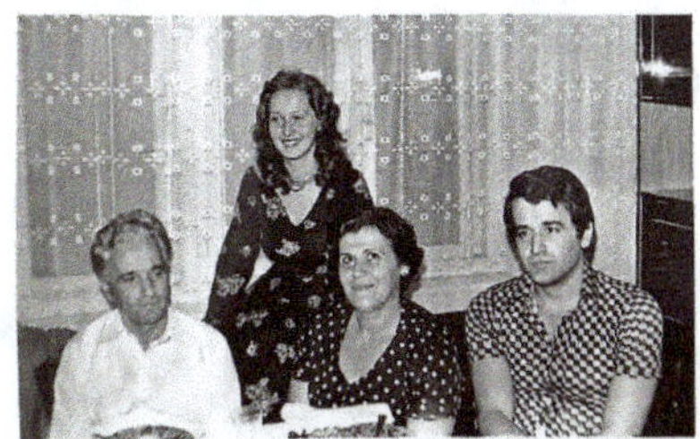

Hasan, Fahrija, Aida and Semsudin, 1974

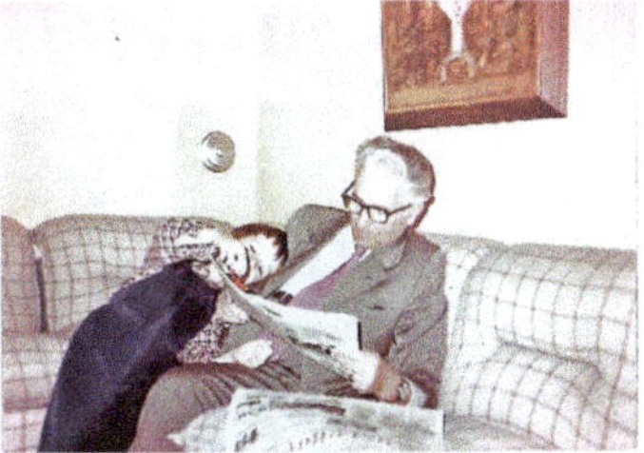

Hasan with grandson Adnan

Semsudin (Dino) Haveric graduated in architecture. His successful career as an architect was evident in his projects in Yugoslavia, Italy, Russia and Iraq. He worked for the well-known companies 'LIK' and '**Sipad**' Sarajevo. In his youth, he played handball in Ilidza.

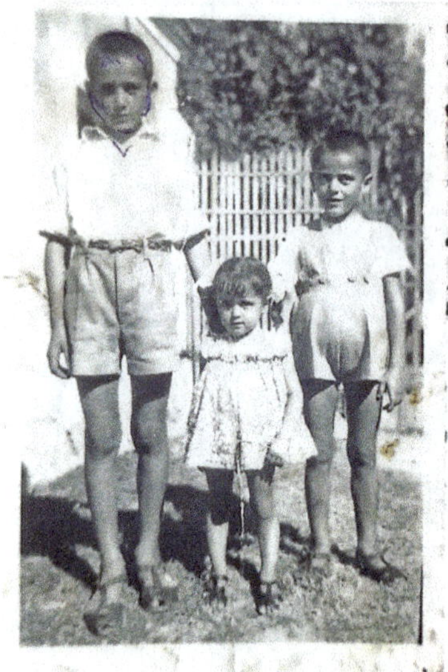

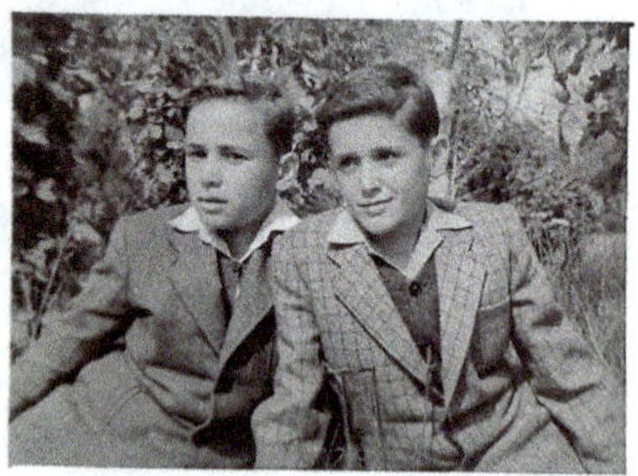

Semsudin (Dino), Rifet with Zineta (Dinka), Albania, 1954
Semsudin (Dino) (right) with friend Pjerino, Albania, 1954

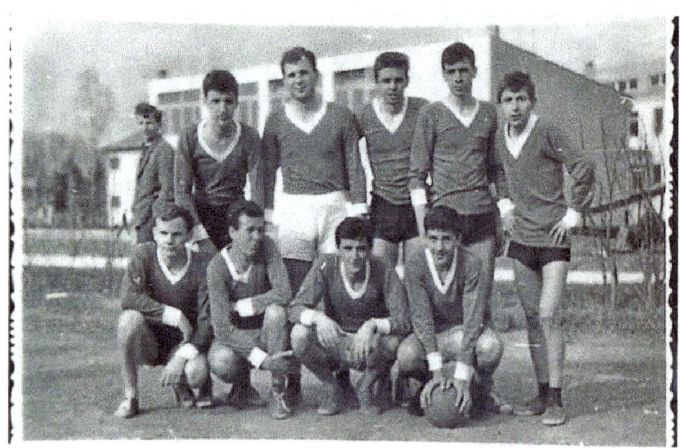

Dino Haveric, Rukometasi, Ilidza, Sarajevo, 1973

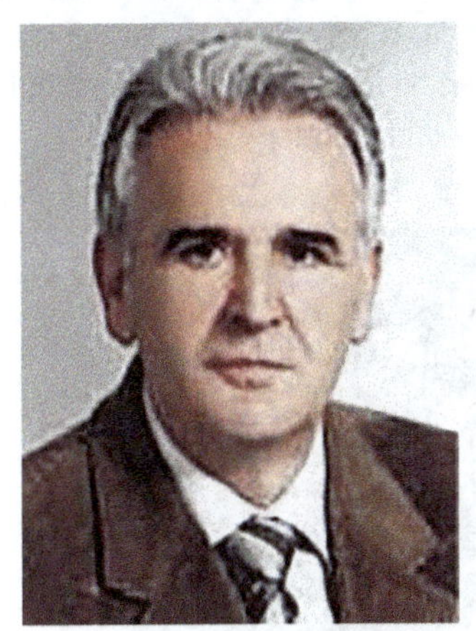

Semsudin Dino Haveric

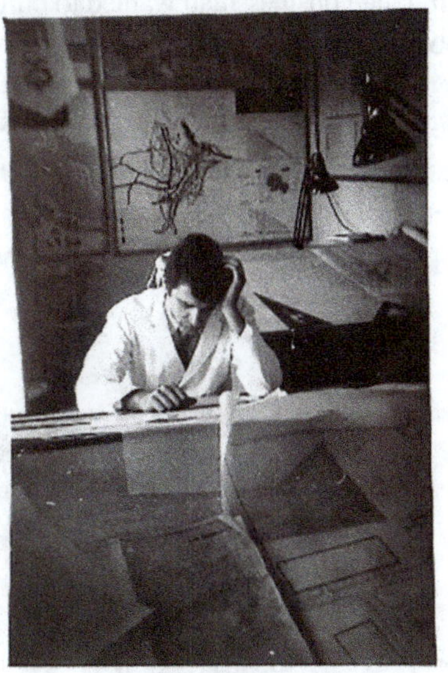

Architect Dino in his studio

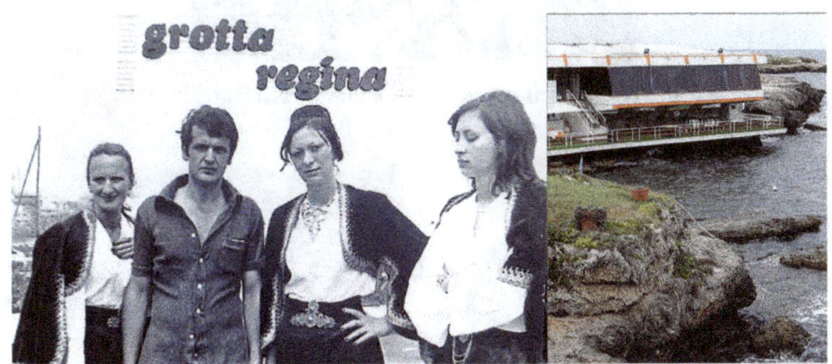

Dino with Bosnian folk group, Bari, Italy Hotel, Grotta Regina, Bari, Italy

An Italian businessman wanted to build a hotel on the rocks, which would look like an anchored ship. The hotel was a wedding gift to his daughter. **Semsudin** was the chief designer. He spent a year in Bari working on the project, whose contractor was a Bosnian company 'LIK'. Since the designer and contractor were from Bosnia, it was decided that the girls from Bosnia and Herzegovina in Bosnian national folk costumes would appear at the opening ceremony of the hotel held in 1973.

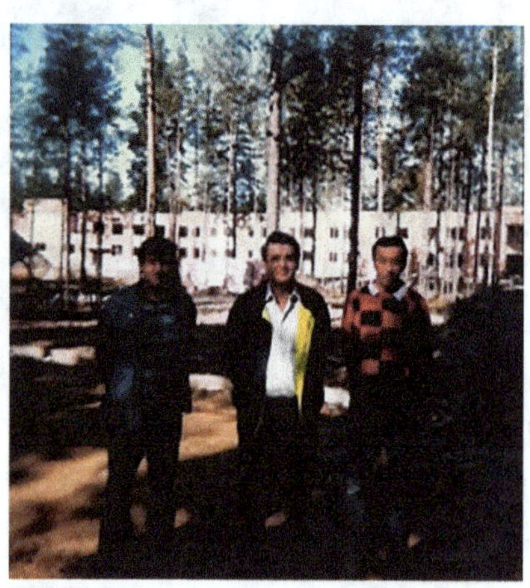

1989 residential project in the city of Kirishi, Russia

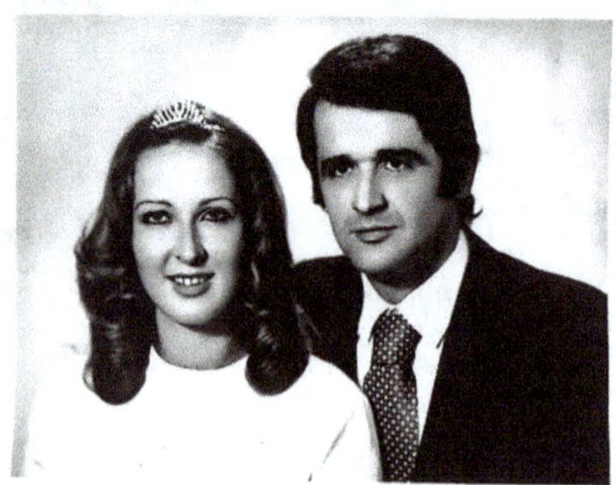

Aida Ibrahimagic Haveric and Semsudin Haveric

Dino married **Aida** Ibrahimagic Haveric in 1974. Aida graduated from the Faculty of Economics in Sarajevo. She built a successful career in the well-known publishing house, 'Svjetlost'. In 1997-2000 and 2002-2012, she held the position of Minister of Finance for the Sarajevo Canton. She also worked at the Clinical Centre of the University of Sarajevo and served as a member of the board of directors at the Institute of Health Insurance.

After finishing his career, **Dino** designed a summer house, where he spent his time. He loved fishing. He died in 2021 at the age of 77 and was buried in the city cemetery of Bare.

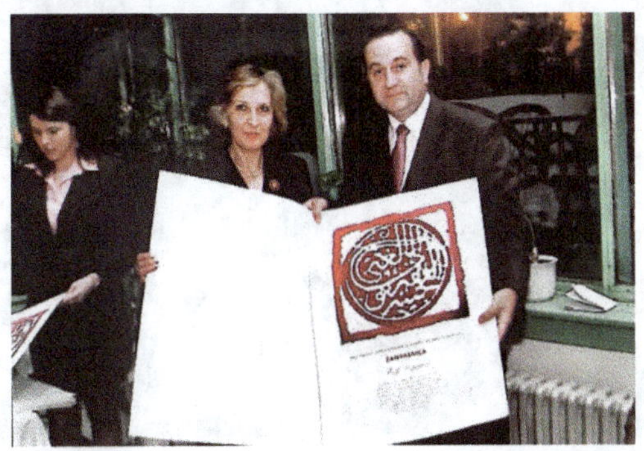

Aida Haveric, Financial Minister of Canton Sarajevo, 2000. Aida was receiving an award for her contribution to the field

Dino and **Aida** had two sons, **Nedim** and **Adnan**. After the war (1992-1995), Nedim and Adnan finished university in Sarajevo. In 2002, Nedim received a degree in economics, and in 2005, Adnan obtained a degree in architectural engineering. **Nedim** and **Adnan** stated:

> We always believed that trust is the foundation of every relationship – whether it is work, friendship or family. Family solidarity and mutual support are also deeply

rooted in our culture. Regardless of the circumstances, our family members were always there for each other.

Rifat Haveric graduated from the Faculty of Economics in Sarajevo. In 1979, he married **Gorana** (née Jusić) Haveric. From 1988, he worked in Italy, the city of Trieste, until 2008. They had a daughter, Amila, who was educated and married in Italy to Paolo Fabricio. They had two children: Matteo born in 2012 and Melissa born in 2014.[317]

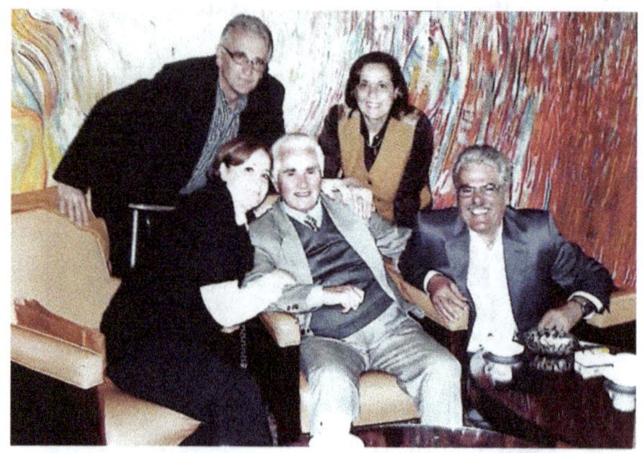

Munevera (Vera) Kulenović, Semsudin Haveric, Zineta (Dinka) Ramadanovic, Rifat Haveric (right), in the middle is a cousin, Fadil Borca

Semsudin and **Rifat**'s sisters are **Munevera (Vera) Haveric Kulenovic** and **Zineta (Dinka) Haveric Ramadanovic**. They both graduated from the high school of economics. **Munevera (Vera)** married Emir Kulenovic. They had two children, **Elda** and **Alen**. **Zineta (Dinka)** married Dr Selman Ramadanović. They also had two children, **Fuad** and **Belma** Ramadanović.

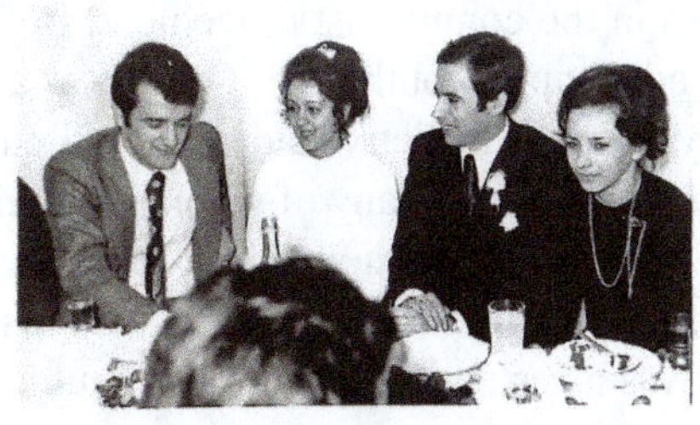

Semsudin, Zineta (Dinka), Selman Ramadanovic and an unknown person

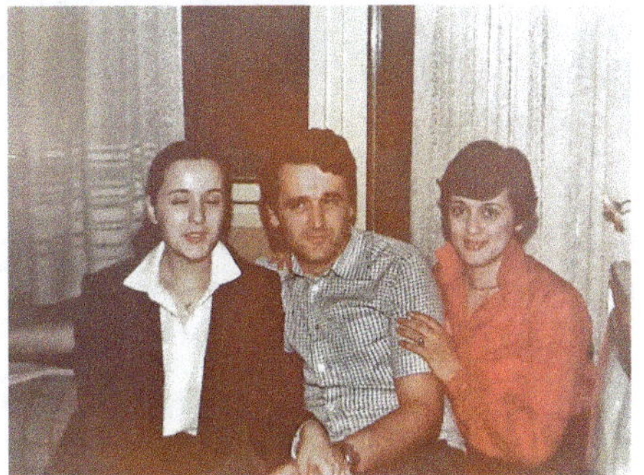

Munevera (Vera) Kulenovic, Semsudin Haveric and Zineta (Dinka) Ramadanovic

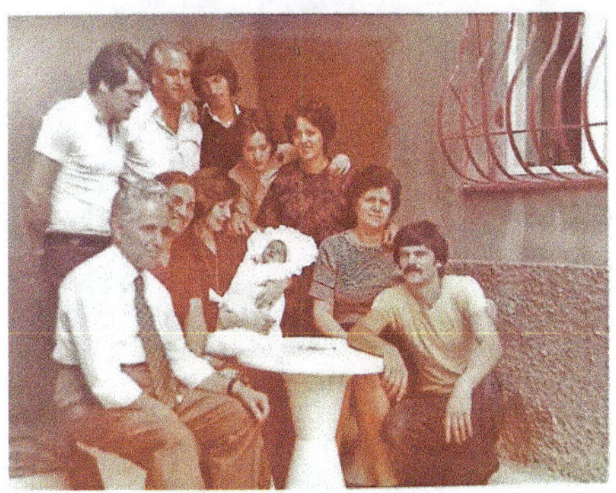

Semsudin Haveric, Asim Ibrahimagic, Bekir Ibrahimagic, Munevera (Vera) Kulenovic, Zineta (Dinka) Ramadanovic and [?]

Fetah (Feto) Sulejman bey Haveric promoted democratic ideals and was involved in the communist movement. Before the Second World War, he had a happy youthhood. **Fetah** was a member of the communist party and took military leadership of Podgorica. He was among many known illegals, many of whom were interned or died. He was credited for his contribution to anti-fascist war.[318] When the war started, he came to Shkodra and stayed with his cousin, Teufik Haveric. **Fetah** was arrested in Shkoder, but Teufik intervened and **Fetah** was released.

Tahir bey was the son of **Hasan bey Kadi** and the younger brother of **Sulejman bey**. He married **Nuria** Hadzic, a sister of Sulejman's wife, Hanifa. They had three daughters, **Saliha, Arifa** and **Halima**, and three sons, **Murat, Sherif** and **Dzemal**. His wife Nuria died and left six small children. She died in childbirth when the committee came in to loot. The committee pulled the carpet off the floor so the children became scared and rolled around. Fortunately, no one was hurt. However, **Tahir bey**, otherwise a good merchant, fled to Albania then came from Albania to Trebinje where he met several Haveric families, including **Hamza Ibrahim bey**.[319]

Apart from the relatives, his friends helped **Tahir bey** by taking care of the children. They lived in Trebinje with their uncle and sometimes with their aunt, until **Tahir bey** married for the second time to **Zarifa**. From this marriage, he had a son, **Ahmed**. He worked with his father as a tanner. He ate something there and this resulted in blood poisoning, causing his death at the young age of 26.[320]

In Trebinje, **Tahir bey** opened a leather shop, and later, apparently, went on Hajj (pilgrimage). It was said, 'the eldest daughter of Tahir bey, **Saliha,** was a wise and beautiful girl'. She married Halil Dubruzovic and they had four sons and two daughters. The second daughter of Tahir bey, **Arifa**, married in Skopje and raised three daughters, while the third daughter, **Halima**, stayed in Albania. **Tahir bey** moved to Zagreb, where his son **Serif** managed to open a successful trading business. His son, **Murat**, died there and was buried in the Mirogoj Cemetery.[321] **Tahir bey** Haveric and his sons lived in Zagreb for some time before arriving in Sarajevo.

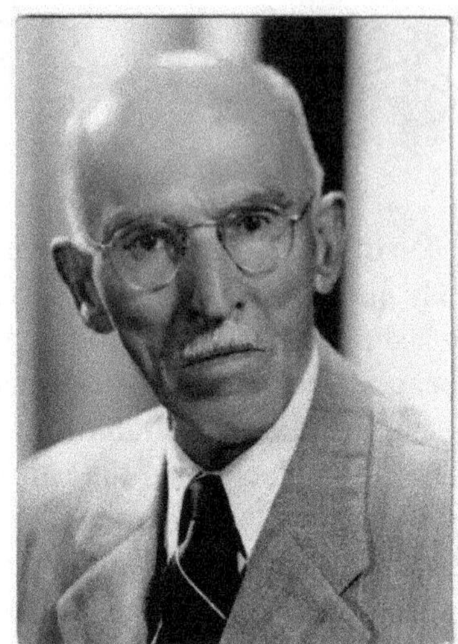

Tahir bey Haveric

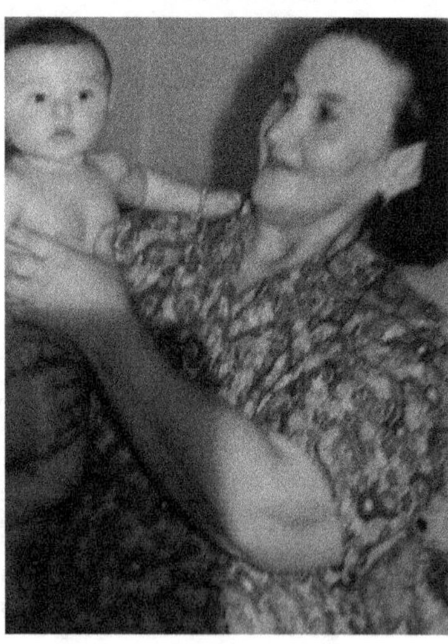

Tahir bey's daughter Saliha Haveric Durbuzovic

Dr Fadil Durbuzovic, whose mother was **Saliha Haveric** Duzrbuzovic, recalled an anecdote in Podgorica: 'When the pashas and viziers came to the house of Haverics, they would tie their horses in the houses of other family'.

Serif Tahir bey Haveric lived in Trebinje, Bosnia and Herzegovina, then Zagreb, Croatia. In Zagreb he worked a furrier, where ran his shop in Zagreb for many years. During the war, Serif imported from Finland about 2,000 pieces of 'silver fox' furs, paying a favourable price. He preserved them after the war to keep them from being damaged, so they could wait for some time for sell. At the time, a pre-war crook, fraudster and vagabond from Sarajevo, who had escaped from Bosnia, because of his cheating and stealing a lot from people, came across **Serif Haveric** in Zagreb, Croatia.

At that time, with the change of government, it was clear the private economy would be liquidated. To save his investment and goods, Serif gave a bribe, intending to transfer the furs to Rijeka, Croatia, and from there to Trieste, Italy. Meeting that crook but unknown to him, **Serif** made a mistake by paying him all bribed, travel expenses, transportation and expenses in Italy.

Before transporting the furs to Italy, the crook lied to **Serif** that he had good connections who could offer him a 'solution' for dispatching the furs to Italy. The crook presented himself to a communist general as a 'business partner of Serif'. Then, 'If I were to approve an export license for 2,000 furs, I would need 2,000 dinars', said the general. Serif took out two packages of above 2,000 dinars from his bag and placed them on the general's desk. Shortly after, the general dispatched a permission notification in the name of 'both business partners'. Subsequently, the goods were transported to Milan at the 'Magazzini Generali' railway station. A quick sale was expected at the set percentages, but to Serif's surprise, the crook did not agree with 20% commission, but asked for 50%, so half the total fur value. Serif was forced to ask for his rights in court. However, in Italian courts, legal matters last for years. The fur was already damaged by lying for too long in the magazines. When the court gave their verdict, Serif gave the crook part of the goods and a 20% commission. The crook continued to lie and steal from the people of Yugoslavia and from Italians. It was found out that he was an English spy who would eventually die miserably in Trieste.[322] **Serif** then indignantly decided to migrate to Turkiye. Settling in Istanbul, **Serif** would say, 'Turkiye received me so well that for goodness I should have immediately gone there'.[323]

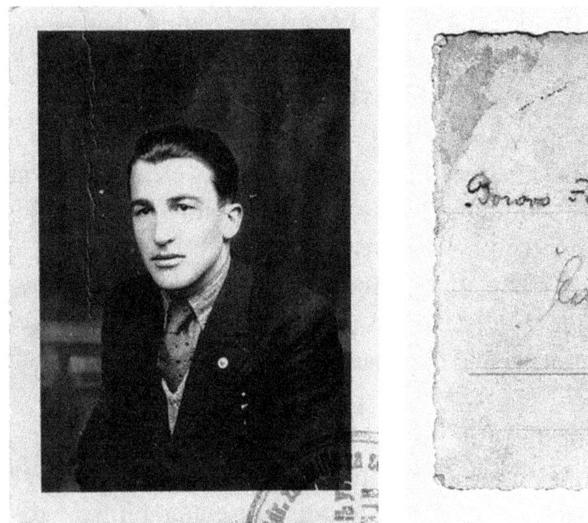

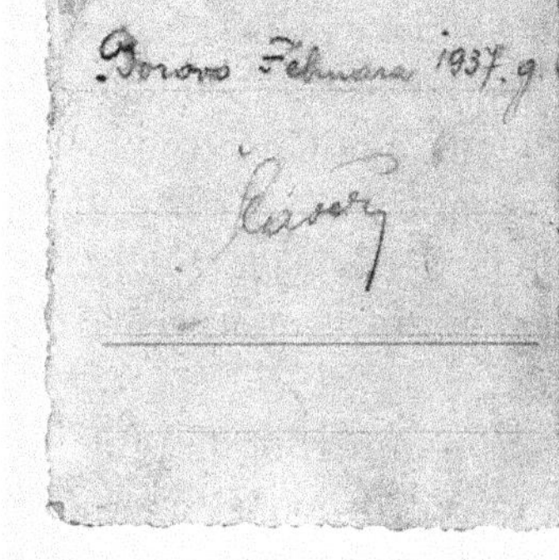

Serif Haveric, Borovo, Croatia, 1937

In Istanbul in the 1950s, he worked in trade and goldsmithing, becoming a known and respected businessman. He had his own jewellery shop in the centre of Istanbul, *Kapalıcarsı* (Kapali Bazaar), which was once the oldest and largest bazaar in the world. The name of his shop was 'Bosna ve Hersek' after Bosnia and Herzegovina.[324] **Serif Haveric** maintained contacts with his family in Bosnia and Herzegovina and Albania, and his relatives were happy to visit him and his family in Istanbul. He had a son, **Murat**, who was also a successful businessman, and worked in a bank. Serif also had a daughter.

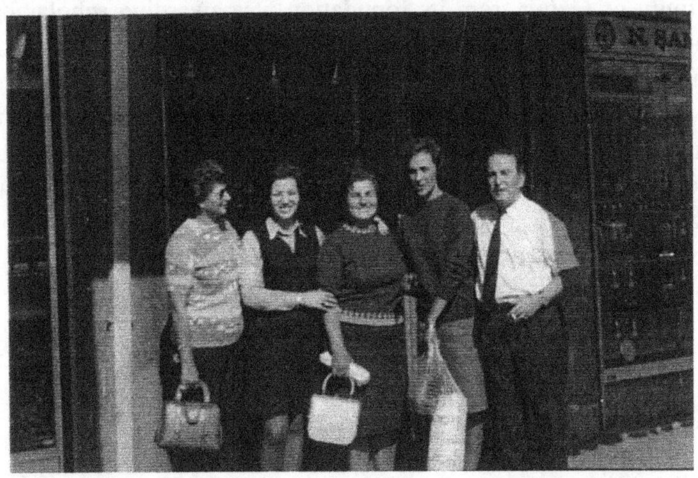

Serif Haveric's goldsmith shop: *Bosna ve Hersek*, Istanbul
(Serif on right with visiting relatives from Bosnia)
At the top of his store in Kapali Carsiji (T. Kapalıçarşı)
was written *Bosna ve Hersek*
Tanbay

Dr Dzemal Tahir bey Haveric was a well-respected member of the Haveric family. In Trebinje where young **Dzemal** lived, three buildings of *Gajret* were owned by the local Council, which had dormitories, classrooms, kitchen, laundry, a playground and a garden within a large yard surrounded by walnut trees. *Gajret* cadets organised a literary section called the *Students' deed*, which achieved visible results. Almost every Saturday the cadets organised various lectures and recitations. *Gajret* used to visit *Reis-ul-Ulama* Spaho in Trebinje.[325]

The effort to include the Muslim population in Bosnia and Herzegovina and the region in the framework of Western European cultural standards resulted in the establishment of the Sarajevo *Gajret* in 1903, whose first president was Safvet bey Basagic. The activity of *Gajret* from its foundation was awarding scholarships and loans to pupils and students and helping apprentices in various trades. According to the statute of *Gajret*, scholarships were awarded to Muslim students from Bosnia and Herzegovina, and the Austro-Hungarian monarchy, who were certified by the board as 'necessary, capable and diligent'. Among the cadets of *Gajret* was **Dzemal Haveric**, 'born in Trebinje with eight years education in Podgorica'. He was noted on the *Gajret*'s list in 1938/9.[326]

Spisak Gajretovih stipendista u 1938/1939 godini

| Redni broj | PREZIME I IME | Mjesto rodenja | Mjesto škole | Škola | Razred | Isplaćena stipendija Dinara |

Redni broj	PREZIME I IME	Mjesto rodenja	Mjesto škole	Škola	Razred	Isplaćena stipendija Dinara
60	Kulenović Džemal	Sarajevo	Sarajevo	Gimnazija	VII	375
61	Kapetanović Kemal	Sarajevo	Sarajevo		VII	950
62	Lipničević Atifa	Bijeljina	Bijeljina		VII	450
63	Muhurdarević Berija	Banjaluka	Banjaluka		VII	950
64	Mehmedbegović Rifat	Bijeljina	Bijeljina		VII	900
65	Mandžić Jusuf	Tuzla	Tuzla		VII	950
66	Nuhbegović Alija	Sarajevo	Sarajevo		VII	475
67	Šarić Husref	Sarajevo	Sarajevo		VII	475
68	Zečević Fuad	Sarajevo	Sarajevo		VII	650
69	Azabagić Mustafa	Tuzla	Tuzla		VIII	750
70	H. Halilović Ahmed	Banjaluka	Banjaluka		VIII	1000
71	Haverić Džemal	Trebinje	Podgorica		VIII	500
72	Muhedinović Zekija	Banjaluka	Banjaluka		VIII	500
73	Sarač Ibrahim	Banjaluka	Banjaluka		VIII	1000
74	Arnautović Ekrem	Sarajevo	Sarajevo	a	I	250
75	Hodžić Emira	Tuzla	Tuzla		I	500
76	Keserović Salih	Zavidovići	Doboj		I	150
77	Mešić Hasan	Zavidovići	Doboj		I	675
78	Midžić Fadila	Sarajevo	Sarajevo	k	I	500
79	Sadžak Mehmed	Sarajevo	Sarajevo		I	285
80	Sandžaktarević Mahmut	Sarajevo	Sarajevo		I	285
81	Bašić Muharem	Banjaluka	Banjaluka		II	475
82	Bajagilović Mehmed	Banjaluka	Banjaluka		II	475

Dzemal Haveric (No 71) Gajret, 1939: 160 Year XX, Sarajevo, July 1939, No 7-9

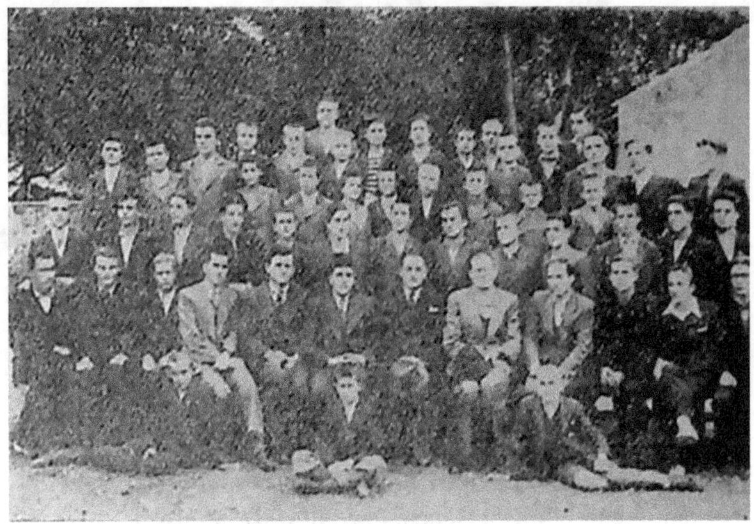

Gajret in Trebinje, Bosnia and Herzegovina, 1939

There was brief information about **Dzemal's** academic and professional career:

> **Dzemal** was born in Titograd in 1919 into a craftsman's family. After three years of living there with his family he moved to Trebinje.
>
> In 1939, Dzemal graduated at the high school in Podgorica. In the same year he enrolled in medical studies in Belgrade, where he studied until the beginning of the war. He continued his medical studies in Zagreb in 1941 and studied until his graduation in 1946.
>
> During the war, **Dzemal** was constantly in Zagreb and studied as a foreign citizen. He was not a member of any enemy organisations. He completed military service after the liberation. He graduated from the Sanitary

Officers' School (SOS) in Belgrade in 1952 and had the rank of reserve second lieutenant. Since the end of the war, he was permanently employed in Bosnia and Herzegovina.

Dzemal specialised in paediatrics in 1955 at the Military Clinic. After professional training, he also completed a course in social paediatrics in Paris in 1957. This training helped him in his later work of 12 years leading similar courses organized by the clinic in Sarajevo. Under his lecturing these courses were completed 140 domestic and some foreign students.

In 1955, **Dr Dzemal Haveric** spent a month at a children's clinic in Genoa, Italy. In 1967, he also worked for half a year in Algeria at the 'Hospital Parnet'. Being appointed to hospital in Sarajevo, he worked as the head of the pulmonary department. Then, for several decades he worked as a head of department at the Paediatric clinic in Sarajevo.

He spoke French, Italian, English and German, and published 38 professional papers, a few of which were in German and French.

During his successful career, Dzemal held several positions in the fields of healthcare, but also as a councillor of the Sarajevo Centre Assembly and the Sarajevo City Assembly. For his outstanding contribution to the social care for children, **Dr Dzemal Haveric** received an outstanding recognition from the Assembly of the Republic of Bosnia and Herzegovina for the International Year of the Child.[327]

Dr Dzemal Haveric married **Razija (Raza)** Niksic, an English language teacher. They had two sons. The first was a great intellectual, **Dr Tarik Haveric**, a university professor, philosopher, polymath, political scientist and author. He married **Sanja** Basagic, a granddaughter of a famous writer, Safet bey Basagic. The second son was **Dr Namik Haveric**, a radiologist in Washington, US, with a previous medical (surgical) career in a Sarajevo hospital. He married **Alma** Brankovic.

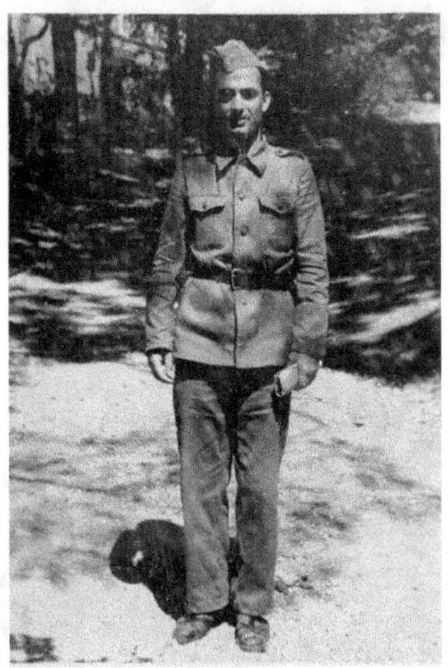

Dr Dzemal Haveric, serving in Yugoslav army in 1951/1952 in the Medical Officers' School ('Sanitetska oficirska škola')

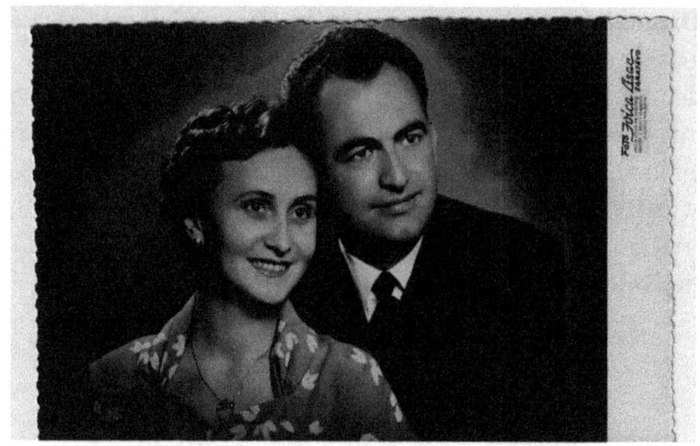

Razija (Raza) Niksic Haveric and Dzemal Haveric

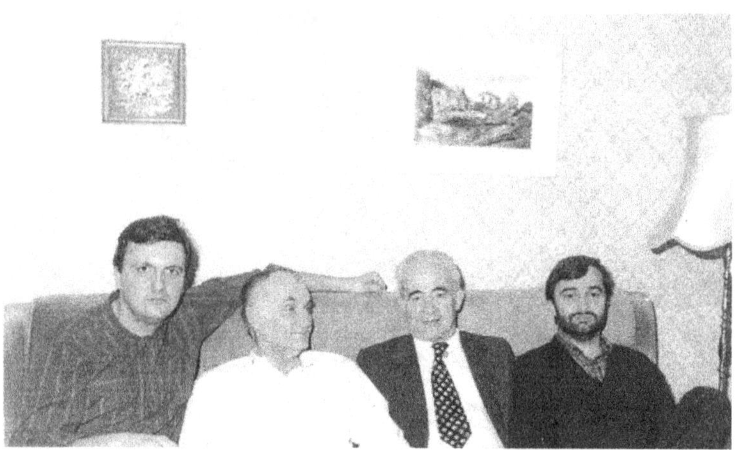

Amer, Sado, Dzemal and Namik Haveric

The following is the family brunch of the Tanbays (Haverics) in Turkiye.

Tahir bey Haveric's descendants:
Mehmet Haveric
Ali Rıza Tanbay's sons are **Aydın Rıza Tanbay** and **Erdogan (Edward) Tanbay**
Aydin's children are **Haver, Betul** and **Zeynep Tanbay**
Erdogan's children are **Dilara (Lara)** and **Cem Tanbay**
Haver's sons **Dogan** and **Yunus** and daughter **Leyla Tanbay**
Cem Tanbay has three daughters

In Turkiye, **Mehmet Haver Tanbay** said that 'his surname was given by my grandfather who was not able to register Haveric as the family last name during new formation of Turkish Republic where the state allowed Turkish surnames only'. About his ancestors in Turkiye, he continued:

> I learned from my father **Aydın Riza Haveric** that my grandfather **Ali Riza** Haveric was born in Shkodra (Iskodra) in 1880 and came to Istanbul when he was only 7 years old to attend a military school. His father was **Mehmet bey** Haveric, who was born in Podgorica. He moved to Istanbul after the independence of Montenegro and died in Istanbul. His father **Tahir Bey** was from Podgorica. They were working for the Ottomans.[328]

Haver's sisters were **Dr Betul Tanbay**, a university professor and the first woman president of the Turkish Mathematical Society, and **Zeynep Tanbay**, an artist of international reputation and 'one of the most significant pioneers of modern dance in Turkiye'. Dr **Betul Tanbay** also said:

> To my recollection there was indeed a disagreement with the choice of the Turkish family name. Our grandfather, **Ali Rıza** chose 'Tanbay', and I thought the others chose Tanyer or Tanyeri. I am not sure (not Tanver, I think) which would mean the place (Yer) of the sunrise (Tan).[329]

Fadila Methadzovic, from Podgorica, wrote to **Haver** and his daughter **Leyla Tanbay**, saying she is double connected to the Haveric family. 'My mother is a daughter of **Alija**, son of **Hamza bey** Haveric'.

> My father's grandmother was one of two daughters of **Tahir bey Haveric**. He also had a son who disappeared at age of 14-15. We don't know what was his name. At that time, they lived in Shkoder. I wonder could this lost boy be your great grandfather **Mehmet**?
>
> My great grandmother's name was **Havusa** and she was married in Methadzovic family in Podgorica, her sister Mahmudija was married in Hackovic family in Durres (Albania).[330]

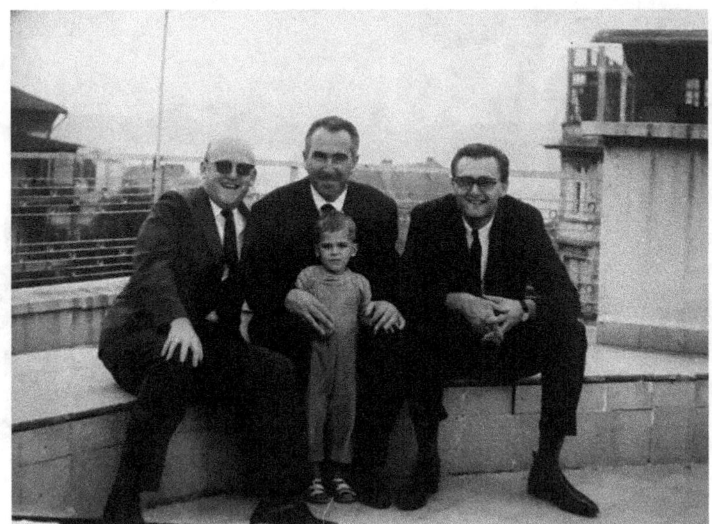

Erdogan, Mehmed (Medo), Aydin and Haver (a little boy), Istanbul

'This photo was taken in Istanbul in Cihangir (near Taksim), where our grandparents lived', said **Betul** and **Haver Tanbay**. **Mehmed (Medo)** used to come regularly in our childhood, as was called a "cousin". His last name might have been Haveric too'.

Dilara (Lara) Tanbay Edward's daughter said:

> My father, **Edward Tanbay**, and his father (my grandfather), **Ali Riza Tanbay**, both worked in tourism in Istanbul. My grandfather's picture shows his company information. His office was in front of the historic and iconic hotel, Pera Palace, located in the Beyoglu (Pera) district in Istanbul known as a 'Little Europe'. It holds the title of 'the oldest European hotel in Turkiye'. My father, Erdogan's company was 'Tourism Transport' on Cumhuriyet Caddesi, overlooking the Bosphorus Straits. I heard that my grandfather, **Ali Riza Tanbay**, got into tourism because he spoke several languages.

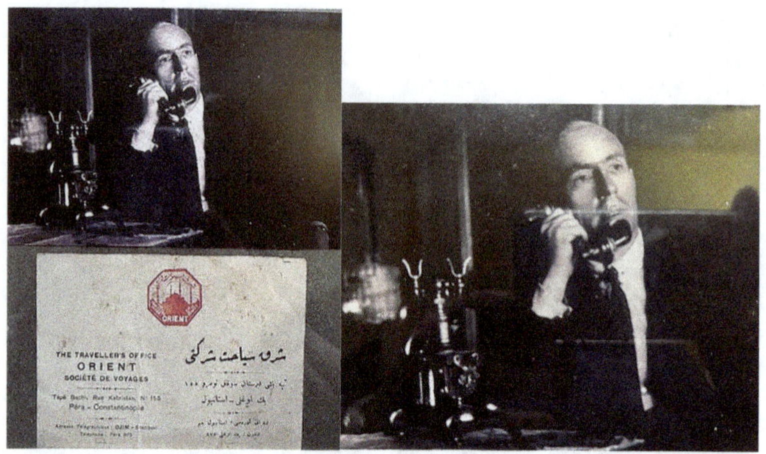

Ali Riza Tanbay

A 92-year-old, **Edward Tanbay (Erdogan Veysi Tanbay)** recalled:

> There was a long history of the 'Ottoman ruling' … and when [many] years later, I went to Podgorica by my two door BMW car and with my wife Kler. Upon arrival there I enquired about the 'remnants of the Haveric's house', but all I found was an old beat-up house with a young kid at the door. As we had no way of communication, we just left off in total disappointment. Sad, but true!

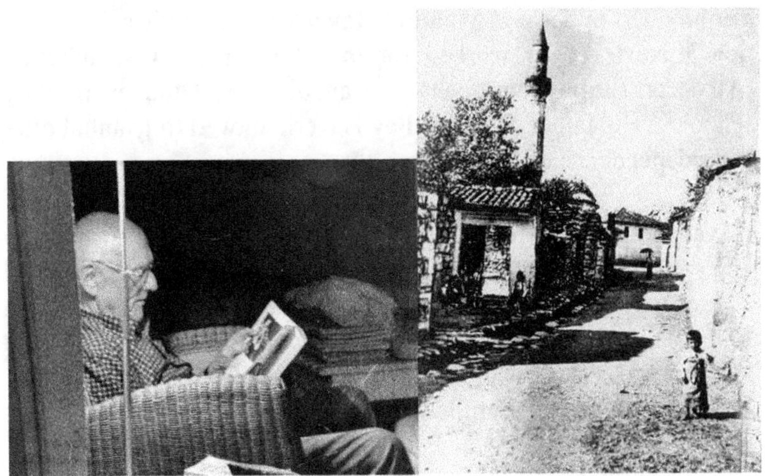

Edward (Erdogan Veysi) Tanbay **Stara Varos, Podgorica**

Erdogan Tanbay further stated: Our family was known only as Haveric. My surname Tanbay was given by my grandfather, who was not able to register the Haveric family according to our surname. During the formation of the Turkish Republic, the state allowed the registration of Turkish names only.[331] The name, Haveric, was changed in Tanbay. The word 'Tan' means sunrise, 'east' (from Farsi) in Turkish, and 'ic' was translated to 'bey', meaning the 'man'. In Ferit Devellioglu's 'Ottoman-Turkish Encyclopedic Dictionary' (*Osmanlica Turkce Ansiklopedik Lugat)* 'Haver' is mentioned as a Persian word for 'east' where the sun rises (while 'Bahter' is 'west'), this is how our last name was derived from Haveric to **Tanbay**; Tan ('sunrise')

Haver Tanbay said, 'My name is **Haver Tanbay**, resembling the family Haveric surname. My father's **Aydın Rıza Tanbay**, my grandfather's name was **Ali Rıza Tanbay**'.[332] From my father I learned that **Ali Rıza Tanbay** (1880) was born around Podgorica. Ali Riza was also the name of Ataturk's father, said **Dilara (Lara)**

Tanbay. His father was **Mehmet Haveric** and his father was **Tahir bey Haveric**. They worked for the Ottomans. My grandfather [**Ali Rıza Tanbay**] was sent to Istanbul to the Ottoman military school.[333] His father **Mehmet bey** Haveric moved to Istanbul after the independence of Montenegro.[334]

Haver Tanbay also recalled that he always searched the internet to find some information, through a brief given by my father. 'I found a letter written to Tahir Haveric by St Petar of Cetinje in 1829. In June 2022, with all my sisters and our children we made a trip to Montenegro, visited also the monastery of St Petar, and even had a chance to kiss his mummified hand'.

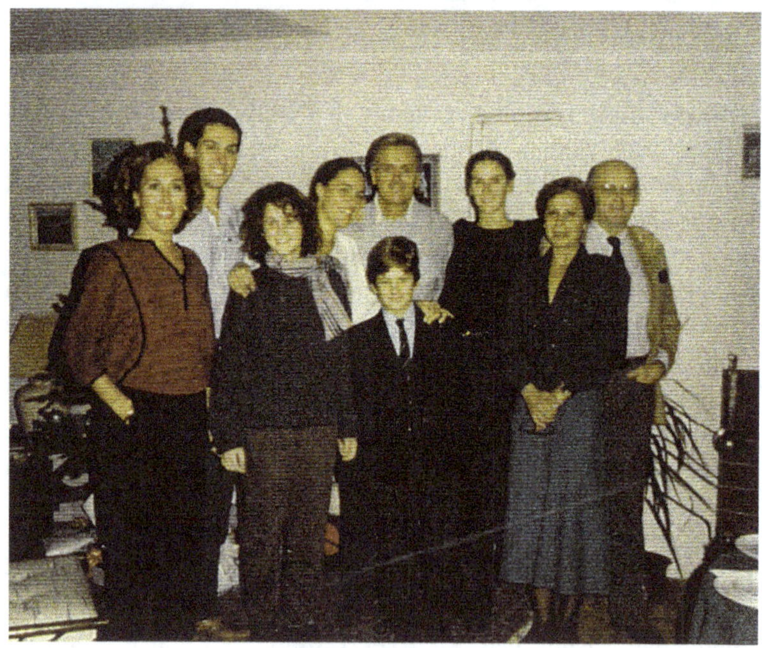

The Tanbays in Turkiye

Haver Tanbay listed family members on the above photo:

Mother Yasemin Tanbay, me (Haver), our cousin Lara Tanbay, Betul Tanbay our father Aydın Tanbay, our cousin Cem Tanbay, my sister Zeynep Tanbay, out aunt Kler Tanbay and our uncle Erdogan Tanbay. The photo is taken in about 1985-86, in Bay Area California.

When **Amer** Haveric from Sarajevo visited Turkiye, he met a Turkish woman, **Beyza Kaftanci**, in Izmir, who told him that 'her mother was **Haveric**'.[335]

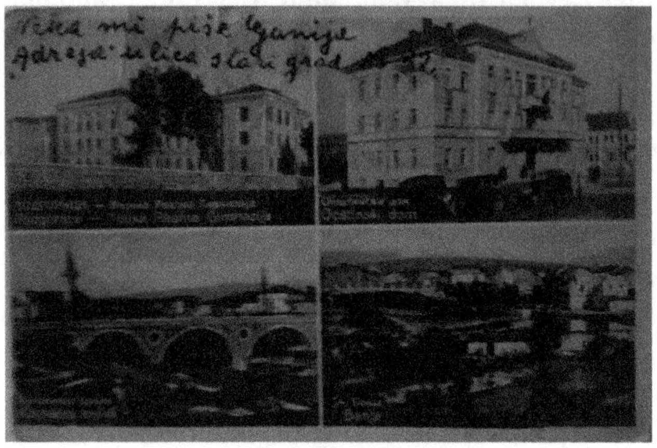

Postcard from Haveric in Podgorica, Montenegro to Haveriq in Tirana, Albania 1933

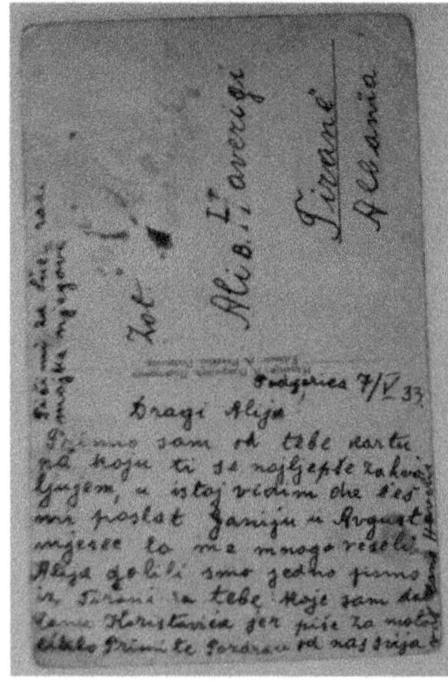

There is a touch base postcard sent by **Haveric** from Podgorica, Montenegro to **Haveriq** in Tirana, Albania. It reflects the connection between relatives.

Podgorica, 7 May 1933
For:
But B. (Bey) Haveriqi
Tirana
Albania

I received a postcard from you, for which I thank you very much. In it, I see that you will send me Gania in the month of August. That makes me very happy. Alija, we received a letter from Tirana for you, which I gave to Cano Koristavic because it is about a motorcycle. Receive greetings from all of us.
PS: Write to me about everything for his Suco's [?] mother's sake.

Hasan (Cano) Haveric

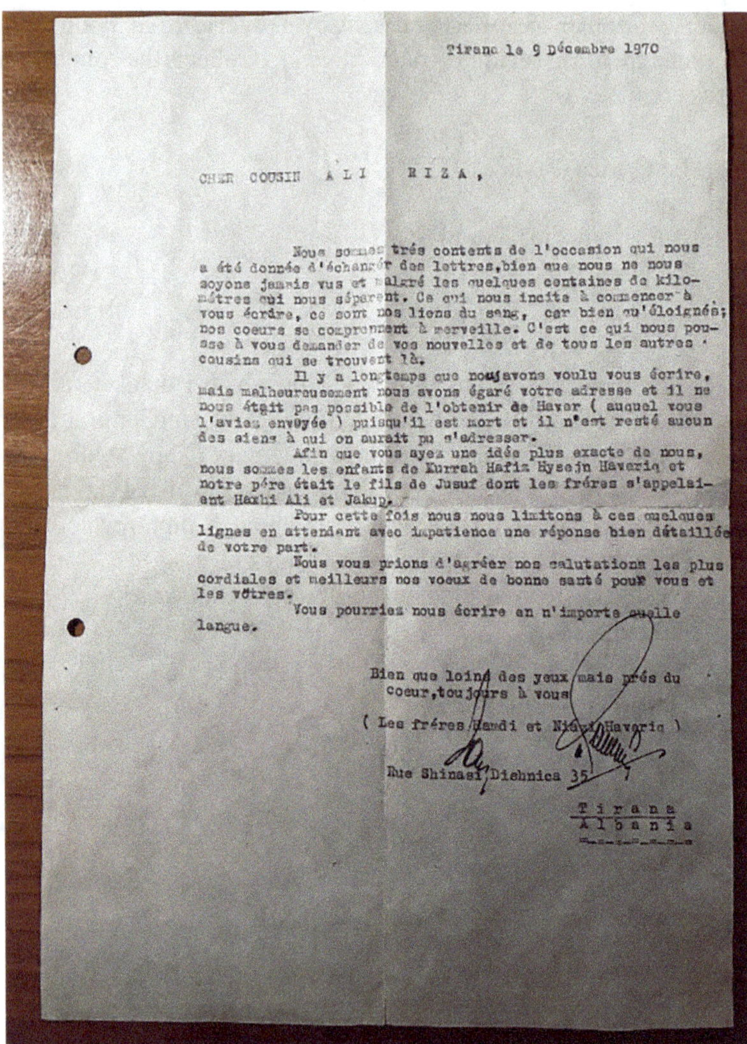

Tirana le 9 Décembre 1970

CHER COUSIN A L I R I Z A ,

Nous sommes trés contents de l'occasion qui nous a été donnée d'échanger des lettres,bien que nous ne nous soyons jamais vus et malgré les quelques centaines de kilomètres qui nous séparent. Ce qui nous incite à commencer à vous écrire, ce sont nos liens du sang, car bien qu'éloignés; nos coeurs se comprennent à merveille. C'est ce qui nous pousse à vous demander de vos nouvelles et de tous les autres cousins qui se trouvent là.

Il y a longtemps que nous avons voulu vous écrire, mais malheureusement nous avons égaré votre adresse et il ne nous était pas possible de l'obtenir de Havor (auquel vous l'aviez envøyée) puisqu'il est mort et il n'est resté aucun des siens à qui on aurait pu s'adresser.

Afin que vous ayez une idée plus exacte de nous, nous sommes les enfants de Kurreh Hafiz Hysejn Haveriq et notre pére était le fils de Jusuf dont les fréres s'appelaient Haxhi Ali et Jakup.

Pour cette fois nous nous limitons à ces quelques lignes en attendant avec impatience une réponse bien détaillée de votre part.

Nous vous prions d'agréer nos salutations les plus cordiales et meilleurs nos voeux de bonne santé pour vous et les vôtres.

Vous pourriez nous écrire en n'importe quelle langue.

Bien que loin des yeux mais prés du coeur,toujours à vous

(Les fréres Hamdi et Nijazi Haveriq)

Rue Shinasi Dishnica 35

T i r a n a
A l b a n i a

Letter from Haveric in Albania to Tanbay (Haveric) in Turkiye, 1970

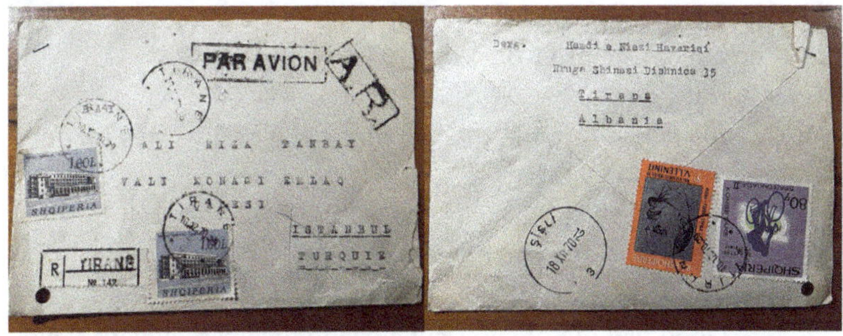

The following is a nostalgic letter written in Tirana in 1970 by Hamdi and **Niazi Haveriq** Haveric in Albania to **Ali Riza Tanbay (Haveric)** in Turkiye.

Dear cousin **Ali Riza**,

We were very happy with the opportunity given to us to exchange letters, although we had never seen each other, despite the few hundred kilometres separating us. What encourages us to start writing to you is our blood ties, because although distant, our hearts understand each other wonderfully. This is what pushes us to ask for your news from all the other cousins who are there.

We have wanted to write to you for a long time, but unfortunately, we misplaced your address and it was not possible for us to get it from Haver (to whom you had sent it) since he died and did not remain. None of his people could be contacted.

So that you have a more accurate idea of us, we are the children of **Kurrah Hafiz Hysein Haveriq** and our father was the son of Jusuf whose brothers were called **Haxi Ali** and **Jukup**. This time we limited ourselves to these few items while impatiently awaiting a very detailed response from you.

Please accepts our most cordial greetings and best wishes for good health to you and yours.

You could write to us in any language.

Good that out of sight but close to the heart, always yours.
(The **Hamdi** and **Niazi Haveriq** brothers)
Tirane, Albania

Mirza Sefket Haveric narrated about his grandparents, **Bajram bey** and **Alema**.

> My grandfather, **Bajram bey**, was a tailor. I assume that he was also a merchant considering that the Haveric family was very wealthy and that they were also engaged in trade. They owned land in Podgorica, and today [apparently] the Academy of Sciences of Montenegro is located on a part of it.
>
> Regarding my grandfather's exodus in the time of the war, I only know that one part of the family went to Albania, the other part of the family went to Bosnia. My grandfather **Bajram bey** managed to evacuate his family by car from Montenegro while fleeing from the Chetniks. You can only imagine how much money he spent to pay for that trip and to pass the Chetnik and the Ustasha barricades, and German occupational check points.
>
> **Bajram** did not live in Albania, nor did my father ever mention Albania. As for Montenegro, they never mentioned the hard times, but they cherished only nice memories from the time they lived there.

Bajram Haveric together with **Murat Haveric** were among the members of the *Napredak* ('Progress') association contributing to the cultural life of Podgorica.

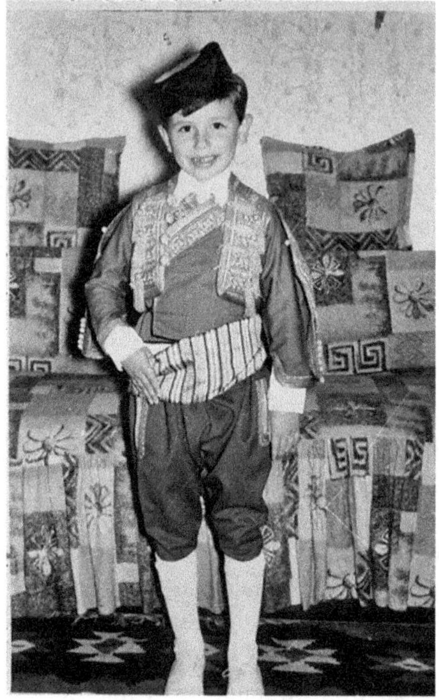

Mirza Sefket Haveric

About his grandmother, **Mirza** said:

> I loved my grandmother, **Alema**, immensely and she loved me too. She was a special woman in every way. She died right before the war in 1991 and lived for over 90 years. She was the pillar of the whole family and she was the one who gathered everything in the family house.

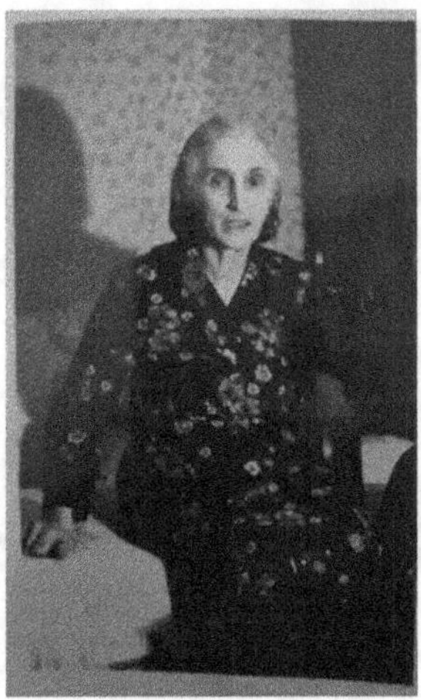

Alema Haveric

> *Eid* was celebrated, sacrifices were regularly offered for the *Eid al-Adha* sacrifice, and Ramadan was carried out according to all Islamic rules and regulations, the grandmother prayed every single prayer until her death. Although my father was in the party, no one ever contested it.

Sefket Bajram bey Haveric was born in Podgorica, in 1922 and died in 1995. He came to Sarajevo in 1943 together with his father **Bajram** and mother **Alema**, brother **Asim (Hasko)** and sisters **Bisera**, **Envera**, **Safija** and **Sabiha**. **Sefket** married **Mubera** and had sons **Mirza, Jasmin** and **Senad**. **Mirza's** wife is **Dr Denita** Imamovic Haveric, a university professor and book author.

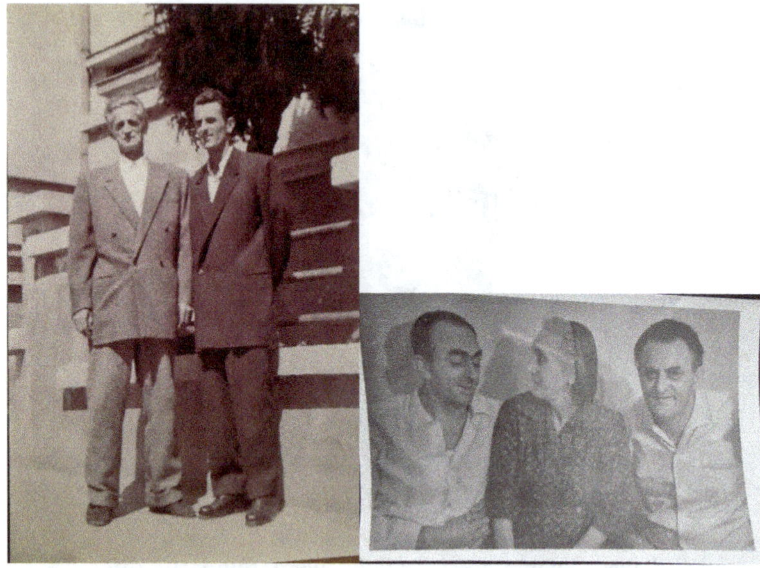

Bajram and Sefket Haveric u Logavina Street, old city of Sarajevo, 1957/8
Hasko and Sefket with mother Alema

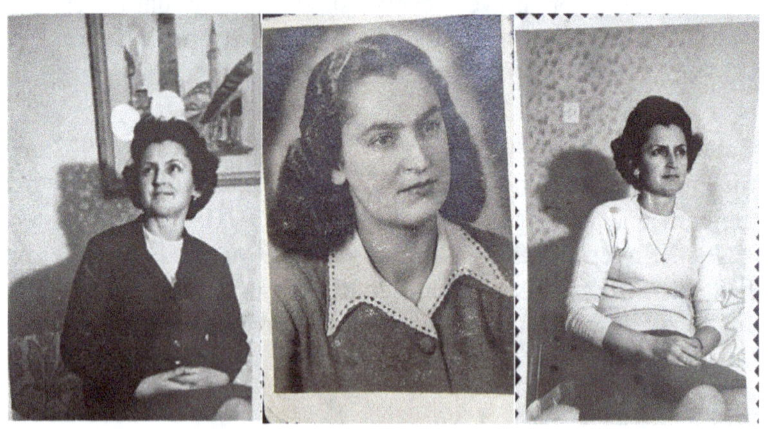

Bisera Haveric **Bisera Haveric** **Bisera Haveric**

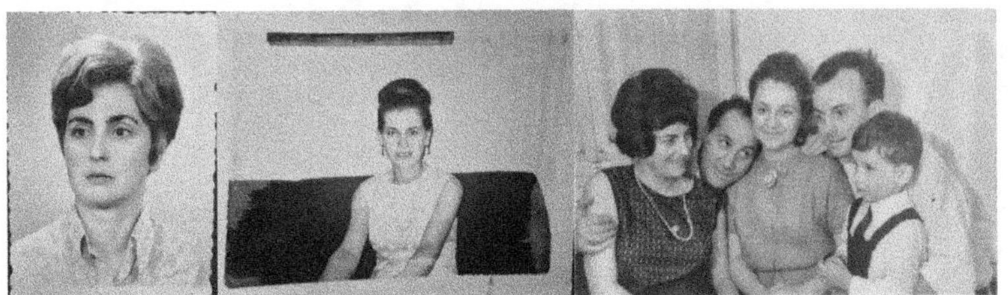

Safija Haveric **Sabiha Haveric** **Envera Haveric and Aleksandar Kalman**

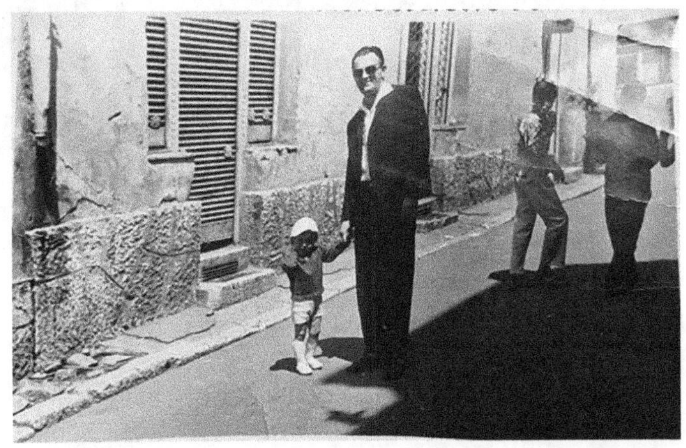

Sefket in front of his tailor shop in Gazi Husrev bey Street, Sarajevo, Bascarsija

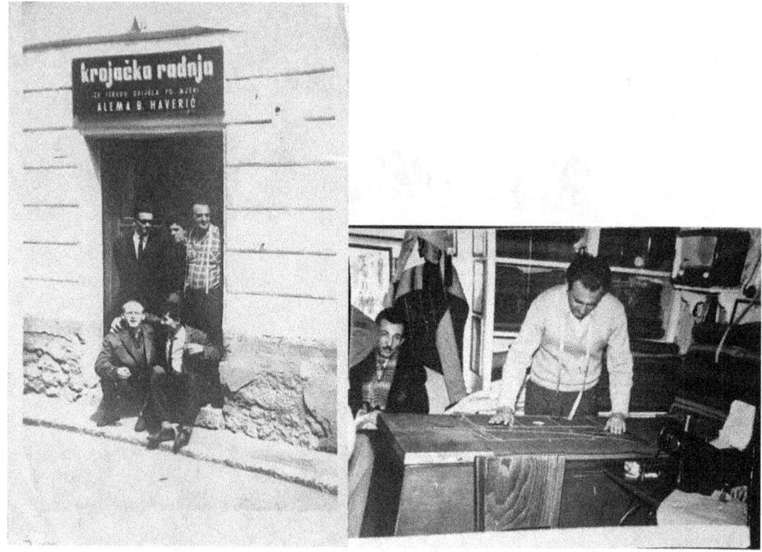

Sefket and his tailor shop 'Alema B. Haveric'

Mirza narrated about father's tailor shop.

> The shop is fondly called the 'Embassy of Montenegro'. The store got that nickname because all the Montenegrins from the city of Sarajevo used to gather there. The shop was registered to grandfather **Bajram bey** because he bought the shop in gold from a Jew. After the Second World War, in 1945, the shop was confiscated by the state and everything was nationalised. After my grandfather's death, the business was transferred to his wife, my grandmother **Alema**, because it could not be otherwise by the law. She was the owner of the shop at the time and my dad **Sefket** was the director of December 22, which was a military textile company. Out of love and respect, primarily for his father **Bajram**, and for his mother and sisters, he continued his family tradition as a tailor, as

he earlier completed his tailoring trade in Podgorica. He didn't want to lose the shop, left his current job and took over the work in the shop. Because of his skills in tailoring and his tailoring patterns, **Sefket** later received an invitation to work for an Italian company. He also worked as a marriage celebrant at the city council.

His shop was also a kind of club, not only for Podgorica residents, but also for respectable Sarajevo residents, who gathered there until late evening. Among the visitors there were many artists. Since my uncle, **Hasko**, was the director of 'Beograd Disk', 'Diskoton Sarajevo' and the music manager, numerous singers came to the shop, such as singers Safet Isovic, Halid Bešlic, Arsen Dedic, Halid Mandic, Himza Half and others. There were also other well-respected Sarajevians with whom he was a great friend and who sewed suits for them, such as visual artist Ismet Rizvic, actor Drago Popovic, mathematician Veselin Peric, Dr Dusko Milisavljevic, politicians Dzemal Bijedic, Munir Mesihovic, General Jovan Divjak and others.

My father, **Sefket**, never lost his authentic Podgorica accent nor did my grandmother **Alema**, my uncle **Hasko** and my aunts. He always felt like an authentic Montenegrin. He always spoke the Montenegrin language even when he had a problem because of that, because he was a prominent communist cadre. He received a large number of awards and plaques.

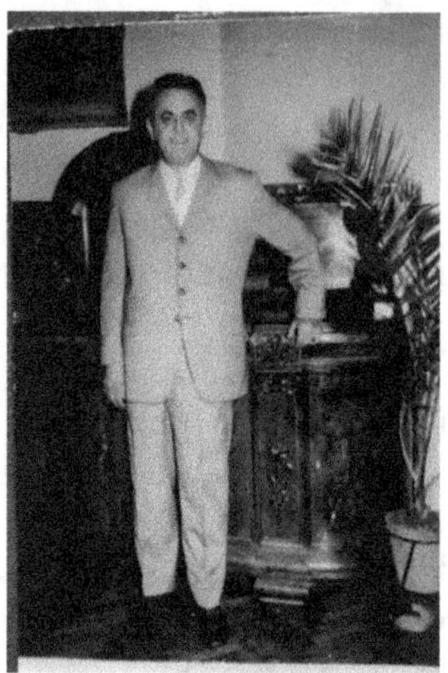

Sefket

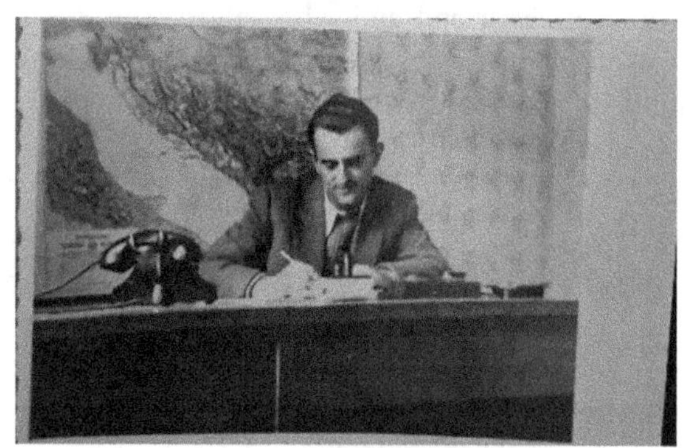

Sefket in his office in the 22 December Company

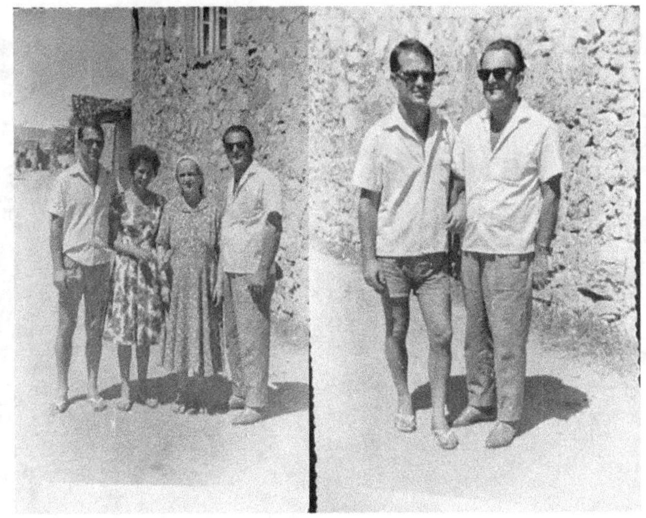

Muniba (second from the left) Sefket's wife and Sefket (first from the right) in front of the house in Podgorica and Mirza's aunty Bira. Sefket in front of the house in Podgorica

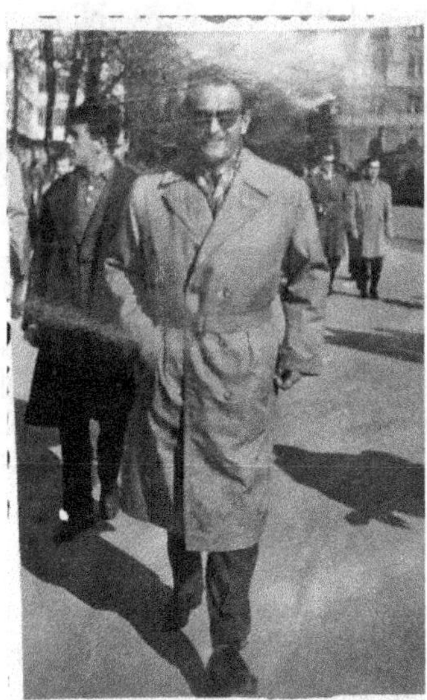

Sefket Haveric

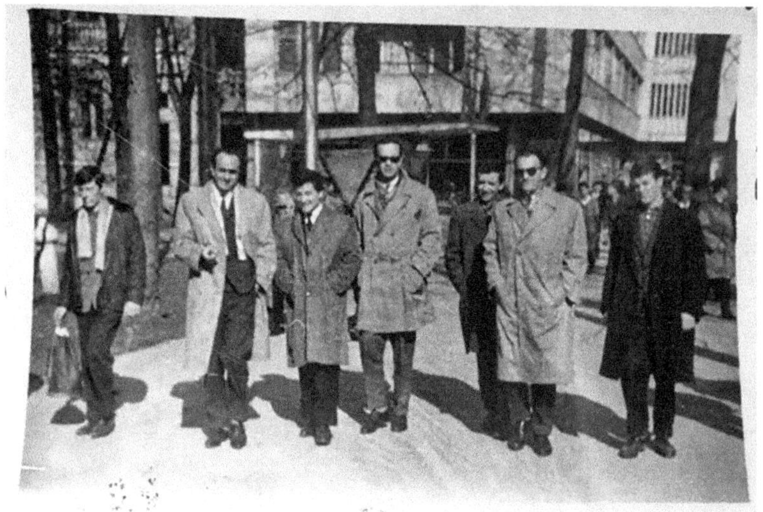

Asim (Hasko) Haveric (the second from the left), Sarajevo

In Bosnia and Herzegovina, **Asim (Hasko) Bajram bey Haveric** was known in the cultural and artistic field. On arriving in Sarajevo from Belgrade, Serbia, in 1973, he worked on establishing 'Diskoton', a music production and record company. He was among the most influential figures in managing music record production. Previously, **Hasko** Haveric was a former employee of the 'Beograd Disk', Belgrade, who contributed to its establishment. In the following ten years, Sarajevo became among the first cities in Yugoslavia to come up with its own interpretation of folk and rock on records. The Diskoton made records and audio tapes of many popular Yugoslav singers and groups. During his time, numerous *sevdalinka* and folk songs from the rich cultural and artistic heritage were also recorded. He used to say, 'Flowers, beauty and music – all go together'.

In the past, **Hasko** Haveric was among the first and active members of the 'Slobodan Princip Seljo Cultural and Artistic Society', which brought together numerous students from Bosnia and

Herzegovina and beyond. The society was founded in 1949/50, when the University of Sarajevo was also founded and **Hasko** was in the first generation of dancers of the society. He was also known for his persuasion of the king of *sevdah,* Safet Isovic, to become a member of the ensemble of folk dances and songs of the student society Slobodan Princip Seljo. During his studies in Sarajevo, Safet Isovic often came to the society during the students' breaks. **Hasko** Haveric, liked Safet's singing, inviting him to become a member of the ensemble of folk dances and songs of the student society Slobodan Princip Seljo, where he auditioned before a committee that included some prominent musicians. Their collaboration continued through Diskoton and Isovic's concerts. Isovic's first appearance abroad was in 1957 at the folklore festival in Geneva, Switzerland, with the support of **Hasko** Haveric. Hasko also participated on juries at various musical festivals, such as popular 'Vas slager sezone' ('Your singing of the season') and the Ilidza Festival. He also recorded a couple of single records for the 'Jugton', a music production and record company in Belgrade.

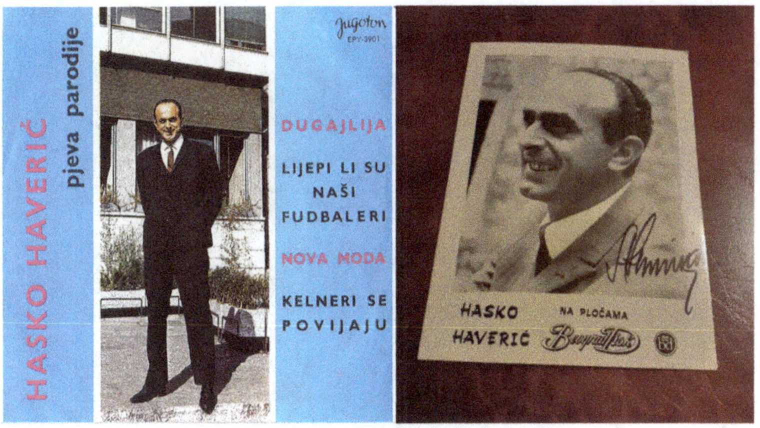

Hasko Haveric (Jugoton, 1968)

Hasko supported many other popular singers, such as Zdravko Colic and Halid Beslic. There were also numerous singers and musicians who fondly remembered him, such as singers Beba Selimovic, Zaim Imamovic, Hasim Kucuk Hoki, Cazim Colakovic, Hanka Paldum and many others. The famous artist and harmonica player Omer Pobric said that **Hasko** Haveric was 'the first manager who recorded and promoted the *sevdalinka* of famous singers like Zehra Deovic'. A singer, Hasim Kucuk Hoki, remembered that 'Hasko Haveric and Vlatko Petrovic gave him his first support at the then RTV (Radio Television) Sarajevo'.[336]

About his four aunties, **Mirza** said:

> **Envera** Haveric, who married Dr Aleksandar Kalmar, was a journalist and worked at newspapers companies *Oslobodenje* and *Vecernje Novine*. **Safija** Haveric, who married Talirevic, was an economist and worked at FZ MIO/PIO. **Bisera** Haveric worked at a company called *Borac Travnik.*

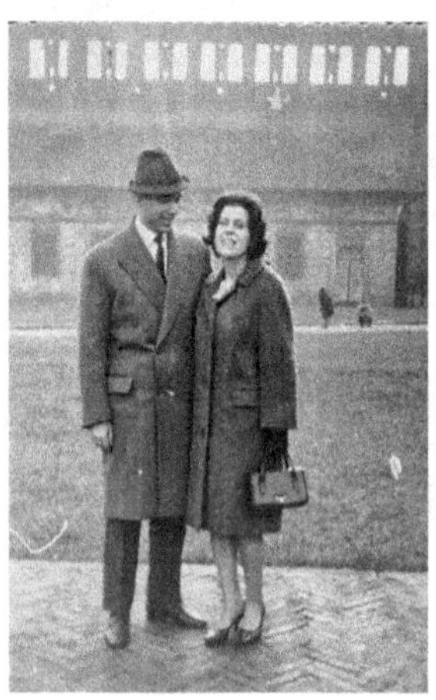

Sabiha Haveric in Milan

Sabiha Haveric went to Milan, Italy, where she married Italian **Ricardo** Albonetti around 1965. She graduated from the Faculty of Philosophy in Sarajevo, Department of English and Italian. She worked at the well-known international company *Energoinvest* as a translator, where she also met her aunt at a meeting. Uncle Riccardo is a former director of the Italian oil company ENI and was very successful in his business.

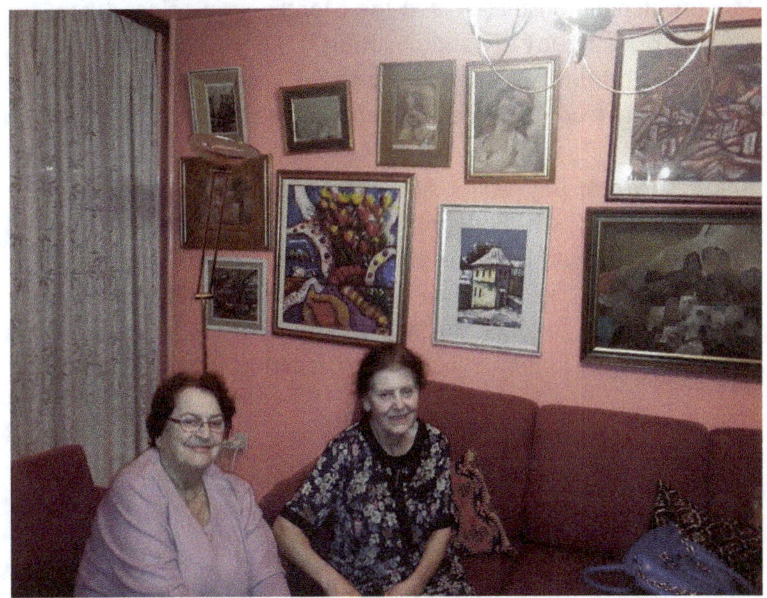

Envera and Sabiha Haveric

Ibrahim bey Haveric was a wealthy merchant and farmer, and an active member in the social life of Podgorica representing the local Muslim community. He was known for his involvement in the Muslim deputation that visited the Montenegrin prince (then, the king) expressing loyalty and devotion.[337] He had five sons, **Selim**, **Hamza**, **Abdulah**, **Zejnil** and **Mahmud**, and a daughter, **Havaja**. The brothers were described as 'four giants'.[338]

Selim Ibrahim bey was a successful merchant in Podgorica. He had tannery shops in Podgorica and Tuzi. **Selim bey Haveric** had sons, **Osman, Velija, Cazim** and **Ibrahim**, and a daughter, **Rabija**. He passed away in 1918 in Podgorica. His son **Osman** owned a tannery shop in Trebinje, where he passed away. When Selim bey's three sons came to Sarajevo, they continued to work in a tannery.[339]

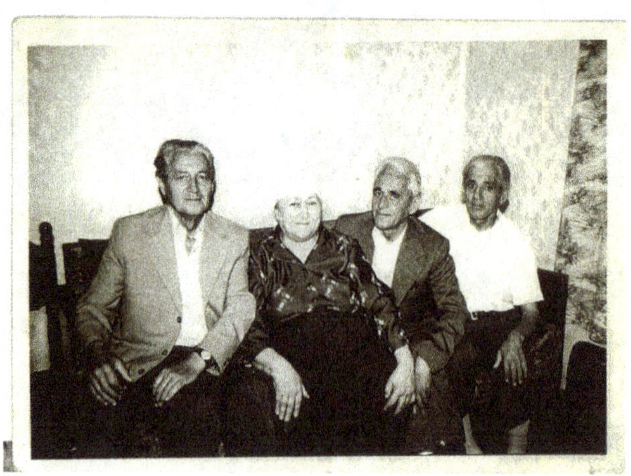

Brothers Ćazim, **Velija and Ibrahim with sister Rabija**

Velija Selim bey Haveric was born on March 25, 1908, in Podgorica in Stara Varos to mother Nurija Haveric née Vranić and father Selim bey Haveric. He was the first child of his parents. He had one sister and three brothers.[340] By his character, he was quiet and calm. He loved history, which he told in his own way, so it was interesting to listen to him. He wrote and read Arabic and learned the Qur'an. He loved nature and long walks to the Kozija Cuprija Bridge, near Sarajevo. He had his own family, his wife Huma Haveric née Krnić and six children, one of which passed away when young. **Veli bey** was 'a good father, husband, son and brother. He loved and cherished his family', said his daughter **Azra**. Being born on March 25, 1908, **Velija** experienced the Balkan wars in 1912 and 1913, the First World War between 1914 and 1918, the Second World War between 1941 and 1945, and the beginning of the war in Bosnia and Herzegovina in 1992. This was the fourth war he had experienced in his life.[341] He and his wife left behind three sons, **Selim**, **Halid** and **Fadil**, and two daughters, **Amira** and **Azra**. **Selim** graduated as a social worker and **Azra** was a logoped (speech therapist) and defektologist (child special education and developmental psychologist).

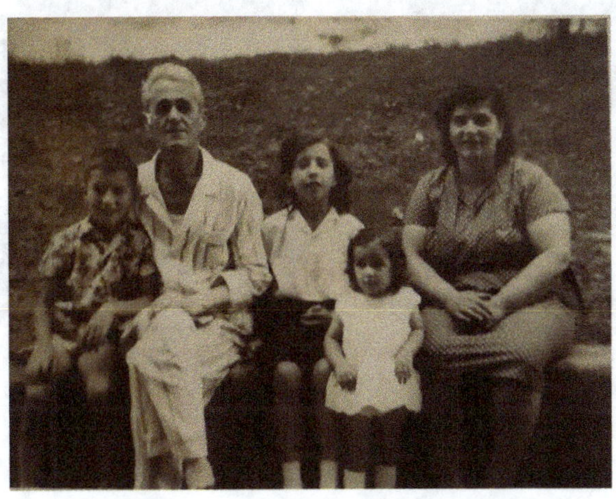

Velija Haveric, his wife Huma and their children

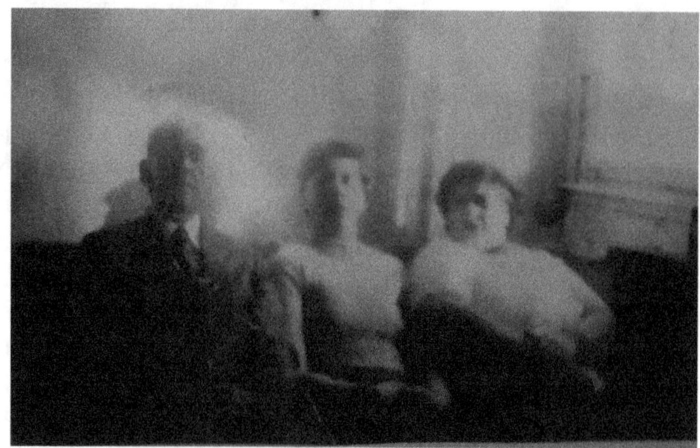

Velija, his oldest daughter Amira and wife Huma

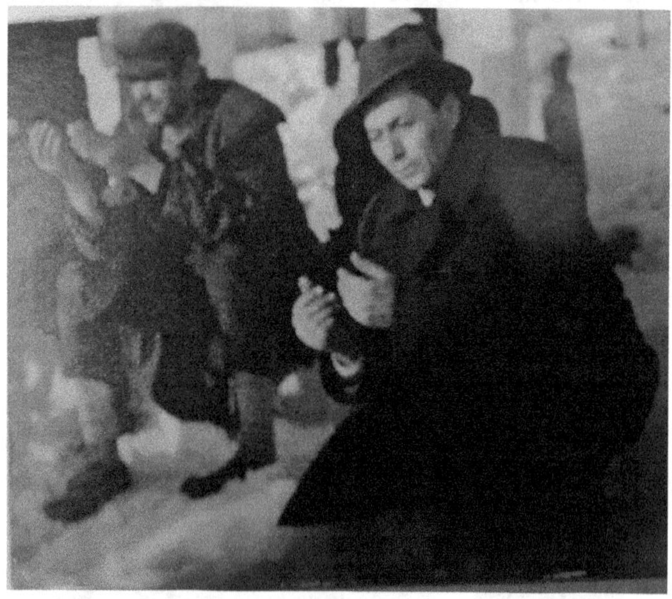

Cazim Haveric

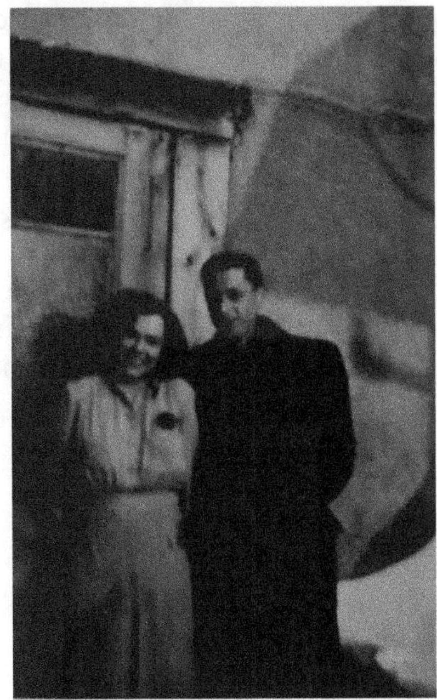

Ulfeta Hadzic Haveric and Cazim Haveric

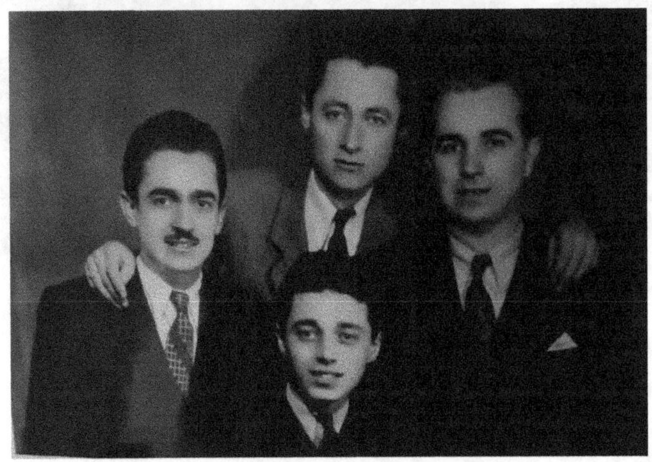

Cazim Haveric above in the middle

Cazim Selim bey Haveric was born in 1911, but he believed it was a bit earlier. **Cazim** took refuge from Podgorica to Shkoder as a 7-year-old boy where his family rented houses. He went to school for 4 years, then another 4 years, followed by a 'small graduation', which was not a small success back then. He lived in Belgrade, Serbia, from April 6, 1941, and came to Sarajevo in 1943. In Belgrade, he worked in a large leather company whose owner was a Greek. **Cazim** was a respected employee and he said the owner was fair to him.[342] He married **Ulfeta** Hadzic and they had one son, **Dr Faruk**, a gynecologist in Bosnia with international experience from Libya, Malta and the US, and three daughters, **Seka (Fikreta)**, **Misa (Faketa)** and **Alma**.

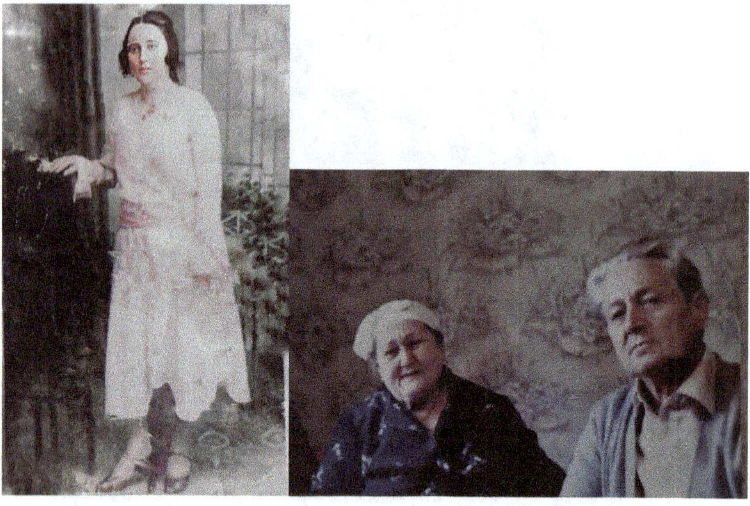

Rabija Haveric Berisa,

Kosovo Brat and sister: Rabija and Cazim Haveric

Rabija Selim bey Haveric was married in Kosovo to a prominent Albanian from the Berisa family.

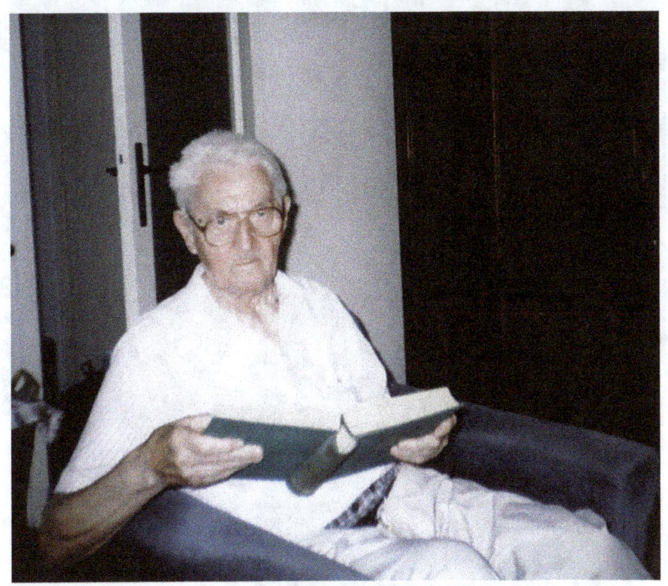

One of the oldest in the Haveric family, Cazim bey, lived close to 100 years

Ibrahim (Ibro) Selim bey Haveric was a professional driver for the Bosnian government. He married **Asima Mahmutovic** from Bijelo Polje, Montenegro, at the age of 49. He died in 1998 at the age of 83. He survived 4 wars. Like Cazim and Velija, **Ibro** was educated in a medresa. There was an anecdote that when **Ibro** went to school he failed an exam. His mother asked him what happened. He replied that he had 'fallen'. 'Did you hurt yourself?', she said. **Ibro** replied 'no'. Then, 'it did not happen', said his mother.[343]

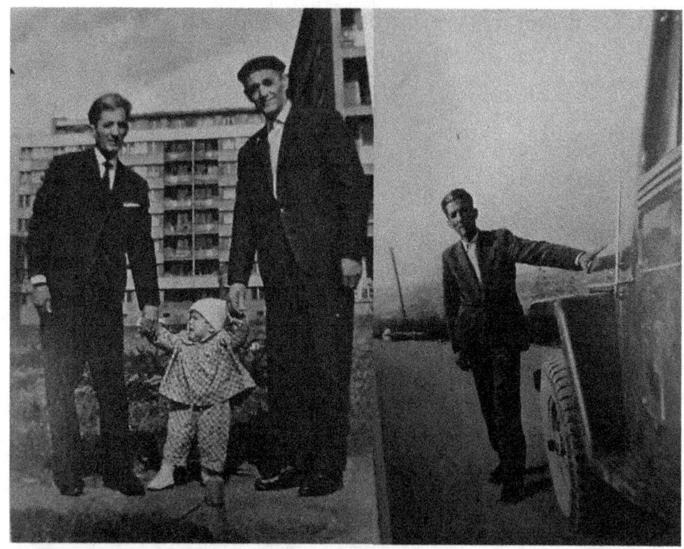

Ibrahim (Ibro) and Velija Haveric **Ibrahim (Ibro) Haveric**

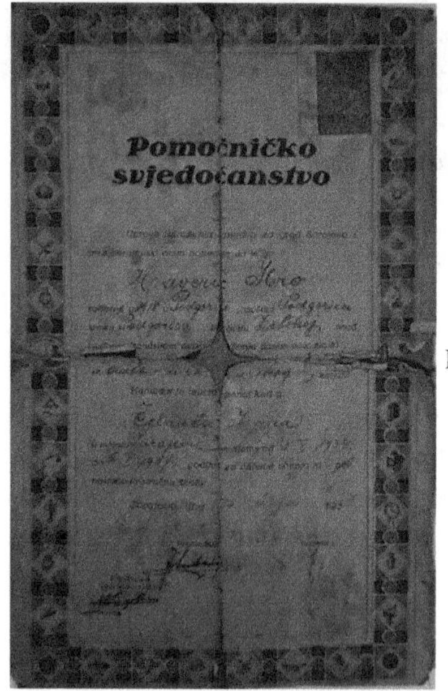

Pomoćničko
svjedočanstvo

Ibrahim (Ibro) Haveric

Hamza Ibrahim bey Haveric married **Zejnepa** Omercahic and they had two sons, **Dzavid** and **Kemal**, and two daughters, **Hatidza** and **Nazira**. He was a wealthy man and had one of the biggest houses in Stara Varoš. At that time, there were no cars but he rode a horse. **Hamza bey** was dressed in national clothes embroidered with gold. He was a merchant, worked hard and would say: 'Our faith is beautiful, which is like honey from the wages'. **Zejnepa** helped people, she was hardworking and strong. My older sister, **Hatidza**, learned skills from her. Their graves are nowhere to be found in Tuzi, everything was deserted, it needed to be investigated, said Nazira Haveric Kerni.

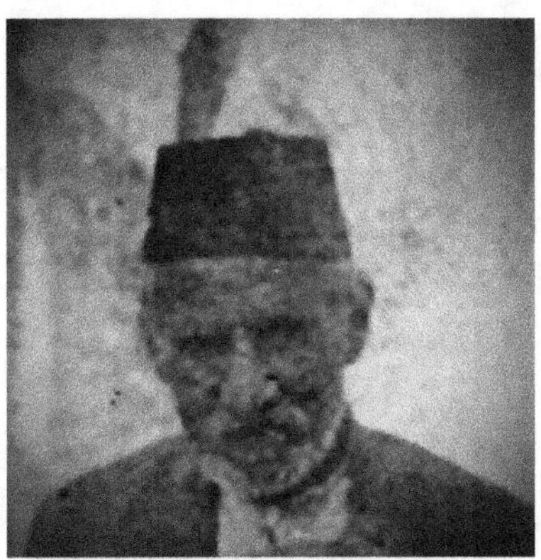

Hamza bey Haveric

Nazira Hamza bey Haveric Keraj (Krnic) recalled:

> My mother's [**Zejnepa** Omercahic Haveric] children were dying during birth. She gave birth to 12 children who died. **Zejnepa's** first daughter was called **Biserka**, who died after two months. My older sister, **Hatidza**, was born in Podgorica. One of the first-born children was **Nazira**, who lived only 13 years, so they gave me the

> same name hoping that it will protect me to live longer. My young brother **Kemo** and I were born in Trebinje.
>
> My parents told me when they first son, **Dzavid**, was born in Podgorica, it was a great joy. They went out of their house, crossing the street and said, 'The she-wolf gave birth to a wolf', a motto to protect him from calamities and to be strong. Their friends also happily said, **Hmaza bey's** wife, **Zejnepa** ('Hamzabegovica'), gave birth to a son! In every mosque the imams greeted the news; sacrifices were slaughtered on one ear, even nine types of shirts were made for **Dzavid** to live long.[344]

Dzavid Hamza bey Haveric was born after 12 infant deaths, when his mother **Zejnepa** (Zepa) birthed him, in 1920. His brother, **Kemal**, was born four years later. For the occasion of the first-born child, **Dzavid**, it was said that 'in every mosque, a *salawat* (prayer) was offered'.[345]

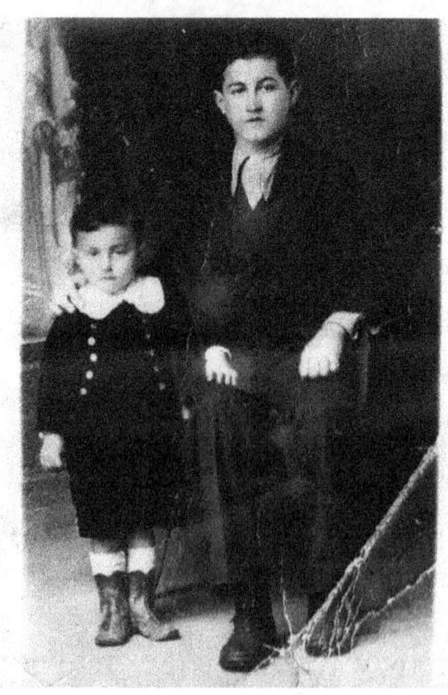

Jakub Ahmet bey Keraj and Dzavid Hamza bey Haveric (right)

The country of Bosnia is my homeland,
that name is known by all the peoples of the world,
God made a nest of heroes.

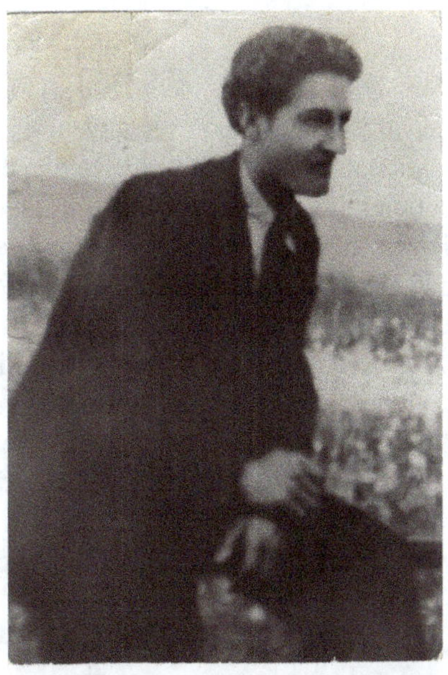

Dzavid Hamza bey Haveric, national hero

Dzavid Hamza bey Haveric (1920-1941), originally from Podgorica, was among the first anti-fascists for the liberation of Sarajevo and Bosnia and Herzegovina. As a young man, he came to Sarajevo in the municipality of Stari Grad Sarajevo (Bascarsija), where he lived and worked until the beginning of the occupation. Before the war, he was, among the progressive youth, a member of the Muslim artisan, craftsmen and business association 'Hurijet' (1908-1945), founded in 1908 in Sarajevo. The association had constitutional rules for the Muslim craftsmen and business association. It issued several written works about organising Hurijet lectures on the expansion of the organisation in the Kingdom of Yugoslavia, the preparation for future self-employed craftsmen, and the cultivation and protection of young artisans. It also published Huriet's pocket calendars.

He was then engaged as a trade union officer in the Leather and Processing Workers' Union and president of the Shoemaker's Branch. He was the leader of the anti-fascist resistance in Bascaršija. In the great epic of the national liberation, **Dzavid Hamza bey** Haveric made his noble contribution to freedom, democracy, social justice, as well as to the preservation of the multi-religious and multi-ethnic identity of Sarajevo and Bosnia and Herzegovina. In August 1941, after a brave and dignified demeanour, he was executed by the Ushashi in Vrace at the age of 21. He was among the first Bosniaks killed in Sarajevo, certainly the first on that execution ground. He was buried at the place with a memorial plaque in his honour, and later at the Vraca Memorial Park – Sarajevo Memorial Park, which was dedicated to all victims of the Second World War in Sarajevo, was built on that place, otherwise declared a national monument of Bosnia and Herzegovina.

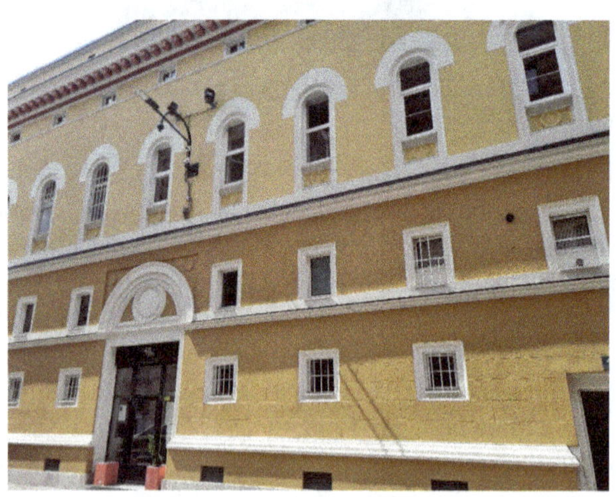

'Beledija' prison in the old Sarajevo

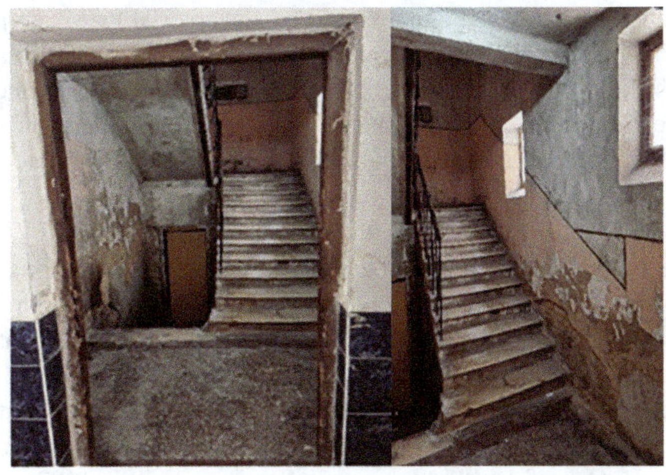

One of entrances to 'Beledija', an interrogation centre, Sarajevo

> ... **Dzavid Haveric**, fell into the hands of the occupier's raid in the old city of Sarajevo. Two agents caught him handing out anti-fascist proclamations. He got into a fight with the agents, knocking one agent to the ground and taking his gun away. Unfortunately, he didn't know how to handle a gun. The agents then overpowered him and subjected him to the harshest torture. He was brought before the court and was sentenced to death. He refused the occupier's pardon and was shot in Vraca in 1941. At the shooting, he refused to be blindfolded, exclaiming the words of freedom for Bosnian (Yugoslav) people. Later, stories were told in Sarajevo about his heroic behaviour during the shooting...[346]

His bravery is recorded in several books, including *Sarajevo in the Revolution* (1981, volume IV) by a group of authors; *Bosniaks (Muslims) of Montenegro* (2002); *Famous Bosniaks of Sandžak and Montenegro* published (1998) by Dr Mustrafa Memic and archives at the Museum of Revolution and Vraca Memorial Park, Sarajevo. In the lineup of the Vraca Memorial Park, his picture was displayed at the entrance. All residents of Sarajevo, Bosnia, and beyond, of different cultures and religions, Christian Catholics and Christian Orthodox, Jews and Muslims remembered **Dzavid** Haveric with respect.

One of the largest primary schools in Sarajevo and Bosnia and Herzegovina was named '**Dzavid Haveric**' in his honour from 1957 to 1992. The school is in old Sarajevo, in a hilly area called Vratnik, above Bascarsija. The symbolic name, after the first hero was given because the city was liberated from the direction of Vratnik. This school was attended by many prominent Sarajevian men and women. One of the oldest streets in Sarajevo, built in 1602, called Dugi sokak in Bascarsija, also bore Dzavid's name. Alija Bejtic in his work 'Streets and Squares of Sarajevo' in 1973, stated Dzavid's name was given to the street on July 31, 1950 (municipality of the old city of Sarajevo).[347] Today, Dzavid Haveric Street also exists in another location in Sarajevo (municipality in new Sarajevo). There is a memorial about him in the Vraca Memorial Park in Sarajevo, which was declared a national monument of Bosnia and Herzegovina.[348] In honour of his brother, **Kemal** Haveric gave his son the name **Dzavid** Haveric.

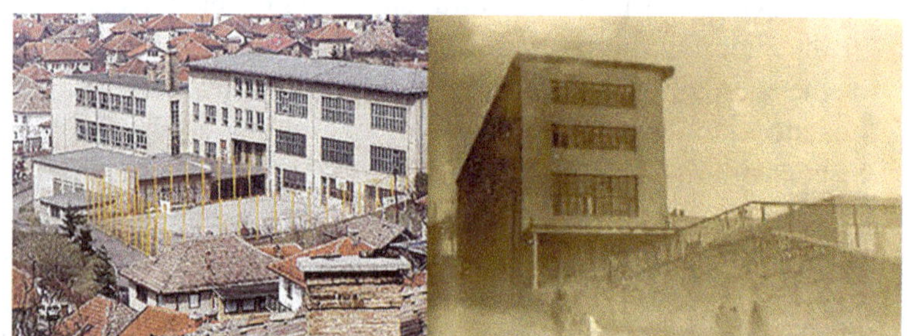

Dzavid Haveric, Primary school, Sarajevo

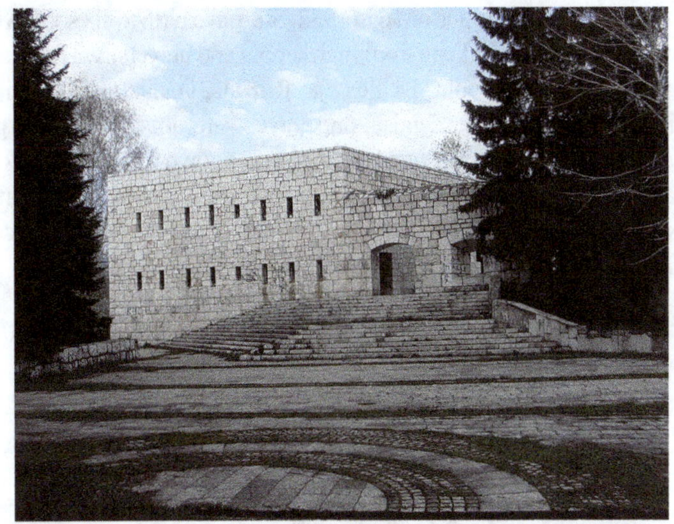

Memorial Centre Vraca to the fallen anti-fascist activists in the Second World War, Sarajevo

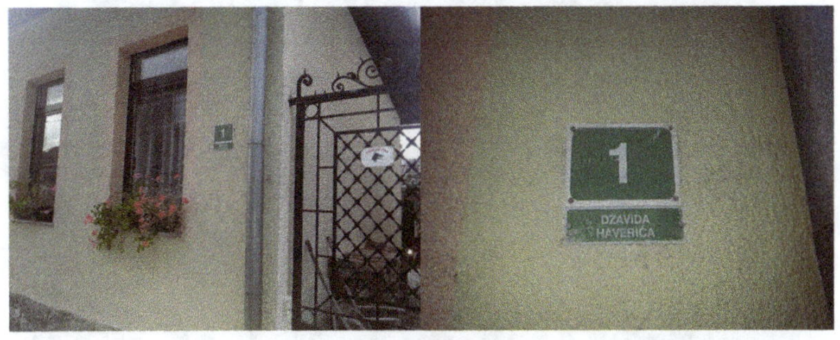

Dzavid Haveric Street, Sarajevo

Hatidza Hamza bey Haveric Keraj (Kerovic) was born in Podgorica. With her family, she took refuge in Shkoder. A couple of years later, her sister **Nazira** also came and stayed in Shkoder. Her brothers **Dzavid** and **Kemal** went to Sarajevo. In Albania, **Hatidza** was described 'a noble cultured woman of the Bosnian [Bosniak] origin'.[349]

Hatidza married at the age of 16 in 1932. She gave birth to six sons. All six brothers went on to graduate from high school and university. Their names were Jakub, Dr Semsudin, Dr Fevzija, Ruzdija, Ganija and Remzija. A couple of them became dentists and three were artists, enjoying great reputations. **Hatidzas**'s husband, Ahmet, was known throughout Shkoder as a 'master of cuisine' and was able to open two restaurants, one in Shkoder and one in Tirana, in the early 1940s, called the 'Bela-Venice'.

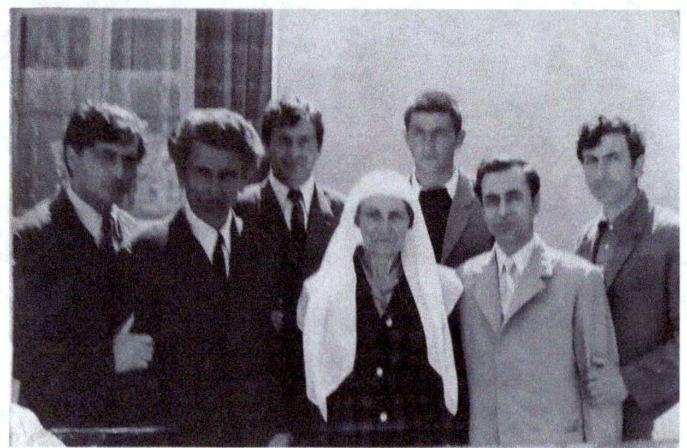

Hatidza Haveric Keraj (Kerovic) with her six sons

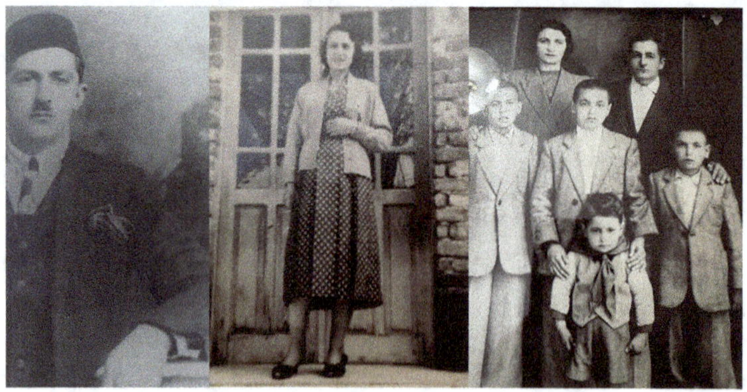

Hatidza's husband Ahmet Keraj (Kerovic); Hatidza; Hatidza and Ahmet Keraj (Kerovic) with sons

The oldest son, Jakub (Pupo), was a national figure in Albanian art. Father, Ahmet, with great sacrifices was able to build a studio in his house. **Hatidza** stayed for hours looking at Jakub bent over the drawing sheets with a pencil in his hand. He studied at the Academy of Fine Arts 'I.E. RJEPIN' of Leningrad (St. Petersburg), Russia. His paintings are displayed at many galleries in Albania and overseas. One of his paintings is displayed at the National History Museum 'Gjergj Kastrioti Skënderbeu', known as the Skanderbeg Museum in Kruja. Jakub's funeral 'in the city of Shkodra was magnificent'. His friend, famous painter Wilson Kilica, reflected this event in a large painting, which is probably 'one of the most successful in the entire history of Albanian painting'.[350]

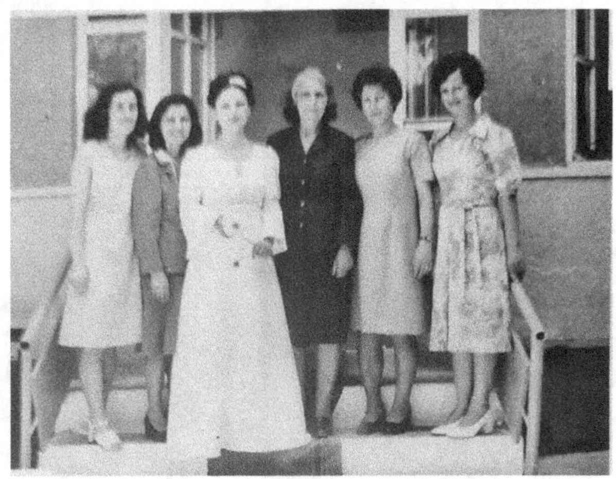

Hatidza with daughters-in-law

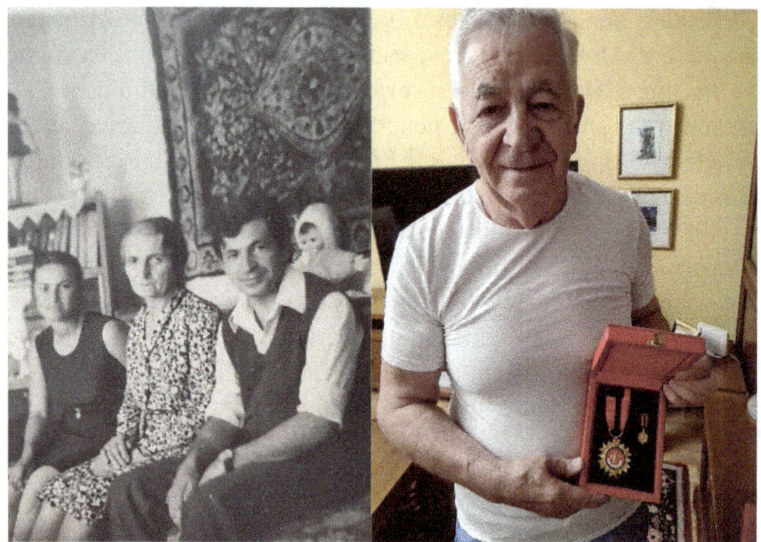

Hatidza Haveric Keraj in the middle **Dr Fejzi Keraj**

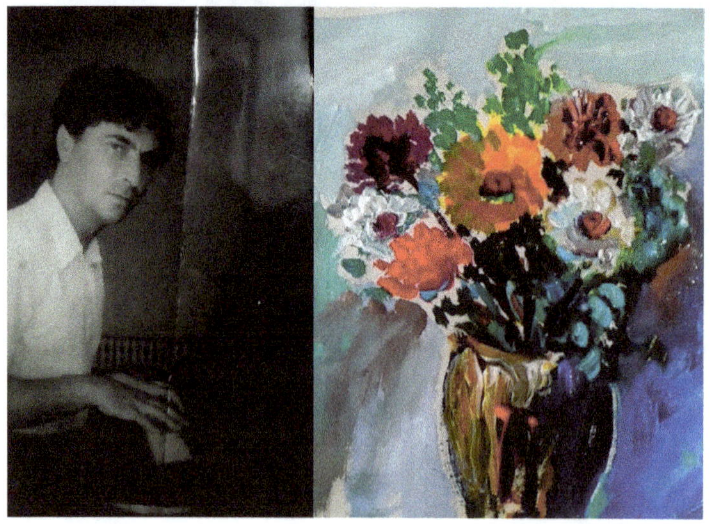

Ruzhdi Keraj **Ruzhdia's painting**

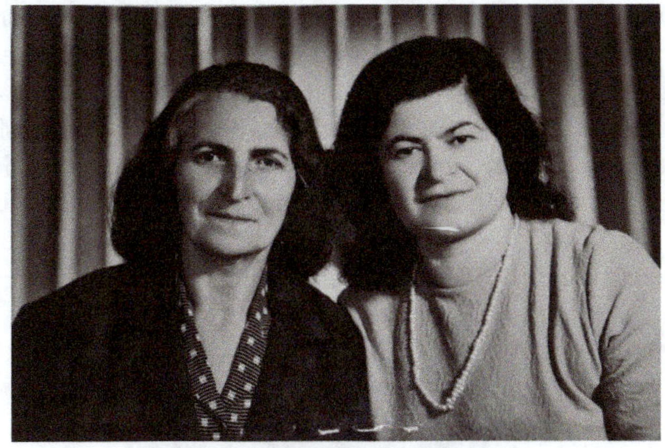

Sisters Hatidza and Nazira Haveric

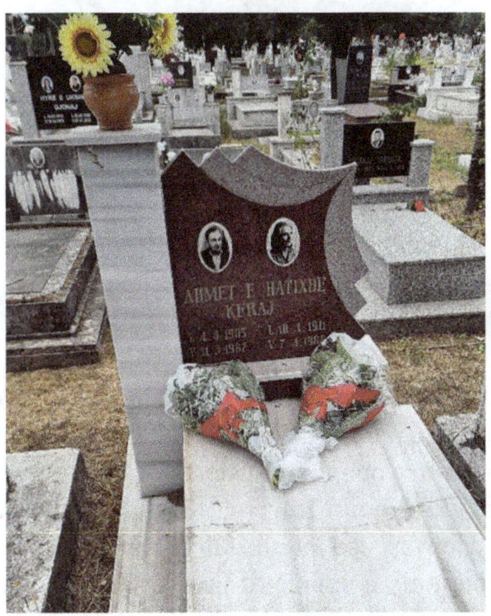

Ahmet and Hatidza Keraj's grave

El Fatiha

Kemal Hamza bey Haveric was born in Trebinje, Bosnia and Herzegovina, in 1924. He lost his parents early. He had an older brother, **Dzavid**, and two sisters, **Hatidza** and **Nazira**. In Sarajevo, he stayed in an orphanage and finished his craft apprenticeship as a shoemaker. He participated in the anti-fascist movement in Sarajevo then in Shkoder. In Sarajevo, together with his brother, **Dzavid**, a national hero, he was imprisoned in Beledija prison. Being not mature enough, he was released from the prison.

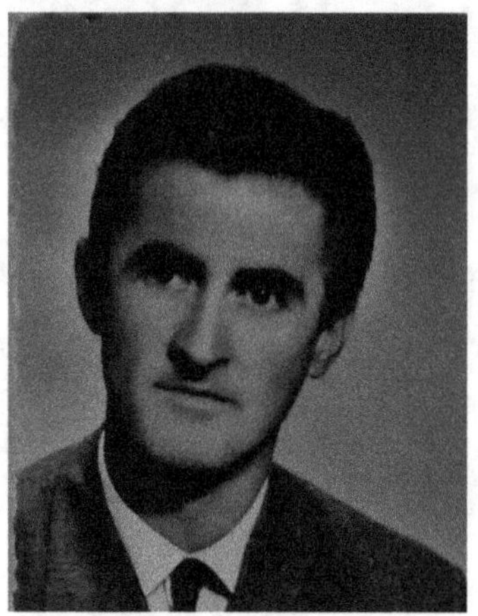

Kemal Hamza bey Haveric

Since he was an anti-fascist according to his conviction, he continued his illegal anti-fascist activities in Albania. In Shkoder, Kemal joined a young anti-fascist group, which consisted of Camo Gradevic, **Kemal** Haveric, Seko Ljumanovic and Mehmed Gokovic.[351] He was also interned in Albania in 1943. While **Kemal** was in prison, only a couple of people were allowed to visit him, including Lilo Zeneli, whose mother was a Haveric.

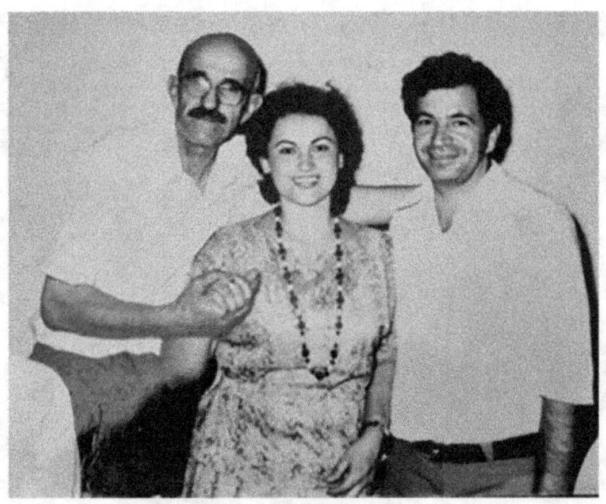

Lilo Zeneli (left)

He returned and continued his life in Sarajevo. He held two recognitions for his wartime merits. After the war, he served in the Yugoslav military service in Ljubljana, Slovenia. Due to the closed borders between Albania and Yugoslavia, he was only able to meet the sisters later. He married to **Hidajeta** Akif Sijercic from an old Bosnian family, whose direct ancestor was Sinan Pasha Sijercic, a general in the Bosnian Eyalet.

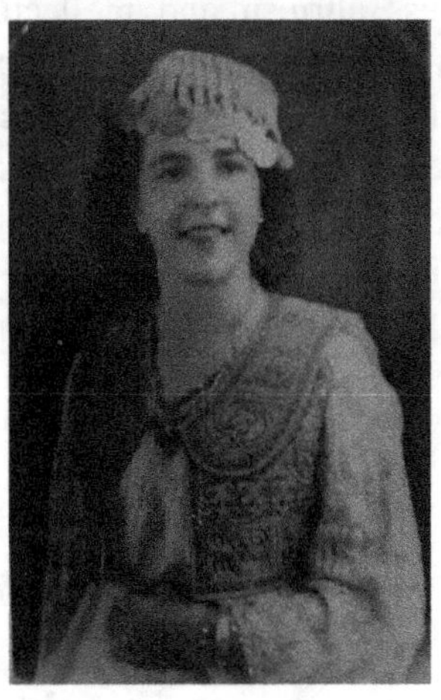

Hidajeta Sijercic Haveric

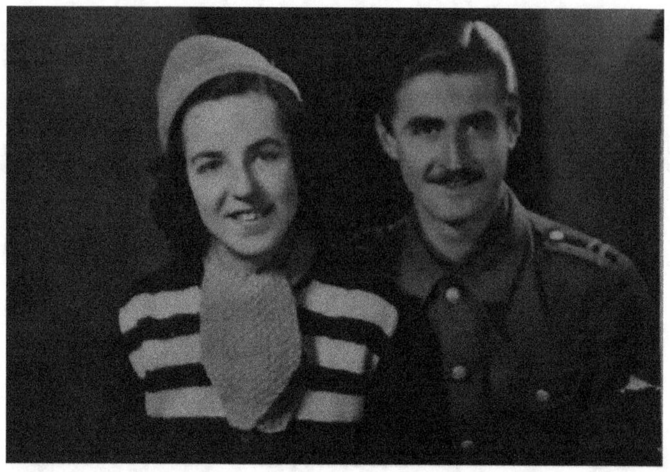

Hidajeta and Kemal Haveric, Ljubljana, 1948, serving in Yugoslav army

In Sarajevo, **Kemal** continued to work as a shoemaker in a few shops, including one behind the Sarajevian Cathedral, then he graduated from school for administrative affairs and worked as a clerk in the companies 'Geoistrage' and 'Unis' in Sarajevo. He enrolled in law studies, but did not complete them due to health reasons. **Kemal** was known for his fairness, altruism and intellectual discussions in his social circles. When he was asked what he thought the purpose of life was, he would answer, 'It is altruism, to serve people'. He spoke Bosnian, Montenegrin and Albanian and liked to read a book, especially history once. He wrote the biographical manuscript about his brother, **Dzavid**.

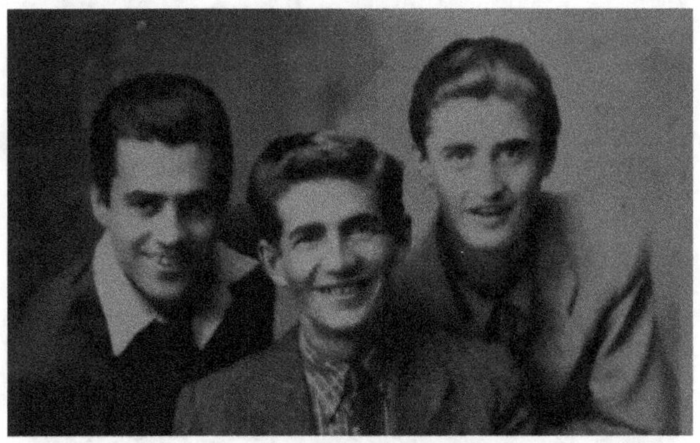

Kemal (right) with friends

Kemal died in Sarajevo due to a traffic accident as a pedestrian in 1979. He was buried at the Bare Cemetery in Sarajevo. About 300 people, family and friends, including distinguished personalities and pioneers from the **Dzavid** Haveric School came together to pay their respects to Kemal Haveric. Kemal and Hidajeta's son is **Dr Dzavid Haveric**, a university researcher, historian, museum researcher and an author. He married **Aida** Piknjac, a teacher and early childcare educator. Kemal and Hidajeta's daughter is **Dzejlana Haveric**, an academic painter and translator.

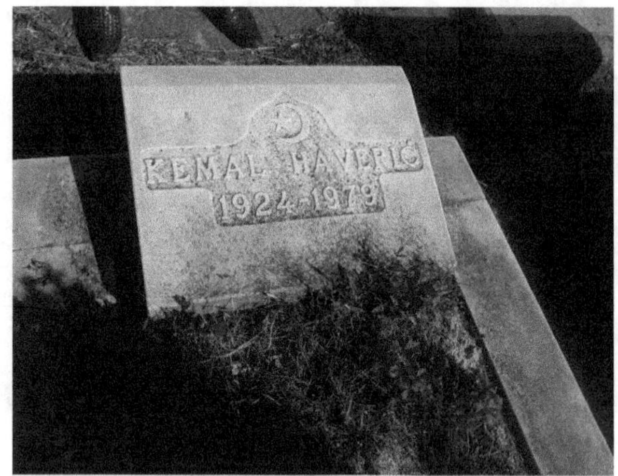

Kemal Haveric's grave, Bare Cemetery, Sarajevo

El Fatiha

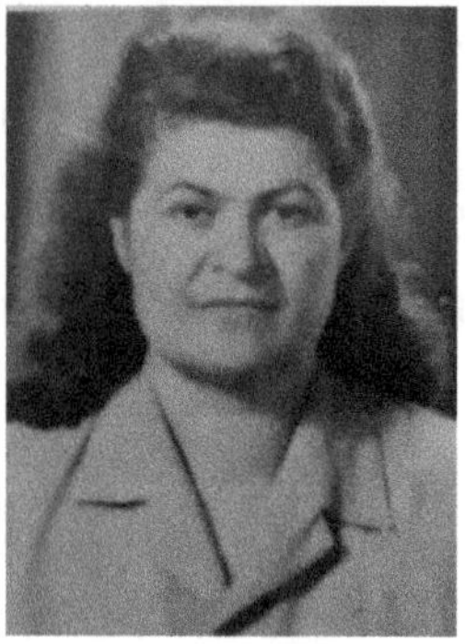

Nazira Haveric Kerni (Krnic)

Nazira Hamza bey Haveric was born in Trebinje, Bosnia and Herzegovina, and married **Hamdija** Keraj (Krnic), a taxi driver. They lived in old Tirana in Ruga Misto Mame street. They did not have children so they adopted a boy named **Gzima**. The street and house where **Nazira** and **Hamdija** lived was inspiration for the artist Ruzdi Kerni's oil painting. Nazira was instrumental in collecting information and stories about various dispersed members of the Haveric family.

In one of her letters, **Nazira** wrote to his Haveric family in Bosnia and Herzegovina: 'We are all fine. We wish the best for you too… *Amanet* (a requested promise, instruction) not even the earth can erase…'; 'We are waiting for you to visit us and fulfill the *amanet* of our parents…' Nezira also wrote, 'Brothers, **Dzavid** and **Kemal**, were like two beautiful falcons, but they were destined for too early black soil'.[352]

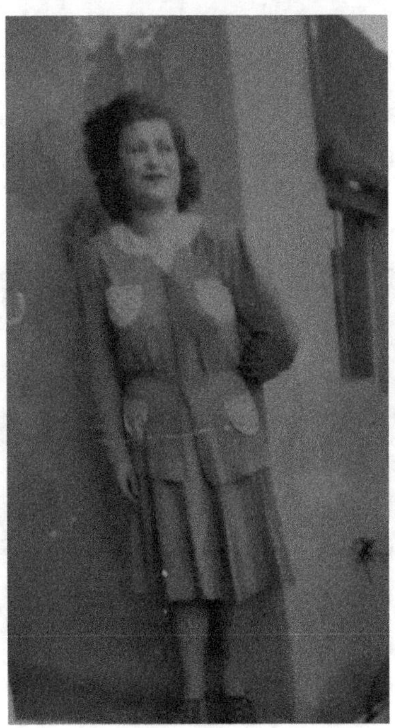

Nazira Haveric Kerni (Krnic)

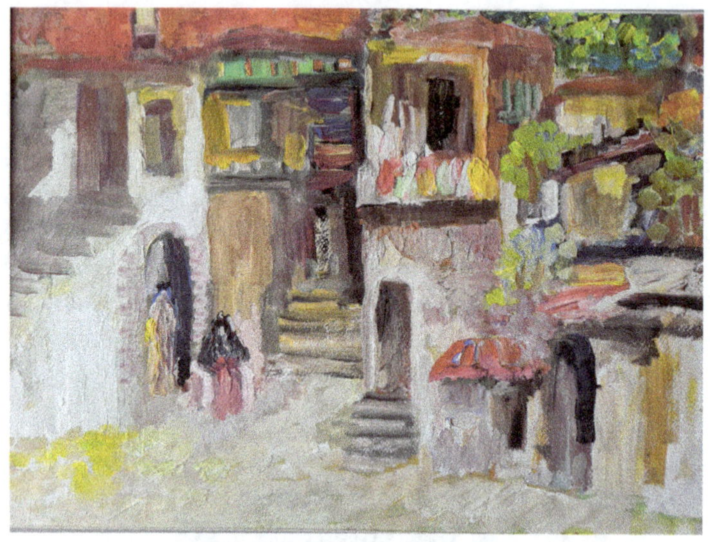

Painting by Ruzdhija Keraj (Ruzdija Kerovic), Ruga Misto Mame, Tirane Street where Nazira Haveric Kerni (Krnic) lived

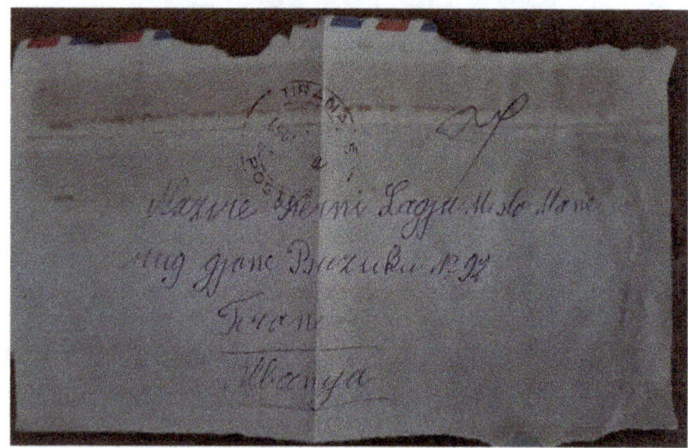

Nazira's address

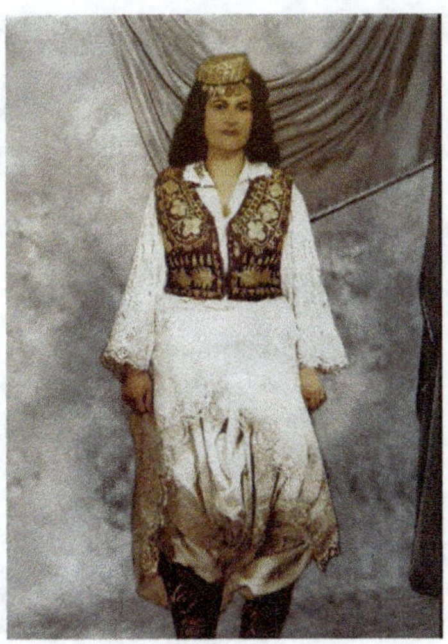

Nazira (Haveric) in Albanian folk dress, 1957

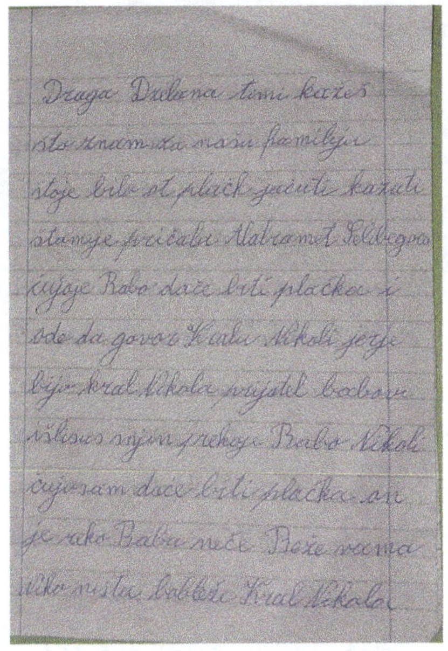

Draga Dželana timi kažeš
što znam za našu familju
što je bilo ot plačk začuti kazati
šta mije pričala Alahramet Selbegova
čuje je Babo daće biti plačka i
ode da govori Kralu Nikoli jerje
bijo kral Nikola prijatel babove
išlisu nijim prekoje Babo Nikoli
čujosam daće biti plačka on
je rako Babu neće Boże vama
niko ništa kableći Kral Nikola

A letter written by Nazira

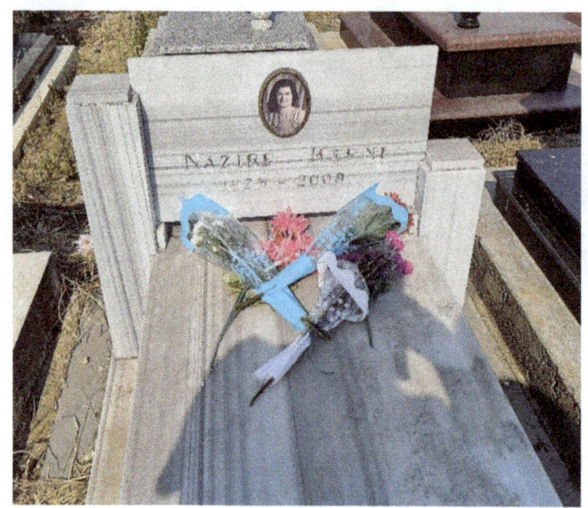

Nazira Kerni's grave

El Fatiha

Abdulah (Duljo) bey Haveric was the third son of **Ibrahim bey**. He was a tradesman and, together with brother Zejnil, traded in Zeta, Montenegro. They were also slaughtering livestock preparing them for sale. Nezire Keraj Haveric recalled:

When they were in Podgorica, all the Haverics used to visit each other. When arrived in Albania, **Abdulah** was probably in Shkoder before me, as he already knew to speak Albanian. When the others went to Sarajevo, he has come to Shkoder for trading. He dealt with trade and had a shop in **Bexisteni** (in Shkoder) where hundreds of trading units were.

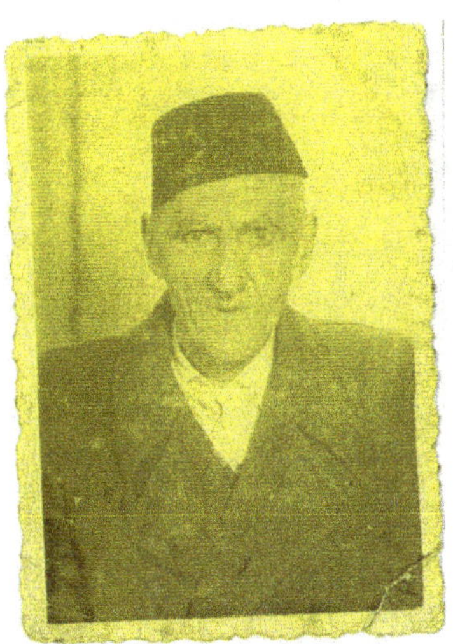

Abdulah (Duljo) bey

A. PARRUCA

Lista emërore e tregtarëve të Shkodrës që kanë patur dyqane brenda Bexhistenit në vitin 1920 (sipas regjistrit të Zyrës së Tatimeve Shkodër)

Shkoder tax register, 1920

In Shkoder, **Dulo bey** often met **Sulejman bey**. According to a register of the Shkoder tax office, on the list of merchants from Shkoder who had shops in **Bexhistent** in 1920, **Duljo bey Haveric** was listed.[353] In front of the units were some places called ‘hladnjaci’ (‘cooling stores’), because they were chilled. There was plenty of cheese and these two ate a lot, so they said an anecdote: '**Suljo** and **Dulo** bringing a hundred of fish [to eat]'.[354] **Abdulah Duljo bey** was involved in the Jewish trade in Sarajevo. **Duljo bey** married Lukacevic. They had a son, **Hajrullah**, and a younger daughter, **Fatima (Fata). Hajrulah (Hajro)** married **Sebija (Bilja)** Lacevic. Their son is **Ismet (Gaga)** and a daughter, **Halima (Limka). Hajrulah (Hajro)** was buried in the Alifakovac Cemetery, Sarajevo.[355]

Zejnil bey Haveric, a fourth son of **Ibrahim bey**, was a merchant who escaped from Podgorica between 1914 and lived in Trebinje, Shkoder, Bihac and Visegrad where his children were born. He married Camila Lukacevic. From the 1930s, they lived in Sarajevo. They had three daughters, **Fahrije**, **Makbule** and **Hava**, as well as two sons, **Enver** and **Shemsudin**. **Zejnil bey** was buried at the Grlica Hill cemetery in Sarajevo.

Semsudin (Semso) Zejnil bey Haveric came with parents and siblings to Sarajevo as a baby from Bihac. He graduated from dental school in Sarajevo. **Semso** first worked as a dentist in the town of Vares, Bosnia. He worked in Sarajevo's dental clinics and had a private practice. He married **Anisa Beslagic** from the town of Visoko.

In the Second World War, **Semso** participated in the 7th Muslim Brigade, which was one of the liberation units. He is mentioned in the book *Sarajevo in Revolution* (1981) During the war, **Semso**'s code name was 'Sane'. In one of the actions, when 'Vladimir Peric Walter was wounded, **Semso** was the first to approach him under crossfire and helped him to get out of the fire line'. That quote was said in the speech of a SUBNOR representative at the Alifakovac Cemetery when Semso's funeral was held.

At the cemetery on Alifakovac, Sarajevo, on his *mezar* states:

El Faitha

Semsudin (Zejnil) Haveric

1925-1997

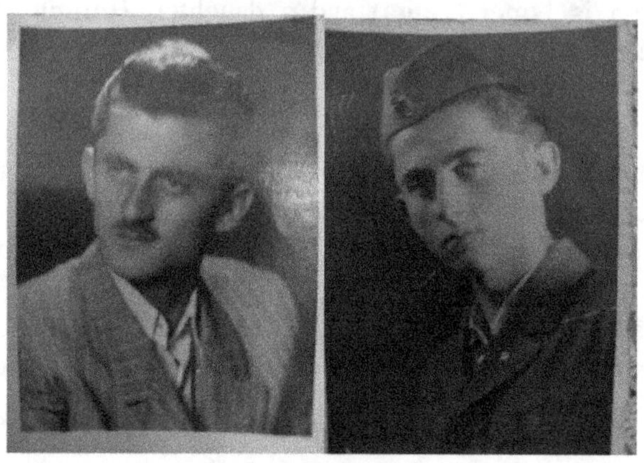

Semsudin (Semso) Haveric

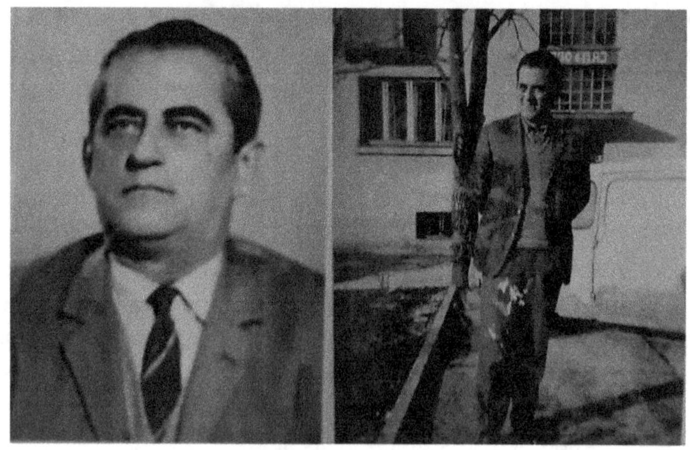

Semsudin (Semso) Haveric

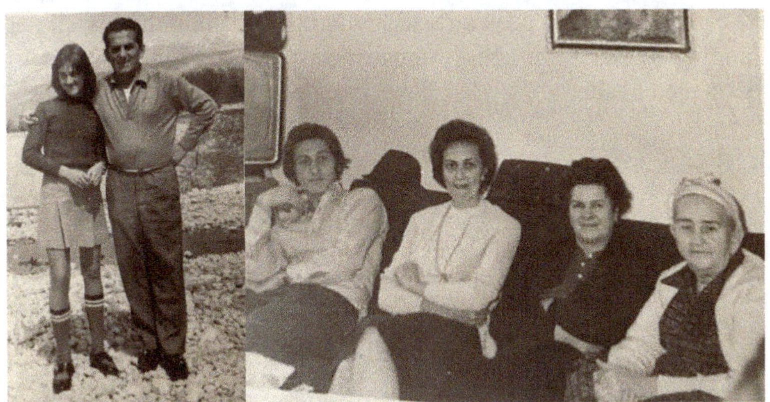

Semso and daughter Alma; Kemal, Enisa, Magbula and Camila (Semsudin's mother)

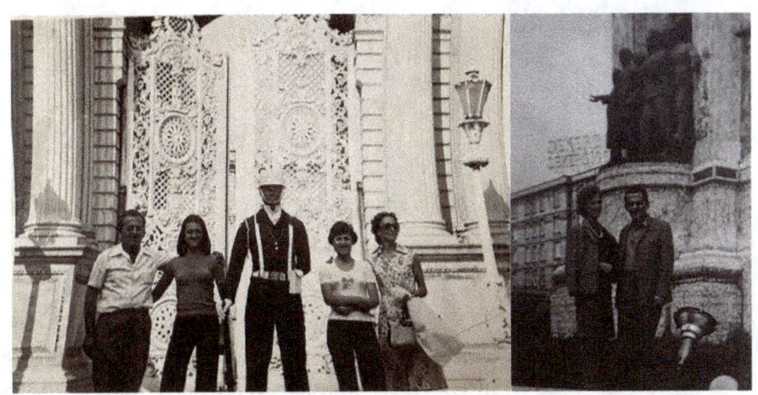

Semso, Alma, Aida and Enisa Haveric visiting Istanbul
Anisa and Shemo in Istanbul, Turkiye

Because of his humanistic ideals and views about freedom of religion, he was misjudged, thus unjustly prosecuted by the communistic authority. His case was set up by a spy, a man of poor ethics. He was sent to Foca prison for ten months. In the Sarajevo tribunal, revolted by the court's decision, **Hidajeta** Haveric exclaimed, '**Semso** is innocent, he didn't do anything wrong!' From the prison, he sent postcards to his family, wishing them well and hoping to see them soon. **Semso** was released from prison with damaged health.

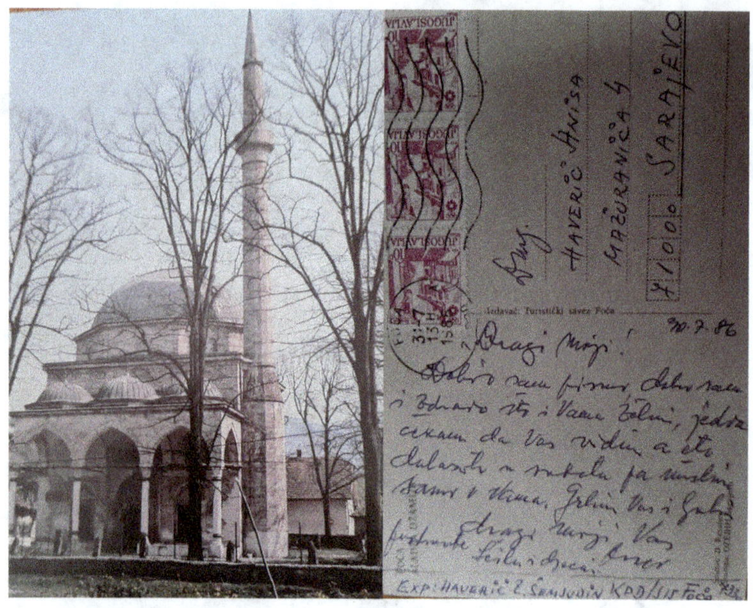

Postcard from Foca prison

Semso loved to read books, often ordering them from the publishers, had a large home library and enjoyed discussing books with relatives and friends. Even unknowing of his death, to his address came information from the publishers, such as 'Slovenacka Mladina', Ljubljana, about releases of new books as he was a regular customer.[356]

Dr Enver Zejnil bey Haveric was born in Trebinje. 'He usually spoke about his father **Zejnil bey** to his mother Camila or my aunts'.[357] The talks were brief but with a great respect. With his parents Enver, as a little boy, moved from Trebinje, Bihac to

Visegrad, so 'all over Bosnia and Herzegovina'. and eventually settled in Sarajevo. He completed his education at the Commercial School in Sarajevo while also working sessional works. He graduated from the University of Zagreb, Faculty of Economics. Enver was a Doctor of Economics and his doctoral dissertation was 'Industrialization of Bosnia and Herzegovina' ('Industrijalizacija Bosne i Hercegovine') in 1974 at the University of Sarajevo, Faculty of Economics. As a professor at the Faculty of Law in Mostar, he taught the subject of political economy. He also taught at the Faculty of Architecture and at the College of Social Work, both in Sarajevo. Towards the end of his working life, he was an Advisor for Economic Affairs at the Architectural Institute in Sarajevo. For his academic work, Dr Enver Haveric received several awards and a plaque.

Enver Haveric married **Nadija (Nada)** Drace from a prominent Mostar merchant family who graduated from the Technical School in Mostar. Enver and Nada's son is **Dr Zlatko Haveric**, a licensed physician who specialised in internal medicine. He also had his medical career in Sarajevo hospital. He married **Inga** Karabeg, a daughter of a respected journalist and editor-in-chief of Oslobodjenje in Mostar, Mugdim Karabeg. Enver and Nada's daughter was **Amra (Manja) Haveric,** a graduated **economist,** who married Aid Valjevac. **Amra** worked in the Privredna bank and an insurance company.

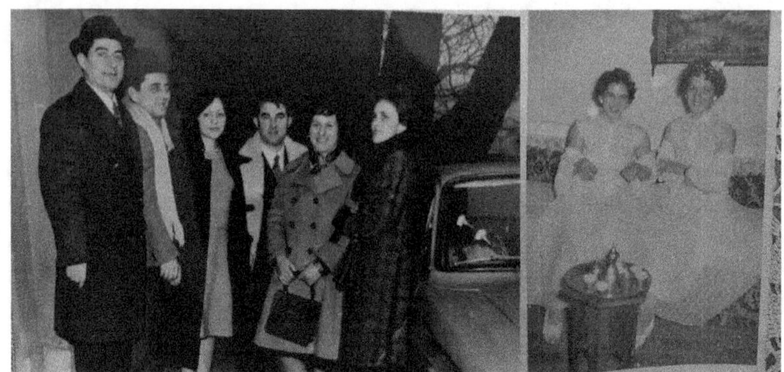

Dr Enver Haveric (first from the left), Nadija (Nada) Haveric (second from the right)

Nadija (Nada) Haveric (left)

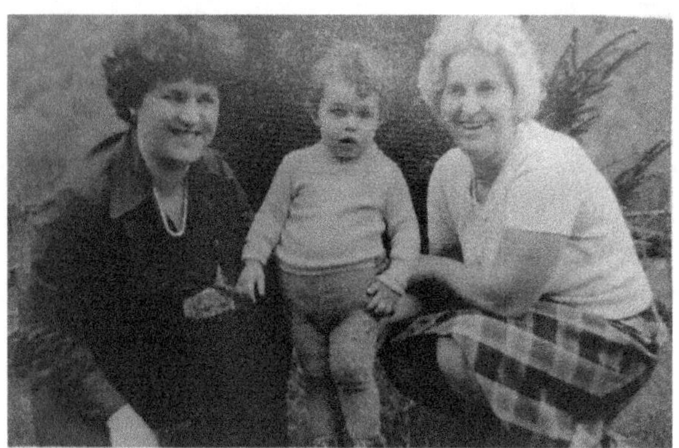

Nada, Ever's wife (left)

Zejnil bey's daughter **Fahrija** was born in Shkoder like Ismaili bey's **Fahrija**. In Shkoder, to distinguish them because of the same name and surname, Zenel's daughter **Fahrija** and Ismaili's **Fahrija** were called 'Fahrija no. 1 and Fahrija no. 2'

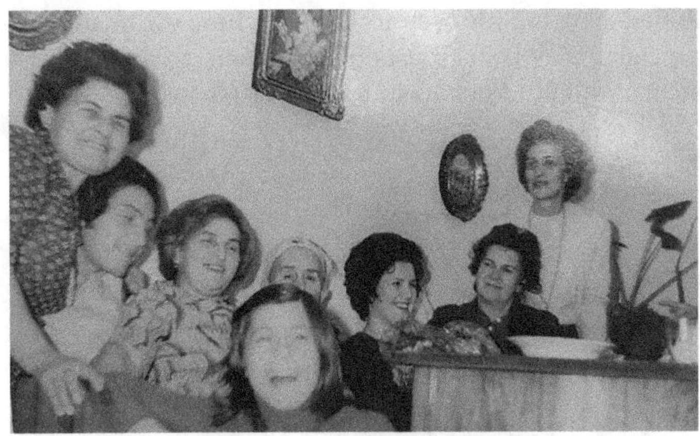

Sisters Fahrija (Faka) Hava, Magbula Haveric with mother in the middle, Nada Envers' wife and Enisa Semso's wife

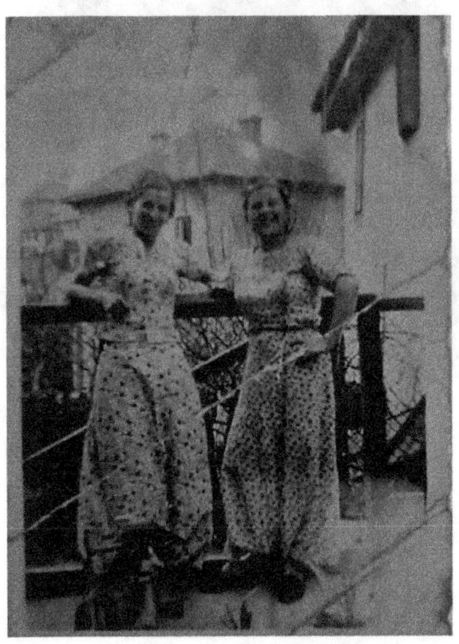

Magbula (left) with her friend Dzemila in Jelica Street in Sarajevo where the girls were gathered near the water fountain

Mahmud bey, the fifth son of **Ibrahim bey**, was married to [?] Osmanagic. They had a son who died young, around two or three years old. **Mahmud bey** was a capable merchant.[358]

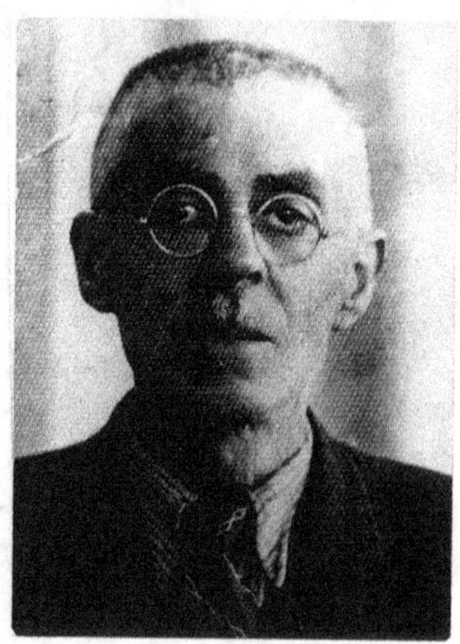

Mahmud bey

Havaja, the daughter of **Ibrahim bey**, married Nezira Keraj Haveric's uncle, Ibrahim Omercahic. They had no children.[359]

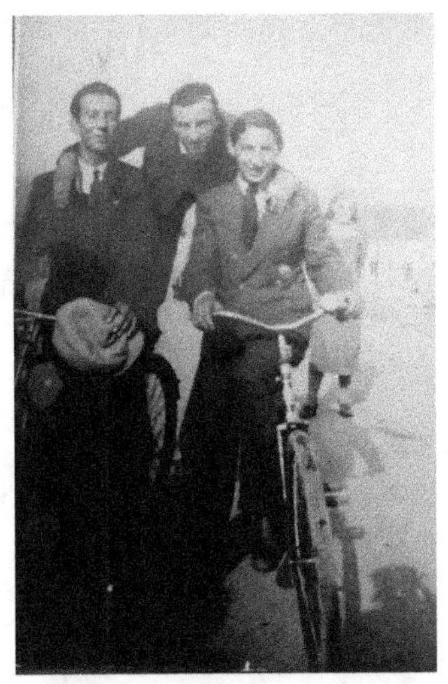

Sukrija (Suco) Haveric (left), 1950

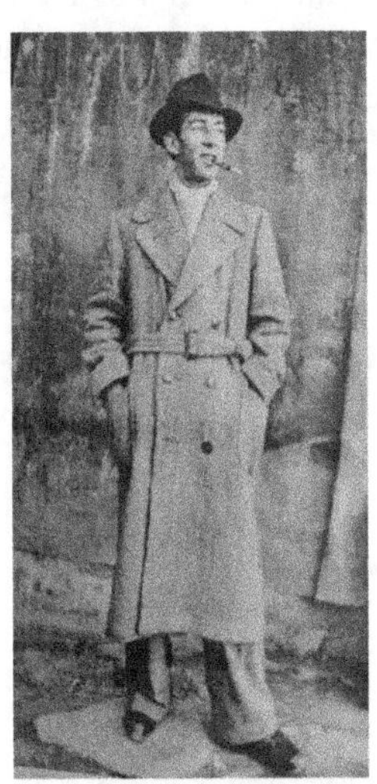

Sukrija (Suco) Haveric

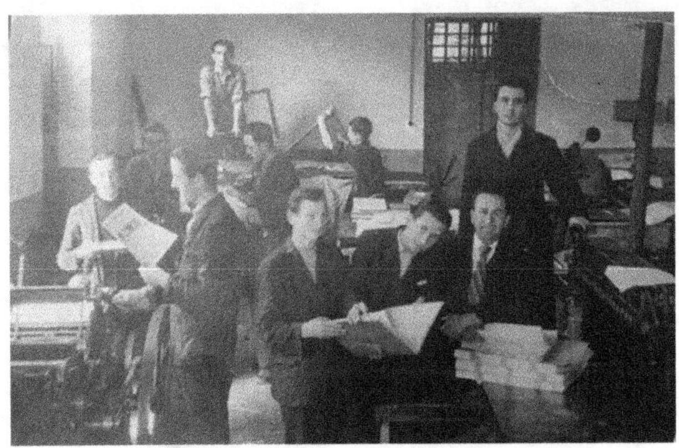

Sukrija (Sućo) Haveric (in the middle-left)

Sukrija (Suco) Haveric worked for the Bosnian (Yugoslavian) authorities. He enjoyed a great respect. He had a son, **Zlatan**, and daughter, **Gordana**. **Zlatan** Haveric worked as a librarian in the great Vijecnica Library in old Sarajevo. **Zlatan** and his wife **Zlata** had two sons, **Dr Sanin Haveric**, an expert in the fields of cytogenetics, genotoxicology and mutagenesis, and **Samir Haveric**.

Zenel bey, was the eldest son of **Hysein bey** (it seems missing in the family tree). He married Dzevahira Limonovic (or Ljumanovic), who was described as an 'authoritative lady and tall'.

Zenel bey worked in the Prefecture (local government) in Podgorica and was thought to have come to Shkodra on a mission, perhaps in the 1990s. It was said he was very good at work so they transferred him to the Prefecture of Shkodera to organise the work there. In Podgorica the first son, **Shyqyi**, was born, around 1874-1875, but he passed away from cholera.

After **Shyqyi** there were five daughters, but a couple died from cholera. Their names are unknown, except for **Mulurija** and **Feride**. They said, 'As soon as one funeral returned, another started, so many deaths occurred, that one was buried, and another was ready (maybe they were sick when they came from Podgorica)'. **Myhurija** married an officer in Turkiye. When there was cholera, they also died. **Feride** died in the city of Vlore, Albania, probably from tuberculosis. She had no children.

In Shkoder around 1897, a boy was born and they named him **Haver**. After a while, **Zenel bey** was transferred to Kruje to work there in administration.

From Kruje in 1878, **Zenel bey** travelled by horse to Durres in 1894. On September 12, 1899, a son, **Qazim**, was born 'on the road'. From there they took him to Kavaje or Durres, where they also had their uncle's son, **Ymer bey**.

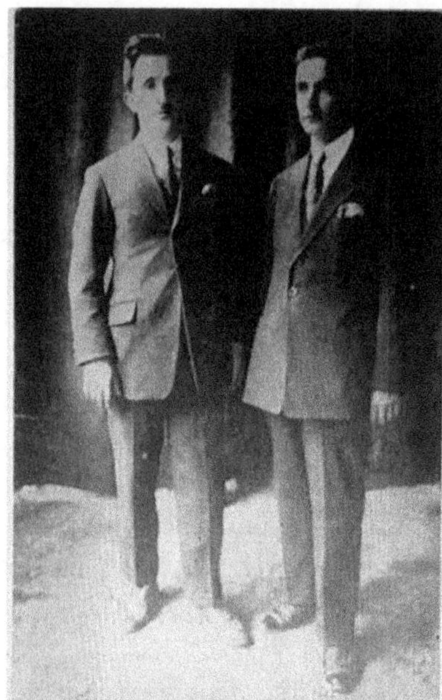

Haver Haveric (right) with a friend

Haver Zenel bey Haveric was born in 1897 in Shkoder. With father and mother Dzevahira and siblings he came to Kruje, where the family stayed for while then settled in Durres. **Haver** married **Hyrie** Drishtin. They had no children. **Haver** was resourceful, a well-talented man. He started dealing with the market and, together with the brothers, expanded the activity over time.

Together with his brothers he ran the trading business 'Bothers Haveric' (**'Vellezerit Haveric'**). During the Great War, Haver started selling soap to Austrian soldiers stationed in Durres, then selling lamb meat and later cars. The three brothers, through Vellezerit Haveric, sold Fiat brand cars from Italy. **Haver** frequently travelled to Italy for business purposes.[360]

In the centre of Durres, at the end of the boulevard of that city in Albania, the Haverik family had a store. It was managed by **Haver Haveriku**, who also had a car factory, large financial possessions, a house and a large cinema in Durres in the 1930s for people watching Hollywood films.[361] It was taken from him during the reign of Enver Hoxha. After the shop was nationalised, it was turned into a movie theatre.

The totalitarian regime of Enver Hoxha expropriated the properties obtained after their hard work and put him in prison. While captured, Haver took on the responsibility to help others even when he was tortured. When he got out of the internment prison in Shkoder, the prison staff told him ironically, 'That's where you were born'. Being freed, **Haver** turned to a new life as a merchant, because 'trade was in his blood'. He started again selling small goods such as trinkets, balloons and lollies. He died around 1960.

With the establishment of democracy, ownership was returned to him, but the cinema continued to function.[362] Later, the Durres newspaper wrote that, in the remodelled and extended place that used to be an old store, 'nowadays American, Italian and Russian films are shown'.

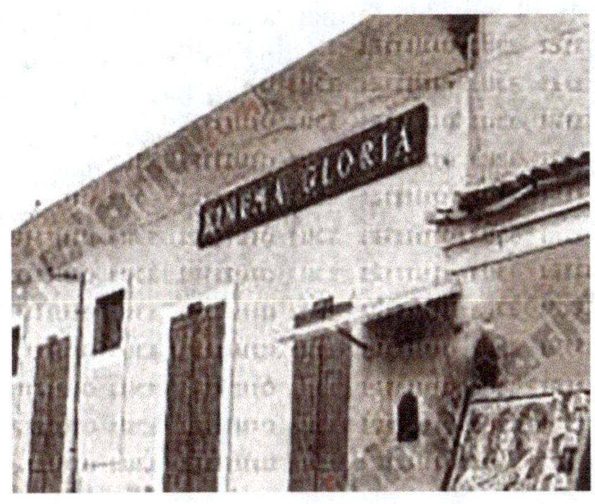

Old store and cinema, Haveriku in Durres

Ismail bey Haveric, after fighting Austria-Hungary, escaped from Podgorica to Shkodra. He fought for Bosnia and held the rank of captain.[363] In October 1918, the Austrians left Montenegro, leaving behind devalued paper crowns. **Ismail bey**, like some others, turned the gold into this paper money, but they say there was so much that he could cover the whole house. Dr Xhevat Repishti, in his book Luffa for the defense of Shkoder in 1918-1920, wrote about this situation: '…but many merchants went bankrupt, after they turned their capital into invalidated crown banknotes'. In Shkoder, very rich at that time, they fell economically. For these families it is said: 'jane fike nga paret austriake' ('are turned off by the Austrian walls').

However, **Ismail bey** told his brother that he still had some houses and shops, planning to travel back to Istanbul. In the meantime, King Nikola was overthrown in 1916. He left Montenegro and come to **Ismail bey**, his former adjutant, who came to Shkoder earlier. Being disordered, the king still 'wondered' about the situation in Montenegro, asking **Ismail bey** 'what's it happening [in Montenegro] the bey?' King Nikola stayed overnight at **Ismail bey**'s house while his wife 'gave him to use a pillow and a blanket embroidered with roses' before he continued to go to Italy.[364] The king left for Italy and went to France at Bordeaux where he established his 'base', still officially representing Montenegro.

Beqir (Becir) Jusuf bey was **Ismail bey**'s brother. He fought in **Gallipoli**. He was wounded heavily but lived and some years after the war resided in Turkiye. He passed away in his 30s.

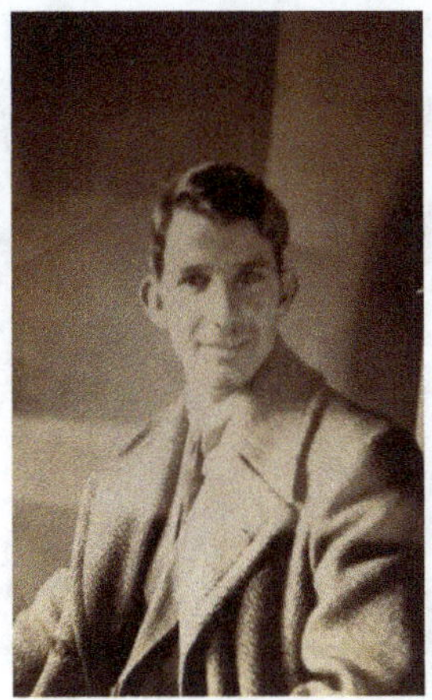

Gani bey Haveri

Gani Ismail bey Haveri was born on March 6, 1913, in Shkoder. His mother was **Rabie Myftar agha Sokoli**. In Shkoder, he finished at the Jesuit high school. Then, in 1930, with his brother, **Ali**, and his sister, **Fahria**, came to Tirana. **Gani bey** worked as an employee in the 'National Defence Command' for King Ahmed Zog (ruled 1922-1939). In 1940 and 1941, **Gani bey** also worked as a secretary in the sub-prefecture of Puka (a town and municipality in northern Albania), as a secretary in its sub-prefecture (a district under the authority of a prefect or governor) and as a pro-activist copyist.[365]

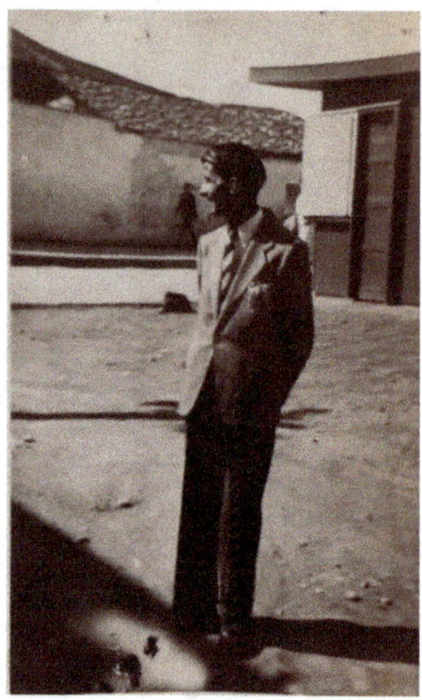

Gani bey Haveri

In 1942, **Gani bey** moved to Tetovo, Macedonia, to probably work as a teacher. There he joined the war and went to the partisan mountain with the 7th Brigade of the Macedonian offensive. He was admitted to the Albanian Communist Party on October 27, 1945. However, after a few years, for health reasons, **Gani bey** withdrew from the service, especially since he could not accept instructions to do espionage because it was not a job that suited his character. After his release, he returned to Albania and worked in different places mainly as a teacher. He married Klimente Kerniqi (Krnic) and they had only one son, **Agim**. Gani passed away in 1961.

> **Gani bey's** nature was calm, while his specialty was oratory. He was also involved in linguistics, collecting material for the Albanian dictionary, which he did not manage to complete.

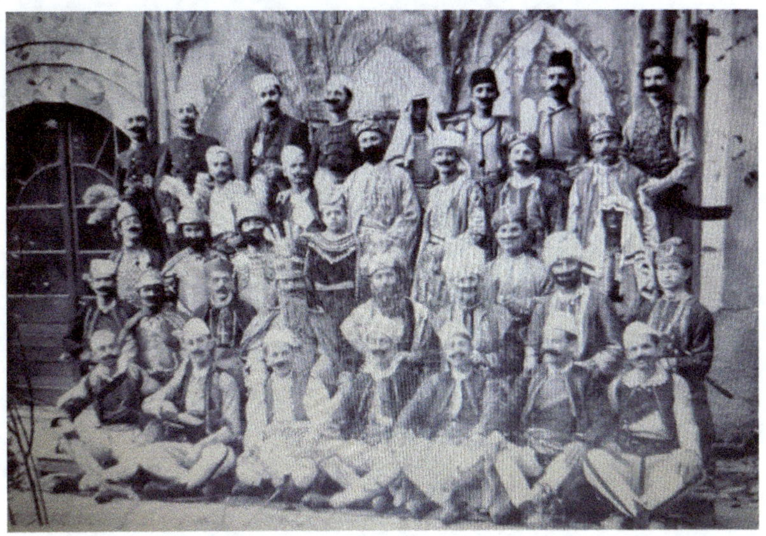

Gani Haveri at Jezuite Gimnazija, 1929 (with a white cap with a moustache, second row from the top, third from the right)

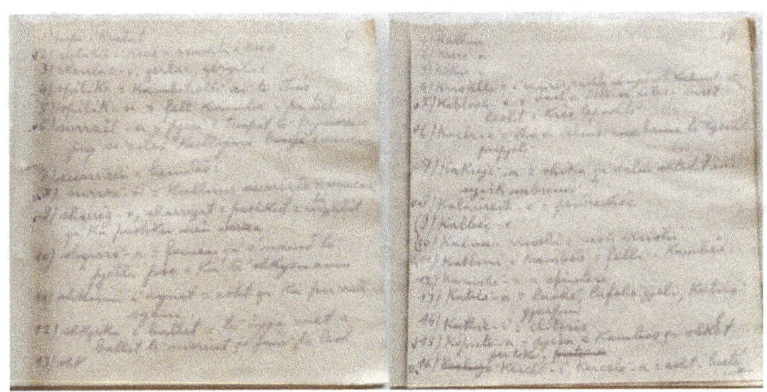

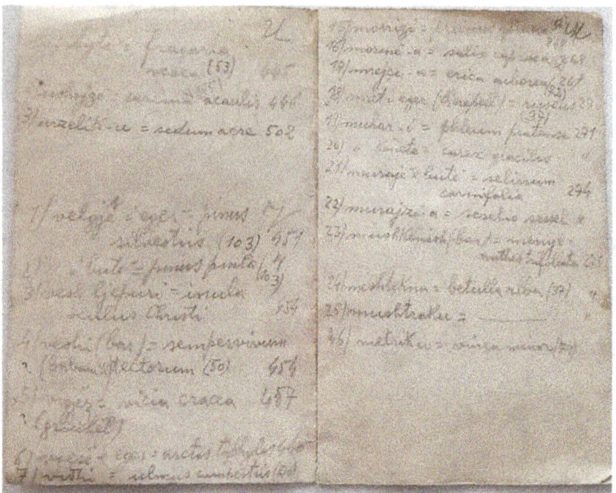

Gani's script: working on Albanian Dictionary Story

Ali Ismail bey Haveriqi was born in 1904 in Podgorica. He was a small child when he came to Shkoder. He grew up in the environment of Shkodra, where he found warmth and peace. He became active in the sport of cycling, where he stood out for his athletic spirit. He took part in the first cycling circuit in August-September 1925 and was a champion in Europe for an amateurs cycling championship.

A series of photographs show the first cycling circuit, starting in 1925, with the departure from Shkoder showing them in Tirana. A photo of this cycling circle has written on it: 'The departure of Zogu cyclists from Shkoder on 28-VIII-1925'.

In 1925, sports articles in Albania reported that **Alija Haveric**, son of **Ismail bey**, took part in a bicycle race, broke his brake, but managed to fix the broken brake while riding thus won first place.

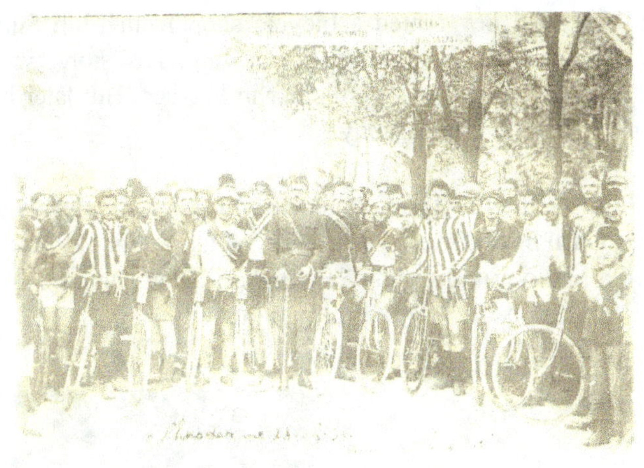

Ali Haveri with cycling glasses (centre right next to a person with a stick) at the championship, Albania, Shkoder, 1925

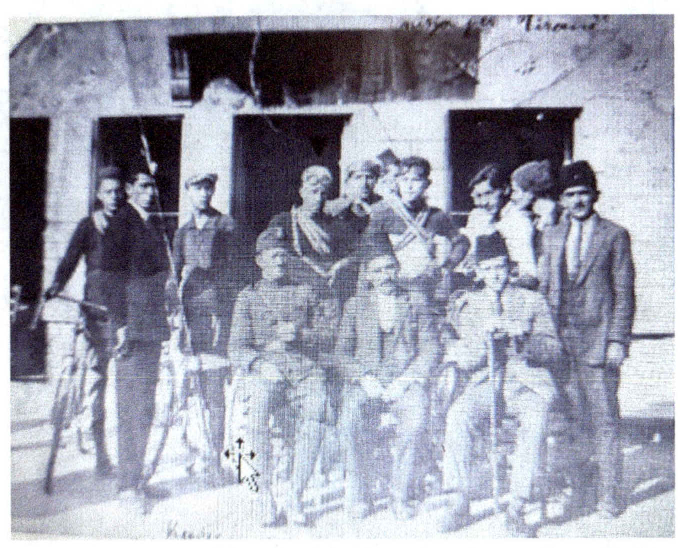

Departure from Kavaje to Tirana

From 1927, **Ali bey** rented a bicycle shop from Filip Suma on Gjane Street. while continuing his cycling. His store was near Car Buburice, which has a public bar in Parruce. But later he was engaged in artistic photography.

In 1930, he settled in Tirana together with his sister, **Fahrija**, and brother, **Gani bey**. Here, in partnership with Sulejman Kelmenti, he opened a photo printing shop: 'Foto Dajti'. The name of the shop was 'Dajti', probably after a nearby mountain.

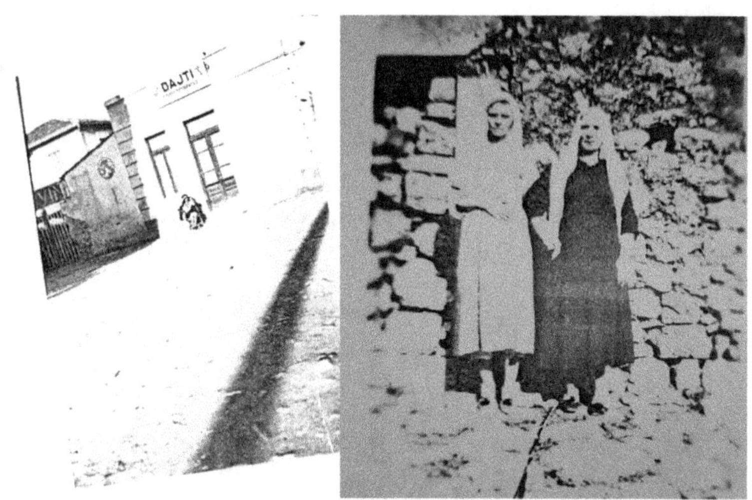

Old photography shop in Tirana

During that time, he also entered the royal court, taking photos of the royal members, so much so that even today there are Albanians who say: '**Ali bey** was the photographer of King Zogu'. **Ali bey** travelled across Europe, sometimes for photo material supplies and other times just for fun. He died at 40 years old, single, on September 27, 1944. Nowadays, his photographic collection is displayed at the 'Fototeke Koleksione Shqiptare'.

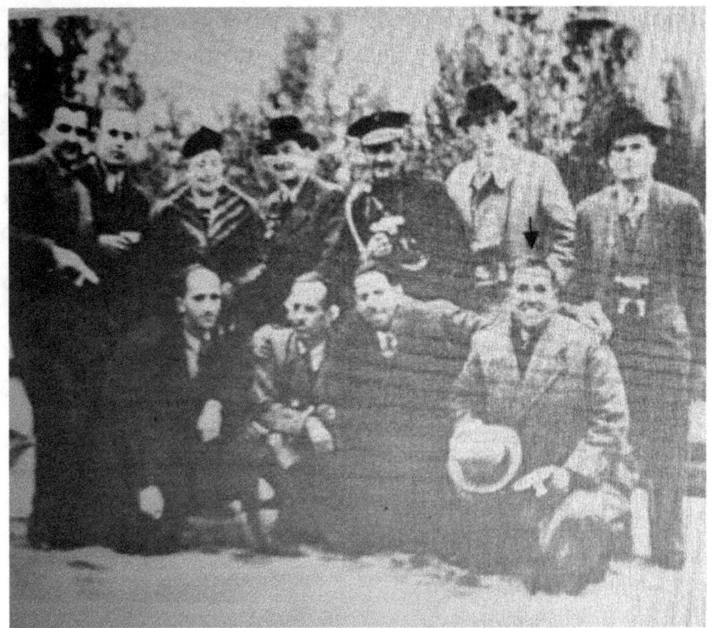

Ali Haveriqi, with white hat on his knee

This photo was taken at the Royal Court in Tirana on the occasion of the 25th anniversary of the Flag Day, that is, on November 28, 1937. It seems that, after the ceremony of the Albanian Declaration of Independence organised by King Zog, the photographers took shots of that occasion. The photo shows 11 men, including **Ali bey** with hats and caps, collared and holding cameras in their hands or around their necks.[366]

Fahrija Ismail bey Haveriq, was born in Podgorica and lived in Shkodra. The mother was Rabie Sokoli from Shkoder. She came to Shkoder in 1909 with grandfather **Ismail bey**, sister **Sanija** and brother **Alija**. With his sister, she stayed for while at Sulejman bey Haveric's house. **Fahrija** eventually married Dervish Kerniqi

(Krnic), who died at the age of 33. Then, she settled in Tirana in 1930. In 1935-6, **Fahrija** completed her schooling in Sarajevo. She attended a course for sewing women's clothes. In Turin, Italy, she graduated as a seamstress for sewing women's clothes. She further specialised in this field, working as a teacher. While travelling to Yugoslavia, Italy and France, she brought from there the latest fashions, which attracted the girls and women in Tirana, who chose this modern clothing.

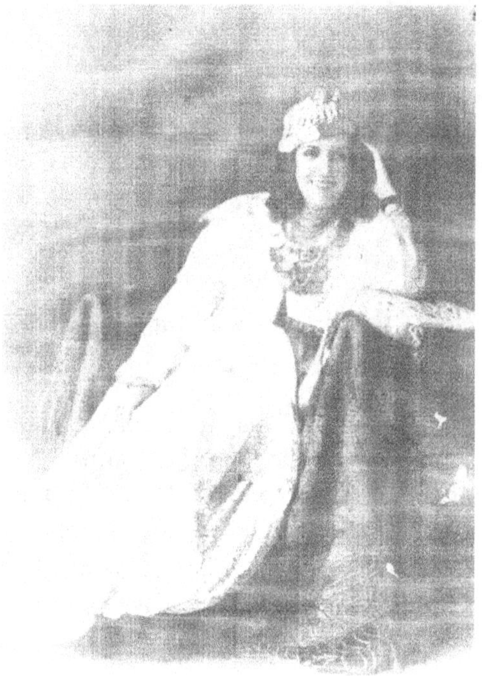

Fahrie Haveriqi (Fahrija Haveric)

During the Second World War, the Jewish engineer, Mark Menahem, found a shelter for Lef Nosi in the **Fahrija**'s house in Tirana. **Fahrija** was aware that Lef Nosi was not a traitor, as the propaganda presented him, but an Albanian patriot and for this reason she refused to receive money to house him.[367] In 1946, 'as an opponent to the communist government', she was arrested in Albania under totalitarian rule and sent to a prison for three years. She managed to escape. In the meantime, **Fahrija** lost her political and civil rights and together with his brother, escaped from Albania to other European countries.[368] It was reported that in 1951 **Fahrije Haveriqi** crossed the Yugoslav border near Dzakovo.[369]

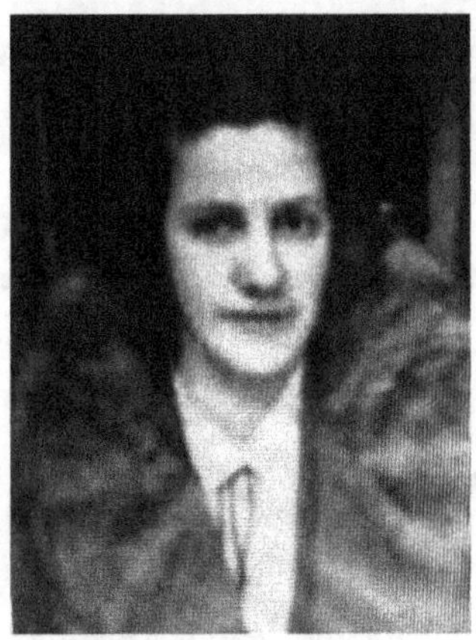

Fahrie Haveriqi, 1935

In the book by Zef Luka, *One hundred Albanians who came with pure freedom*, a few lines described **Fahrija**'s escape from Tirana to the mountain, 'after being holding an exponent of the old government'.[370] During her exile, she lived for a while in Sarajevo, left for Torino, Italy, in 1943 then moved to France in the 1950s where she worked as a fashion designer and stylist. In Italy and France, **Fahrija**'s name was known among the Albanian refugees because 'she had helped theme during her time there'.[371] From a girl who relied on religion and prayed, **Fahrija** completely changed into a new Western society lifestyle.[372]

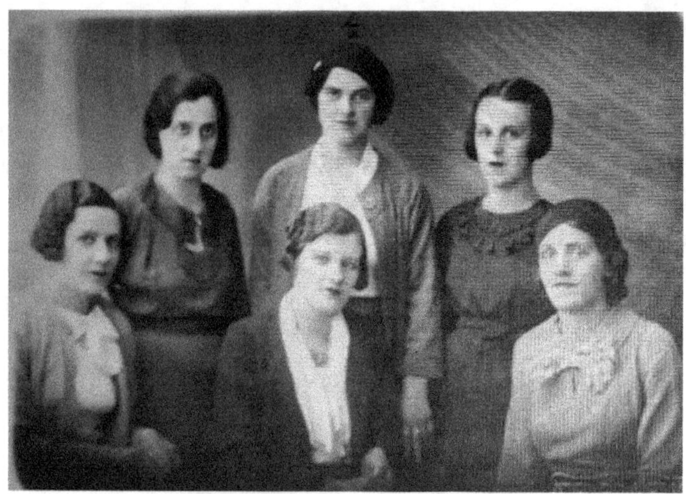

Fahrie Haveriqi first from the left (and on the top in the middle another Fahrija Haveric)

Agim Gani bey Haveriqi was born in 1952 in Tirana. He graduated from '7 Nentori' Vocational High School, mechanical department and graduated as a Mechanical Technician. He worked at the Tirana Geophysical Company for the search for minerals with geophysical methods, but later, in the repair and production of new devices. **Agim** was decorated with the *Labour Medal* from the Presidium of the People's Assembly of the Socialist Republic of Albania dated December 1, 1990, by decree no. 7430, regarding his: 'hard work and conscientious discipline in completing and exceeding the tasks of the plan on time and in quality'. He participated with Fori Zicishti and Duro Kuci in the production of an electric device for measuring the distortion of drilling wells, thus being called *Novatore* ('Innovator'). Since 2004, he has been working at F.S.H.N. in the Department of Physics. He married **Elvana** Ali Doci and they had a daughter, **Semirada**.

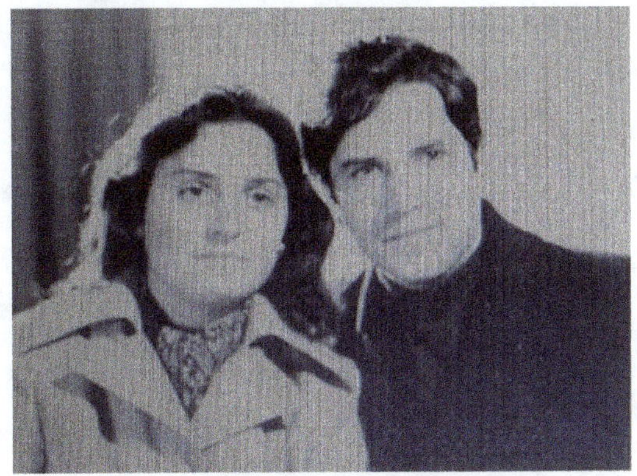

Agim and Elvana (Doci) Haveri

Agim's Family Anthem

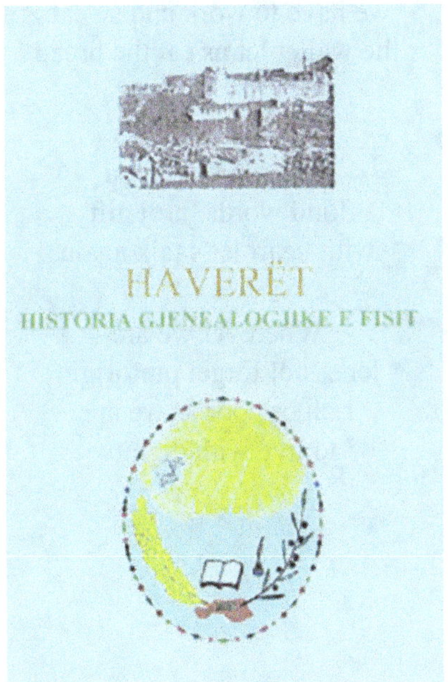

**'Haveret': Genealogical history of the kinfolk by Agim G. Haveri, Tirana
Symbol: A feather-pen, book and an olive branch and birds under the sun
On top is an old fortress in Podgorica.**

Dzavid Haveric

The anthem of the Haveric kinfolk[373]

With the name of God in the heart
and exemplary wisdom forever
to act every man and woman
to show that we are Haveric

Do not approach evil
virtue always gathers you
with a pure heart like a child
to always spread kindness

We live our lives in honour of them
just like the first ones,
we have to work and sweat,
the wallet let us eat the bread

Peace be with us
peace be with you
kind words [are] gift
with heart let's talk again

Wherever we are
let's 'not forget our origin
rich or poor as we are
to live with dignity

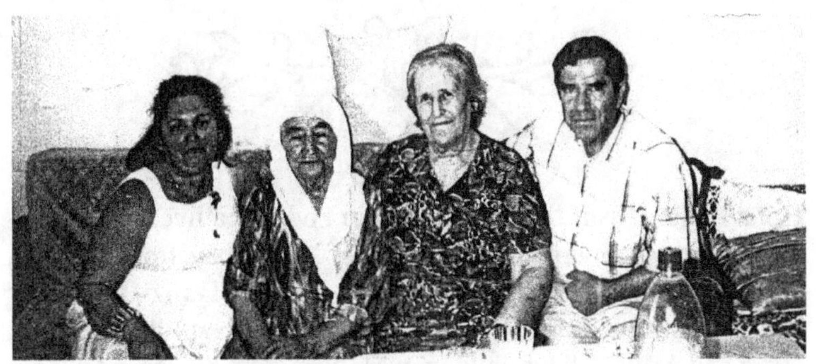

Haverics in Tirana

Hafiz Hysen Jusuf bey Haveriq from Podgorica lived in the mid-19th century and married the daughter of Manco bey, from Shkodra, but they separated after six months. After this, **Hafiz Hysen bey** married **Esma** Zyber Metaj and had a family: **Hamdi**, and **Halit**, **Niazi** and **Adile**. All his children were born from his second wife in Podgorica. However, after the *komitas* looted Podgorica, including their home, they moved to Shkoder where the fifth child was born. The following family narration was preserved:

> When she was pregnant with her first child, **Hysen bey** heard a spiritual message in a dream, who said to her: 'You have kept her pregnant, she is going to give birth to a boy, you are going to give him the name **Hamid**, and he is going to have a long life'. And, indeed, a son was born and they named him **Hamid**. It was probably in 1908. Then they had a daughter, who was named **Adile**. A few years later, on May 13, 1918, a boy was born again, and they named him **Halit**. Not even a year after Halid, in February 1919, a son was born again, and he was named **Nijaz** (Nijazi).

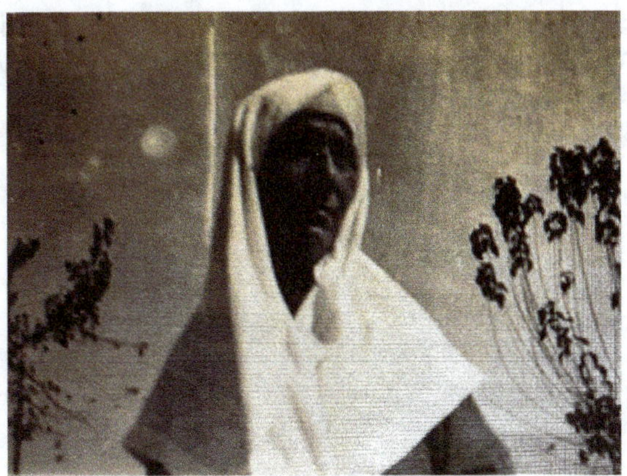

Esma Metaj Haveriq

When the Austrians came out of Montenegro, the Montenegrins started violence and looting in Podgorica among Muslims. They even raped women in [front of] the eyes of men. Maja, Husein bey's wife, kept the *florins* (money) at a neighbor's house, because she heard that there was going to be looting. **Hysein bey** was in the mosque in the morning. They caught him and beat him. So, exhausted, he came to Shkoder over the mountains, 'step by step'. The neighbor protected his wife and children. They had the order to leave for 24 hours. When the family found safety and peace, **Hysein bey** worked as a manufacturer. He died around 63 years old.

Hamdi Hafiz Hysen bey Haveriq, the eldest son of **Hysen bey**, took up the carpenter trade and was very good at this profession. Hamdi went to school, but had no job and changed his profession. Sanija's son, the daughter of his uncle, **Ismail bey Haveriq**, Niazi Bushati, learned the trade from him. But it is said that '**Hamdi** was also a good tailor, and also that 'he built the first floor of the house in Tirana alone'. So, he had to wait for everything with concern.

However, Hamdi's work was useful. Some archival documents from 1937 and 1938 also mentioned '**Hamdi bey Haveriq** as a carpenter on Washington Street and Queen Geraldine Street in Shkoder'.

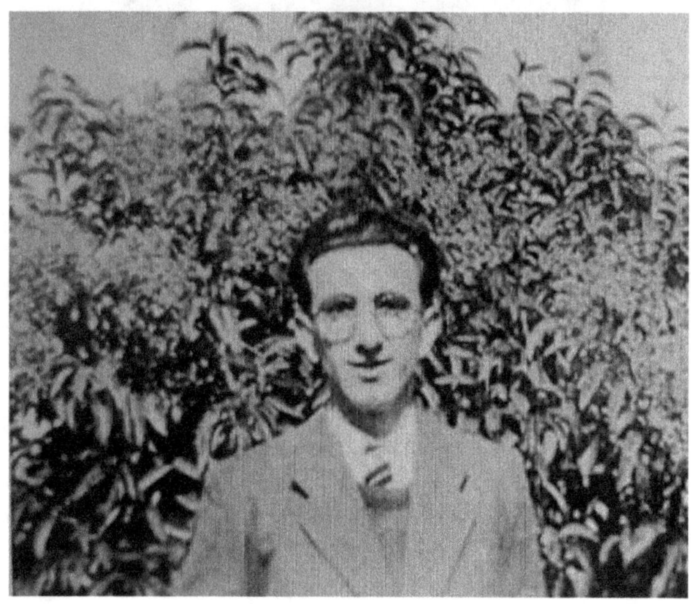

Halit Haveriq, a poet

Halit Haveriq a son of **Hafiz Hysen (Gurrahi) Haveric**, was a talented poet. Poetry was one of the most widespread literary forms in the magazine the *Culture of Islam Review* and Halit's poetry was published in almost every issue along with other poets.[374]

Adile Haveriq, a daughter of **Hafiz Hysen Haveriq**, was born in 1923 in Durres. Haji Hafiz Muhamet Bektashi, one of leaders of the Tixhani Sufi order, wrote a poem about this 'beautiful girl named **Adila'**, a sister of poet **Halit Haveric**, who passed away at not even 20 years old in Shkoder. At the funeral, family and friends wanted to open the coffin to see her beautiful face once again.[375] The poem reads:

What is howling, what is thundering,
It started with a drizzle of rain
What is that bird that dies?
No one knows its problem.

The Hoxha climbed into the minaret:
Take a look mum who has died!
A girl from the village:
That girl that I loved.

Bring out my new clothes, mother,
Bring them out, so I may wear them!
I want to wear them and go out to the door,
And sit on that deserted stone
So, I may cry into a handkerchief.

Ethem bey was born in Podgorica. He was the first son of **Jusuf bey**, described as having an 'average body'. He lived near the old Doganjska Mosque.[376] **Edhem bey** together with his brothers, **Husein, Smail, Muhtar, Zajnel and Becir**, were engaged in trade. He was also a *zabit* of Podgorica. He married **Hjarija** Sokol, the daughter of Myftar agha Sokol. Shortly after their marriage, Myftar agha, **Edhem bey**'s father-in-law, died of a complicated infection. After a long time, **Hajria** gave birth to a girl, but after six months she died. When he was nine months old, her son also died. Hajrija fell ill, went into a depressive state and, leaving her properties behind, went to Shkoder, where she died. **Ethem bey** married again soon after the death of his wife. His second wife was **Hajrija**, a daughter of Sulejman bey Osmanagic whose uncle Becir bey Osmanagic was *vojvoda* (duke), in service of King Nikola. It was recorded that when **Hjarija** married, 'she wore a national costume', as a custom in the presence of the king's family.[377] **Edhem bey**'s two daughters were born, but both died when the Spanish flu epidemic spread, 'One died in the morning and the other in the afternoon'.[378]

Zyber Abaz bey Haveriqi was born in 1885 in Podgorica. His life had been close to his brother **Said bey** and in 1918 he came with him to Shkoder. In Shkoder, the two brothers were successful in their business, tailoring men and women's folk costumes. **Zuber bey** later had his own manufacturing business.[379] He married **Hanife** Sulejman Bratovic and they had several children: **Selman**, **Sedike**, **Shyqyri**, **Shefike** and **Ilijas**. **Selman** was born in 1906. In Shkoder, he also followed the fate of his uncle, **Said bey** and his uncle's sons, **Osman** and **Asim.** He died in the same year as them, i.e. in 1920. A year after him, in 1921, **Zyber bey** also passed away. This was the time of the Spanish flu, which spread through Shkoder and took the lives of many residents. The disease was brought by the Austro-Hungarian soldiers, between 1916 and 1918, who carried the infection from the war fronts. Even a couple of years later, the consequences of this disease caused many deaths in many families, especially affecting young women.

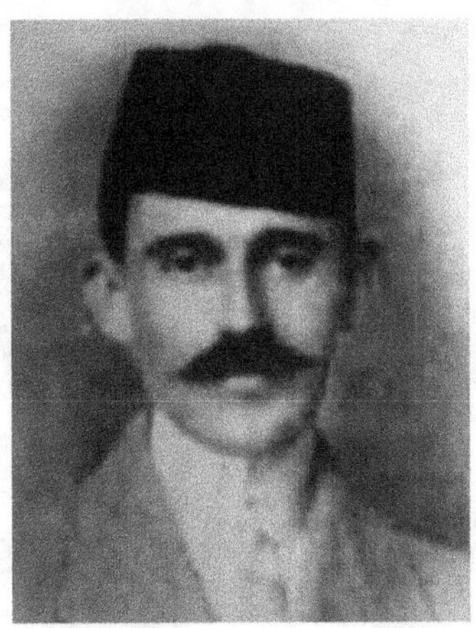

Zyber Abaz bey Haveriqi

Shyqyri Zubey bey (Shykri, Suco Haveric) was born in 1908. **Shyqri** worked in administration in Bashkina and Shkoder, where he certified documents in the municipality of Shkoder. He married around 1938 to **Hafife** Asllan Bektesh and they had four children: **Valdete, Violeta, Said** and **Fatmir**. He was tall man. He lived with his family in Ndocej. Because of his reputation, he was respectfully called 'Shyqri Efendi'. **Shyqyri** died in 1985. His daughter **Valdete** completed high school in Shkoder and graduated from the Faculty of Medicine. She married **Xhevar** Nedan and they had a son.

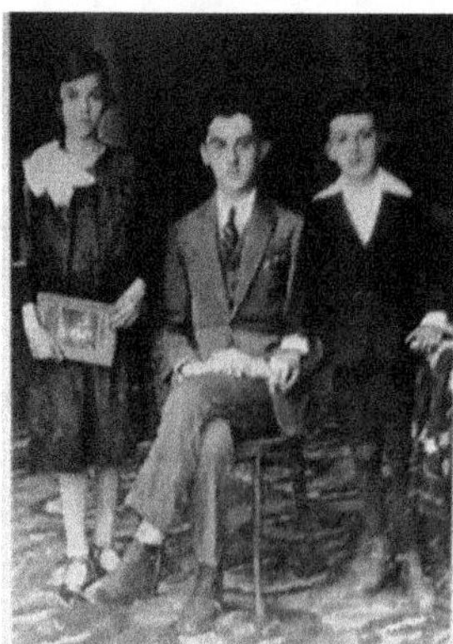

Shyqyri in the middle

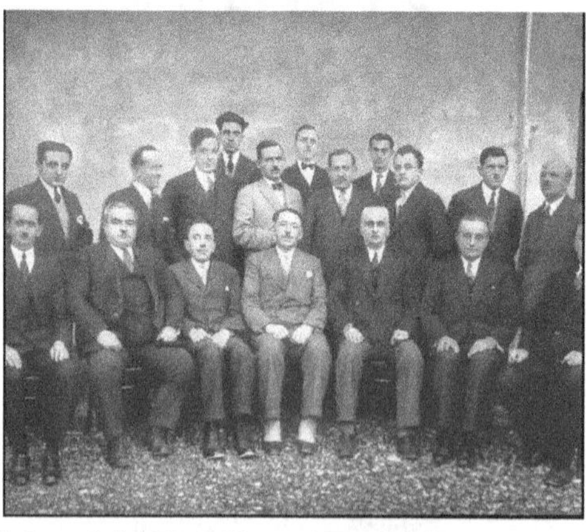

Upper row (left to right) No 3 Shyqyri Haveri City Hall Shkoder, 1931[380]

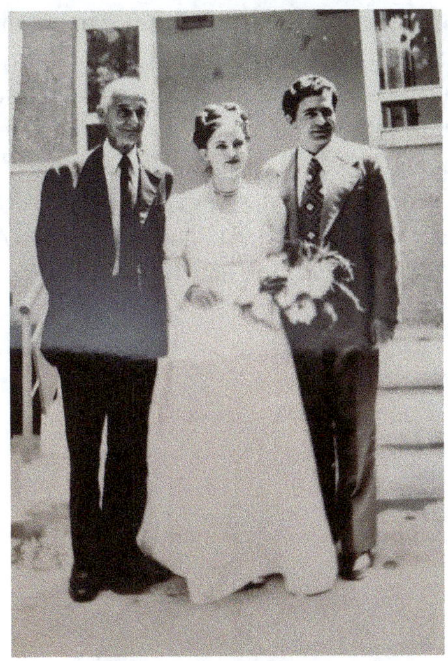

Shyqyri Haveri (Suco Haveric) left

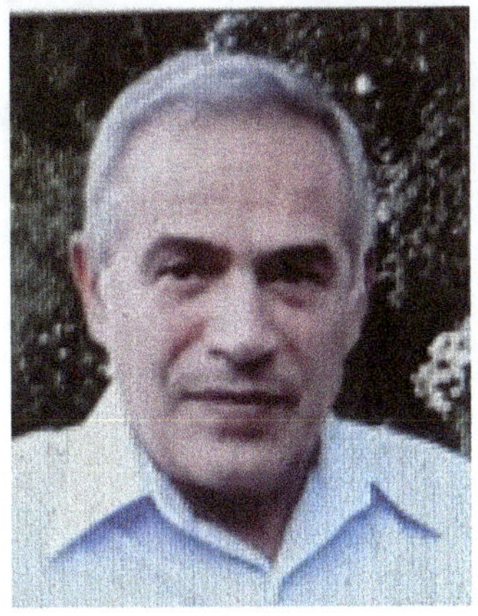

Ilir Ilijas bey Haveri

Ilir Ilijas bey Haveri was born in 1960. His mother was Ismete Spahiu. He attended the 'Avni Rustemi' school, the 'Qemal Stafa' general secondary school, the 'Horticulture' high school, and the Kamez Agricultural Institute, where he later defended his master's degree in banking and finance. He worked at the 'Ali Kelmendi' Food Plant. Then, he worked at an agency for tourism and travel services 'Albexx' and at the 'Besa' fund. He married Anila Gazhelin and they had two children: Ina and Ilijas. His wife died at a very young age.

Suco (brother in Shkoder)

Jusuf Haveric (sons Fadil and Skender) in Shkoder

Fiko Haveric, son of Dr. Omer, Ali and Dr. Hilma Haveric

Zenel Haveriqi was the fifth child of **Jusuf bey**. Like his brothers, he was engaged in trade. He married **Hajrija** Bibezic, 'a good, beautiful girl'. **Zenel bey** and Hajrija had five daughters. Three of them were **Bedrien**, **Sherifen** and **Kimeten**, while others probably died young. The family first lived in Podgorica. **Zenel bey** was known for having his own style. He often wore a green jacket and residents called him a 'Green [Jeshili] bey'.[381]

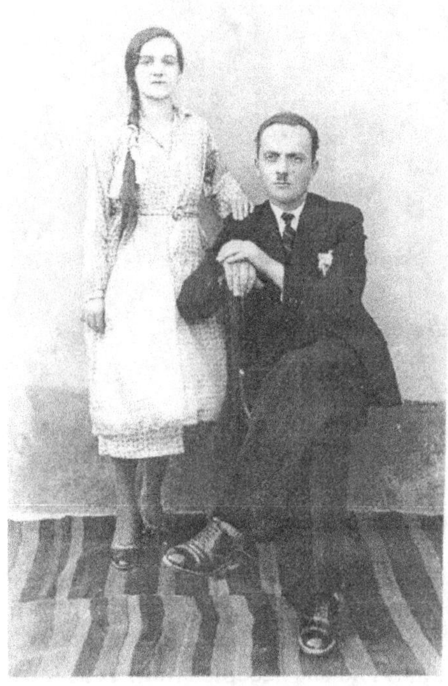

Hajrija Bibezic and Zajnel bey Haveric

During the First World War, when King Nikola fled to Italy because he lost the war, the new ministers gave orders to loot Muslims. They also looted **Zenel bey**. **Zejnel bey** came to Shkoder with **Bedrien** for three months, bought some houses near **Dervis bey** and lived there. However, **Zejnel bey** was depressed and a little later in 1918 he died from a mental breakdown soon after his mother passed away. After the death of **Zejnel bey**, Hajrija lived with her children for a while finding a home in Podgorica. **Zenel bey**'s eldest daughter, **Bedrija**, married Mehmed (Medo) Lacevic in Podgorica and they had five children: **Sadik**, **Fahrija**, **Cazim (Cako) Sherif (Sheko)**, **Ismet (Iso)** and **Adlija**, all born in Podgorica. In 1944, shortly before the bombing of Podgorica by the Anglo-American allies, Medo settled in Shkoder with his business selling shoes near the old tourist house and a bookstore.

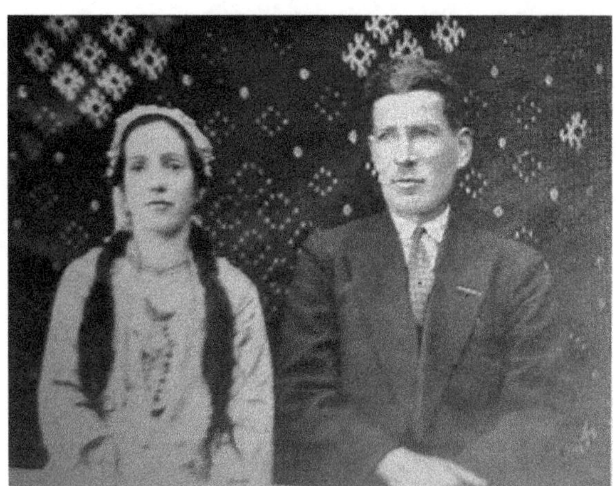

Bedrie and Mehmed (Medo) Laceviqi

Teufik Aqif bey, immediately after the death of **Said bey**, for the sake of custom, that the 'woman should not leave the house, especially since she was a widow and with two children', was recommended by relatives and friends to marry to **Hasiba** Ali Efendi Sanxhaktari and she accepted him. **Teufik bey** was a young, single boy, about 22 years old, and they married around 1921.

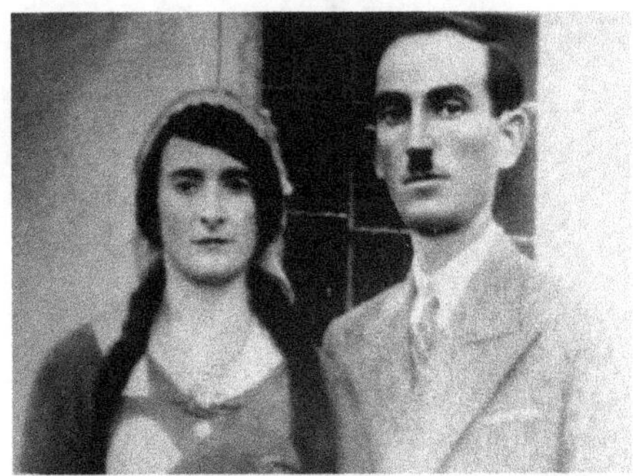

Teufik Aqif Bey with his wife Hasiba

Said bey's widow kept her daughters, **Aisha** and **Hrjrija**, as well as two boys, **Asim** and **Osman**, who died very early. With **Tufik bey**, she lived in a house in the Ndocej neighborhood, where **Said bey** left them his inheritance. They had five sons, **Ymer**, **Beqir**, **Ali**, **Hiviziu** and **Hilmiu**, as well as twin daughters, **Bahrija** and **Munira.** Munira died young, maybe around two years old. The couple maintained strong family ties and **Teufik bey** always cherished nice memories about his partnership work with **Said bey**.

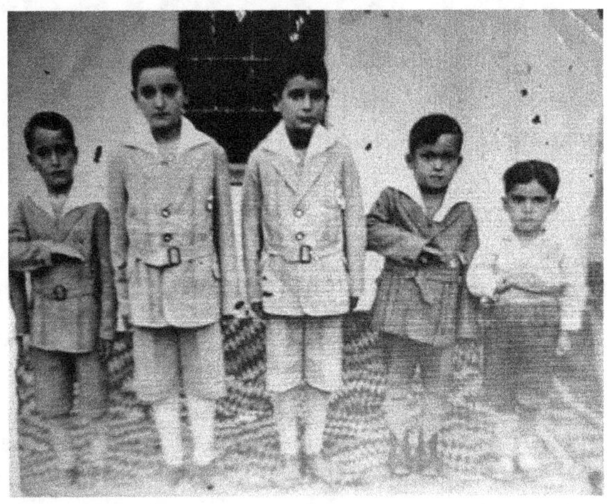

Ali, Ymer, Beqir, Himzi, Hilmi, c. 1935

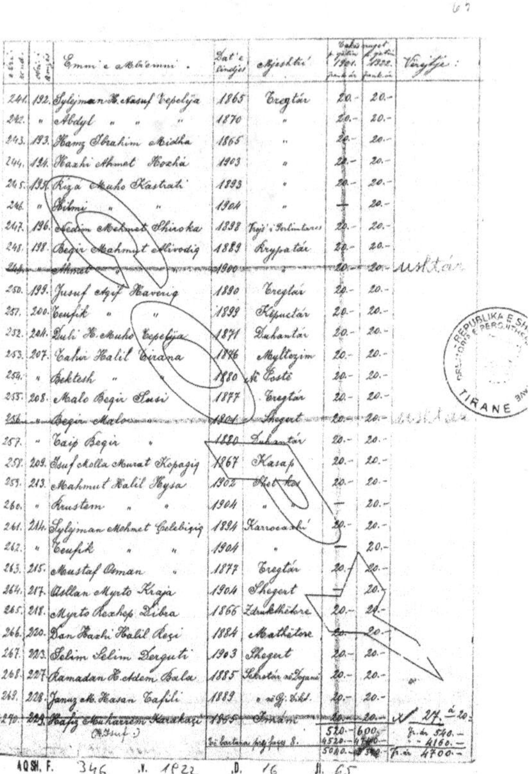

65

[illegible]	[illegible]	Emni e mbiemni.	Dat'e lindjes	Mjeshtri	1921	1922	Vërejtje:
241.	192.	Sylejman H. Nasuf Tepelija	1865	Tregtár	20.-	20.-	
242.	"	Abdyl " " "	1870	"	20.-	20.-	
243.	193.	Hamz Ibrahim Midha	1865	"	20.-	20.-	
244.	194.	Hazhi Ahmet Hoxha	1903	"	20.-	20.-	
245.	195.	Riza Muho Kastrati	1893	"	20.-	20.-	
246.	"	Hilmi " "	1904	"	—	20.-	
247.	196.	Nedim Mehmet Shiroka	1898	[illegible]	20.-	20.-	
248.	198.	Beqir Mahmut Mirodiq	1889	Kryjpatár	20.-	20.-	
~~249.~~	~~"~~	~~Ahmet " "~~	~~1900~~	~~"~~	~~20.-~~	~~20.-~~	[illegible]
250.	199.	Jusuf Aqif Haveriq	1890	Treglar	20.-	20.-	
251.	200.	Teufik " "	1899	Këpuctár	20.-	20.-	
252.	204.	Duli H. Muho Tepelija	1871	Duhantár	20.-	20.-	
253.	207.	Tahir Halil Tirana	1896	Myltezim	20.-	20.-	
254.	"	Bektesh " "	1880	N' Postë	20.-	20.-	
255.	208.	Malo Beqir Susi	1877	Tregtár	20.-	20.-	
~~256.~~	~~"~~	~~Beqir Malo~~	~~1901~~	~~Shegert~~	~~20.-~~	~~20.-~~	[illegible]
257.	"	Taip Beqir "	1880	Duhantár	20.-	20.-	
258.	209.	Isuf Molla Murat Kopaqiq	1867	Kasap	20.-	20.-	
259.	213.	Mahmut Halil Hysa	1902	[illegible]	20.-	20.-	
260.	"	Rrustem " "	1904	"	—	20.-	
261.	214.	Sylejman Mehmet Çelebiqiq	1894	Karrocaxhi	20.-	20.-	
262.	"	Teufik " "	1904	"	—	20.-	
263.	215.	Mustaf Osman "	1877	Tregtár	20.-	20.-	
264.	217.	Asllan Myrto Kraja	1904	Shegert	—	20.-	
265.	218.	Myrto Rexhep Dibra	1866	[illegible]	20.-	20.-	
266.	220.	Dan Hazhi Halil Rexi	1884	Mathëtore	20.-	20.-	
267.	223.	Selim Selim Derguti	1903	Shegert	20.-	20.-	
268.	227.	Ramadan H. Adem Bala	1885	Sekretár në Dogane	20.-	20.-	
269.	228.	Januz M. Hasan Tafili	1889	" në Gj. [illegible]	20.-	20.-	
~~270.~~	~~229.~~	~~Hafiz Muharrem Karakaçi~~ (M. Isuf.)	~~1895~~	~~Imam~~	~~20.-~~	~~20.-~~	27. a 20.
					520.-	600.-	Fr. ar 540.-
			Të bartuna prej faqes 8.		4520.-	4740.-	" 4160.-
					5040.-	5340.-	Fr. ar 4700.-

AQSH. F. 346 .V. 1922 .D. 16 .Fl. 65

Jusuf (Akif) and Teufik (Akif) Haveriq, 1921-1922

Ali Teufik Haveri was born in Shkoder in 1926. He joined the Anti-Fascist Youth Movement and became a member of the National Liberation War, joining the **Perlat (Pearls) Rexhepi battalion** at the beginning of the war and later was in the 27th Assault Brigade. He was decorated with war medals. **Ali** worked as a business manager, under the main manager, in industries such as fishing and clothing. Around 1953, when he came to Tirana, he worked as a branch chairman in the 'Central Union of Handicrafts'. But he returned to Shkoder, where he married **Shyrete**, the daughter of Ismail Axhem, and they had four sons: **Arben**, **Ardian**, **Artan** and **Alban**. During this period, he also worked in the 'Vaut Dejes', Fierzes hydropower plants, until he retired. **Ali** was very devoted to the family and community. He died suddenly in 1995.

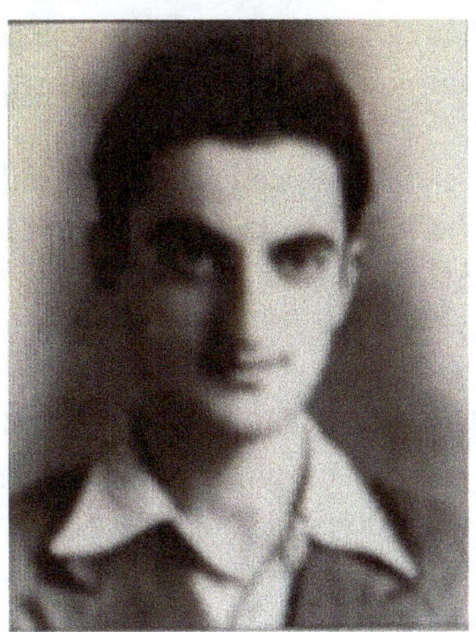

Dr Ymer Teufik bey Haveri

Dr Ymer Teufik bey Haveri was born in Shkoder in 1923. He finished schooling at the State Gymnasium of Shkodra. Soon he found a job as a Secretary of the Health Section. Then, he went to Belgrade, where he stayed for a year and returned. It was a time when relations with Yugoslavia were broken. Later, he was sent to Czechoslovakia to study as a 'General Physician'. He graduated from the Faculty of Medicine at the University of Prague in 1953. When he returned, the Ministry of Health assigned him to work in Puka.

After two years, he returned to Tirana as a teacher at the Medical High School and as a sub-inspector for the technical department. He married **Atilie** Sami Kaduin, who died soon after of leukemia. During that time, he had many ups and downs. He went to Vlora to work as a teacher, because the school where he taught had been transferred there. Later, he married **Suzana** Llagami from Tirana, who worked as a teacher.

Dr Ymer Haveri is one of the first doctors who opened the Endocrinology Gland Disease Cabinet, where he worked for some time. When he returned from Vlora (southwestern Albania), he continued to work as a doctor. In 1983, when he retired, he came up with the idea of creating day centres for the elderly. In the former Pioneers' Palace, he created the Albanian Gerontology-Geriatrics Association (SH. SH. G.G.), becoming its director, but shortly after he passed away.

After his death, **Dr Ymer Haveri** was made honorary president of SH. SH. G.G. for his special merit in the international arena. He was awarded the title of 'Candidate of Distinguished People' by the University of Cambridge and his name was entered in the university's fundamental register.

Interestingly, **Ymer** was nostalgic for his origins and wanted to work for recognition of his family origin, but his initiative was not strong and vigorous enough to work on. Ymer had two children, **Edmond**, an economist, and **Miranda**, a medical doctor.

Beqir bey Haveri was the second son of **Teufik bey** born two years after **Ymer** in Shkoder in the house in Ndocej, Teufiku. As a young boy he was described as a 'handsome man with wavy hair'. He was a wise, loving, attractive, brave man and had a lot of friends. **Teufik bey** took the children, including Beqir, as apprentices to teach them about life, give them work skills and provide some experiences.

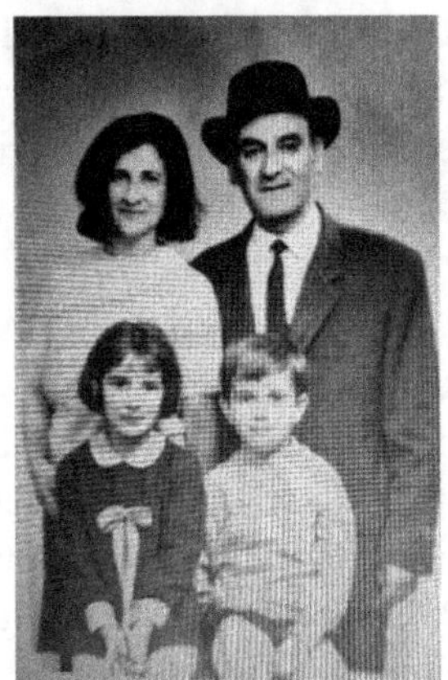

Beqir Haveri

Beqir Teufik bey Haveri worked in the factory of sweets, making hot cakes, candies, chocolates and cookies. During the time of the Italian invasion, when **Teufik bey** opened his own shop after receiving a permit in Beqir's name. The store was in front of the Albanian National Bank in Piace, selling fruits and their by-products. Because Teufik occasionally went to Italy, the main business person was **Beqir**. **Beqir bey** was married and had two children.

Dr Hilmi Teufik bey Haveri was born in Shkoder in 1932. He finished high school and worked as a teacher during a time of widespread illiteracy. To educate people, he worked in villages such as Hajmel, Shenkoll, Pllane and Manati. A remark was made about his childhood:

> **Hilmi** was a skilled and nice-looking child as such recognised in his neighbourhood. When boys played in the yard, or in the alley in front of the house, or in the yard where many kids played, he was called a 'commander'. He was brave, but also had support from

> his brothers. However, he has suffered blows. He was hit by a bicycle and a car, and had other injuries. Despite his struggles, he and his brothers and friends have had a lot of friendships with the girls and they have protected them like their sisters from gangs.

After serving in the army, he graduated from the Faculty of Medicine in the Department of Dentistry. They assigned him to in different places to work, such as in the neighborhood clinic no. 2, in Ndroq, in New Tirana. He also became the director of the ward clinic no. 3 e 10. He specialised in oral diseases and practiced this until he retired. For his merits, Dr **Hilmi** was decorated by the Presidium of the People's Assembly of the Republic of Schippers with a medal: 'For good service to the people', issued by decree no. 7287, dated February 8, 1989. He also received a 'medal for service to the military on the occasion of the 10th anniversary of the formation of the Staff of Pergj. Ush. Na-Ci from the Minister of National Defense'. A street in central Tirana was named after him, 'Ilmi Aver' (**Hilmi Haveri**). He married Sadie Xhevat Llukaci and had a family: Illiriana e Kujtim, who died very young.

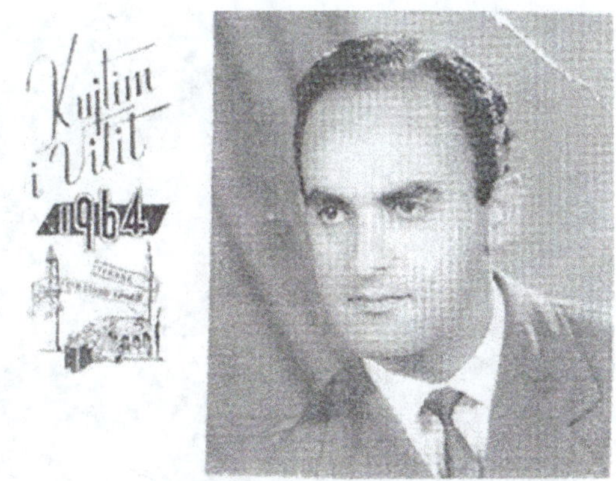

Dr Hilmi Teufik Haveri
***Kujtim i vilit*, Memory of the villa, Tirana, 1964, Albania**

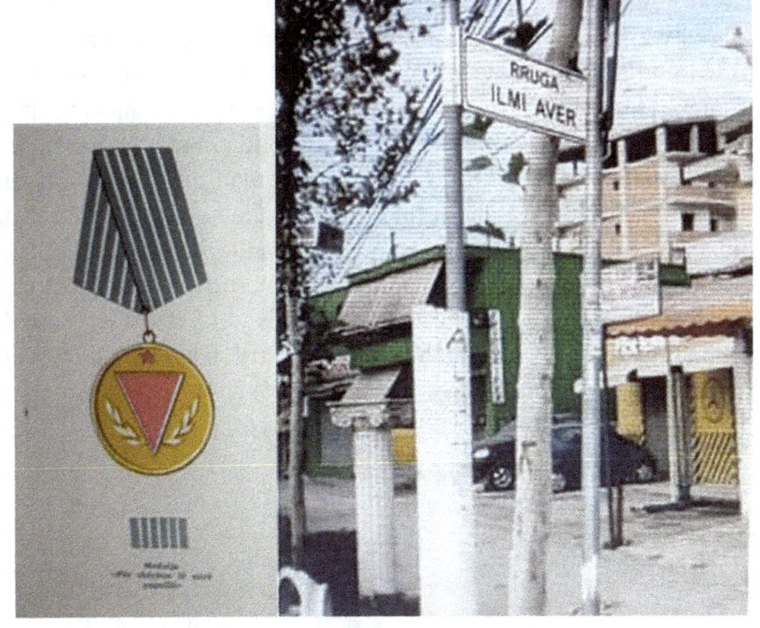

Hilmi Haveri, Medal and Street (Ilmi Aver)

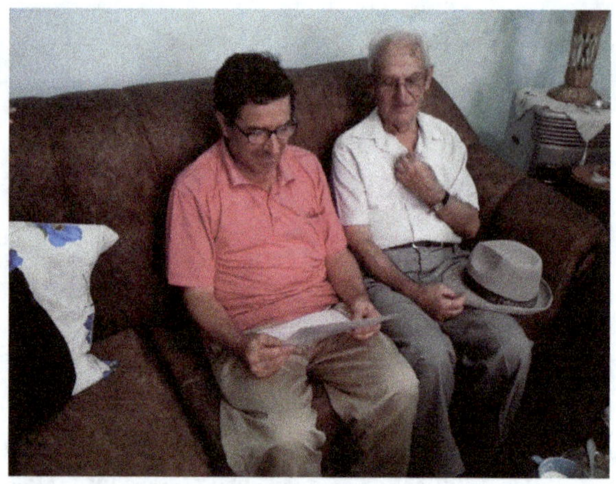

Agim and Dr Hilmi Haveri (Tirana)

Hivzi Teufik bey Haveri was born in Shkoder. He went to high school while working at the same time. Then, he studied a course to work in a bacteriological laboratory, held at the Tirana Sanitary Center. This laboratory has done a great job of diagnosing and curing serious social diseases, such as syphilis, malaria and other diseases, which affected most of the Albanian population. **Hivzi** also has received great merit for beginning the field laboratory that did analysis of infectious diseases. Based on the diagnoses, the sick received the corresponding treatments from the designated doctors. **Hivzi** specialised in Czechoslovakia in this field. Then he started the Faculty of Medicine, but he could not finish it because he fell ill with acute leukemia and died young in 1959.

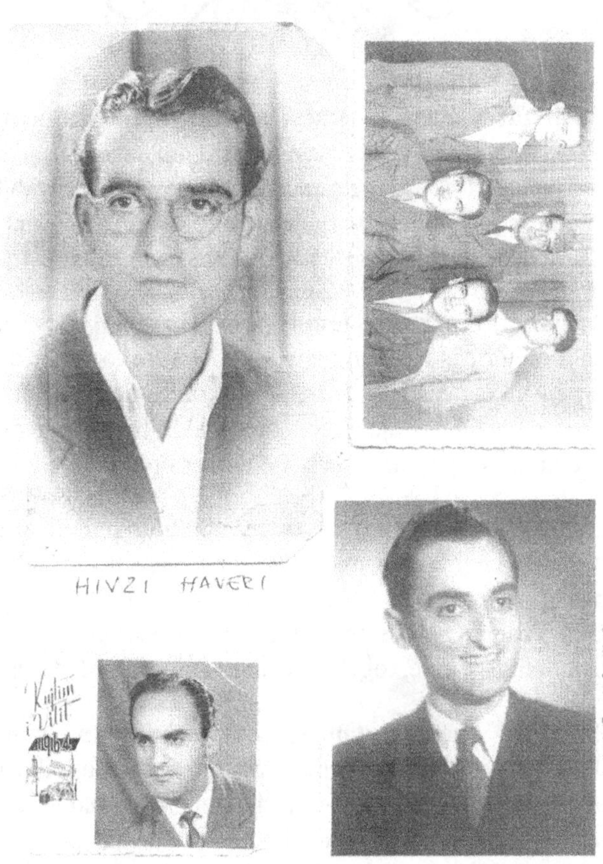

Photos of Haverics, Memory of the villa, 1964 (Kujtim i vilit, Tirana, 1964) Albania

Mahmut Ymer (i.e. Omer) bey Haveriqi was born in Podgorica. He may have been married in Podgorica and had a daughter. It is said he came to Shkoder together with his brothers. He worked as a clerk. Later he went to Istanbul, Turkiye, perhaps together with his brother, **Osman**.

Ibrahim Ymer (i.e. Omer) bey Haveriqi was born in Podgorica. He completed military school, because when he came to Albania, he was an officer. He spent some time in Kavaja and went to Pekin (town in central Albania). Apparently, there he was assigned for a job.

Ymer (i.e. Omer) bey Haveriqi was born in Podgorica. He was engaged in trade. He may have been married when he came to Shkodra. He had two sons, **Ilijaz** and **Ymer**. **Osman** bey later left Shkoder and went to Istanbul, Turkiye, together with his brother, **Mahmud**.

Mehmet Ymer (i.e. Omer) bey Haveriqi was born in Podgorica in 1850. There he completed a religious school, a madrasa, and promoted the Muslim religion in Montenegro. Due to his religious activities, his life was threatened by local gangs and this made him leave Podgorica with his mother and all five brothers: **Mahmud bey, Osman bey, Ibrahim bey, Mehmet bey** and **Sulejman bey. Mehmet bey**. Being quite young, he then migrated to Kavaja. They came around 1870, so before the Congress of Berlin in 1878. The mufti of Podgorica directed **Mehmet bey** to the mufti of Kavaje, Ibrahim Kaduku, giving him a recommendation to help **Mehmet bey**.

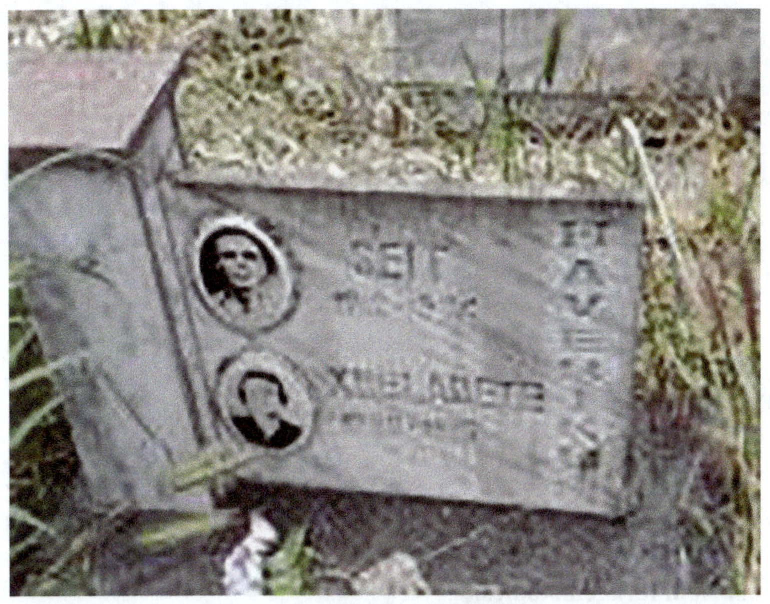

Seit Haveriku (1910-1974) and Xheladete Haveriku (1920-1987), a joint grave at the cemetery in Shijak, Durres

Mehmet bey was the first Haveriku to settle in Kavaja and appointed as *bashqatip* or chief secretary of the Kavaja court. He was married to **Adilja** and had seven boys and two girls.[382]

> **Mehmut bey** devoted himself to administrative work and made a lot of money after his profession. The residents of Kavaja called him and his family fondly after his role in the bashqatib office, as 'the family of bashqatip', not Haveri or Haveriku. In Kavaja he maintained very good relations with the citizens there, working honestly, helping them, so that he created a name that was inherited by his descendants.[383]

Mehmet bey's wife died very young, around 32 years old, leaving behind her small children. Thus, **Mehmet bey** decided to marry again.[384] Three of his boys, **Reshat**, **Fadil** and **Hysen**, went to Istanbul for their studies.

The first son, **Reshat**, studied law and was appointed a governmental position in Turkiye. He was married and had two daughters. Unfortunately, the family lost contact with him in 1957. It is uncertain sure why this happened. He either moved locations or another plausible option is that, since Albania at that time was under a communist regime (the family was persecuted), all letters going out of the country and coming from outside were controlled and filtered. **Reshat** never returned to Albania and to this day, it is unknown what happened to him or his daughters.[385]

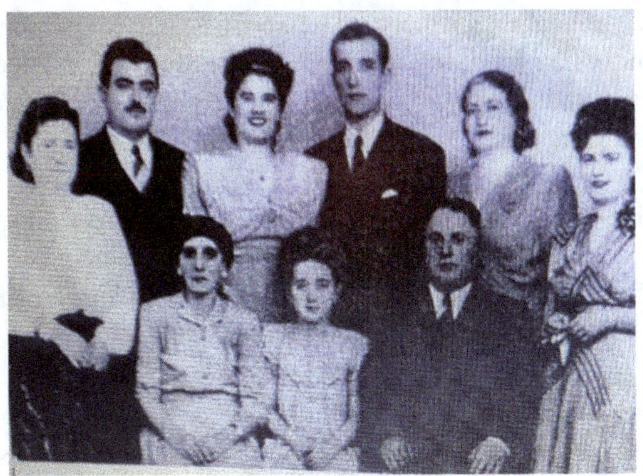

Reshat Haveri (Adenis) sitting right

In Turkiye, **Reshat** changed his last name in '**Adenis**', which in Turkish means: 'I came from the sea'. His address at that time was: Reshat Adenis Mehallesin 'Murat Pasha Sector no 2. Istanbul'. Many Bosnians, Montenegrins and Albanians lived there. Today, that area became a highway. **Reshat** was a general or worked for the Ministry of Defence. In Turkiye, he got permission to visit her other brother on vacation. However, in 1956, the connection with family in Albania was lost. **Reshat** had only two daughters, **Melahet** and **Sabahet**. They were educated in Istanbul. One daughter's husband owned a shoe factory. **Reshat Adenis** died there in 1962 or 1963. He was buried in the old cemetery inside of Istanbul.[386]

The second son, **Fadil**, studied in a military school, but during exercises in school, he fell from a horse and lost his life.[387]

Fadil graduated from the Military Academy. On one occasion, probably training, he needed to cross a 3m

> wide canal with water by a horse. The canal was slippery and when the horse turned Fadil, he fell to his knees. Fadil damaged his knee, which later became infected and gangrenous…soon he passed away.[388]

The third son, **Hysen**, studied in Istanbul to become a telegraphist. Having finished his studies, he returned from Istanbul to Kavaja and left as descendants one boy, **Fehmi**, and two girls, **Lirie** and **Adile**. His descendants lived and worked in Kavaje.[389]

The fourth son, **Tahsim**, was born in 1900, lived in Albanian and left three boys and two girls: **Mehmet** (the first boy who was named after his grandfather), **Fadil**, **Eqerem**, **Fiqirie** and **Pranvera**. **Mehmet** and **Eqerem** worked as agronomists, **Fadil** and **Pranvera** were teachers in the local secondary school, and **Fiqirie** was a tailor.[390]

The fifth son, **Mustafa**, born in 1905, was married but he had no children.[391]

The sixth son, **Aqif**, born in 1910, was an officer during the King Zong I monarchy. He was imprisoned and executed in 1947 by the communist regime in Albania.[392] He is an Albanian national hero.

The seventh son, **Qemal** was born in 1912, worked in agriculture and left seven children, one girl and six boys.[393]

The two daughters of **Mehmet** were **Naxhie** and **Ismete**. They married and left descendants in Kavaja.[394]

Hafiz Miftar (Muhtar) bey was born in Podgorica in 1870. He was educated in Istanbul. He returned to Podgorica as a madrasa graduate and *hafiz*. He worked as an imam. In 1896, he married **Hanka** Beciragic (1885-1968) from Niksic. **Hfz Miftar bey** and **Hanka** formed a family: **Halil** (1900-1980), **Rizah** (1903-1944), **Ibrahim** (1905-1928), **Mustafa** (1908-1990) and **Cazim** (1916-1947), and sisters **Havusa** (1917-1944) and **Hatidza** (1923-2009).

A brief story about **Rizo** Haveric, **Ismail Hfz Halil bey**, recalled:

> **Rizah (Rizo) Miftar bey Haveric**, a farmer from Bar, at the age of 40 went with a mule through gorges, steep serpentines and fell. He was also an olive grower and had a large land holding. When the mule came home alone to the city, his family realised that something wrong may have happened to **Rizo**. Then they went to search for him and found him lying dead on the road…

Cazim Miftar bey Haveric was born in Leskovac, Serbia. He graduated from economics school in Austria. He was not married. He ran a trading business with food and other goods, and supplied the region of the Boka of Kotor with food. He also supplied corn, flour etc. to Albania, as at one time there was nothing in this country.[395] At some point in the 1930s, **Cazim** Haveric was a vice-president of the 'Waqf Commission in Stari Bar'. As a member of the commission, he managed and checked the book records of the local Muslim community, and consulted its elderly and prominent members to help the community.[396] About **Cazim Haveric**, **Ismail** and **Fahro** narrated:

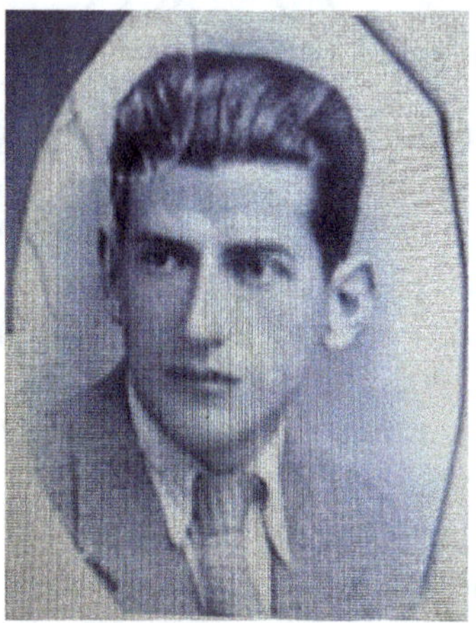

Cazim Muftar bey Haveric

Cazim Haveric was a great businessman and sheep farmer. He had a couple of blocks of land and a farm with 200 goats. He also had 3 shops, all named 'Braca Haveric' in Bar created when **Cazim** hired his brother **Murat** as an assistant. It included a trading shop in old Bar, the second shop 20 metres down was a manufacturing shop with a small 'grocery centre' and the third shop in the port of Pristan in Bar. **Cazim** owned a hotel in Shkoder in the centre of Tirana opposite the residence of Albanian President Enver Hoxha. The only surviving 'relic' from this hotel is a plate used with a logo, which was made in Germany. He also had a warehouse/shop in Shkoder.[397]

During the wartime, **Cazim** took the surrounding road on the Bar-Albania-Italy route. In his warehouse in Shkoder, he would bring the earned bags of gold and goods from where they were taken to Tirana in his 'business empire'.

That illegal road went from Mount Rumelija along a road called Bijela Skala to Shkoder. Although he had several cars, he couldn't use them on this road.[398]

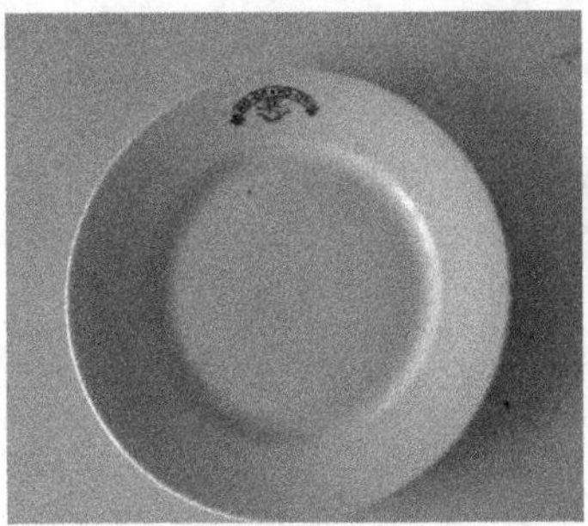

A plate from Cazim's hotel in Albania

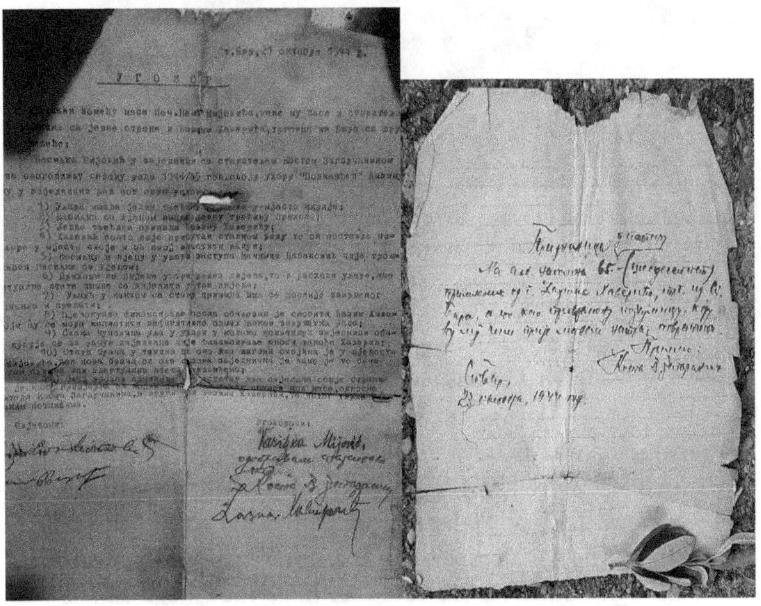

У Г О В О Р

Trade agreement with Cazim Haveric and others
Debt contract for money borrowed from Cazim Haveric

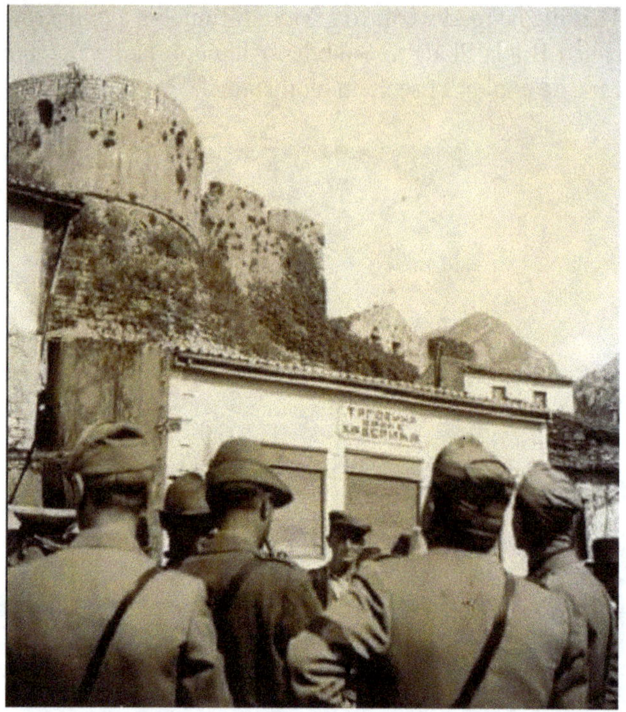

Italian soldiers in old Bar surrounding the front of a closed Cazim's shop the 'Braca Haveric' (the 'Brothers Haveric')

El Fatiha

Fahro Haveric further narrated:

> After the war, in order to protect the fruit of his hard work from the greed of the communistic authorities which imposed the nationalisation of property, **Cazim** hid the olive oil he produced. He dug holes on his properties during the night so that no one could see him, filled metal barrels of 200 litres with olive oil and buried them in the ground.

Because of the wealth he had, Cazim was targeted by the local communist authorities who persecuted his brother too, **Mustafa** (1908-1990). **Mustafa** (**Bayazit**'s father) suffered torture in the sea with electric shocks. They also threatened to stab **Musftafa**'s little son **Haver** with a bayonet if he did not reveal where Cazim was hiding. **Mustafa** did not even agree to that.

Later, those old barrels were found in several locations. Cazim's hidden treasure of ducats was also found in his second shop in the basement. He hid gold in many places, so there is an anecdote that 'they found ducats among the goat manure'.

Cazim was found after 2 years of hiding. Because of his oppression and continuous suffering, he used to say 'I love more one goat than 50 enemies'. He was killed with two friends in 1947 on the top of a hill in Bar, the place where Bayazit Haveric built his grave together with two of Cazim's friends in the early 1990s. Then, **Bayazit** hid the money obtained in the court case from Cazim's hotel with Fahro's mother **Hafiza (Naka)** under Fahro's bed without Fahro's knowledge. One day, when Bayazit took out the money, **Fahro**, then a high school student, was not only surprised that the money was under his bed, but he had never seen more sums of money in his life.

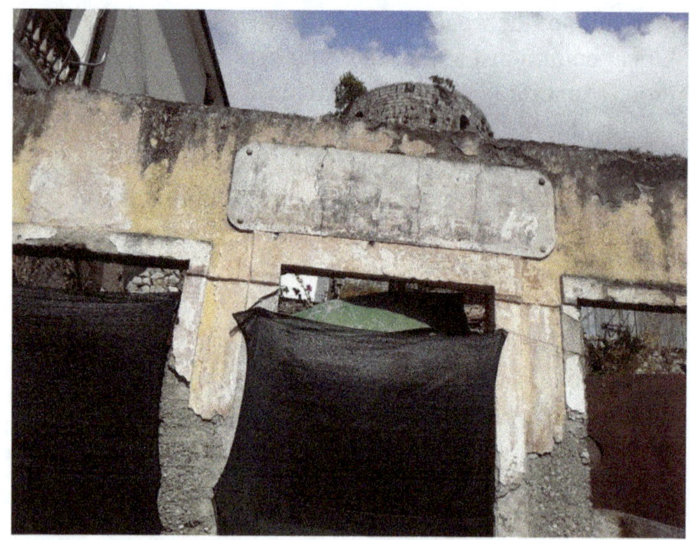

After the war, Cazim Haveric's ruined shop, old Bar

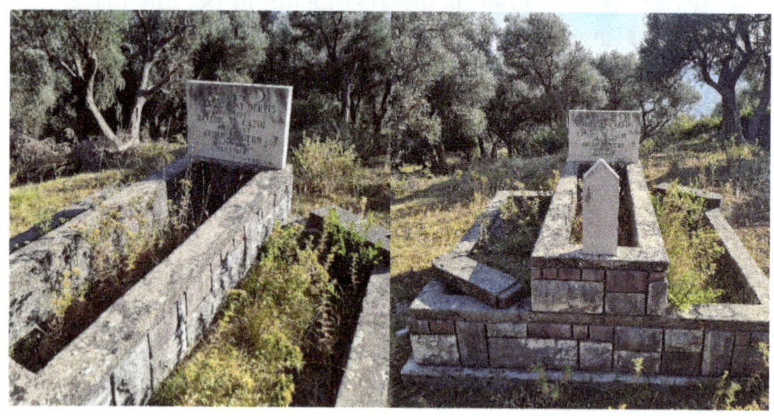

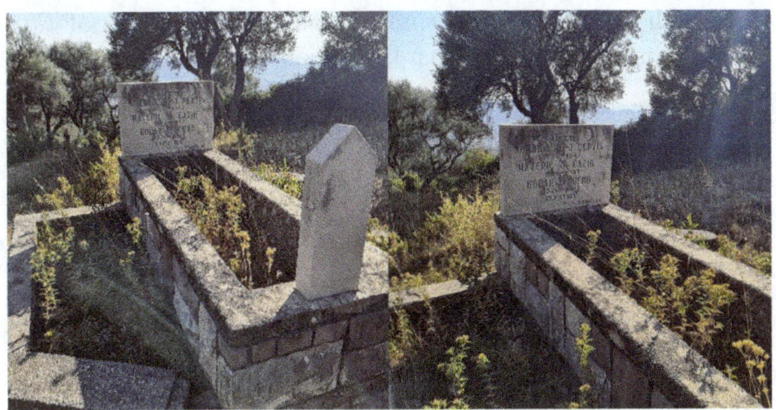

Cazim mezar with his two friends *El Fatiha*

Hfz Halil bey and his wife **Havaja** had several children: **Teufik** (1927-2001), **Dzevahira** (1930-1949), **Jusuf** (1932-1943), **Mehmed** (1934-1966), **Ismail** (1936-), **Hajrija** (1939-), **Rukija** (1941-) and **Muhtar** (1943).

About his brother **Mehmet**, **Ismail Haveric** wrote:

> On October 12 in 1966, **Mehmed bey** was killed in Sarajevo, where he lived and worked. He had almost married Semsa Čerkez and they had no children. He was killed out of the blue by retired Serbian officer Ariton Dukovski, with a firearm (pistol), who was thirsty for Muslim blood. He killed him because of an argument about the laundry room, in an apartment building on Cengic Villa in Sarajevo. He was sentenced to 14 years in prison but was immediately transferred to Serbia with his family. The question is, did he even spend a day in prison? The murdered Mehmed was transported to Bar, his funeral was held, and he was buried at the Belbeder city cemetery in Bar – 'May the dear Allah reward him

with the blessings of *Jannah* (Paradise)'. The murder of Mehmed hit everyone hard, especially his parents.[399]

Dr Ismail (Smajo) Hfz Halil bey Haveric was born 1936. He finished running Gazi Husrev bey' madrasa in Sarajevo. He obtained a master's degree in economics, then a doctorate in Islamic studies at the Faculty of Islamic Sciences, Sarajevo. For a time, he worked as the secretary of the Bosnian Islamic headquarters in Sarajevo. He wrote columns for Bosnian Muslim newspaper *Preporod.* He went to Hajj in 1979/80. In his successful business career, **Ismail** was a Director of the Institute of Statistics, Sarajevo Canton, an Assistant to the Mayor of the Municipality of Novi Grad Sarajevo, the well-known companies *Energoinvest* and *Elektroprivreda.* As a hobby, he liked to make audio recordings of his loved ones. He loved science, reading and writing. He collected interesting information for his books and typed day and night on the Olympia machine. He was especially devoted to Islamic learning. He published several Islamic books, from those one with his father Hafiz **Halil** and another with his wife, **Izeta Devic Haveric**, about Islamic marriage and family.[400] He and his wife have a son, **Haris**, a social worker and a director of the SUMERO organisation, and a daughter, **Harisa**, who is a graduated electrical engineer.

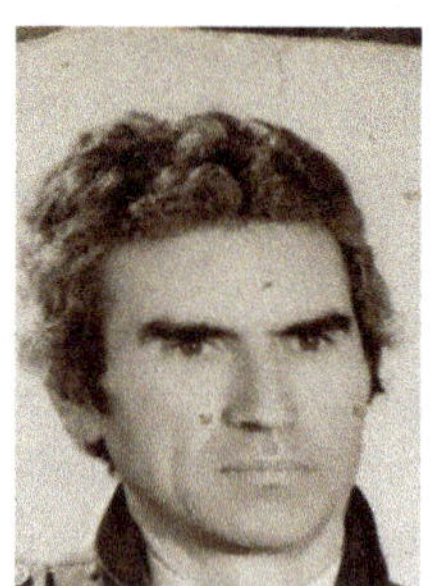

Dr Ismail Haveric

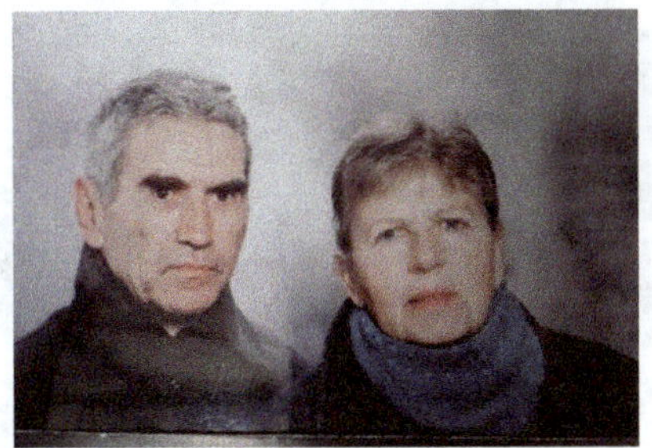

Ismail and Izeta (Devic) Haveric

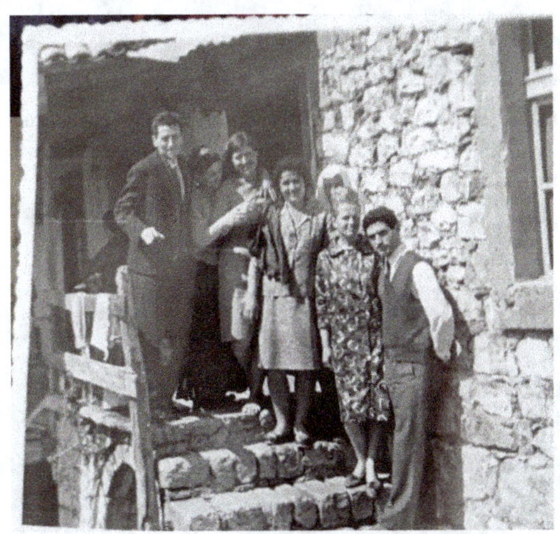

Ismail and Izeta, Hafiza, then Baflija (Hajrija) Nafija and Teufik in old Bar

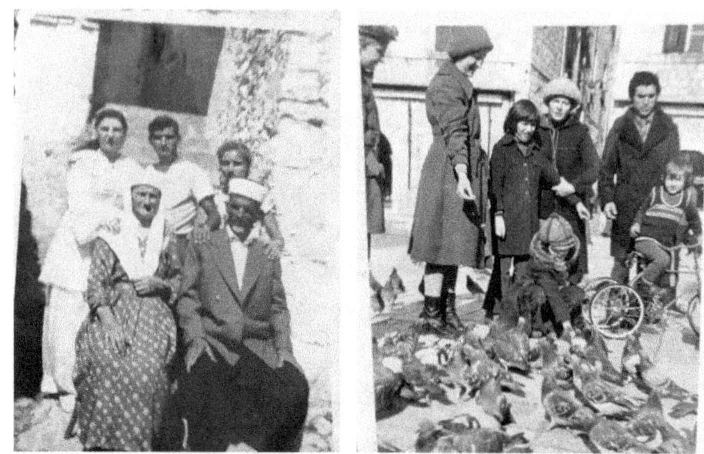

In the first row is Halil and his wife Havaja. Behind them stands Ismail in the middle, to his left (behind Havaija) is Nafija's daughter-in-law and to the right (behind Halil) is Ismail's sister, Rukija

Izeta, Ismail, Harisa and Haris with a bike

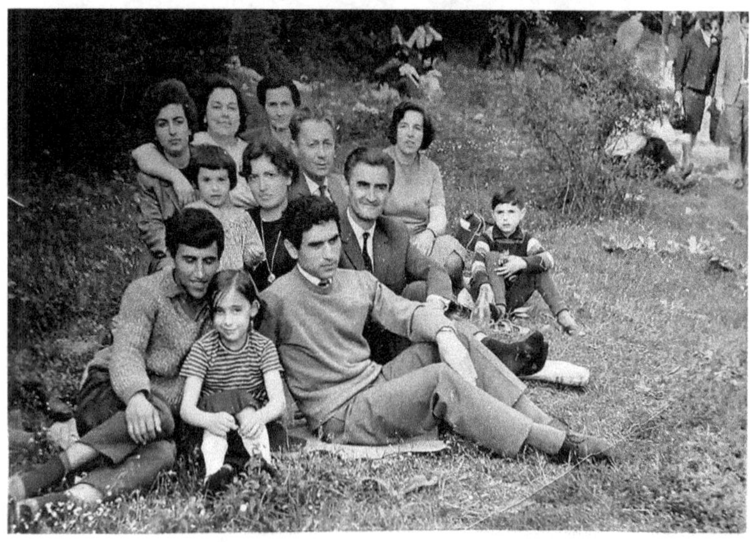

Muhtar, Rukija, Hajrija, Cazim, Ismail, Kemal, Ulfeta, Hidajeta Haveric and their children

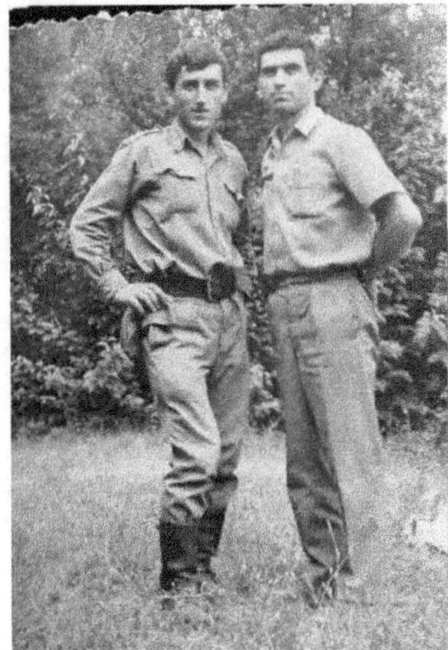

Brothers Muhtar and Ismail

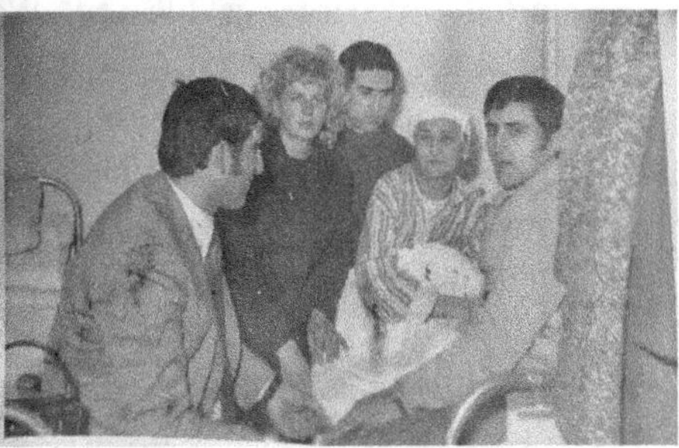

Mother Havaja with her sons Muhtar and Ismail, daughter-in-law Izeta and their cousin Bato

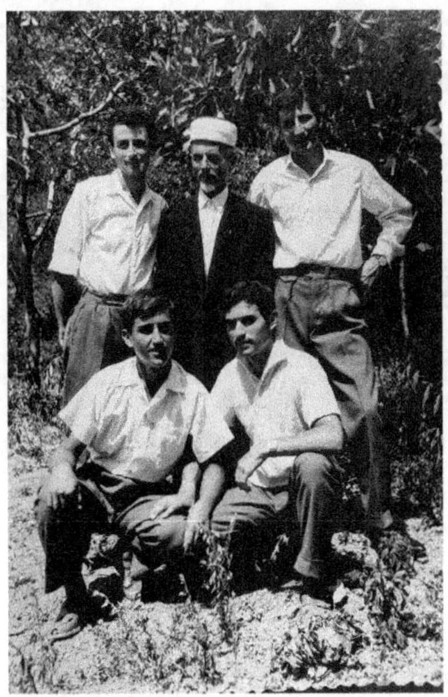

Hfz Halil bey with sons in Bar, 1961

Ismail's brother, **Dr Muhtar (Muho) Haveric**, recalled:

> I grew up like a child among olive trees. The olive tree is a sacred tree. The place where I was born and started my career is blessed. We lived from farming and cattle breeding until I graduated in 1968 from the Faculty of Dentistry in Sarajevo and started a career at a clinic (Dom Zdravlja) and later had a private practice. I worked for 3-4 months in Sjenica, in Urosevac, for 11 years and then continued to work in Bar until retirement. **Muho** and his wife **Fevzija** have two sons, **Almedin** and **Almir.**[401]

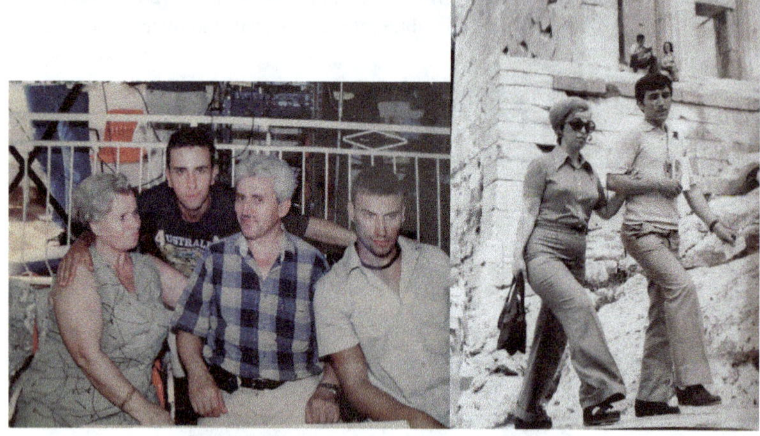

Muhtar with Fevzija and their sons

Muhtar with his wife Fevzija in Athens, Greece

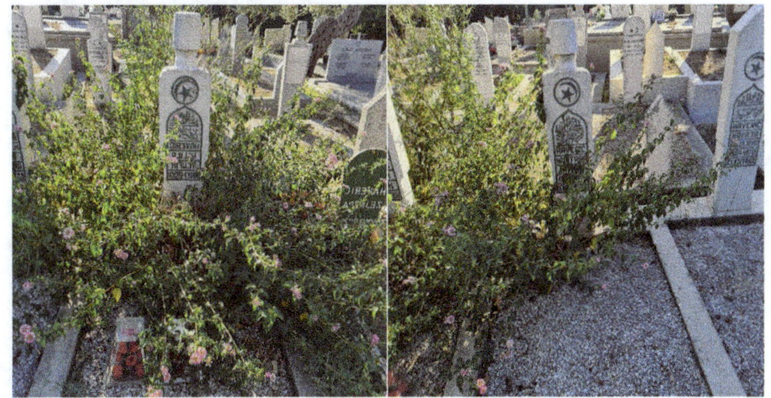

Haveric Halila **Teufik Haveric Muhtara 1927-2001**

El Fatiha

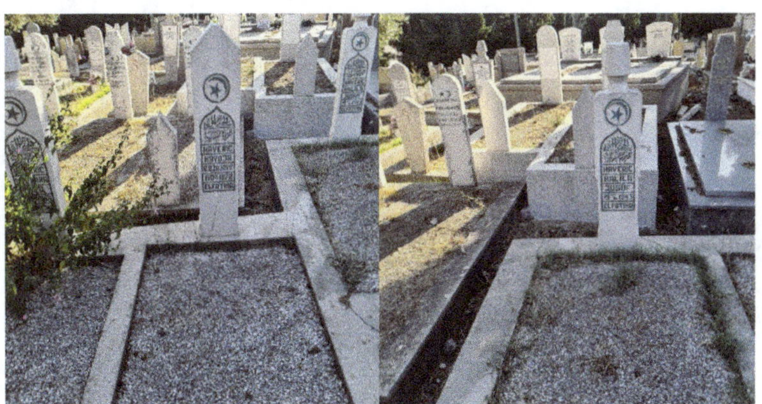

Haveric Havaja (R. Dzajovic), 1904-1972 **Haveric Halila Jusuf, 18??-1943**

El Fatiha

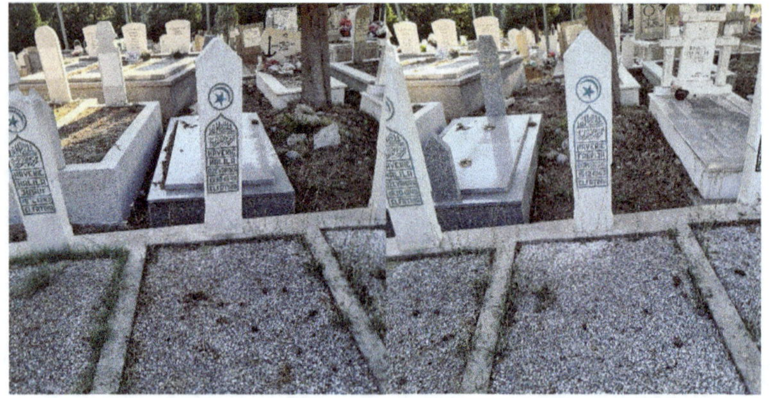

Haveric Halila Dzevahira, 1930-1949 **Haveric Fahrija (R. Kapisazovic), 1912-1943**

El Fatiha

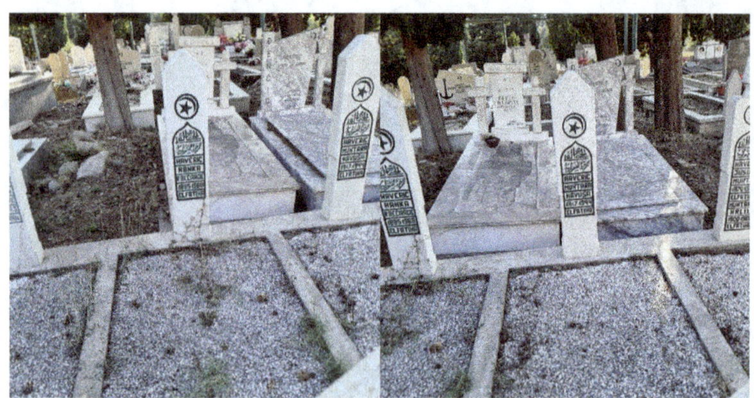

Haveric Hanka (R. Beciragic), 1885-1968 **Haveric Muhtara Havusa, 1917-1944**

El Fatiha

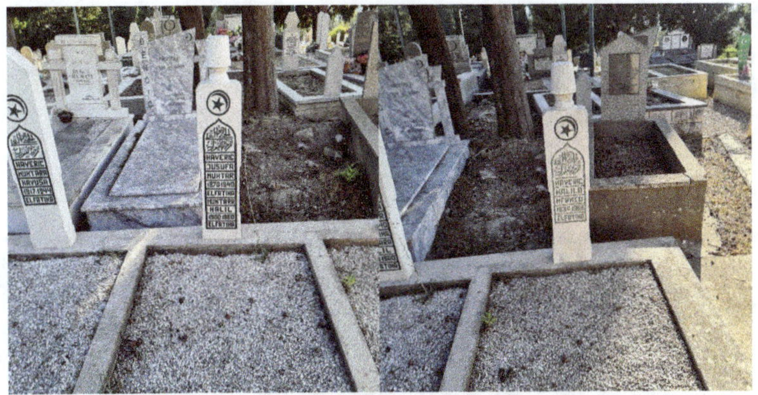

Haveric Jusufa Muhtar, 1870-1940 Haveric Halila Mehmed, 1934-1966
Muhtara Halil, 1900-1980

El Fatiha

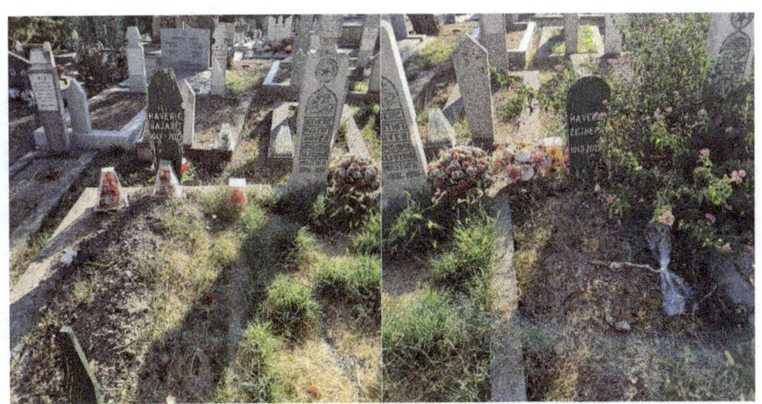

Haveric Bajazit, 1947-2022 Haveric Zejnepa, 1943-2022

El Fatiha

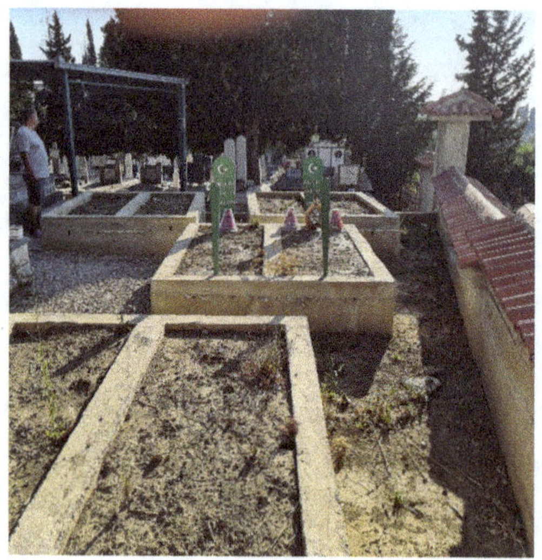

Haveric Sabaheta

El Fatiha

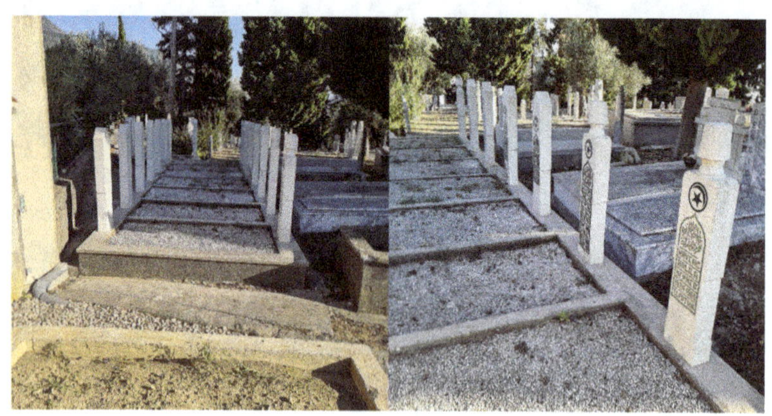

Collective picture of the Haverics' mazars

El Fatiha

Bajazit Mustafa Haveric was born in 1947 in Bar. After working in a company in Sarajevo as a graduate economist, **Bajazit** returned to his native town of old Bar. In Bar he was one of the largest olive growers and the most reputable producers of olive oil. For 30 years, on the family estate in Velembusi, he actively engaged in olive growing and other agricultural crops, improved and modernised production, and showed exceptional dedication to this occupation. **Bajazit** was the recipient of significant awards and recognitions in the field of agricultural production. He received awards at numerous domestic and international fairs, and he was also the winner of the award for the most successful olive grower in 2019, which was given to him by the event 'Maslinijada' (olive festival). He was the winner of the highest state award, the award for the record holder in agricultural production, for the field of olive growing in Montenegro. **Bajazit** was the founder and member of the 'Board of Directors of the Olive Growers Association' since 2002 and the founder and member of the 'Olive Growers Association Antivari-Stari Bar' since 2018.[402] A long hilly street, named **Zejnel bey** Haveric, in old Bar leads to his long farming property, a manufacture for olive oil and making cheese.

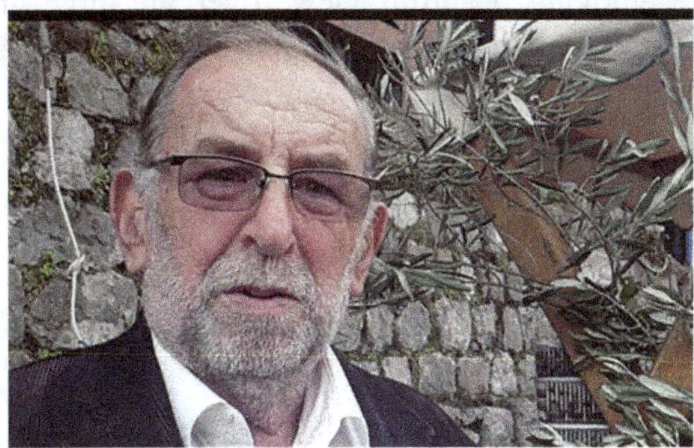

Bajazit Haveric

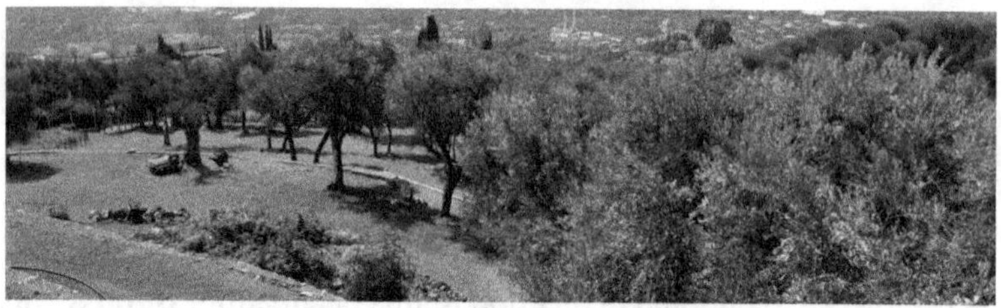

Oliv trees: A view from Bajazit's house

It was also recorded:

> **Bajazait Haveric**'s ancestors, most notably **Zejnel bey**, first started to grow olive trees centuries ago. Today, the Haveric olive grove covers 6,000 square meters and comprises some 600 olive tree roots; it produces some 3,000 litres of high-quality virgin olive oil each year. The **Bajazit'**s two-storey house has a terrace large enough to host many guests, who can sample the various olive products, as well as traditional goats' cheese, pomegranate juice and other Montenegrin specialities while enjoying beautiful views over the olive grove. Close to the old city of Bar, the grove is surrounded by sites of culture and heritage.[403]

Bajazit's brother, **Haver**, died of an infectious disease in Bar at the age of 5 or 6.[404]

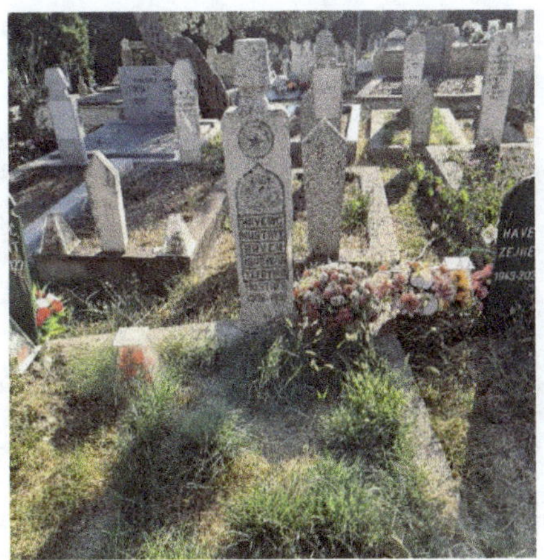

Haveric Mustafe Haver, 1940-1946
Mustafa
1908-1990?

El Fatiha

Fahro Haveric recalled, 'My grandfather, **Halil**, spoke old Turkish language, *Osmanli*. My father, **Teufik,** who became blind after a traffic accident also knew old Turkish'.

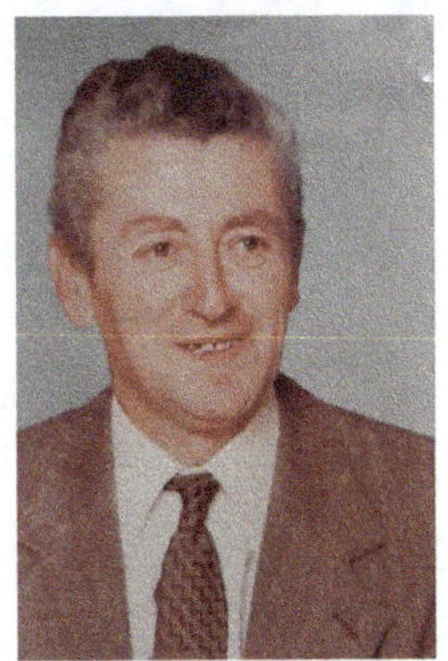

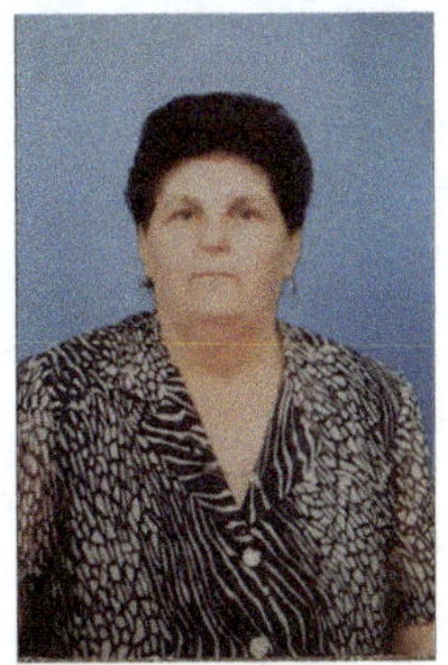

Teufik Haveric and his wife Hafiza

Nowadays, in old Bar, the shop is run by **Fahro Haveric** and it is called **'Braca Haveric'** ('Brothers Haveric').

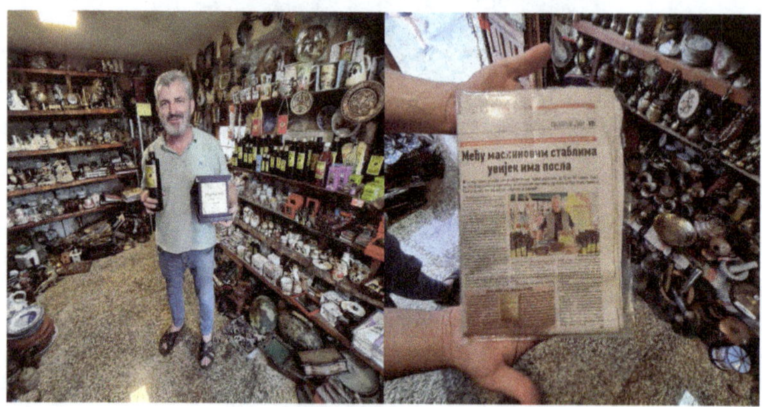

Fahro's shop 'Brothers Haveric'

With economic development and urbanisation, in the new part of Bar, Pristan, the *Society* of *Rumija* was formed. In 1936, the main annual assembly of the *Society of Rumija* for the Promotion of Tourism and Hospitality was held at Pristan. Government representatives, prominent Barani and successful businessmen were elected to the new administration; among them was **Nazim Haveric**.

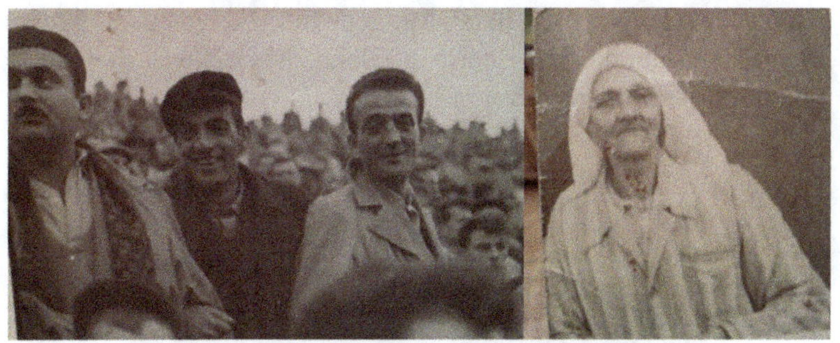

Redzep (Redzo) Haveric in the middle
Redzio's sons are **Jakub (Pupo), Fuad** and **Enver (Vero)**, and a daughter **Munevera (Vera)**

Fuad Redzep Haveric worked for the Montenegrin government. He married **Radmila** Kasalica and have three sons, **Damir**, **Irfan** and **Alen**.

Enver Haveric lived in Ulcinj, Montenegro. His father was **Murat bey** and his mother was born in Ulcinj. **Murat** was the son of **Osman bey**, who came from Podgorica.

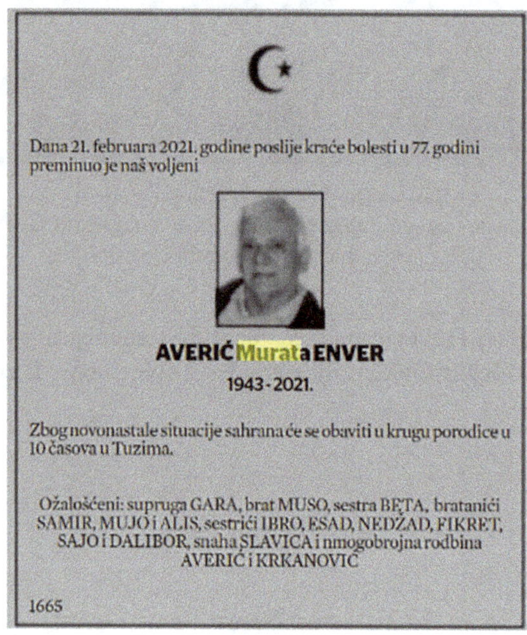

Dana 21. februara 2021. godine poslije kraće bolesti u 77. godini preminuo je naš voljeni

AVERIĆ Murata ENVER

1943 - 2021.

Zbog novonastale situacije sahrana će se obaviti u krugu porodice u 10 časova u Tuzima.

Ožalošćeni: supruga GARA, brat MUSO, sestra BETA, bratanići SAMIR, MUJO i ALIS, sestrići IBRO, ESAD, NEDŽAD, FIKRET, SAJO i DALIBOR, snaha SLAVICA i nmogobrojna rodbina AVERIĆ i KRKANOVIĆ

1665

(H)Averic Murata Enver
1943-2021

El Fatiha

Mustafa, a son of **Osman bey**, lived in Podgorica.

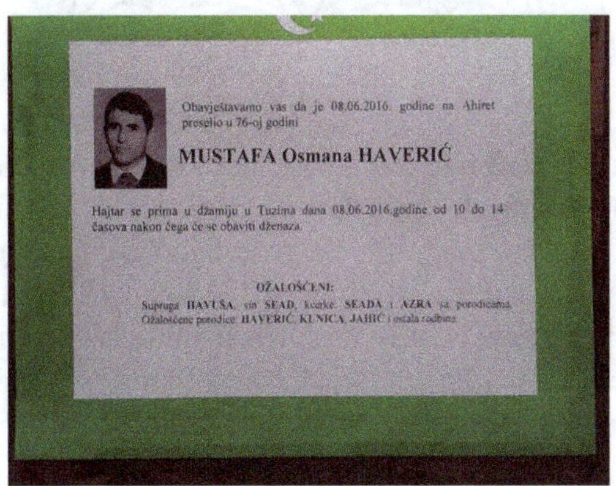

Obavještavamo vas da je 08.06.2016. godine na Ahiret preselio u 76-oj godini

MUSTAFA Osmana HAVERIĆ

Hajtar se prima u džamiju u Tuzima dana 08.06.2016.godine od 10 do 14 časova nakon čega će se obaviti dženaza.

OŽALOŠĆENI:

Supruga **HAVUŠA**, sin **SEAD**, kćerke **SEADA** i **AZRA** sa porodicama. Ožalošćene porodice: **HAVERIĆ**, **KUNICA**, **JAHIĆ** i ostala rodbina.

Mustafa Osmana Haveric
1940-2016

El Fatiha

The Haveric who lived in Prijedor was **Muhamed**. His sisters are **Sabiha** and **Dika**, who lived with addresses in Sarajevo.

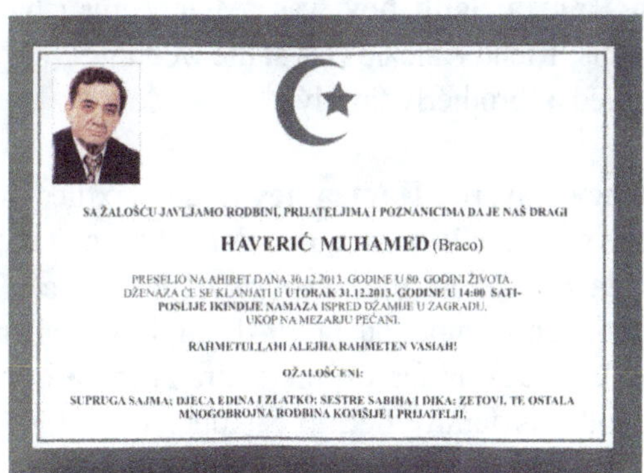

SA ŽALOŠĆU JAVLJAMO RODBINI, PRIJATELJIMA I POZNANICIMA DA JE NAŠ DRAGI

HAVERIĆ MUHAMED (Braco)

PRESELIO NA AHIRET DANA 30.12.2013. GODINE U 80. GODINI ŽIVOTA.
DŽENAZA ĆE SE KLANJATI U **UTORAK 31.12.2013. GODINE U 14:00 SATI-POSLIJE IKINDIJE NAMAZA** ISPRED DŽAMIJE U ZAGRADU.
UKOP NA MEZARJU PEĆANI.

RAHMETULLAHI ALEJHA RAHMETEN VASIAH!

OŽALOŠĆENI:

SUPRUGA SAJMA; DJECA EDINA I ZLATKO; SESTRE SABIHA I DIKA; ZETOVI, TE OSTALA MNOGOBROJNA RODBINA KOMŠIJE I PRIJATELJI.

Haveric Muhamed
1933-2013

El Fatiha

Salih Alija bey Haveric was a merchant in Podgorica and had sons **Hamza** and **Abdulah**. **Saih bey** and his sons lived in Goricani. They had a property there 'from a generation to generation, until the Chetniks expel them away between 1914 and 1916'. The mosque in Goricani was active until 1952 when someone set fire to it. The Haveric cemetery was in Goricani and **Salih bey** and **Abdullah bey** were buried there.[405]

When King Aleksandar Karadzordevic, with his *Decree*, allocated land to the landless, so large estates in Bar and Zeta became nationalised. That naturalisation was further implemented by the agrarian reform in 1927/8 in Goricani, Vukovci and Golubovci. However, even today, some descendants of the old Christian residents said that 'this bey's area belonged to the Haverics'.[406] After the land was taken, **Hamza Salih bey** returned to Podgorica, where he lived previously. Around 1910, when **Hamza Salih bey** was a flagbearer ('bajraktar'), he married, and his 'friend Kalezic was at the wedding', who came from what they called a 'brotherly family'.[407]

With **Omer bey** Haveric, **Hamza bey** traded textiles in Podgorica. They had three stores in Podgorica, one store in the city of Danilovgrad and another in Kokota on the outskirts of Podgorica. The actions continued until the occupation in 1941. In 1941, when Podgorica was bombed by the Axis forces, the entire **Hamza bey** family and **Omer bey** with his family fled to Shkoder until 1945 when they returned to Podgorica. **Hamza bey**'s daughter stayed in Albania. **Hamaz bey** died in 1947. '**Hamza bey** was authoritative and with a high reputation could reconcile quarrelling people, brotherhoods and religious communities'.[408] **Hamza bey**'s sons are **Alija** and **Cazim**.

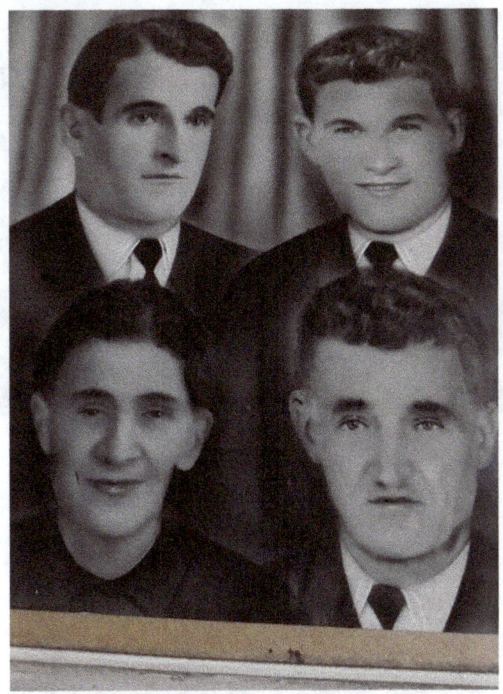

Alija and Cazim (top)
Wife of Hamza bey and Hamza bey (below)

Alija Hamza bey Haveric was born in 1912. He graduated from business school in Zagreb and worked in Podgorica in trading companies like 'Beogradski Vracar'. He was a manager of several textile stores from 1945 until 1972 when he retired. Being a successful businessman, he often traded in textiles with his business associates in Dubrovnik and other areas of the region. At one time he was the secretary of the Municipality in Podgorica. Alija also spoke Albanian.

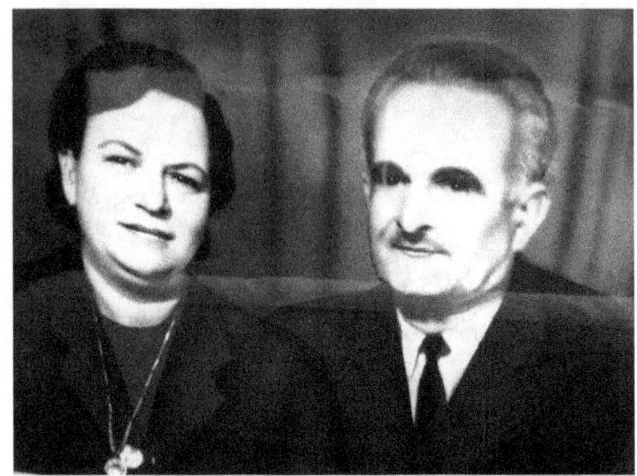

Hajrija and Alija (Podgorica)

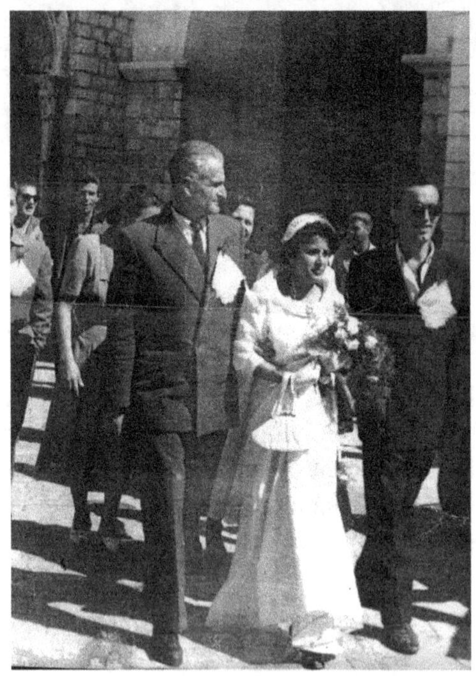

Alija Haveric (left) and Dzavit Haveric in Dubrovnik, Croatia

After the war, **Alija** often came to **Sefket**'s shop in Sarajevo, and he also visited **Alija** and a company where he worked. After **Sefket** from Sarajevo, **Hamza** and **Nezo**'s brother was named **Sefko (Sefkija)**. A remark that was typical for many Haverics of that time, when the people of Sarajevo were sitting in front of shops or in cafes, they saw **Alija** and other Podgoricans, recognising them by 'their good manners, elegance, stylish clothes, and lacquered shoes'.

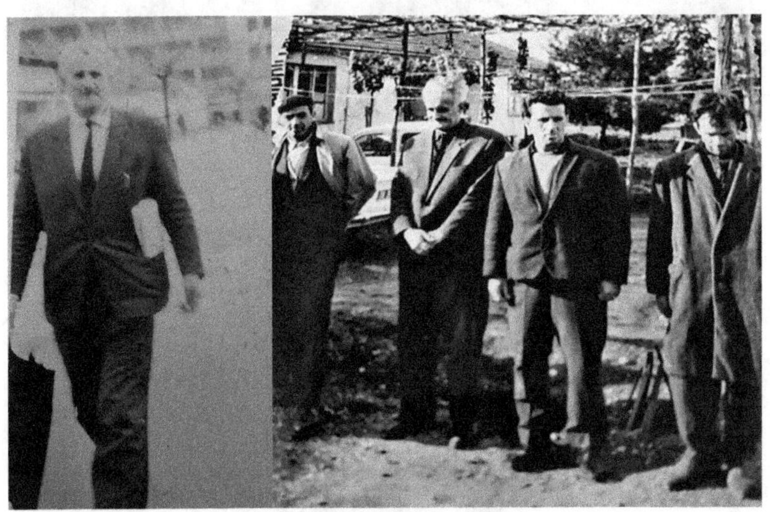

Alija Haveric **Haverics attending at a *janazah* (funeral)**

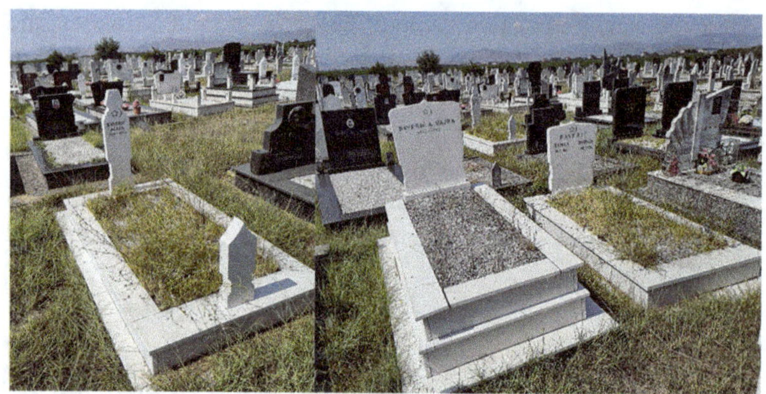

Alija and Hajra Haveric

El Fatiha

Cazim (Cako) Haveric was born in 1922. He was a member of shoemaking cooperatives that worked illegally against the occupiers. He worked as a shoemaker in one of those cooperatives. **Cazim** had a natural gift for singing and was known as a merry man, an organiser of entertaining evenings. He was two metres tall and one of the most beautiful residents in Podgorica.

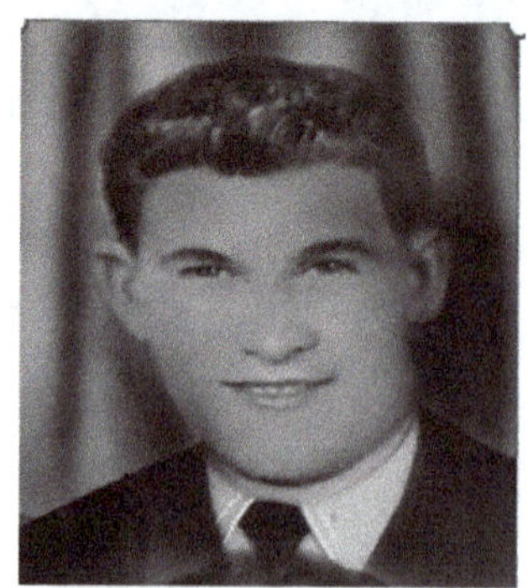

Cazim (Cako) Haveric

In 1948, during the resolution, under unclear circumstances (although he was not a supporter of Stalin), **Cazim** was sent to Goli Otok from 1948 to 1952. After 4.5 years of torture spent in the notorious prison, he returned to Podgorica, where he showed psycho-physical weakness from his experiences. After one year of care from his brother **Alija** and children, with agreement from his parents and brother, **Cazim** was given help in the psychiatric hospital in Kotor. He was housed in the Risan nursing home. On the way to Kotor, he sang old Podgorica songs for the last time and beautifully. Exhausted from his terrible experiences in the past, he never mentally recovered and died in 1992. **Alija** did not have the strength to visit **Cazim** in the psychiatric hospital, so he also died of grief behind him. Like several Haverics, **Cazim** was buried at Cijevna Cemetery.[409]

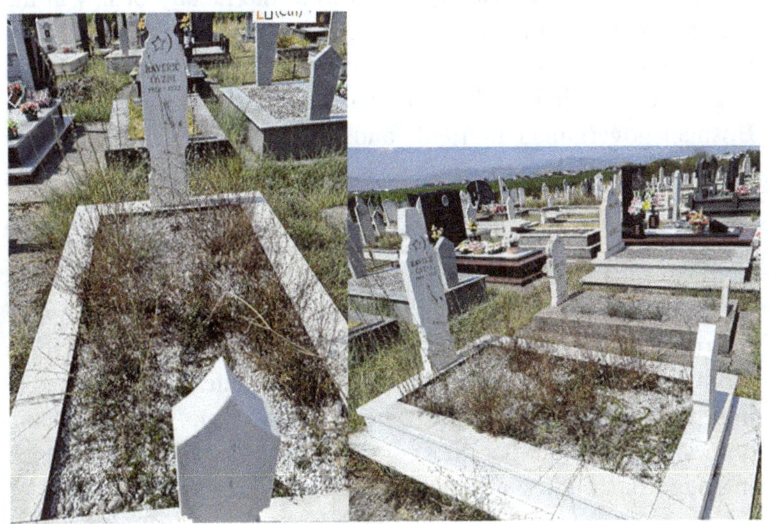

Cazim Haveric

Ef Fatiha

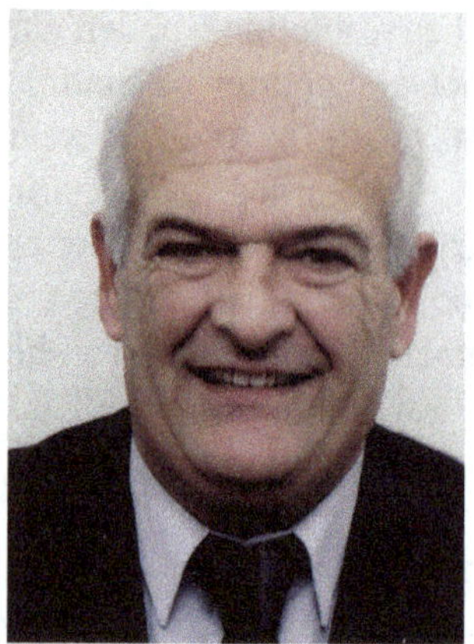

Fadil Haveric

Fadil Alija bey Haveric graduated from the faculty of law at the University of Novi Sad, Vojvodina. He married Decevic and they have two daughters, Aida and Sabina, known to be chosen for Miss Pageant of Bosnia and Herzegovina. **Fadil** Haveric worked for the Bosnian government in 1990s and 2000s. His government posts included Deputy President of the State Government, Minister in the Ministry for Human Rights and Refugees and General Secretary of the Ministry Social Politics. During the war years in Bosnia, he was also engaged in humanitarian activities. Fadil was noted during an international conference titled 'With the truth to the sustainable returns' in Banja Luka on January 30, 2001.[410] **Fadil** worked in prominent companies 'Pismolik' and later 'Interneon' dealing in lighting and flashing advertisements and designs for shops and offices. With his brother **Nezir** he established an Interneon branch in Podgorica. **Fadil** passed away in 2024.

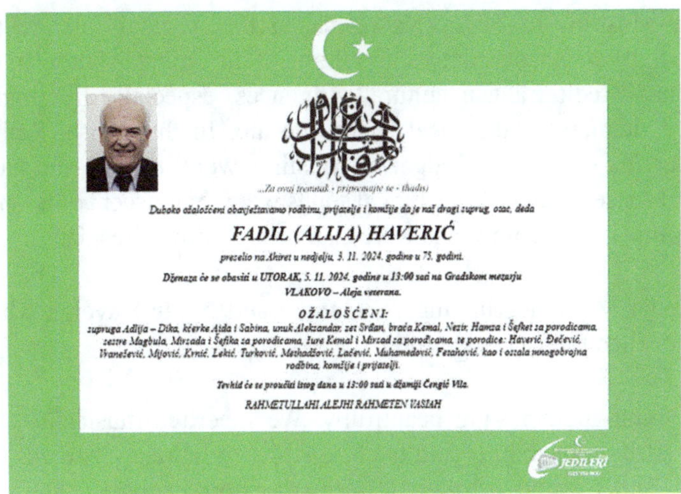

...Za ovaj trenutak - pripremajte se - ibadis)

Duboko ožalošćeni obavještavamo rodbinu, prijatelje i komšije da je naš dragi suprug, otac, deda

FADIL (ALIJA) HAVERIĆ

preselio na Ahiret u nedjelju, 3. 11. 2024. godine u 75. godini.

Dženaza će se obaviti u UTORAK, 5. 11. 2024. godine u 13:00 sati na Gradskom mezarju VLAKOVO – Aleja veterana.

OŽALOŠĆENI:

supruga Adlija – Dika, kćerke Aida i Sabina, unuk Aleksandar, zet Srđan, braća Kemal, Nezir, Hamza i Šefket za porodicama, sestre Magbula, Mirzada i Šefika za porodicama, šure Kemal i Mirzad za porodicama, te porodice: Haverić, Đečević, Ivanešević, Mijović, Krnić, Lekić, Turković, Mehadžović, Lačević, Muhamedović, Fetahović, kao i ostala mnogobrojna rodbina, komšije i prijatelji.

Tevhid će se proučiti istog dana u 13:00 sati u džamiji Čengić Vila.

RAHMETULLAHI ALEJHI RAHMETEN VASIAH

JEDILERI

El Fatiha

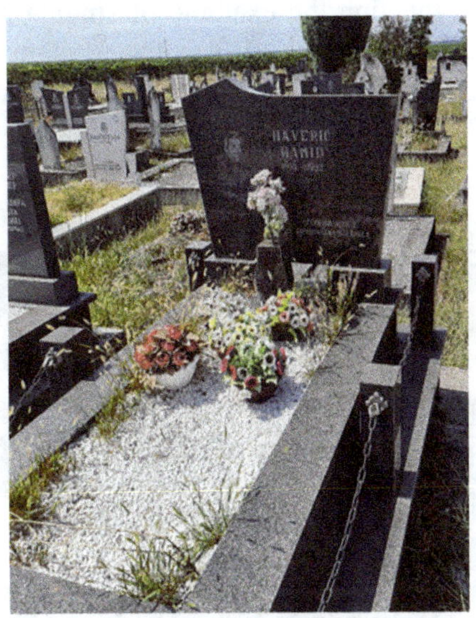

Hamid Haveric's grave

Ef Fatiha

Non-Muslims of Podgorica respected the original folklore and creativity of Bosniak artists. Synthesis of the Oriental-Ottoman and Balkan-Mediterranean cultural influences, especially by singers, gave richness to the local social mosaic. In this sense, Zelimir Rukavina explained, Podgorica Muslims were musical and had a great sense of song. Their lyrical songs were reminiscent of Bosnian *sevdalinka* and epic songs were also brought from Bosnia.

Popular Montenegrin singers, **Hamza** and **Nezir** Haveric, whose fans called them 'beys', said:

> Our mother sang beautifully. We inherited musicality from our mother and uncle Cazim. Podgorica, Sandjak and Bosnia had their *sevdah* (traditional songs). Each one is specific in its own way. However, the Podgorica's *sevdah* is the softest and it is sung quietly. It is good enough to mention the example of singing by a great singer Ksenija Cicvaric. When the Muslims of Stara Varos held concerts in the fortress, at that time young Ksenija joyfully listened to them by climbing the walls. We have very inspirational singing and music.

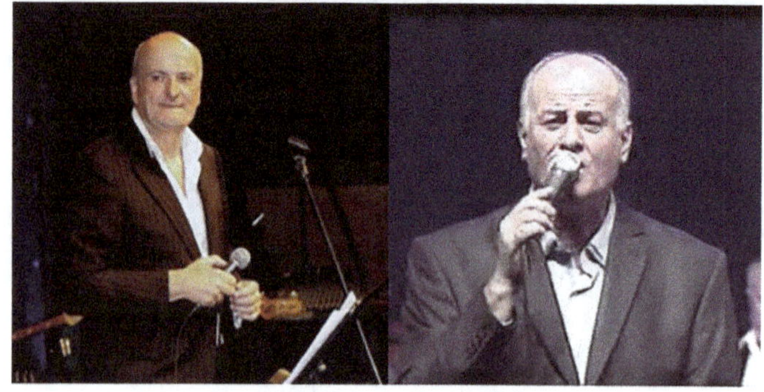

Popular singers Nezir (Nezo) and Hamza Haveric

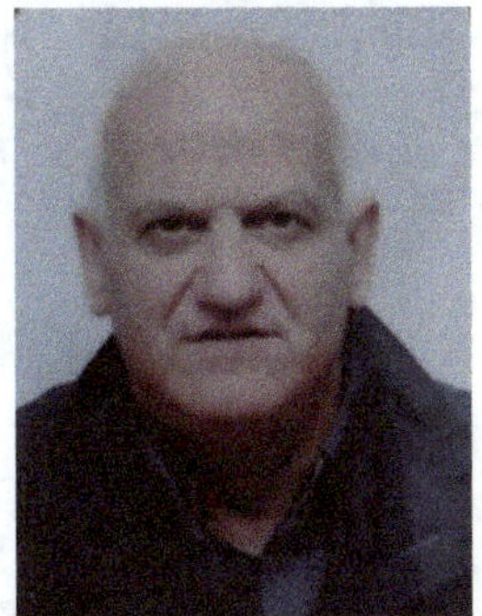

Sefket Haveric

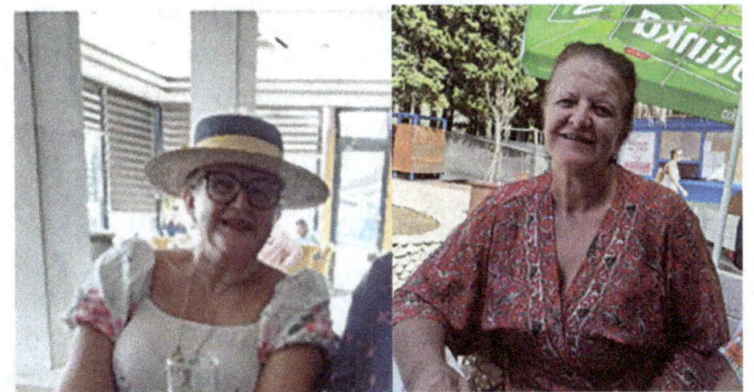

Sisters, Mirsada and Sefika

Conclusion

After years of research this book revealed the rich tapestry of the Haveric family's genealogy and historiography. By tracing relevant sources, this research covered more than five centuries back in history, and to different Balkan areas of a glorious history. Up to now it was almost forgotten part of family history, especially an unknown part of the Balkan history, not to mention transoceanic countries, where nowadays genealogical works get greater attentions, such as Australia. In Australia it is quite a new historical project that may inspire other Muslim immigrant families to write their genealogies and historiographies.

This genealogical work is not only related to the 'trunk of direct ancestors' but to multiple branches which makes this work very complex. Moreover, the historiographical part of the work, by avoiding romanticising ancestors, examined evidence of important events, migrations, and notable individuals critically. Evidently, it is not merely about names, dates, and family relationships. Thus, in their interplay a genealogy served as a 'skeleton' while historiography is the 'flesh' filled through rounding out the places and events of the family where they lived. It should be mentioned in another part of the research complexity about the presence of Haverics in several countries they lived, namely Montenegro, Albania, Bosnia and Herzegovina and Turkey. These cross-roads of history created the record of events of the past and their significance – 'facts without significance are not enough; and significance without facts is hollow'.

Besides available literature and journals, the research contains a treasure of primary sources, such as schematic representations of family trees, immigration records, old documents, tax registrars, archival censuses, civil indexes, statistics, manuscripts, old photos, post cards, letters, valuable stories, testimonies, old articles, medals, poetry, headstones and paintings. Here, the oral family tradition is a stalwart of its own history. Like many of the world's greatest books, this book also has its roots in oral tradition. At some point, some ancestors took the time to write down those oral accounts to preserve them, like other affluent families who chronicled their histories.

All these components also helped to find new links within the Haveric own family tree. Every member of the family is given equal consideration and respect. Traditionally in the Balkans and beyond, family genealogy takes on a paternalistic tone, thus the lineage often follows male lines. It is because most families inherit male surnames. However, the females in this work are not misrepresented, indeed, they are included as an integral part of historiographical narrations.

Looking back at history, it is evident that the Haveric family emerged in the Balkan social mosaic as an old Muslim family of the 15th century when Islamisation began from the gradual conversion of local inhabitants, the Bogomils. It reveals the authenticity of its ethnic origin and identity free from ideologies. There is also a possibility that the Haveric family was even older Muslim family. Nevertheless, they were recorded as the first Muslim family in Podgorica, Montenegro. At any rate, that region actually gave birth to the family history.

The book offers the discovery of previously unknown relatives and highlights a noble family tradition. The title of 'Bey' historically indicated nobility, often within the Ottoman Empire, retained even in time of the Montenegrin and Yugoslav kingdoms. The Haverics were known for their military prowess and service in the Ottoman Empire and later as influential figures affiliated as members of distinguished representatives such as the royal offices, or appointed judges or adjutants or a senator in Montenegro and Albania.

The Haveric family was among the Balkan bey families which mostly lived in the urban cosmopolitan centres of Podgorica, Bar, Sarajevo, Tirana, Shkoder, Kavaja, Durres, Istanbul and Izmir under specifically adopted surnames Haveri, Haveriku, Haveraj, Tanbay and Adenis. They gave many notable members. Seven Haverics held the title of Pasha, one of the highest titles in the Ottoman Empire. Numerous hold title of Bey due to their services as military commanders, judges, secretaries, philanthropes, imams and scholars. Their noble ancestry appeared in a number of historical records, important documents, received Sultan and King's awards and some were mentioned in the famous epic poetries. Indeed, it reflects those ancestors of the Haveric family who had an influence in certain regions of the Balkans.

Among the Haverics there were a few national heroes in their states. Many Haverics were wealthy landowners and merchants and craftsmen others were achievers in their fields. They all left their imprint on time and place where they lived. In particular, this family history also reflects their challenge in justice, especially in the time of wars or exoduses, which started after denials of their authentic identity. Their endeavour and contribution to freedom, social justice, social and interfaith cohesion and democracy are also notable qualities. The book let the narrations speak. Thus, this allowed to give on behalf of those long-forgotten ancestors the chance to give their side of the story.

By connecting personal family stories to historical events, the research adds depth to the understanding of the circumstances of the past and the world around them. It provides a framework for individual members to connect with their past, offering insights into cultural, religious, ethnic, and national identities and an understanding of social evolution, including migrations and mixing with host populations over time. It is also important to keep in mind that those Haverics who lived more modestly were also often called 'beys' by others as an act of respect for their ancestorial tradition.

A motto says, 'Family is a little world created by love'. Many families pride themselves on identifying their lineages. Now having a clear and expanded knowledge about the Haveric family tree, the book provides reflection on the ancestry, religion and culture, which are important aspects of historical succession known as beys. Their continuity and legitimacy create a family pride. Even after new historical regulations, it lost its title of bey becoming known as a distinguished family when the title of bey, became only the curtesy title as part of family tradition.

For me as the author, it was truly staggering research by documenting rich family history and noble ancestry. But it was not measuring only the status, wealth or titles but human virtues they shared with others either rich or poor. The Haverics also were always part of a great diversity of all social classes, either as local residents or immigrants to other countries. Their ancestral tradition is what made their distinctiveness important in genealogy and historiography.

Forgetting ancestors is a sad reality. However, certain details about the ancestry get lost over time with a hope it unfolds in the future. It will be the further building up of facts into a comprehensive whole, a coherent picture of the family history. There is a hope that this book may inspire future generations to continue exploring their family roots and tradition and share their stories, enriched with less known branches or individuals.

Endnotes

---

[1] Amira Turbic-Hadzagic i Đenita Haveric, 2023, *Kroz prezimena progovara naš višestoljetni identitet*, interview in *Stav* newspaper, Sarajevo
[2] Cirgic 2007: 75
[3] English-Arabic-Hebrew mini-Dictionary, Mideastweb Middle East
[4] Noble Titles, Royal Titles, 2018
[5] Mijović and Kovačević, 1975: 138
[6] https://shkoder.net/malesoret/
[7] Ismail Haveric, 2015
[8] Mustafa Memic cited in Bosnjaci.net, 2003
[9] https://www.montenegro.org.au/bjelopavlici.html
[10] Haveric, 2005
[11] Muhic, 2013:329
[12] Ibid, 2013:329, Haveric, 2005
[13] Haveric, 2005
[14] Marianne van Twillert, 2017
[15] Čelebić, 2022
[16] https://golubovci.me/
[17] Rukavina, 12
[18] Haveric 2005
[19] http://www.paundurlic.com/forum.vlasi.srbije/index.php?topic=236.0
[20] Muhic, 2022: 109
[21] Rastoder, 2010: 11-85
[22] Muhic, 2022: 117
[23] Hrabak, 90
[24] Kalezic, 2002: 44-5
[25] Vukanovic, 1974: 310
[26] Ismail Haveric, 2015
[27] Rukavina, 12
[28] Folić, 2013: 57-8
[29] Radusinović, 1991
[30] Agim Haveri, 2008
[31] Hrabak, 207
[32] https://golubovci.me/
[33] Noble Titles, Royal Titles, 2018
[34] Garnett, 1904: 5
[35] Salih Yucel, 2025

[36] Turbic-Hadzagic and Haveric, 2023
[37] Noble Titles, Royal Titles, 2018
[38] Fadil Haveric, 2013
[39] https://www.refworld.org/legal/legislation/natlegbod/1982/en/17317
[40] Kujovic, 2005
[41] Cirgic, 2007
[42] Rukavina, also Memic, 2002: 49
[43] Hadžiabdić, 2018: 203
[44] Muhadinović, 149
[45] Brković, 162-3
[46] Halit Đečević, n.d.
[47] Brković, 162-3
[48] Brković, 162-3
[49] Tuzovic, 2019: 36
[50] Agim Haveric, 2013
[51] Ismail Haveric, 2013 and 2015
[52] Fudo Haveric, 2013
[53] Agim Haveri, 2013
[54] Nesic, 1912: 5
[55] Radusinovic, 1991: 20
[56] Jasavić, S., 2009
[57] Memic, 2002: 45
[58] Name list of owners of lands [houses] from the city of Podgorica, 23. II. 1879
[59] Cukic, 287
[60] Nazira Haveric, n.d.
[61] Radusinovic, 1991: 20
[62] Tuzovic, 2019: 63 Mandic Sead, 2024
[63] Gradska TV Podgorica 2025
[64] Zlatko V. Zlaticanin, 140
[65] Gradska TV Podgorica, 2025
[66] Enver Backovic, 2024
[67] Pulevic, 2009: 82
[68] https://golubovci.me/stranice/istorija
[69] Ismail Haveric, 2013 and 2015
[70] Hrabak, 195
[71] Cirgic 2007: 136
[72] Burzan, 2011: 186
[73] Hrabak, 187
[74] Hrabak, 194
[75] Stari Bar: Prica na tri jezika, 2009
[76] Dacić, 2019: 154
[77] Agovic, 2001
[78] Ibid, 2001
[79] Rukavina, n.d., broj: 57: 12
[80] Ibid 12
[81] Rastoder, 2010, 11-85

[82] Lipovina, 2004: 182
[83] Agic, 2002: 95
[84] Rifat Haveric, 2024
[85] archive: Library Svetozar Markovic, Belgrade
[86] translated by Ismail Albayrak
[87] Ismet Busatlic, 2013
[88] Nazira Haveric, n.d.
[89] Agic, 2002: 77; 88; 95
[90] Ibid, 71: 93; Drzavni arhiv CG, 1906K. br. 35 dok. 2067/1-2
[91] Agovic, 2002: 225
[92] Vukić, 2004: 141
[93] Drzavni Arhiv CG, Cetinje, 1906, godine, K br35 dok. 2067/1-2
[94] Agovic, 2001: 82; 229
[95] Glasnik, no. 7., 1935
[96] Muhtar Muho,.2024
[97] Amedin Haveric, 2024
[98] Fahro Haveric, 2024
[99] Agovic, 2001:34
[100] Agim Haveri, 2024
[101] https://myftinia-shkoder.org/wp-content/uploads/2018/09/udha-islame-web-187.pdf
[102] Agim Haveri, 2024
[103] Clayer, 2009
[104] https://memorie.al/en/enver-hoxha-massacred-the-muslim-clergy-in-albania-in-the-most-barbaric-way-and-there-was-no-tolerance-towards-him-as-they-say-reflections-of-the-renowned-researcher/
[105] Six Centuries of Institutional Islam in Balkans, 2016, pp. 11-25; https://isamveri.org/pdfdrg/G00180/2016/2016_MEHDIUF.pdf
[106] https://blokukombetarindependent.com/biographies-cara-hoxha/; Biographies – Cara thru Hoxha – BLOKU KOMBTAR INDEPENDENT (blokukombetarindependent.com)
[107] Agim Haveri
[108] Agim Haveri; https://blokukombetarindependent.com/biographies-cara-hoxha/; Biographies – Cara thru Hoxha – BLOKU KOMBTAR INDEPENDENT (blokukombetarindependent.com)
[109] Clayer, 2009
[110] Forumi Musliman i Shqipërisë, Tirane, 2008
[111] From the Kemal Bey's narrative, 1970s
[112] Cirgic, 2007: 368 *...Ako nikada nešto ne pokušate objasniti, nikada ništa nećete spoznati.* Howard Zinn, 2002.
[113] Vujosevic, 2015
[114] Sead Mandic
[115] Abdić, 2023
[116] Enver Backovic, 2013
[117] T. Tuzi Sehitigli Ve Nizam Camisi
[118] Maurits, 205: 604
[119] Hrabak, 45
[120] Hrabak, 45
[121] Ronald, 1979

[122] Wael, 2009: 175-6
[123] Hrabak, 45
[124] Hrabak, 45
[125] Muhadinović, 144-8
[126] Halit Đečević
[127] 'Bog ih kaznio', Feljton, Polis, p. 37, Podgorica
[128] Irina Deretić
[129] Muhic, 2022: 125
[130] https://www.lektire.rs/gorski-vijenac-petar-petrovic-njegos/
[131] Ibid
[132] https://www.bosnjaci.net/prilog.php?pid=47283
[133] Kazaz cited in Hadžiabdić, 2018: 199
[134] Jovanović, 2021: 291-300
[135] http://www.institut-genocid.unsa.ba/pdf/GORSKI%20VIJENAC.pdf
[136] https://www.rastko.rs/knjizevnost/umetnicka/njegos/mountain_wreath.html
[137] https://sofiografskaskola.com/
[138] Zlaticanin, n.d. 'Bog ih je kaznio', Polis, p. 37, Podgorica
[139] Zlatko Zlaticanic, 139
[140] Brković, 2006: 221
[141] Agovic; https://www.broj19-number19.org/?s=Haveric
[142] Ismail Haveric; https://www.onlinepeticija.com/obnova_haverica_dzamije_goriani_podgorica
[143] 'Damaged walls of the old Haverić mosque in Golubovci', 2014
[144] Kurgas, n.d.
[145] Ismail Haveric, 2015
[146] Dacić, 2019: 154
[147] Rastoder, 2010: 92
[148] Ibid 2010: 96
[149] Ismail Haveric, 2010
[150] Rastoder: 2010, 85-121
[151] Fahro Haveric, 2024
[152] Dacić, 2019: 154
[153] Odluka MZ Stari Bar I MZ Bar, CG, 2009
[154] https://en.wikipedia.org/wiki/Kubelie_Mosque
[155] http://prishtinapress.info/wp-content/uploads/2012/02/Aqif-Averiku.jpg
[156] Alba Haveriku
[157] Edukata Islame Revistë shkencore, kulturore islame tremujore, 2002: 172-3
[158] Rastoder 2010: 12-3
[159] Rukavina, n.d.
[160] Memic, 2002: 49
[161] Zlaticanin, 1938:17
[162] https://montenegrina.net/wp-content/uploads/2014/05/ILIJA-ZLATICANIN-Svjedocanstva-podgorickog-hronicara.pdf
[163] Basagic, 1900: 89
[164] Brkovic, 2006: 153-4
[165] *Zeta*, godina ?; Br. 17, strana 6, Podgorca; Brković, 2006: 165
[166] Ilija Zlaticanin

[167] *Zeta*, godina ?; Br. 17, strana 6, Podgorca; Jevrem Brkovic, 2006: 165
[168] Brković, 2006: 165
[169] Brković, 2006: 165
[170] Ismail Haveric, 2015
[171] https://archive.org/stream/letopisslovensk01matigoog/letopisslovensk01matigoog_djvu.txt
[172] Mitar Bakic, 1913: 295
[173] Archive Istanbul University – İstanbul Üniversitesi'nin Arşivihttps://eliber.me/poslanici-turskog-poslanstva-na-cetinju/
[174] https://www.liverpoolmedals.com/product/order-of-the-medjidie-5th-class-badge-european-made-2
[175] https://www.medalbook.com/europe-east/turkey/ottoman-empire-1299-1922/orders/order-of-osmania/civil-division/order-of-osmania-civil-division-iv-class-6/order-of-osmania-civil-division-iv-class-0
[176] https://en.numista.com/catalogue/exonumia300056.html
[177] The State Archives of Turkey (BOA, Prime Ministry Ottoman Archive,17 Rabi'u'-Ewvel 1324 / 5 April 1322
[178] https://incubator.wikimedia.org/wiki/Wp/cnr/Vasilije_Popovi%C4%87
[179] Zlaticanin
[180] https://popforum.rs/legenda-o-bajramu-drickovicu/
[181] https://www.njegos.org/petrovics/avericen.htm
[182] Iz knjige, "Petar I Petrović – DJELA" 1999
[183] Jovicevic, 1999 https://www.montenegrina.net/pages/pages1/istorija/dokumenti/barjaktari_i_barjaktarstvo_u_cg_m_jovicevic.html
[184] Cukic, 2018: 2249; 39
[185] Ibid, 249-50; 239
[186] Ivic, 2020
[187] Tuzovic, 2019: 62
[188] Ibid, 2019: 129
[189] Martinović, 2020: 83
[190] Ibid 2020: 110
[191] Ibid
[192] Mirsad T Kurgas, 2013, 'Kraljevi gosti' https://www.broj19-number19.org/kraljevi-gosti/
[193] Martinović, 2020: 84; 86-7
[194] Tuzovic, 2019: 136
[195] From the data left by Jusuf Aqif Bey Haveri and from Skender Haveri and others told Agim Haveri
[196] Fadil Haveric
[197] Proceedings, 2015: 31
[198] Agim Haveri, Archive, 2024
[199] Memic 2002; 178-9
[200] Agic, 2002: 95
[201] Rastoder, 2010: 74; Memic, 2002: 56
[202] https://dergipark.org.tr/en/download/article-file/2328775
[203] Agim's grandfather
[204] The digital State Library of Upper Austria
[205] Ibid

[206] Ibid
[207] Tuzovic, 2019: 64
[208] Scekić, 2017: 216
[209] Lara (Dilara) Tanbay
[210] Tuzović, 2019: 152-5 I
[211] Tuzović, 2019: 157
[212] Mehmeti, 2021
[213] Enver Backovic
[214] Murat and Enver Backovic
[215] Rastoder, 2010: 42-3
[216] Cetinjski Arhiv, proslijedio Enver Backovic
[217] ARCHIVAL NOTES, 2019: 41-2
[218] Ibid 2019: 48
[219] ARCHIVAL NOTES, 2019: 49; https://dacg.me/wp-content/uploads/2021/02/Arhivski-zapisi-broj-1-2-za-2019-godinu-2.pdf
[220] Ibid
[221] Rastoder, 2010: 49
[222] Konjević, 2018: 399-401
[223] Cukic, 2018: 287
[224] ARCHIVAL NOTES, 2019: 53
[225] Rastoder, 2010: 42-3
[226] Ibid, 2010: 51
[227] Martinović, 2020: 69
[228] Ibid 2020: 69
[229] MUD, 1882, https://eliber.me/
[230] Ibid, 1882
[231] Ibid
[232] Ibid
[233] Rastoder, 210: 83
[234] Ibid, 210: 31
[235] Fadil (2009) and Ismail (2010) Haverić
[236] Spisak pravnih birača iz opštine varoši Podgorice za izbor narodnog poslanika za 1905 god, Cetinje Arhiv
[237] Glas Crnogoraca in Lipovina, 2004: 106
[238] Rastoder, 2010: 78
[239] Ibid 2010: 79-80
[240] Ibid, 2010: 80
[241] Glas Crnogoraca cited in Lipovina, 2004: 106; Rastoder, 2010
[242] Enver Backovic Cetinje Arhiva
[243] https://www.blic.rs/riznica/100-godina-podgoricke-skupstine-sta-se-dogodilo-na-dan-o-kome-se-i-danas-pricaju/kzkgxhb
[244] Fadil Haveric
[245] Memic, 1998: 69
[246] Smajic, 2019: 164
[247] Muhic, 2022: 115
[248] Smajic, 2019: 208

[249] Agim Haveri, 2024
[250] Ibid, 2024
[251] Tedeschin, 2021
[252] https://bosnae.info/index.php/progon-bosnjaka-iz-crne-gore-ustanka-1875-1878-2
[253] ARCHIVAL NOTES, 2019: 41-2
[254] Rastoder, 2010: 204
[255] cited in Lipovina, 2004: 180
[256] Abla Haveriku, 2024
[257] Konjević, 2018: 399-401
[258] see works by Rastoder, Imamovic, Muhic
[259] Voloder, 2018: 8
[260] Fadil Haveric
[261] Voloder, 2018: 9
[262] Vukić, 2004: 277
[263] Number 629 V. 1909. 12. Knjaž. Ministry of Foreign Affairs Works of Cetinje
[264] Vukić, 2004: 283
[265] Rastoder, 2010
[266] Sead Mandic, 2024
[267] https://core.ac.uk/download/pdf/51100309.pdf
[268] Tedeschin, 2021
[269] Dzavid's note 2013
[270] Smajic, 2019: 155
[271] Cazim Haveric 2013
[272] Smajic, 2019: 70
[273] Dzavid's note
[274] Enisa Haveric, 2024
[275] Dzavid's note, Fadil Haveric
[276] Azra Haverić, 2024
[277] Alija Nametak, 1962
[278] Nezir Haveric, 2024
[279] Tuzović, 2019: 157
[280] According to the data of their relatives in Mustafa Memic
[281] Rifat Haveric, 2024
[282] Ibid, 2024
[283] Nezir and Hamza Haveric, Dzavid's note
[284] Cirgic, 2007: 368-9
[285] Ibid 2007: 345
[286] Ibid, 345
[287] Abla Haveriku, 2024
[288] FK Leotar, Trebinje
[289] Mustafa Memić, Sarajevo as a Migration Centre
[290] Pulevic, 2009: 82
[291] Abla Haveriku, 2024
[292] ARTICLE: Nga: Neki Babamusta, Londër, 14 shkurt 2012 Aqif Averiku stone castle in immortality (1910 – 1947), Albanian News, 2012: 17

[293] Online Archive of Victims of Communism https://en.kujto.al/personat/alma-haveriku/; https://en.kujto.al/personat/mehmet-haveriku-2/; https://en.kujto.al/personat/rudin-haveriku/; https://en.kujto.al/personat/xhemal-haveriku/
[294] https://en.kujto.al/?s=Haver
[295] Enver Backovic, 2013, 2024
[296] Ibid, 2013
[297] Ibid, 2024
[298] https://fr-fr.facebook.com/pglegende/photos/a.122318211173468/124603054278317/
[299] Enver Backovic, 2024
[300] Memic, 1998: 69
[301] Amer Haveric, 2025
[302] https://fr-fr.facebook.com/pglegende/photos/a.122318211173468/124603054278317/
[303] Article: P. K., 'Od Kolijevke roda tvoga', 1971
[304] P. K., 'Od Kolijevke roda tvoga', 1971
[305] Ibid, 1971
[306] Amer Haveric, 2025
[307] Lejla Haverić-Sejdić and Emir Haverić, 2024
[308] Ramadan Zaganjor, 2024
[309] Ibid, 2024
[310] Ibid
[311] Djana Osmanagaj, 2024
[312] Ramadan Zaganjor, 2024
[313] Djana Osmanagaj, 2024
[314] Tuzovic, 2019: 72
[315] Abdullah Bato Abdic, 2023
[316] Aida Havereic, 2024
[317] Rifat Haveric, 2024
[318] Tuzović, 2019: 149
[319] Cazim Haveric, 2013
[320] Agim Haveri, 2013
[321] Fado Durbuzovic, 2013
[322] Memnun Idzakovic, 2008
[323] Fadil Durbuzovic, 2013
[324] Semso Haveric, 1990
[325] Gajret, 1939: 129; https://www.preporod.ba/wp-content/uploads/2022/08/Gajret-1939-broj-7-8-i-9.pdf; Izvjestaj glavnog odbora Gajreta za godinu 1938-9, Gajret, juli, 1939
[326] Ibid, 1939: 160
[327] from Dr Dzemal Haveric's biography
[328] Haver Tanbay, 2024
[329] Betul Tanbay, 2024
[330] https://www.facebook.com/groups/22307609761/
[331] Erdogan Tanbay, 2024
[332] Haver Tanbay, 2024
[333] Lara Tanbay, 2024
[334] Haver Tanbay, 2024

[335] Amer Haveric, 2024
[336] https://www.limundo.com/kupovina/Kolekcionarstvo/Ostalo/ORIGINAL-POTPIS-HASKO-HAVERIC/114952433; https://estradalist.blogspot.com/2012_11_23_archive.html
[337] Tuzovic, 2019: 132
[338] Nazira Haveric Kerni, nd.
[339] Cazim Haveric, 2013
[340] Fadi Haveric, 2013
[341] Azra Haverić, 2024
[342] Cazim Haveric, 2013
[343] Edina and Aida Haveric, 2024
[344] Nazira Haveric Kerni, n.d.
[345] Ibid, n.d.
[346] 'Vojno Delo, 1964: 95
[347] Bejtić, 1973
[348] Kanton Sarajevo, *Ministarstvo za boračka pitanja*, Komisija za očuvanje nacionalnih spomenika, 2005
[349] https://memorie.al/en/student-of-the-russian-puzanova-and-master-simon-rota-graduated-excellently-in-leningrad-but-in-shkodra-was-left-in-an-8-year-school-brothers-testimony-for-the-great-master-of-portrait
[350] https://memorie.al/en/student-of-the-russian-puzanova-and-master-simon-rota-graduated-excellently-in-leningrad-but-in-shkodra-was-left-in-an-8-year-school-brothers-testimony-for-the-great-master-of-portrait/"Student of the Russian Puzanova and master Simon Rota, graduated excellently in Leningrad, but in Shkodra was left in an 8-year school" / Brother's testimony, for the great master of portrait.
[351] From the testimony of Alit Selhanović, said Sead Mandic
[352] Nazira Haveric, n.d.
[353] Agim Haveri, n.d.
[354] Nazira Haveric, n.d.
[355] Dzavid Haveric
[356] Anisa Haveric, 2024
[357] Amra Haveric, 2024
[358] Nazira Keraj Haveric, n.d.
[359] Ibid, 2024
[360] Agim Haveric, n.d.
[361] https://www.reporter.al/2020/08/21/ne-kerkim-te-bibliotekes-se-re-dhe-kinemase-se-munguar/
[362] Nazira Haveric, n.d.
[363] Agim Haveri grandfather
[364] Shkoder archive/ Agim Haveri
[365] Agim Haveri, archives, 2024
[366] Ibid, 2024
[367] Malaj, 2014: 2
[368] Ibid, 2014
[369] Gjakovo Kosovo, with a group of dissidents of 25 men and four other women. KABASHI, SHAQIR_0046.pdf; https://www.cia.gov/readingroom/docs/KABASHI%2C%20SHAQIR_0046.pdf
[370] Agim Haveri, archives, 2024

[371] Ibid, 2024
[372] Malaj, 2014
[373] Agim G. Haveri, written 2008
[374] Neziri in Abdula and Koroglu, 2024: 323
[375] Agim Haveri, , 2024
[376] Agim Haveri's letter, Pek histori nga dega gjenealogjike e ethem jusuf beg haveriqit , Tirane, 25. 7. 2007
[377] Ibid 25. 7. 2007
[378] Ibid
[379] Dzavid's note
[380] https://www.flickr.com/photos/111076799@N03/49852736562
[381] Hajrije Efovic
[382] Abla Haveriku, 2024
[383] Agim Haveri, 2024
[384] Ibid
[385] Abla Haveriku, 2024
[386] Agim Haveri, ,2024
[387] Abla Haveriku, 2024
[388] Ibid, 2024
[389] Abla Haveriku, 2024
[390] Ibid,, 2024
[391] Ibid
[392] Ibid
[393] Ibid
[394] Ibid
[395] Agim Haveri record, 2024
[396] Dacić, 2019: 154
[397] Fahro Haveric, 2024
[398] Ibid, 2024
[399] Ismail Haveric, 2013
[400] Haris Haveric, 2024
[401] Muhtar Haveric, 2024
[402] https://www.jedro.bar/info/12932-saopstenje-udruzenja-maslinara-antivari-stari-bar
[403] https://oliveoilmontenegro.me/portfolio-item/bajazithaveric/
[404] Fahro Haveric, 2024
[405] Nezo Haveric, 2024
[406] Ibid, 2024
[407] Local tradition said by Hamza Alija Haveric, 2024
[408] Nezir Haveric, 2024
[409] Nezo and Hamza Haveric, 2024
[410] Members of Ministry for Human rights and refugees in Bosnia and Herzegovina, 2001

Bibliography

Abdulah Bato Abdić, 2023, 'Pobrezje – Podgoricko mezarje kojeg vise nema', Islam Montenegro, https://www.monteislam.com/novosti/pobrezje-podgoricko-mezarje-kojeg-vise-nema

Adnan Cirgic, 2007, *Govor podgorickih muslimana*, Institute of the Montenegrin Language and Linguistic 'Vojislav P. Nikcevic', Cetinje.

Andrija Jovicevic, 1999, *Zeta i Ljeskopolje Skadarsko Jezero*, Fototipska izdanja, CID, 1999, Podgorica.

Andrija Jovicevic, 1999, 'Porodice Podgorickih Muslimana' Podgorica, str. 248-9.

Aleksa Ivic, 2020, 'Fragmenti iz Istorije Bosanskog Ustanka 1875 i 1876', Dionicka Tiskara, Zagreb. https://archive.org/stream/ivic-aleksa-fragmenti-iz-istorije-bosanskog-ustanka-1875.-i-1876.-godi./Ivi%C4%87%2C%20Aleksa%20-%20Fragmenti%20iz%20istorije%20Bosanskog%20ustanka%201875.%20i%201876.%20godi._djvu.txt

Alija Bejtić, 1973, *Streets and Squares of Sarajevo*, Sarajevo City Museum, Sarajevo

Alija Nametak, 'Some folk customs and local traditions of Muslims in Podgorica (Titograd)', Gazette of the Ethnographic Museum in Cetinje, II book, 1962, Cetinje, https://www.rastko.rs/rastko-cg/ljudi/anametak- podgorica.html

АРХИВСКИ ЗАПИСИ ARCHIVAL NOTES 1-2/2019, Издавач: Државни архив Црне Горе/Publisher: The State Archives of Montenegro Цетиње.

Bajro Agovic, 2001, *Dzamije u Crnoj Gori*, Almanah, Podgorica.

Besir Neziri in Edt Sevba Abdula & Ahmet Köroğlu, The Trajectory of Islamic Thought in the Interwar, Balkan Periodicals, 2024: Ajgraf Skopje, North Macedonia.
SHKRIMET LETRARE NË REVISTËN KULTURA ISLAME

Blazo Kalezic, 2002, *Kalezici kroz vijekove: Prilog istoriji bratstva – Rodoslovi*, Udruzenje bratstva Kalezica, Podgorica.

Bogumil Hrabak, 2000, *Istorija Podgorice*, https://www.scribd.com/doc/254908538/Bogumil-Hrabak-Istorija-Podgorice-pdf

Bogumil Hrabak, 2000, *Podgorica do početka XIX vijeka*, Samostalni izdavač, Beograd

Borislav Jovanović, 'Njegošologija; Jedna apoteza i komentari', Matica, br. 88, 2021.pp. 291-300. https://www.maticacrnogorska.me/files/88/12%20Borislav%20Jovanovi%C4%87.pdf

Bosna i Hercegovina, Federacija Bosne i Hercegovine, Kanton Sarajevo, *Ministarstvo za boračka pitanja*, Komisija za očuvanje nacionalnih spomenika, 2005

'Damaged walls of the old Haverić mosque in Golubovci', Online Vijesti, Montenegro, 2014 https://www.monteislam.com/nouallimciscena-dzamija-u-goricanima.

Danilo Burzan, 2011, *Podgoricki toponimi i znamenja*, Pobjeda, Podgorica.

Dragan Kujović, 2005 u *Tragovima Orijenalno-Islamskog Kulturnog Nasljeđa u Crnoj Gori,* Almanah, Podgorica

Dzavid Haveric, 2005, *Islamizaciaja Bosne: Rani bosanski uticaj na bosansko drustvo* (Deakin University), Bellarine Print, Victoria.

Edmond Malaj, 2014, *Persekutimi dhe ekzekutimi i Lef Nosit nga diktatura komuniste*, Revista Kuvendi. Reviste e shoqates Kuvendi, Michigan; Gazeta Dielli, Bronx, Universiteti 'Aleksander Xhuvani', Elbasan) https://memorie.al/en/after-nako-spiro-was-in-moscow-we-took-lef-nosi-to-hide-him-at-the-nephew-of-a-friend-of-his-a-prominent-personality-but-he-handed-him-over-to-sigurimi-memoirs-of-the-jew-marko-menahem/\

Edukata Islame Revistë shkencore, kulturore islame tremujore Viti XXXI nr. 66 / p. 172-3, 2002 Prishtinë https://forumimusliman.org/simpoziumi.pdf

Famous Podgorica Muslims, Haveric and Osmanagic. (Ilija Zlaticanin 'Znameniti podgoricki muslimani – Zeta (IX/ 1938, br.17 (1. V) str. 6 cited in Ljiljana Lipovina, 2004: 183)

Ferid Muhic, 2022, *Ontologija Islama*, BANU, Novi Pazar-Rozaje, Srbija – Crna Gora.

Ferid Muhic, 2013, in Edukata Islame Revistë shkencore, kulturore islame tremujore Viti XLIII nr. 107 / 2014

Forumi Musliman i Shqipërisë, Tirane, 2008, 'Integration of Albanians in Europe and the values that Islam convey in this integration' (Integrimi i shqiptarëve në Evropa dhe vlerat që ka Islami përcjell në këtë integrim) Kavajë shkurt, 2008, pp. 1-294 https://forumimusliman.org/simpoziumi.pdf

Garnett, Lucy Mary Jane. *Turkish Life in Town and Country*. G. P. Putnam's Sons, 1904. phttps://en.wikipedia.org/wiki/Bey

Glas Crnogoraca XXXVII/1908, br 51(31.IX) str. 3; br. 52 920. IX str. 3 cited in Ljiljana Lipovina, 2004: 106

Glas Crnogoraca XXXVIII/1909, br 10 (1.III) str. 1 cited in Ljiljana Lipovina, 2004: 106; Rastoder, 2010.

Gradska TV Podgorica 2025; Emisija 'Gradski vremeplov', Branko Vukelic, Gradska TV Podgorica, 2025

How much have the Highlanders ruined Shkodra?!, 2014 …https://shkoder.net/malesoret/

Husein Ceno Tuzovic, 2019, *Podgoricka historijska citanka*, Savez undruzenja boraca NOB-a i antifasista Crne Gore i JU Narodna biblioteka 'Radoslav Ljumovic, Podgorica

Ilija Zlaticanin, 2013, Svjedocanstva Podgorickog Hronicara https://www.scribd.com/document/396514681/ILIJA-ZLATICANIN-Svjedocanstva-podgorickog-hronicara-pdf

Ilija Zlaticanin, n.d., 'Bog ih kaznio', Feljton, Polis, Str 37.

Ismail Haveric in Islam Montenegro, Islamski Web Portal u Crnoj Gori, 2013, https://www.monteislam.com/historija/porijeklo-porodice-haveric)

Jevrem Brkovic, 2006, *Ljubavnik Duklje*, DANU, Padova.

Lejla Voloder, 2018, *A Muslim Minority in Turkey: Migration, Ethnicity and Religion in a Bosniak Community*, L.B. Tauris, London.

Ljiljana Lipovina, Slobodan Scepanovic, 'Porijeklo kolasinskih Muslimana', Vijesti III/1999 2004

Members of Ministry for Human rights and refugees in Bosnia and Herzegovina; https://www.bridgemanimages.com/en/noartistknown/bosnia-s-ministry-for-human-rights-and-refugees-meet-in-banja-luka-2001-01-30-photo/photograph/asset/8160608

Memnun Idzakovic, 30. 6. 2008, 'Podzemni rat spijuna: Ustaski agenti u partizanima', Oslobodenje

Milan Jovičević n.d. in *Barjaktars and the banner act in Montenegro* (*Barjaktari i barjaktarstvo u Crnoj Gori*, https://www.montenegrina.net/pages/pages1/istorija/dokumenti/barjaktari_i_barjaktarstvo_u_cg_m_jovicevic.html

Milan Šćekić, Crnogorski Muslimani u Crnogorskoj Vojsci Tokom Prvog Svjetskog Rata (1914-1916) u *Časopis Montenegrin Journal for Social Sciences upisan je u evidenciju medija*, Ministarstva kulture Crne Gore pod rednim brojem 782., Volume 1, 2017. Issue 2. Podgorica December 2017, p. 216

Mirsad T. Kurgas, n. d., 'Ambijetalne Cjeline u Barskom Kraju'

Mitar Bakic, 1913 'Izvjestaji Mira Bakica crnogorskog poslanika u Carigradu 1885-1887, Knjiga 1 Zbornik Dokumenata' https://www.youtube.com/watch?v=yv8sqVR0IHk

Mountain Wreath, Reading Analysis/ Petar Petrovic Njegos, https://www.lektire.rs/gorski-vijenac-petar-petrovic-njegos/

Mustafa Memic, 2003, 'Sarajevo Kao Imigracioni Centar' cited in Bosnjaci.net, 2003.

Mustafa Memic, 2002, *Bosnjaci (Muslimani) Crne Gore*, Almanah, Podgorica.

Mustafa Memic, 1998, *Poznati Bosnjaci Sandzka i Crne Gore*, Matica, Sarajevo.

Nadir Dacić, 'Pljevljansko Muftijstvo (1930-1936)' u Husein Pasa Boljanic I Njegove Zaduzbine (*povodom 450 godina od izgradnje Husein-pašine džamije u Pljevljima)*, ISLAMSKA ZAJEDNICA U CRNOJ GORI, MINS, NIKŠIĆ, pp. 137-160

Name list of owners of lands [houses] from the city of Podgorica (23. II. 1879) Podgoricain Tuurks, Cetinje Arhiv, dao Enver Backovic.

Nathalie Clayer 2009, 'The Tijaniyya: Reformism and Islamic Revival in Interwar Albania', Journal of Muslim Minority Affairs Volume 29, 2009 - Issue 4: European Modernity and Islamic Reformism among Muslims of the Balkans in the Late-Ottoman and Post-Ottoman Period (1830s–1945)

Nešo K. Stanić, 1910, *Monument to the Shadows of Podgorica Serbs* – printed in Cetinje at the KR printing house. CR. Ministry of the military.

Novo Vujošević, '*Crnogorke u vizuri Toma P. Oravca, Njegošev spomenik: Imaju koga viđet i Ini na nebu'* , Dan online, 2015; https://old.dan.co.me/?nivo=3&rubrika=Feljton&clanak=520710&datum=2015-11-24

Paul Tedeschin, Dec 4, 2021, *Familjet nga Podgorica, Ulqini dhe Kraja që jetojnë në Shkodër*, Ulqini Online, https://ulqini-online.com/sajti/?p=30772Paul Tedeschini from the book "Shkodra and the weather" by Hamdi Bushatihttps://www.shkodraweb.com/dossier-shkodra-dhe-motet-familjet-shkodrane-me-prejardhje-te-huaj/

Pavle Mijović i Mirko Kovačević, 'Gradovi i utvrđenja u Crnoj Gori', 1975, str. 138

Pavle S. Radusinović, 1991,Stanovništvo i naselja Zetske ravnice od najstarijeg do novijeg doba', Nikšić. Genealogy of the Mohammedans of Podgorica, 1894 and Muslims in Zeta ('Muhamedanci u Zeti') Prilozi, Titograd

Pavle S Radusinovic, 1991, *Stanovnistvo i naselja zetske ravnice od najstarijeg do najnovijeg doba*, Druga Knjiga, Titograd.

Petar I Petrović – Djela, 1999, CID Podgorica Vojna štamparija, Beograd

Predrag Vukic Iseljavanje Muslimana iz Podgorice u Toku 1909 godine (Dokumenti) Almanah, 27-28 ISSN 0354-5342 Podgorica, 2004. PP. 277-287

P. K., 'Od Kolijevke roda tvoga', 1971 (novinski clanak)

Proceedings, 2015: 31, 'New Year greeting from Muslim parties from Bijelo Polje to King Nikola, 14 January 1914, ABO NMCG, NI, no. 29. MONTENEGRO IN THE FIRST WORLD WAR Proceedings, Matica Crnogorska, Cetinje – Podgorica 2015 https://maticacrnogorska.me/files/1%20sv%20rat.pdf

17 Rabi'u'-Ewvel 1324 / 5 April 1322 The State Archives of Turkey (BOA, Prime Ministry Ottoman Archive), BOAR (Prime Ministry Ottoman Archive Guide), BOA.DH. SAID (Dahilie Nezareti Sicill-Ahval İdare i Umumiyesi), BOA.DH. SAID.d. – --- DH_SAİD_109_246; 489) (Ministry of Internal Affairs Registry Books Index)

Ramiza Smajic, 2019, Migration Flows, Socio-Political Circumstances in the Bosnian Eyalet (1683.-1718.) PhD Thesis, Faculty of Philosophy, Zagreb. http://darhiv.ffzg.unizg.hr/id/eprint/11026/1/Smajic_Ramiza.pdf

Safet Bandzovic, 2011, Iseljvanaje Muslimana Crne Gore u Tursku, Knjiga I, Matica Muslimanska Crne Gore, Podgorica.

Salih Mehmeti, 2021, 'The double-headed Albanian – the freedom-loving symbol from Byzantium to today', KOHA Ditore, Albania.

Safvet Beg Basagic-Redzepasic, 1900, *Kratka Uputa u Proslos Bosne i Hercegovine, (1463-1850),* Vlastita Naklada, Sarajevo.

Slobodan Cukic, 2018, *Podgorički brevijar: skica za istoriju Podgorice do 1900. Godine*, Nova Pobjeda, Podgorica.

Spisak pravnih birača iz opštine varoši Podgorice za izbor narodnog poslanika za 1905 god, Cetinje Arhiv

Srđa Martinović, 2020, Policijska Organizacija u Crnoj Gori do Nestanka Kraljevine , Matica Matica časopis za društvena pitanja, nauku i kulturu, God. 21, br. 84, 2020, str. 53-166 https://maticacrnogorska.me/files/84/08%20srdja%20martinovic%2084.pdf

'Stari Bar: Prica na tri jezika', 2009, https://turistickadesavanjabar.blogspot.com/2009/04/stari-bar-prica-na-tri-jezika.html

Turkish and Ottoman Nobility and Royalty, 2018, https://nobilitytitles.net/turkish-ottoman-nobility-royalty

Šerbo Rastoder, 2010, *Bosnjaci/Muslimani Crne Gore izmedu proslosti i sadasnjosti*, Almanah, Podgorica

Šerbo Rastoder, 'Bosniaks-Muslim of Montenegro Between Past and Present', Podgorica 2010, pp. 11-85

Šerbo Rastoder, 2010, 'O Vakufima u Crnoj Gori s Kraja XIX i Prve Polovine XX Vijeka.'u Bosnjaci-Muslimani Crne Gore Izmedu Proslosti I Sadasnjosti, Podgorica, 85-121

Tatomir Vukanović, 1974, 'Poistovjecivanje Srpsta sa Pravoslavljen', Ethnogenesis of Southern Slavs, Vranje, p. 310.

Ustanak Naroda Jugoslavije 1941: Zbornik, Vojnoizdavacki Zavod JNA 'Vojno Delo', Beograd, 1964: P. 95
Veselin Konjević, 2018, 'Iseljavanje Muslimana Crne Gore', Matica, br. 74.

Vukić Pulevic, 2009, Degradacija Vegetacije u toponimiji Crne Gore, Lingua Montenegrina br. 4, Cetinje Institut za crnogorski jezik i jezikoslovlje, Vojislav P. Nikčević.

Zelimir Rukavina, Podgoricki muslimani u proslosti, Muslimanska Svijest, Broj: 57. Str. 1-3.

Zlatko V. Zlatičanin, 2025, *Čiča Ilija N. Zlatičanin – hronika podgoričkog vremena*, Unireks, Podgorica

Zvezdan Folić, 2013, 'Islamizacija – Osnova nastanka Muslimanskog naroda', Matica Muslimanske Crne Gore, Istorija Muslimana Crne Gore: 1455 – 1918 Knjiga I, Podgorica.

https://eliber.me/podgoricki-kapetan-becir-beg-osmanagic-pozdravlja-u-ime-ekonomskog-drustva-u-kojem-su-pripadnici-svih-vjera-zdravi-dolazak-knjaza-nikole-u-petrograd-mud-avgust-1882/

https://eliber.me/naredba-barskom-kapetanu-da-omoguci-zejnel-begu-upravljanje-njegovim-dobrima-mud-maj-1882/

https://www.limundo.com/kupovina/Kolekcionarstvo/Ostalo/ORIGINAL-POTPIS-HASKO-HAVERIC/114952433; https://estradalist.blogspot.com/2012_11_23_archive.html

https://www.aktuelno.me/crna-gora/kaludjer-u-decanima-prije-400-godina-zapisao-da-su-turci-izgradili-tvrdjavu-podgorica-a-ne-nemanja/

https://snv.hr/wp-content/uploads/2021/12/srbi-u-cetinskoj-krajini.pdf

https://www.ucg.ac.me/skladiste/blog_23602/objava_73797/fajlovi/Risto%20Kovijanic%20_%20Crnogorska%20plemena%20u%20kotorskim%20spomenicima_knjiga%20II.pdf

https://www.iskultur.com.tr/osmanlica-turkce-ansiklopedik-lugat.aspx?srsltid=AfmBOop2Oi1PEQ_ytyX8VzRG6y5hMaDFm7a3hBov8KswXfqU3c6V9V7U

An addition to my family branch:

Endorsements

The book's timeframe primarily focuses on the Haveric Bey's family, from its beginnings in the 1480s to the end of the 20th century, spanning over 500 years. It illustrates the evolution of the family within cultural, religious, and socio-historical contexts. This groundbreaking work is a meticulously researched and deeply engaging exploration of one of the most enduring and influential Muslim families in the Balkans's history.

'Bey' is a Turkish honorific originally used for military nobles and later for wealthy or reputable chieftains. Beys in Ottoman history played a crucial role in social, spiritual, educational, political and military affairs which the author found in the historical tree of the Haverics. This research shows that the Haveric family is one of the Beys who played a significant role in the Balkans which were deep in the memories like 'pieces of hidden pearls'. The author made Haveric Bey's history unhidden. This research is the first in-depth study in English on the genealogy and historiography of an historical family within the context of the Beys' history of the Ottoman Empire.

One of the book's greatest strengths lies in its ability to contextualise the Haveric Bey's family within broader historical dynamics—from the Ottoman era to modern times. Rather than presenting genealogy as a static listing of names and dates, the book engages with questions of identity, power, and memory. It invites readers to consider how family narratives are shaped by and in turn shape the forces of history, governance, and cultural evolution. This research illustrates how the Haveric Bey's family built interfaith relations in the region and contributed to social harmony during the Ottoman era. The author also provides a brief historical overview of the religions, architecture, education, arts, culture, and geography of the Balkans, where the Haveric Bey family and their descendants resided.

What makes this book particularly compelling is its fusion of archival rigour with narrative richness. Drawing on rare manuscripts, official records, oral histories, and ancestral correspondence, as well as pictures, the author reconstructs the lineage and legacy of the Haveric Bey's family with both academic precision and storytelling grace. The result is a vivid portrait of how a single-family thread has woven itself through the religious, political, social, and intellectual fabric of Bosnia, Albania, Montenegro, and Turkiye since 1480.

This work will be of great interest not only to scholars of history and genealogy but also to general readers with an appreciation for legacy, heritage, and the enduring influence of the Haveric Bey's family. It serves as both a scholarly resource and a tribute to the enduring legacy of generations. The care and attention poured into this research are evident on every page, making it a valuable contribution to regional historiography and beyond.

Prof. Salih Yucel
Centre for Islamic Studies and Civilisation
Charles Sturt University
Australia

....

Like his previous works, this captivating book finds Dr. Haveric tracing the remarkable 500-year journey of the Haveric Bey's family—from Bosnia to Turkiye, and Montenegro to Albania. Blending personal memories with major historical events, he offers a unique window into a family shaped by rich cultural, religious, spiritual, and political influences. A warm and engaging read for anyone interested in family heritage and regional history.

Prof. Ismail Albayrak
Australian Catholic University
Australia

....

Dr Dzavid Haverc's book, 'The 530 years of the Haveric Bey's Family: Genealogy and Historiography', saw the light of day to my personal joy and satisfaction. The light of the book illuminates hundreds of years of a history which in the labyrinths of time had begun to lose its lustre and clarity. Previous too fragmented works on a similar theme were mostly methodologically inaccurate and interpreted in a false way, often maliciously.

The author made a great effort to clean the obscured facts from the dust of oblivion with which time has covered them, to 'green the desert of our forgetfulness', to rescue facts and to tell the truth from the historical labyrinths in which the Haveric ancestors wandered for 530 years.

The work of Dr Dzavid Haveric has manifold value because it reveals to us who we are, where we come from and what and why we are. It explores how the Haveric Bey's family played its role in the history. It also illuminates for us the paths that we are walking now and that the descendants and future generations of this honorable family should walk. I wrote this comment, not because of my mother's Haveric side, but guided by an old Latin saying, *Fiat iustitia, et pereat mundus* ('let there be justice [truth] and let the world perish')! Therefore, I congratulate Dr Dzavid Haveric from the bottom of my heart!

Dr Enver Backovic
Formerly Professor at the Faculty of Economics and Business
Sarajevo
Bosnia and Herzegovina

....

About the Author

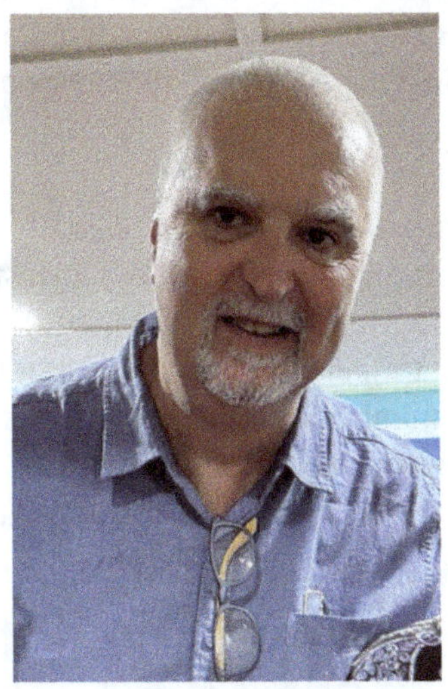

Dzavid Haveric's direct ancestry:
Kemal, Hamza, Ibrahim, Mahmud, Mehmed, Adnan, Zejnil, Alija, Mustafa, Omer, Mahmud, Alija, Murat, Haver and Junuz.

Dr Dzavid Haveric is an Adjunct Research Fellow, Historian and Author at the Centre for Islamic Studies and Civilisation (CISAC), Charles Sturt University. He is a leading expert on history of Islam and Muslims in Australia. He worked as a Reporter at the Special Broadcasting Service (SBS) Radio Program for the Bosnian Community and as a Journalist for Bosnian community newspapers. Dr Haveric worked as a Project Officer and Program

Assistant at the Parliament of the World's Religions within the Victorian Multicultural Commission. He was a Research Assistant and Project Worker at the Institute for Community, Ethnicity and Policy Alternatives, Victoria University. He is an Honorary Researcher at the Victoria Museum contributing to the Museum's image and story collections. He is a member of Charles Sturt University's Public and Contextual Theology Research Centre and the Australian Association of Islamic and Muslim Studie (AAIMS). He is also a member of the Bosniak Academy of Sciences and Arts (BANU) and the Bosnian Academy of Science and Arts 'Kulin ban' (BANUK).

Dr Haveric has written widely and influentially. He is the author of fourteen books, including Muslims making Australia home (2019), History of Islam and Muslims in Australia (2019) and A History of Muslims in the Australian Military from 1885 to 1945 (2024). He has also written a number of academic articles, numerous reports and community newspaper articles. In 2023 he was awarded Australian Muslim Professional of the year at the 16th Annual Australian Muslim Achievements Awards (AMAA).

www.ingramcontent.com/pod-product-compliance
Lightning Source LLC
LaVergne TN
LVHW020503100826
845148LV00003B/687

* 9 7 8 0 9 5 8 0 1 0 3 7 5 *